Praise for
Lethal Choice

"Fast-paced and full of suspense, ***Lethal Choice*** captures essential controversies surrounding end-of-life issues. Dr. Terman's clear insight is timely. Heated debates continue over legalizing Physician-Assisted Suicide at the state and federal levels. On an individual level, court cases feud over refusing nutrition and hydration to patients with greatly diminished consciousness. A successful dramatization of both sides of these issues, this medical thriller as informative as it is exciting."

—**Philip S. Cifarelli**, MD, JD, FACP, FACG, FCLM, Attorney at Law; Past President of the American College of Legal Medicine

"The story reveals brilliant insight into the controversies surrounding Physician-Hastened Dying. Its memorable, well-developed characters also teach us much about human nature. Although I had intended to sleep on the flight back to Melbourne from Toronto, I couldn't... the story was just too engrossing."

—**Rodney Syme**, MBBS, FRACS, President, Dying with Dignity, Victoria; Past Chairman,Victorian Section, Urology Society of Australasia

"My interest in 'Death with Dignity' led me to this novel. I was delighted by the way it revealed in depth, the rarely shared thoughts in the minds of professionals who work in this controversial field. Dr. Terman has woven the most salient ethical, legal, and religious issues into a story so wonderful that I read it again (and again)."

—**Dennis G. Kuby**, M Div, President, the Socrates Fellowship of Death Acceptance; former head, Hemlock Society of California, Berkeley, CA

"Wonderful twists and surprising turns make ***Lethal Choice*** so compelling that I could not put it down. But there is another reason why this book is a 'must read.' Though fictional, it is based on facts relevant to one area that we all must face. This stimulating book will provoke much discussion."

—**Irene J. Morris**, RN, University of California, Irvine, Student Health Infirmary & Emergency Room (retired)

"***Lethal Choice*** is at the cutting edge of ethical and public policy issues in end-of-life health care. Over fifty concepts in ethics, medicine, law, and public policy are seamlessly woven into the plot without any contrivance or awkwardness. Despite the conceptual content, I found it difficult to pause for meals, much less to sleep after I began reading. Then I had to struggle with the impulse to skip ahead as the action changed to learn if, or how, the characters could overcome their intriguing challenges. In a word, this medical thriller is a masterpiece of suspense."

—**Ronald B. Miller**, MD, FACP, Director Emeritus of the Program in Medical Ethics, Clinical Professor of Medicine, University of California, Irvine

Praise for

The BEST WAY to Say Goodbye:
A Legal Peaceful Choice at the End of Life

by

Stanley A. Terman, Ph.D., M.D.,
with Ronald Baker Miller, M.D., and Michael S. Evans, M.S.W., J.D.

"Offers a close to ironclad strategy, even for those individuals who may ultimately suffer from severe brain damage or dementia. This book is so good that our organization keeps copies at every office. Knowledge is power; read this book!"

—**Barbara Coombs Lee**, PA, FNP, JD; President, Compassion & Choices;
Chief Petitioner for the Oregon Death with Dignity Act

"A very insightful analysis of the President's Council on Bioethics' report, 'Taking Care: Ethical Caregiving in an Aging Society' Dr. Terman's detailed suggestions for wording Advance Directives are very important."

—**Janet D. Rowley**, M.D., D.Sc.; President's Council on Bioethics member;
Albert Lasker Clinical Medicine Research Prize recipient

"A comprehensive look at the medical, legal, and spiritual aspects of the dying process. Highlights the often-overlooked process of voluntary refusal of food and fluid. Adds depth and sensibility to an area that is rampant with controversy. "

—**Judith F. Daar**, J.D., Professor of Law, Whittier Law School; Clinical Professor
of Medicine; University of California Irvine, College of Medicine

"A wise, medically well-grounded, and even witty book. Illustrates the middle course of refusing tube feeding and hydration, a way to die that is relatively painless, effective, legal, and in keeping with many religious traditions."

—**Elliot N. Dorff**, Rabbi, Ph.D., Distinguished Professor of Philosophy,
University of Judaism; author of *Matters of Life and Death*

"African-Americans are wary... Dr. Terman must be commended for examining this area. The section on religion is just awesome... should be required reading."

—**Cecil L. "Chip" Murray**, Rel. D., Tanzy Chair of Christian Ethics, U.S.C.;
Pastor Emeritus, First African Methodist Episcopal Church, Los Angeles

"If had only one book to read in the right-to-die field, I'd choose ***BEST WAY***... [It] renewed my interest in [Refusing Food & Fluid]... fun reading despite a grim subject."

—**Bill Fagan**, Board Member of Hemlock Society of San Diego;
Senior Exit Guide for Final Exit Network

Lethal Choice

Other books by Stanley A. Terman, Ph.D., M.D.

The *BEST WAY* to Say Goodbye:
A Legal Peaceful Choice at the End of Life

with
Ronald Baker Miller, M.D., & Michael S. Evans, J.D., M.S.W.

(www.BestGoodbye.com; 800 64 PEACE)

LAST WISHES:
Memoirs and *Professional Advice* on *Peaceful Transitions*
Editor (expected in 2007)

Lethal Choice

a novel

by Stanley A. Terman, Ph.D., M.D.

Life Transitions Publications
Carlsbad CA 92009

Back material: Acknowledgments; Legalizing Physician-Assisted Suicide: a position statement; Why also a self-help book with memoirs on the same topic?; and, How can competent patients hasten dying by refusing food & fluid?

This is a work of fiction. Names, characters, places and incidents either are the product of the author's imagination or are used fictitiously, and any resemblance to any actual persons, living or dead, events or locales is entirely coincidental. Names of real people have identifying footnotes, unless the identity is obvious.

Cover Design by Jonathan Pennell

Author photograph by Beth Gardner

Typesetting by K. Lorraine Graham and Janelle Diters

Publisher's Cataloging-in-Publication

(Provided by Quality Books, Inc.)

Terman, Stanley A.

Lethal choice : a novel / by Stanley A. Terman.--

1st ed.

p. cm.

ISBN 1-933418-20-6 (soft cover)

ISBN 1-933418-21-4 (hard cover)

ISBN 1-933418-22-2 (large type, soft cover)

LCCN 2005936403

1. Terminal care--Fiction. 2. Medical ethics--Fiction. 3. Life and death, Power over--Fiction. 4. Patient advocacy--Fiction. 5. Death--Moral and ethical aspects--Fiction. I. Title.

PS3620.E75L43 2007 813'.6

QBI05-600180

Life Transitions Publications * Post Office Box 130129 * Carlsbad CA 92009
www.LifeTP.com

www.LethalChoice.com www.CaringAdvocates.org

Dedicated to Dr. Ronald Ferris,
who knew how to live and taught us how to die.

Foreword

By Ronald Baker Miller, M.D., F.A.C.P.
Clinical Professor of Medicine, Emeritus
Director, Emeritus, of the Program in Medical Ethics
University of California, Irvine

The premise of **Lethal Choice** is as frightening as it is compelling: Will we be denied the right to choose when and how we die? And, will promoting this right lead to the exploitation of society's most vulnerable?

At the cutting edge of ethical and public policy issues in end-of-life health care, **Lethal Choice** is a medical thriller based on the hopefully fictional (but plausible) economic greed of insurance companies. Given the rapidly increasing number of elderly people who will need expensive acute and chronic long-term care, the time when we must face the real challenge of fiscal necessity is not that far off, given that a new case of dementia occurs every seven seconds [Reuters, December 2005].

While this is Dr. Stan Terman's first novel, he has previously written essays and memoirs, and published contributions to the end-of-life clinical literature, especially in the areas of decision-making capacity (mental competence) and quantifying the loss of ability to enjoy life. He was formerly on the medical faculty at the University of California, Irvine. He has also provided expert testimony and submitted declarations on a variety of contentious legal issues in this field.

The questions posed in **Lethal Choice** are as challenging as they are profound: May a person whose care is extraordinarily expensive consider forgoing that treatment so that the funds can be spent instead on what the individual considers more noble purposes? How does a physician resolve the conflict between "do no harm" and "do only what the patient believes to be a benefit"? Should physicians preserve life or reduce suffering, if both are not possible?

In its balanced presentation of such issues, **Lethal Choice** is a morality play in the classical sense. It boldly illustrates the dark side of the slippery slope: the mercenary motivation to encourage individuals to hasten their dying is to increase the profits of health insurance and long-term care insurance companies.

Dr. Terman has applied his psychiatric skills to show the motivation of every character in the novel. For example, the physician who treats terminally ill patients becomes complicit in crimes due to devious schemes of a male nurse with whom he is forced to collaborate. A naïve young doctor, just ten months out of medical school, finds that romantic love leads him to risk his own life as he attempts to save the life of his future father-in-law. Along the way, he learns more about end-of-life ethics and physician bias than he ever anticipated. The targeted patient, a victim of Lou Gehrig's disease, finds his last great challenge in life is spiritual, and he devises an ingenious strategy as he hopes to assuage his daughter's the survivor's guilt after he dies.

Over fifty concepts in ethics, medicine, law, and public policy are seamlessly woven into the plot of **Lethal Choice**. Without contrivance or awkwardness, the story includes euthanasia, physician-assisted suicide, palliative (comfort) care, substituted judgment, double effect, palliative (terminal) sedation, and forgoing life-sustaining treatment (unplugging a ventilator). The novel also presents refusal of food and fluid as a peaceful, legal means to hasten dying that is often the only available option for patients who are irreversibly descending into dementia, and for those not dependent on life-sustaining technology that they could legally refuse.

The novel contrasts unrealistic hopelessness that can lead to preventable suicides with the rational basis to hasten dying when existence becomes intolerable. It reveals the personal and social challenges of patients and families who must cope with Lou Gehrig's disease, Alzheimer's dementia, coma, and cancer. The story provides insights into Buddhist and Catholic teachings on end-of-life issues and it shows how physician bias may lead to disrespecting patients' Last Wishes and Living Wills. Finally, it illustrates with compassion, the importance of having a trusted proxy who will end terminal suffering by faithfully honoring the request to discontinue medical treatment, or nutrition and hydration, under specified circumstances.

Despite its robust conceptual content, the story is so compelling that I found it difficult to pause for meals much less to sleep once I began reading it. I had to struggle with the impulse to skip ahead as the scene changed, to learn if, or how, the characters could overcome the intriguing challenges of the action I had just read. In one word, this medical thriller is a masterpiece of suspense.

As a bioethicist who contributed to a multi-authored amicus brief submitted to the U.S. Supreme Court on Physician-Assisted Suicide (1997), and as a son whose mother died peacefully by voluntarily refusing food and fluid (which story I relate in our book, **The *BEST WAY* to Say Goodbye: A Legal Peaceful Choice at the End of Life**), I believe **Lethal Choice** is an excellent vehicle for enlightening readers about end-of-life options that are as important as they are controversial.

The novel will appeal not only to those who love medical thrillers; but also to professionals in fields that touch on the ethics of end-of-life care. Many will find the drama as provocative as it is exciting.

In the years ahead, most of us will be forced to deal with agonizing decisions about whether to extend the lives or to hasten the dying of our loved ones. Using Treatment Directives (Living Wills) and Proxy Directives, we should also make such decisions in advance, for ourselves. **Lethal Choice** stimulates us to think about our preferences and to discuss them with our proxy, our loved ones, and our physicians. It presents these profoundly challenging issues via a story that is, from beginning to end, thoroughly gripping.

Ronald Baker Miller, M.D.
2006

Chapter 1

Norman Cameron walked down the hospital corridor towards his patient's room. His stride was longer than usual, perhaps because he was anxious to learn the answer to a question he had been asking himself for days: *How much longer would she hold on?*

He opened the door, glanced toward the bed, and felt relief that Vivian Barretino's eyes were shut. He would not need to force a smile. Her thin body remained motionless as he approached her bed. As he raised her stiff hand and gently stroked her cold, curved fingers, Vivian opened her eyes and rolled them toward him. Brilliant turquoise, they were the only animate parts of a body that was literally turning to stone.

Cameron kept his voice gentle. "Vivian, dear, how is it for you, this morning?"

"I hurt, Doctor. I hurt all over. This is... It's the worst it's ever been."

In his thirty years of medical practice, Cameron had witnessed the ravaging effects of many diseases, but when severe, Scleroderma was among the worst. The "scarring" disease progressively stole flexibility from every tissue. Strikingly visible in the skin, it also slowly destroyed critical internal organs. Barretino had the worst variant of the disease. Calcium deposits kept on erupting through her skin. —Like miniature shards of ice.

"I'm sorry you had such a painful night, Vivian. The nurses called me—"

"I know. They increased the IV, but it didn't help." She swallowed hard. "I hate to complain, Doctor, after all the time you've spent with me. I know you're doing all you can."

Cameron gazed at her in silence.

Vivian was not quite fifty. Her long limbs and elegant hands were testaments to the ghost of beauty past. Until twelve years ago, she worked as an exotic dancer. Now, silver gleamed at the roots of her sparse auburn hair. Tiny spots of red dotted her parchment-like skin. Over the past few days, the subdued glossy sheen on her face had turned to an unnatural purple hue.

"I know your pain *is* terrible. Give me a moment to read your chart, okay?"

As Cameron sat down, he let every muscle in his face go limp except for a conscious frown. He knew doing this made him appear compassionate. He opened the chart but his eyes refused to focus. Instead he recalled the magnificent sunrise across the Washington, DC, skyline that he had just enjoyed from his new office... from *his* Palliative Care Center... from the very room where, in addition to the daily routine of reducing the suffering of his terminal patients, he'd soon make the greatest medical contribution of his life.

Cameron never worried about how long he sat in front of a patient's chart. Unless she was anxious about potentially bad news, the longer he took, the calmer she became. Of course, she imagined her "wise doctor" was absorbing data and trying to figure out the best way to treat her.

After a few moments, Cameron finally focused on the nurses' notes. After making a separate memo in his Palm Pilot, he looked up at his patient. Again, he wondered, *How much longer would she hold on?*

Vivian had been suffering from Scleroderma for eight years. Her symptoms worsened after the court trial. The jury refused to hold the manufacturer of her silicone breast implants liable for causing her Scleroderma. So she became depressed, and that made her disease worse.

Three weeks ago, when Cameron admitted Vivian to the Palliative Care Center, she expressed little interest in living. The social worker's detailed report indicated that Vivian had no family. When her mood unexpectedly improved, Cameron wondered why. Was it was the social worker's excessive visits? Did that do-gooder give *his* patient false hope? Cameron always told his patients the truth. And the truth about Scleroderma, is that for advanced cases, any remission is temporary.

He looked up. "Vivian, I'm sorry. There's nothing new here. I wish I could give you more hope."

Vivian sighed. "At least I have your support. You've spent more time talking to me than any other physician." Her look softened with appreciation. "And your promise... Especially your promise... I can't tell you how much that means to me. I'm so grateful. I want to than—"

"Please... don't *thank* me. You don't have to. Helping you through this... your most challenging time... It has been *my* privilege. I only wish I could do more."

Poor Vivian. Trapped in her own body, what kind of life did she have? She was denied even the privacy of showering since she required help from two assistants. Cameron looked closely... why did her face seem shiny? Ah, tiny tears. His sympathy turned to conviction. He knew exactly what he had to do. And why. That is, when she was ready. Only *she* could make the ultimate decision. But she seemed so close.

"I'd do anything to make the pain go away," Vivian said. "Maybe I'm ready to-"

"Good morning!" —A bright voice from the door. Vivian had stopped, mid-sentence. Cameron turned his head. It was Juliana, the Palliative Care Center's charge nurse. Like a reflex, his Palm Pilot shut with a crisp metallic snap.

"I hate to intrude, Doctor, but I promised Vivian I'd stop by while you were here."

Juliana had a curious frown and seemed to focus on Cameron's Palm Pilot as he slipped it into his white jacket's side pocket. Doctors rarely write separate notes about their patients, like businesses that don't keep two sets of books. But then, perhaps the nurse thought he was just checking his calendar? "Not at all, nurse. I'm glad you came. I'm concerned about Vivian's pain. The night nurse's note... the one she wrote at 3:45 AM... 'Severe agitation.' When she called me, I gave clear instructions to increase the rate of Vivian's IV."

"Yes, and she did." The nurse looked intense. "Doctor, isn't there anything else we can give her, to ease her pain?"

Cameron turned toward Vivian. "Please excuse us for talking about you as if you weren't here. You know I wish I could. But you've already received the maximum dose of steroids. Any more would do more harm than good. Of course, I'm not one of those timid doctors who worry that you will become addicted to narcotics. So I did increase your dose of painkillers. The problem is, your type of pain—from crystals of calcium that pierce your skin—it is so very difficult to treat."

Vivian seemed satisfied and turned to the nurse. "I'm glad you came in." Her voice strengthened with determination. "But I'd like to talk to Dr. Cameron alone, now. Okay, Juliana?"

"Of course." The nurse moved closer and lightly touched her shoulder. "Shall I return in an hour?" She waited for the nod, turned and then closed the door.

Vivian's lips barely moved as she whispered, "I'm thinking about Michelle. She's very worried about me."

"Of course she is. That's her job. That's why hospitals hire social workers—to worry. But you haven't—? I mean, *have* you discussed your options with her?"

"No, I couldn't. She wouldn't like it. She so much wants me to get better."

"We all do. Of course. But you must be realistic. The question is, what do you want? Not, what does she want? That's not relevant. What do *you* want, Vivian?"

"Doctor, I've lived most of my life alone. Over the past few days, I've come to realize that I will have to make my final decision alone."

"Whatever you decide, Vivian, you'll have my total support. If you like, we could talk more about it. I'll make the time. We can even talk more now."

"Dr. Cameron. We've been over it so many times. I bet I can remember some of your exact words. I don't need more talk. But your promise... it has... well, it's... it's been such a great source of comfort. It's the *only* thing that brings me comfort."

Cameron retrieved his Palm Pilot, flipped it open, made a final note, and slipped it back in his jacket. Then he took Vivian's hand. "I've devoted my entire professional life to minimizing suffering. I just wish I could reduce yours."

He studied her face to detect any hint that she would say something else. Her eyes seemed focused but her tight facial skin hid her emotions. After another moment he said, "Okay, then, Vivian. I'll see you tomorrow morning." He turned and walked toward the door.

"Doctor, may I ask?"

Cameron looked back. "Yes?"

"Could you possibly come back this afternoon?"

"This afternoon? What is it, Vivian? You've never asked for a second visit before."

"I don't know, Doctor. Maybe today—" Vivian's eyes focused intensely on his. "I don't know for sure, but maybe I'll decide today... Maybe today will be the day... the day that I will hold you to your promise."

Chapter 2

David Grainger slid between the doors of the hospital elevator to avoid being late for rounds. As the elevator rose, he mused on the wide range of doctors' motivations as they hustled from patient to patient, making diagnoses and designing treatment plans. Was it the opportunity to show off their clinical acumen? To assert their sense of importance? To prove their prowess as they fought disease?

Now ten months out of medical school, the intern had come to learn that cures were rare. The true goal of internal medicine was primarily to slow down the progression of diseases. For example, controlling blood sugar doesn't cure diabetes. Patients rarely left physicians better off than before they became ill. That was one reason why he had decided on a career in research. He would devote himself to the prevention of disease.

The elevator doors opened to reveal Tom Mendendorf, the third-year resident whom the Director of Graduate Training had paired him with. His broad shoulders filled out his white coat as if it had been tailored for him. He sipped coffee as he leaned against the nurses' counter of the Internal Medicine ward. For mental alertness on their schedule from hell, Tom and he counted pots, not cups of coffee. "Good thing you got here before Franklinstein."

"Thanks." David took a gulp from the cup that Tom had just handed him.

Dr. Franklin, their faculty physician, was a stickler on punctuality. Interns and residents secretly called him "Dr. Franklinstein"—which made Tom and him, his "Igors."

"Closing arguments should start today," Tom said.

"Huh?"

"You know, the Kenard trial," said Tom.

"Oh, yeah." David grimaced.

"What do you predict?"

"Life," David said.

"Life? Really? Want in on the pot to guess the closest number of years Kenard gets?"

"Sorry. I'm not a betting man."

David turned when he heard the sound of slapping feet. Dr. Franklin's pronounced stoop emphasized his basketball-center height and bald head. "Good morning, Doctors."

David's task was to gather the patients' charts. He did not resent the chore, although a clerk could have done it. Instead, he was always thinking. As he removed each chart from its metal shelf, he mused on the source of the patient's malady. Some had conditions that could not be circumvented—like the colon cancer patient with a family history. Others had preventable diseases—like the stressed-out, beef-eating, sedentary "Type A" personality who had a heart attack. Finally, there were self-inflicted patients—like Kelly, the eighteen-year-old girl in liver failure. She had overdosed with Tylenol after her boyfriend dumped her. David had talked to her at length one afternoon. She never wanted to die. She only wanted to get her boyfriend back. Of course, now *she* wouldn't take *him* back.

David never judged patients harshly because their illnesses were preventable or self-inflicted. He felt they deserved more compassion. Millions of middle-aged men eat red meat, and millions of teenagers are rejected in romance, but most live long, healthy lives. But he did find it draining to deal with terminally ill patients and their families. He was inclined to be supportive, but he knew he'd be safer keeping his distance, so he'd feel less loss when they died. He knew about the pain of loss and how much it hurt.

David looked up. They were standing in front of Kelly's room. Tom rattled off the lab results. His energy lifted as Franklinstein pronounced the obvious conclusion, the one he had been hoping for. "Good. Her liver function tests have improved significantly. Tom, you can remove her name from the list of patients waiting for liver transplants."

Rounding on patients was an emotional roller coaster. David's energy faded as he approached Donald Becker's room. He noticed that his two colleagues remained behind so he had no choice but to open the door and be the first to step inside. The drawn curtains created a darkness that enveloped him. He walked in, inhaling the smell he hated most: Dying.

Becker's medical history was sad, but far from unique. A once-successful photojournalist, this forty-three-year-old had been admitted to Memorial five times in the last three months. He had dropped from an aerobic-lean 165 pounds to less than 95 in the past year. His face sported square jaws that once evoked comments on its strength. Now his cheeks were so sunken that his eyes appeared ready to burst from bony sockets.

"Hurts," Becker murmured, rocking back and forth. His skeletal mouth gaped to emit a low, grating moan. David felt the hairs rise on the back of his neck. Becker continued, "Stop it. Stop it stop it stop it stop it—"

Franklin stepped forward and shook his head. "We'll see what we can do."

David despised the constellation of ailments from AIDS—skin cancers, blindness, untreatable pneumonias, progressive dementias. No part of the body or mind was safe from assault. While research on new drug cocktails was increasing survival time for newly diagnosed HIV-positive patients, even the most brilliant physicians who treated patients with advanced stages of AIDS were frustrated by the limitations of their science.

"—Stop it. Stop it—"

Franklin motioned to David. "Administer a Mini-Mental Status."

In other circumstances, David would have argued that this test was a poor choice to determine patients' mental ability to make medical decisions. But he just did what was asked. To get the man's attention, he leaned forward. He tried to disregard the stench of slow rot. "Mr. Becker, can you tell me the date?" Getting no answer, he asked, "The day of the month?"

"I'm not sure. Monday?"

"How about the year? What year it is?"

"Nineteen hundred and—? No, I mean two thousand and... I don't know. Sorry. It just hurts so bad."

"It's okay, Donald. Can you tell me where we are?"

"This place here? It's very large—"

"All right. Can you tell me what my job is?"

"You'd know that." Becker closed his eyes. He seemed exhausted.

"Rest easy now, Donald. We'll see what we can do," Franklin spoke softly and slowly. He nodded for Tom and David to move toward the door.

For a moment, the three men stood motionless in the hall. The huge deterioration in both Becker's mental and physical condition had shaken them all. Donald's score was so low, there was no reason to administer a better test.

"Dr. Grainger, did you inform Donald's parents that his end was near?"

"No." David's neck flushed warm with embarrassment. "I haven't had a chance."

"*Haven't had a chance*?" Franklin's eyes burned. "That's no excuse. If you didn't want to do it, at least you could have been honest with me. And with yourself. Tell me now, exactly why did you NOT want to tell them?"

"Well, I can't predict the future... and I figured, maybe there was a chance Donald would respond... We just started his IV nutrition." More softly, he said, "You never know."

Franklin was condescending. "Dr. Grainger, you still see 'Death' as the enemy, don't you?

Grainger hesitated. "I see my role as a doctor to do everything to prolong life."

"Sometimes that's too narrow a view." Franklin turned. "Dr. Mendendorf, what would you recommend for Mr. Becker?"

Tom hesitated. "Should we transfer him to our PCC?"

"At this point, the Palliative Care Center can't do anything more for him than we can."

Tom nodded as if responding to a standard cue. "Poor guy's really hurting. What about us raising his morphine dosage by, say... fifty percent?"

David stepped forward. "That much, so fast? It could be lethal." He looked at Tom. "What are you saying?"

Tom glanced at Franklin.

Franklin's head was bent into Becker's chart as he flipped through its pages. "Ah, here is his Proxy Directive. He designated his mother to make medical decisions for him if he no longer can." He turned the page. "And he checked the box to indicate that he is willing to risk dying to relieve his suffering if his pain is extreme—as long as two doctors consider his terminal condition to be hopeless." Franklin stared down at David. "His condition is hopeless, isn't it?"

David felt forced to nod.

"One reason why his pain is so extreme, David, is that he is tolerant to lower doses of narcotics." Franklin turned toward Tom. "Let's double his morphine and add a barbiturate. Sedation will help ease his pain."

David gulped. Could he go along with this plan? He'd witnessed doctors interpreting patient's Advance Directives to impose *their* wishes on patients, but this was worse. Franklin and Tom were colluding to give Becker a combination of medication that would definitely stop his breathing. It was common knowledge that such scenarios played out thousands of times a day nationally, but David never thought he'd find himself center stage, playing an active role.

As if Franklin could read his thoughts, "Doctor Grainger, please define *Double Effect.*"

"Okay. When an action is likely to have two consequences, one good and the other evil, it is possible to perform the act as long as the intention is solely to bring about the good effect."

"Your memory is perfect," Franklin said, "but how would you apply that now?"

David tried to sound like he believed his next words. "In trying to reduce a patient's suffering, we know there is a possible but *un*-intended side-effect, in this case, we might bring about the patient's death."

"Well said. And do you by any chance know who introduced this concept?" asked Dr. Franklin.

"I think so. Wasn't it Thomas Aquinas, in the thirteenth century?"

"Right again." Franklin rubbed his chin. "I'm impressed with your knowledge of facts. You just need to learn how better apply to apply them to clinical reality."

David was indebted to his mentor, Dr. Solomon, for educating him. But his knowledge, and their discussions, led David to a different opinion. He bit his tongue as other words seared through his mind, words that he dared not say. *But you* ***are*** *intending it. You are deliberately prescribing enough meds to end this patient's life. Intentional active euthanasia is immoral, unethical, and illegal. I'd call it,* ***Managed Death****.*

David could not be totally honest and use this term. Directly confronting a faculty physician would end David's internship, and he had only two more months to finish. He had to finish to get his medical license. And he had to get a medical license to start his fellowship. So he had no choice but to be diplomate. "I just wanted to be absolutely certain that Becker really wished to die now," he said.

Franklin raised his voice in anger. "But that is NOT our intent. We only want to provide him adequate relief for his extreme suffering. It's called Terminal Sedation. You administered the Mini-Mental Status, Doctor. Do you think we need to ask a psychiatrist to confirm that he has lost decision-making capacity?"

"No. He can't even articulate a choice, let alone a consistent one. But—"

"Then who better than the physicians who know him best, who are providing his treatment, should decide what is in his best interest?"

David's right eye started to throb. His unique type of headache usually didn't start until late afternoon. He had nothing to say. For some reason, Franklinstein's stare softened. Now what?

"David, your combination of idealism and denial, though inappropriate, has inadvertently led me to consider a relevant legal point. Given the daily news coverage of the Kenard trial right now, it's not a good time for me to take any risk, even if my delay prolongs Becker's suffering."

David wondered where Franklin was going with this remark as the tall doctor handed him the chart. "Check the medication log. Has Becker needed to increase his dose of analgesics?"

Glad for the excuse to look away, David flipped through some pages. "He was on Vicodin on admission but we had to switch him to morphine. Since then, we've increased his dose about every other day, including yesterday."

"He's definitely tolerant. Tom, document that point in Becker's chart. David, get an informed consent form for 'Controlled Sedation for Refractory Suffering' from the file cabinet." Franklin's stare was relentless. "I want *you* to sit down with his parent to get written permission."

David felt a shiver inside. "Me?"

"Yes. You," Franklin said. "You can find Becker's parents in our cafeteria."

"All right, I'll speak to them," David said, "but I must admit, I consider it my duty to convince them not to—" He stopped and wondered, *Had I already said too much*?

"Were you about to say, 'NOT to agree'? If so, that's precisely why I chose you." Franklin smiled. "If you obtain their informed consent, I surely won't have to worry about any legal repercussions."

Franklin motioned for them to move on to the next room. After a few steps, he stopped and asked, "Dr. Grainger, would you be surprised if the Beckers do give their consent?"

David's jaws welded together.

Franklin grunted and turned to Mendendorf. "Doctor?"

Tom straightened up. "If his mother signs, I'll write the orders."

"Good." Franklin motioned to his Igors to move on to their next patient.

⁂

Fifteen patients and ninety minutes later, David pulled Tom over to a quiet corner of the nurses' station. "Can I ask you something, Tom?" He waited for a nod. "Has Becker been a burden to you?"

"What do you mean?"

"You know. All those fever work-ups in the middle of the night, and—"

"So?"

"It's so frustrating treating him. The extra stress on us, hardly any sleep—"

"Just what are you implying?" Tom's expression hardened.

"Nothing, I was just wondering—"

"Look, my work load has absolutely nothing to do with—"

"Then why did you volunteer to take him out? Isn't Kenard standing trial for what you're planning to do?"

"How can you ask that? This is totally different."

"But you stood in that hallway and concocted a plan to take Becker out. How is that different from what Dr. Kenard did?"

"We only ordered sufficient meds for suffering so extreme that we couldn't control it any other way. In contrast, Kenard committed active euthanasia right after the patient's priest informed his congregant that it would be a mortal sin. Our hospital's ethics committee approved the protocol for treating refractory suffering. But Kenard thumbed his nose at the Catholic Church."

"If all that's so, how come Franklin admitted he would have made this decision to take out Donald without asking his parents if Kenard's trial had not been in the news?"

"David, it's not that we believe, 'Doctors know best.' But if we could make the decision ourselves, it would spare Donald's parents from a lot of guilt." As he placed his hand on David's shoulder, Tom no longer looked defensive. "Listen my young colleague: as you ask Becker's parents to sign that form, try not to make them feel as though they are granting permission to kill their son. Otherwise, they'll be guilt-ridden for the rest of their lives."

David swallowed hard. "How can I avoid that?"

Tom hesitated. "Say it was *our* decision. That it was hard for *us* to make."

"But it didn't seem that hard for Franklin." David brushed Tom's hand away. "—Or for you! How can you live with yourself after making the decision to give him an overdose of meds? Don't you ever wonder if you're playing God?"

"Becker was pleading for relief, David. You heard him."

Becker's muffled moaning came from down the hall as Tom paused.

Tom pointed toward Donald's room. "Listen to him suffer. You call yourself a doctor? How can you live with yourself, if you ignore his request and allow his suffering to be prolonged?"

Chapter 3

"You look absolutely fabulous." Cameron extended his hands and gently pulled Wendy up from the oriental hand-carved mahogany bench near the maitre-d's podium. He remembered to restrain his hug. His wife had left the house twice this week, but this was the first time she had enough energy to dress up.

"It doesn't feel like me. Not completely." Wendy pointed to her wig.

"As far as I'm concerned, you could have worn one of your silk scarves. I particularly love the royal blue one. The way it contrasts with your skin—"

"Be serious. I wouldn't—"

"You're doing so well, dear. Soon, you'll be your old self again."

By arriving just as they opened for lunch, they were offered a window table. *Jeffrey's at the Watergate* was their favorite DC restaurant. It was here that Norman had proposed marriage.

"I'm glad you decided to come here. Look at the sailboats on the Potomac!"

Cameron was amazed at how Wendy's spirits rose so quickly. "I know. See that beautiful tall ship with flapping sails? At night, we'd only see a string of lights."

But he really suggested lunch because Wendy's energy could not last if they had waited until he left the PCC that evening. Still, she was getting stronger every day. Chemotherapy had extended her life. But still, he worried. For how long?

Wendy had been so beautiful when they'd met twenty-seven years ago. He could hardly believe she agreed to marry him. To his eyes, she became even more beautiful as the decades passed. There were many challenges. Her greatest disappointment was infertility. Not having children must have made it harder to be the wife of an obsessed medical researcher. She helped his work by scanning the popular media for articles related to his research interests. But it was her keen interest in pets and designing jewelry that channeled her nurturing and creative energies. After all these years, he had to ask, how much happiness had all his late hours and the resulting eighty-three published articles really brought them?

"These new brochures excite me," she said. "Indonesia, Thailand, Singapore, and Myanmar. I wouldn't mind if we spent all our time in the Far East."

Cameron loved the way her face glowed when she talked about traveling. Her eyebrows arched as she envisioned a visit to these places. He had to look more closely now since her hair had grown back so light. "I want you to have the best trip possible."

Cameron's mind flashed to Wendy's struggles during her last round of chemotherapy: memories of her 106-degree temperature, her trembling in the ice bath, her bouts of nausea. These images would fade, like those from prior treatments.

He looked at the many rows of fine lines that surrounded her hazel eyes. He mused, like the marks on a tree to keep score for each of her battles.

A question from a waiter startled him as if he'd been in a trance. "Yes, yes. I already know what I want. An order of your Jumbo Lump Crab Cakes, please."

"And I'll have the Chopped Cobb Salad." She smiled. She knew he'd eat half of her salad in exchange for two small bites of crab cake. "I can't wait to see the floating market near Bangkok. But you know what I'm most looking forward to? Spending time with you without your worrying about patients or being frantic to finish a grant application by the deadline."

His thoughts drifted back to the challenges of the last five years: the *dotcom* crash that wiped out their life's savings. Wendy's cancer. His hope for a cure... but when it recurred, feeling shaken to his core. Then his research grant was not renewed. No further funding. Shortsighted, goddamn government, slicing at the top, at the brains, at the source of lasting discoveries, at Norman Cameron, B.A., M.P.H., M.D., Ph.D.

His reprieve came from headhunters searching for a physician to lead Memorial's PCC. Cameron feigned more delight than he felt when they offered to double his Walter Reed salary. He knew he wouldn't stay long enough to replenish his life's savings. But late in the interview process, his interest was piqued when the headhunters introduced him to key members of the Good Life Committee. In return for his participation in their special project, they offered Cameron a bonus large enough to take Wendy around the world and to retire in comfort.

But it wasn't just the money. Cameron had long disdained the overuse of high-tech medicine and its appalling waste of resources. For many illnesses, fifty percent of lifetime medical costs are spent during the last year of life. That's futile when the patient's quality of life is virtually nil. As members of the Good Life Committee confirmed their impressions of Cameron's clinical pragmatism, the doctor began to read between their lines. He didn't ask if they represented the CEOs if health-insurance or long-term care companies whose salaries were based on performance, who felt forced to reduce costs to maintain high profits...

The CEOs' mercenary motivation did not bother Cameron because he could see a scenario where everyone would win. His work would encourage doctors to decrease expensive, futile end-of-life care. Patients and caregivers would be saved from needless suffering. A huge potential monetary drain on insurance companies, including Medicare, would be averted. And, if the timing worked as he planned, Cameron would receive the recognition he deserved for being the courageous outspoken physician who put a stop to inappropriate, excessive end-of-life care, just as Wendy and he retired by taking a dream-come-true around-the-world trip.

Perfect, he thought, as he locked in on these images.

He squeezed Wendy's hand under the table. "I also want more quality time with you dear. It won't be long now."

But as he moved his fork over to her salad plate, he worried if her strength would endure. Never religious, he surprised himself by hearing what he mumbled next. "I just pray my bonus comes before it's too late."

Chapter 4

Years ago, David learned he could block out intrusive painful thoughts by focusing on something concrete. So he decided to go to the library. He needed to read a few more research articles so he could write the paper required to complete his fellowship application. But on his way, his cell phone vibrated. From the prefix of the phone number, he knew the caller was from Georgetown.

"Hello, Dr. Grainger? This is Ryan Leary. You saw me in the Outpatient Oncology Clinic about two months ago. Remember me?"

"Ryan Leary.... It sounds familiar, but I'm not sure."

"I'm sixty-eight and have advanced prostate cancer. You explained why my energy was zero—because all my testosterone was wiped out, remember? And you gave me the phone numbers of some prostate cancer support groups."

"Oh yes, of course. Sorry. It took me a minute to remember." David recalled wondering why Leary's doctor had failed to inform him that decreased vitality was a common side effect. Of course, he could say nothing since interns are not permitted to criticize their faculty physicians. Now he said, "Did you find a group?"

"Yes. I met some nice people at the group. Thanks. Dr. Grainger, I was quite impressed with the personal way you related to me. So may I ask... Would it be possible for you to refill—"

"Mr. Leary, aren't you a patient of Dr. Moskowitz?" David interrupted.

"Yes. I am, but—"

"Are you calling me because he's out of town?"

"Listen, I need to speak to someone who really cares, and you—"

"Before you go on, may I say something? I appreciate your confidence in me, but I'm just an intern. Until I get my medical license, everything I do must be signed off by a faculty doctor." David sighed. "Still, Mr. Leary, I'll try to help if I can. What going on?"

"Doctor Grainger, please, could you just renew my pain medications? I'm not asking you to make any changes from what Emmanuel Moskowitz prescribed. Can you, could you please just do that?"

"No. I wish I could, but Dr. Moskowitz must approve. I'm truly sorry."

"I've tried to get in touch with Dr. Moskowitz, but—"

"If he's out of town, I could get another physician at Urology Associates to call you."

"That's okay." His volume tapered off. "I'll try phoning Moskowitz one more time."

After the click, David was struck with the contrast between the steadiness of the dial tone and the uncertainty of his own conviction. Did he feel drained because he had to say "No"? Or because Leary was so needy? Or because Leary's request tapped right into his conflict about Becker, who would soon feel no pain—at the expense of not feeling anything else, ever again?

David wished he could have prescribed more pain meds for Leary. Helping others was what originally motivated David to enter clinical medicine. He recalled the prayer his mother had posted on their refrigerator door:

> *I expect to pass through this world but once.*
> *Any good that I can do, or any kindness that I can show,*
> *Let me do it now . . . for I shall not pass this way again.*

Somehow he no longer had any motivation to do library research. He changed his direction toward the cafeteria. If the Beckers weren't there yet, he could make up for missing breakfast.

❧

Swarms of doctors, nurses, residents, and visitors. Scrub suits, smocks, white shirts, ties, Bermuda shorts, T-shirts. Wan complexions and sunken eyes. Dishes clattering, isolated bursts of laughter. A droning television mounted high in the corner.

David stood at the entrance of the cafeteria, scanning the crowd for Becker's parents. They were easy to spot, huddled together over a table in the farthest corner. David took a deep breath and walked toward them. He considered asking them to move to the Quiet Room. However, the cafeteria might be a better place to discuss their son's fate. With its constant chaotic rush and the smell of fried potatoes, stewed tomatoes, and coffee, the room was a churning sea of life that might remind the Beckers there was more to the world than the sinking island that was their son.

Or was David just finding an excuse? In the public glare of the cafeteria, this dreaded conversation would likely be shorter.

Joseph Becker was shaped like a fifty-gallon drum: no neck, no waist, his arms as thick as most people's legs. David had learned the construction contractor specialized in refurbishing historic homes to meet the strict specifications of the Washington, DC Historical Society. His snowy-haired wife, Angeline, sat beside him. They were holding hands. Mrs. Becker watched David approach through thick-lensed glasses.

David took the chair across from Mr. Becker. "I don't know if you remember me. I'm one of the doctors from the third floor, where your son is. Dr. Grainger?"

Mechanically, Joe Becker extended a massive hand. Its strength and roughness were a stark contrast to his son's skeletal, quivering fingers.

"Mr. and Mrs. Becker, we need to talk. Would you prefer to go to the Quiet Room?" David gulped, realizing that question heralded him as the bearer of bad news.

Joe glanced at his wife. She didn't move. "No," he said.

"I was sent—It's about Donald. Remember, you signed a DNR order?"

For several heartbeats there was no response. Angeline finally said, "Yes." Her voice, soft as a pussy willow, somehow slipped through the noise of the cafeteria.

Joe remained silent, his posture unchanged.

"As you know," David said, alternating eye contact between the parents, "Donald's condition is not improving. This morning, his pain was worse."

Joe's face frowned deeply. Angeline's mouth curved down.

"During rounds, the other doctors... and myself... we considered the options." David squeezed his thighs together. "These are difficult decisions. One option was to raise the amount of his morphine and add a sedative.—To reduce his pain. But there's a risk." David twisted in his chair. "These meds could stop his breathing, and—" He had to say it. "There's a possibility your son might not make it."

Joe remained still. Angeline looked at her husband, then turned to David. Her eyes were sunken and swollen, her skin looked as if it had been dredged in ash. "So what do you want from us? To approve increasing his medications? To accept the risk he'll die?"

"Is that it?" Joe interrupted "You want us to agree to possibly killing our son?"

Joe's directness shook David. "No, it's not. I mean not I. Not what I want. But I have to—Yes. I do have to ask you if you'd agree."

He couldn't believe what he just said. Exactly what Tom advised him not to. He wished he could take it back. Their faces dropped, proving his words had made them feel guilty. He wanted to run and fade into the crowd. Or hide in the library. But he had to stay. And suffer with them. "This was a very, very hard decision for us, at rounds today. There was even some difference of opinion among the doctors. But we want to do what's best for—"

"Best for yourselves!" Joe Becker's voice rang like a hammer blow on cured concrete. He turned his huge rectangular head and stared hard at David. "Tell me, Doctor, how long will Donald have, if we don't increase his medications?"

"Well, I wouldn't want to—"

"I'm sure you wouldn't. So try this one. How many days ago, even weeks ago, could you have given him enough medications to stop his pain and end his misery? What were all those goddamn forms we signed for, anyway?"

"We tried to ask your son this morning, but he can no longer—"

"Tell me straight." Joe rose from his chair. He was solid like a tree stump. "For once, I want one of you quacks to give me a straight answer. How long has our son been suffering up there while you and your buddies only discussed—only talked about—helping him? Instead of doing something to relieve his misery? How long, Doctor?"

"Mr. Becker," David said, "as physicians, we must preserve life and—"

"And cover your asses!" Joe shoved the table forward with his thighs. His eyes were red-rimmed, swollen. Angeline's hand rose toward him.

"Oh, Jesus, Jesus, you damn doctors. And my poor son."

As startling a sight as water springing from stone, tears poured down his flat cheeks. David wanted desperately to look away, but the sight held him. Joe's hands rose and extended, then swung back up to his face with an audible slap. Through them came the sound of weeping.

On all sides, the cafeteria noises continued.

Angeline rose and stood beside her husband. Standing a half-head taller than Joe, she put one arm around his shoulders and turned to David. "Do what you have to do," she whispered. "Please! Just do it." Tears poured down her face, too.

"I'm sorry. I really am. It hasn't been easy on any of us."

As they continued to cry, David forced himself, "I'm sorry, but I have to ask. This form—Could you sign it? It explains the risks we just talked about."

He handed the clipboard to Angeline, but couldn't watch her sign. A moment later, she handed it back to him.

"Thank you. I'm really sorry." He hated hearing the way his voice sounded with ineffectual words. But he did feel sorry... Sorry for making them decide, sorry for being unable to relieve their guilt, sorry for failing to prevent Donald's imminent death. Sorry for failing so miserably.

As he walked through the cafeteria, David kept his head down for fear that shame might show on his face. Then a boy in a baseball cap caught his eye. He was sitting with a woman, probably his mother, in front of a dish of melted ice cream.

Had the boy lost his appetite because his father was sick? Had he visited his Dad and said the wrong thing? Had he nagged him to get out of bed, reminded him that he had promised to take him to the zoo? Worse, had he wished for another father, one who wasn't too sick to play with him? Did the boy feel guilty now? And would he feel guilty for the rest of his life, as David did, every time he thought of his own father?

A female voice snarled from the boy's direction. "What are you starin' at?"

David shook his head and mumbled, "Sorry." Before he looked away, he noticed the hairless skull underneath the baseball cap.—Chemotherapy, for cancer. No appetite, even for ice cream. David hurried on, his face burning with shame.

Near the exit of the cafeteria he looked up at the television set. The face on the screen looked familiar. Thinning hair and black horn-rimmed glasses. Below the image of Dr. Kenneth Kenard floated the CNN logo and the words "Breaking News." David moved closer to hear the TV over the noise of the cafeteria. "The defense has rested. Closing arguments begin next week."

David wished he were at the courthouse at that very moment. He'd walk right up to Kenard and explain how his actions had shaken the sanctity of medicine, how they had tarnished the whole profession. Doctors were supposed to heal, not kill.

Still under his breath, but louder, "I'd like to punch you in the mouth."

David rushed to the house-staff lunchroom. The sooner he found Tom and gave him Becker's signed consent form, the sooner this whole ordeal would end.

He looked around and saw Michelle Wintress, Tom's girlfriend.

"Hi!" she said brightly. "Tom just called. He'll be down in a few minutes."

He often enjoyed lunching as part of this trio. Today though, despite Michelle's chipper attitude, his spirit was down.

"How's Slowpoke?" asked Michelle.

He forced himself to answer. "Either sleeping or running forty miles per hour."

He appreciated her changing the topic. She convinced him to own a pet even though it seemed stupid for a medical intern whose entire life revolved around the hospital and didn't even have enough time to sleep. Michelle told him that Animal Rescue had a Greyhound that would be "put to sleep" if no one adopted her. Gentle creatures; rich ass holes make them race until they get hurt. She claimed she wasn't allowed to have dogs where she lived and promised to feed and walk her whenever he couldn't.

Later, Tom admitted that Michelle had sensed David's loneliness. Part of her social worker's talent was her knowing when to implement what intervention. Now David couldn't imagine coming home without being greeted by that leaping bundle of bones, sloppy tongue, and unbridled affection. And Michelle kept her promise. She walked Slowpoke every third night.

David yearned for a girlfriend but he didn't envy Tom. He liked Michelle's golden hair and was tempted to flirt with her green eyes, but he couldn't get past her sharp chin and angular physique. They seemed to match her personality. Too aggressive for him.

A chair squeaked. "How did it go?" Tom asked, as he sat down.

Without a word, David handed over the clipboard.

"What else?"

"That's all you need, isn't it?" David said flatly. "Now you can write your orders."

David felt a light hand on top of his. "What's wrong? Why so angry?"

"Not now, Michelle." David resented Michelle's friendly advice when it turned into intrusive psychotherapy. She had accused him of holding back his feelings so many times. "Please, not now."

She took her hand away.

Tom turned to Michelle. "Dr. Franklin forced David to... to do something that'd be very hard for anyone." He caught David's eyes. "Why don't you tell her?"

David wanted to yell, *Stop messing with my mind!* Instead he said, "I appreciate your offer, but now's not a good time. I need to work in the library." More than ever, research was calling him. He wanted to distract his thoughts by focusing on his fellowship paper.

Michelle looked at him with lowered eyes, head cocked, and hair falling at an angle. "David, you can't run away from things."

Again. David stood up. "If there's anyone who knows that running doesn't help, it's me."

⁂

Tom watched David leave with concern. "Ease up a little, Michelle. If he's not ready, don't pressure him."

"But we've got to get him to talk. He's avoiding his issues."

"But you're not his official psychotherapist."

"But I know him and I care about him.—Like a friend."

"Maybe you care too much. That's one reason I love you. But sometimes—"

"I know, that is a problem for me. Tom, can I talk to you about something else? It's the PCC. I'm starting to worry about transferring patients there."

"Why's that?"

"Before I transferred them, my patients were doing okay... not happy of course, but coping. But after being on the PCC, every single one became severely depressed. I know you can't predict exactly how long 'terminal' patients will live, but their previous physicians had predicted much longer survivals. I know because I went back and checked their charts."

"Doesn't the PCC force patients to give up their hope for a cure?" Tom asked.

"No. Patients do best when they come to terms if a cure is no longer possible. You know, *acceptance,* it's so important—"

"Yes, but I heard that the PCC staff forces their patients to sign DNR forms."

"I don't need to hear your 'The rare success of cardio-pulmonary resuscitations in terminal patients' argument. Besides, it's not true. They only ask," said Michelle.

Tom hated the PCC's deal. To receive *Comfort Care,* including expert pain management and treatment to relieve other kinds of suffering, patients had to agree to forgo diagnostic testing and curative treatments. The expertise of the PCC's new head provided Memorial with instant fame in this area. Yet two weeks ago, Tom was forced to ask Donald Becker to choose between *Curative Care* and *Comfort Care* because his insurance company refused to pay for both. And Michelle's concern was warranted. Research showed that depression shortens lifespan. "Telling patients that there's nothing more we can do for them must be depressing. Could that explain why they do so poorly?"

"No way. We never say, 'There's nothing more we can do.' While we don't offer false hope, there *is* much we can do. We never stop caring, and we never write them off. We only encourage them to accept the last chapter of their lives. And try to finding meaning in it. But there is still something I can't figure out. Dr. Cameron takes such a strong personal interest in every patient. Other than psychiatrists, I've never seen a physician spend so much time talking to patients."

Tom softened. "For a department head, that's really rare."

"But my point is, with so much extra attention, plus my extra time, why do they do so poorly?"

Tom just looked at her. He had no answer.

"Today, I came in early to make sure I'd have time to visit Vivian Barretino," she said. "I fear she might be slipping into a severe depression."

"Michelle, did any PCC doctor write an order for a social worker consult?"

"No... but I don't think one is needed. Vivian's in the same hospital—"

"Be careful—"

"Something's wrong on the PCC, Tom. I've got to find out what."

"May I ask, who appointed you? Remember *your* Child Guidance Clinic? I believed you, but what was the bottom line? They fired you and nothing changed. Right?"

Despite his note of caution, Tom admired Michelle's commitment. She showed him an article on how patients survive sixty percent longer after heart attacks if their social workers called them every week. Michelle told him she hope that her extra attention would similarly extend the lives of her terminal patients after they were transferred to the PCC.

"Be careful," Tom said. "Once the physicians you work with transfer a patient to the PCC, she's no longer officially yours. I admire how much you care, but some of the PCC doctors might see your continued interest as intrusive."

"But it's still—it's still right, I mean, morally."

"In hospitals, politics carry more weight than morals. I'm worried about you."

"I love that you care about me, Tom. But for just one minute, consider poor Vivian. Who does she have to worry about her? Only me."

Chapter 5

Dr. Norman Cameron opened the lower left-hand drawer of his oak desk and removed an antique leather doctor's bag. He had reviewed the notes from his Palm Pilot. Comparing her responses to those of other patients, he knew she was close. As he walked down the hall to her room, he wondered if Vivian Barretino had decided to finally end her suffering.

For her, that would be best. With Scleroderma, Vivian would certainly suffer another period of unbearable pain. At that point, she'd be suicidal again, like when she first entered his Palliative Care Center. Again he wondered about her unexpected improvement. Was it due to the extra visits from that social worker that had strained his patience. How goddamn long was he supposed to wait?

Cameron saw no crime in hurrying Nature along. He had no conflict in giving Vivian an opportunity to decide how she'd accept the inevitable. Over the past four days, he gradually replaced her painkillers with placebos. So, her pain had increased to the point where now—instead of several weeks from now—she might be motivated to commit suicide. The point was, why make her go through this kind of anguish again and again, if the ultimate result will be the same?

Cameron entered her room, walked over to the bed, took Vivian's hand, waited for her to open her eyes, and then asked, "Tell me, Vivian, why did you want to see me again, today?"

"I've decided it's time, Doctor. I want my pain to go away. Permanently."

"Are you sure, Vivian? Would you like to talk about it some more?"

She merely looked up at him.

"Vivian, this is your call." He took care to speak very slowly. "This is entirely your choice, you know." He held his breath as he waited for her answer.

"Explain it again. How would it work?"

Cameron reached down to remove a stainless steel bottle from his medical bag. He pointed to the flexible plastic straw in the bottle. "*If*... *If* you definitely decide that you want to drink this... And again, Vivian, it's entirely up to you. You must drink quickly, not stopping until it's all gone. That's for your safety. Otherwise you could end up living indefinitely as a brain-damaged person. The last thing you want is to become a 'vegetable,' isn't it? But if you do decide to drink, and you drink all of it quickly, you'll fall asleep. It will soon become a very, very deep sleep... And then, then all your pain will go away. Forever."

Cameron waited for her response, knowing he need not say anything else.

As he waited for Vivian's response, he reflected on his recent research of which Vivian was the last subject in a series of seven. All the other researchers' work was not only ridiculously superficial, they were seriously flawed. How could they correlate pain and suicidal intent by merely choosing a single number from 1 to 10? The point wasn't to rate their "will-to-live," but their determination to die! Cameron interviewed his patients extensively to learn how they grappled with the option of Physician-Assisted Suicide, not as an abstract concept, but as an option they really believed they could choose. Otherwise, why struggle with that lethal choice? Cameron promised to assist their suicides as he was the head of the PCC, a place they had come to only because they were expected to die. So they believed him based on his position. But it also took his courage. This unique combination made it possible for Cameron to contribute greatly—to medicine and to society.

Cameron had not asked the Human Subjects Research Review Board to approve his research project. Not those dummy committee members. He never expected to publish his findings in a professional journal where only a few hundred academicians would read his article. No, his plan would achieve recognition from millions.

Cameron would educate the masses on how pointless it is to prolong lives after they lost all human quality, or were totally consumed by pain and suffering. He'd create a dramatic video documentary that would be widely distributed, a video that would change the behavior of both doctors and patients so that it would become routine for them to discuss various options to hasten dying.

"Doctor." Vivian's voice jarred him. "I'm ready." Her speech, much stronger than he expected. "I can't continue living like this. There's just no letup."

Out of compassion, in the course of his long clinical career, Cameron had helped dozens of patients to end their lives. But in conducting his current research, he was aware of his own conflict of interest. To be honest, he was biased in wanting his patients to decide to hasten their deaths. That's why he deliberately took extra efforts to make absolutely certain that each patient had several opportunities to change their minds. Then, there would be no question that their decisions were both well-considered and independent. He took pride in the meticulous way he followed his self-imposed ethical code.

"Vivian, are you absolutely sure you want to do this?"

She nodded.

"You know, if you want to change your mind now, just say, 'No.' That's completely fine with me. But you must say it." He looked straight into her eyes. He would not proceed unless she said it. "Say 'Yes' or 'No,' Vivian. Tell me what you want. If you're not sure—"

"Yes. I say, 'Yes,' Doctor."

Cameron's shoulders relaxed a notch. "Okay, now, Vivian, drink this. It will end your suffering." He helped her put the straw to her lips. "With Scleroderma, there's much suffering in your future. If you're sure you want to avoid that... really sure... then drink up, quickly."

She looked directly at him. Her eyes filled with appreciation.

Cameron swallowed. He realized that his face would be the last she'd ever see.

She put her lips to the straw and sucked. She winced at the bitterness.

"Quickly, Vivian. Drink quickly."

Cameron watched her throat swell as she swallowed. Again. And again. When the liquid was completely gone, he exhaled a fear he had been holding back: the fear that Vivian might fall asleep before she drank it all. Thank Heaven she didn't.

Cameron held her hand as her eyes closed and she fell asleep.

He reviewed their conversation. Her act was completely voluntary. He repeatedly emphasized she could change her mind. She had said, "Yes," many times. Then she had nonverbally expressed her desire to end her life by sucking in all the liquid. That proved her determination. Beyond any doubt, Cameron had not swayed her choice.

Cameron waited. Then he pinched her under the arm. She did not respond to pain The anesthesia had therefore begun. Right now, her respirations were still strong, but in two to four hours, she would stop breathing. The danger was that during these hours, some do-gooder on the staff might try to resuscitate her.

That was a chance Cameron would not take.

He retrieved a filled syringe from his bag, inserted the needle into Vivian's IV tubing, and quickly pushed the plunger all the way down.

Vivian Barretino's chest contorted in a single upward heave. She gave a final, feeble whimper, and then slumped motionless.

Cameron put his stethoscope to her chest and listened... A moment later, he released a deep sigh. For a moment, he felt a bit queasy. Then he reminded himself of how much Vivian would have suffered and that thought allowed him to settle down and experience instead a profound sense of satisfaction. He felt sorry about Vivian's recent suffering from his substituting placebos, but that was necessary to prove the connection between extreme pain and suicidal intent. Yet compared to the years of suffering that plagues many victims of Scleroderma, her few days of pain were brief.

He was proud to have applied his knowledge so skillfully. How different from the criminal justice system. After significant doubts arose whether executioners had used adequate doses of sedatives, judges in some states stopped capital punishment because the process might be "cruel and unusual punishment." Might be. There was no way to tell. Any indication the prisoner was experiencing pain was hidden due to the administration of a second drug that caused paralysis. That made "writhing in pain" impossible. In contrast, Cameron's technique was transparent. He used an adequate dose of sedative, but no paralytic drug. Since Vivian remained deeply asleep as he administered the final drug. She had definitely died in peace. A job well done!

He replaced the bottle and syringe in his bag, zipped it up, got to his feet, and stretched. Bending over a patient for so long was murder on his lower back.

He left the room, shut the door, and approached the nurses' station. He anticipated the impulse to add, *Please don't disturb her,* so he said only, "Ms. Barretino is resting quietly." He wanted as much time as possible to elapse before anyone discovered she was dead without saying anything that might seem suspicious in retrospect.

As he walked toward the elevators, he had a sense of accomplishment. He had executed every detail with perfection. Cameron's noble goal—to reduce end-of-life suffering—would never be cloaked in the robe of a martyr standing on trial for murder, like that idiot Dr. Kenard. No one knew Vivian's plan. There was no family to request an autopsy, but even if one were performed, he had previously prescribed the same sedative and no one would check its blood level. As a natural substance, the lethal dose of potassium would leave no trace.

Cameron pushed the elevator UP button and waited. The doors opened.

Out stepped Vivian's social worker.

"Oh. Good evening, Dr. Cameron."

He could only manage a nod as he watched Michelle Wintress walk toward Vivian's room. He retraced his steps quickly enough to place himself between her and the door to Vivian's room. Once there, he caught his breath.

"I'm glad to see you, Ms. Wintress." Cameron's voice had fatherly kindness. "I wanted to tell you how much I appreciate the work you've done with Vivian."

She blushed.

"But she's resting now and does not want any visitors."

Wintress looked puzzled. "But I usually visit her around this time."

"Yes, I know, but I just saw her. Today, she was adamant. 'No visitors.'"

"That doesn't sound like Vivian. You know she has no family or local friends. I'm all she has. I just can't believe she wouldn't want to see me."

Struggling to conceal his irritation, Cameron tensed his toes down. "Yes but she was in a lot of pain and needed more medication. That's why I came in. I told you, she is simply just not up to a visit." He forced a smile and toned down his voice. "Your concern and involvement are impressive, Ms. Wintress, but a patient's wishes must always come first. Don't you agree?"

"But... but she's never refused me before. Can't I just ask—"

"Ms. Wintress," his voice resounded with authority, "you're not questioning my clinical judgment, are you?"

"No, of course not. It's just—" Wintress crossed her arms in front of her chest. "Well, when can I see her?"

"Perhaps tomorrow. However, I suggest you call first."

Cameron instantly regretted his last suggestion. He swallowed hard. There was no way to undo it. At least Wintress turned to go back to the elevator. He entered Vivian's room and looked through the slightly ajar door. He watched Wintress push the DOWN button, wait, and get into the elevator. It descended.

Cameron waited another moment, then stepped out of Vivian's room, firmly closed the door behind him, crossed the corridor, pushed the UP elevator button, and waited. Once inside, he pushed "8." Finally, his respirations began to slow.

Close call. He pondered how to inform Wintress that Barretino was dead. Perhaps he'd have the night nurse call her at home and wake her up. An abrupt emotional shock from a deep sleep might erase the memory of his recommending that she call before she came in.

Chapter 6

David accomplished little at the library. Not able to concentrate intensely on the research articles, they failed to distract him. As he walked back to the Internal Medicine Outpatient Clinic, he ruminated about Becker: Was he feeling guilt, grief, frustration, compassion for his parents, or conflict with Tom and Franklinstein? Did he even want to sort it out? Now he hoped focusing on his patients' problems would provide the distraction he sought. He looked at the white board to see where his first patient was, and entered a small alcove by pulling on its curtain. There sat Joan McCarthy, a woman in her sixties, for her third appointment since her heart attack in February. An attractive nurse had just finished taking her blood pressure and jotted down, "145/92" in her chart.

Ms. McCarthy had spruced up for her doctor's visit. Pearly pink lipstick highlighted her wrinkled lips and a hint of blush shaded her cheekbones.

"How is it, Doctor?" Her voice quavered.

"Tell me, Joan, did your ex-husband give your cats back?"

She blinked. "Why, yes, he did. How did you know?"

The young nurse who assisted Joan looked back as she hung the blood pressure cuff on the wall, obviously eavesdropping. After noticing her great calves, David turned to Joan. "Last time, you were extremely upset about losing your cats."

"I didn't lose my cats! Harry stole them."

"Well, I'm glad you got them back. You know, studies show that caring for small pets significantly lowers the risk of patients having a second heart attack."

"Really?" Joan's eyes brightened with surprise.

"In fact, if you had been petting your cat as the nurse measured your blood pressure, it would have been even lower."

"So, I'm better?" she exclaimed.

"Better, yes. But wait a few more weeks before going to a disco."

She beamed and was suddenly quite lovely. David wondered if her husband left her for a younger woman, but dared not ask. Volumes of research proved that lonely hearts have an increased risk of heart attacks.

David stood by the main desk writing notes in Joan McCarthy's chart as the nurse approached. A gingery dusting of freckles complemented her green eyes and a large bun of hair perched on the back of her head. David wondered how her hair would look if she let it down.

"Can I ask you a question, Dr. Grainger? Every month, you must see hundreds of patients. So how did you remember Joan's cats?"

"Maybe because I have a dog." David glanced briefly at her badge. "Slowpoke definitely saved me from having a heart attack this year, Cathy."

"But I've seen you recall special things about other patients." Her smile revealed great teeth. "You'll be a good clinician. It's a pleasure to see you work."

"Thanks for the feedback. My mentor taught me—the best way to take care *of* a patient is to care *about* the patient."

"I agree! Who was your mentor?"

"Dr. Gerald Solomon."

"Our Chief of Staff?"

"Yes. It was a great loss to teaching when he went into administration." For a moment, David felt some guilt, then he knew why. He decided to explain. "I'm planning to spend next year as a research fellow. That will take me away from patients."

"For a while. But many fellows return to clinical medicine. I predict you'll come back"

"Why?"

"Because you do care."

David said, "Thanks, I'll have to think about that," but what he really thought was how nice it was to receive appreciation from an attractive female. It had been a long time. He wondered if Cathy's interest in him extended beyond clinical medicine. "Cathy, if you happen to be free, I'm invited to a party at Dr. Solomon's, this Saturday night. They're celebrating his son's return from India. He and I were roommates at Brown, and—"

She giggled softly. "I'm sorry, Dr. Grainger, I'm married. I don't wear a ring when I'm working. But thanks... really."

David felt awkward. "Okay. I still enjoyed working with you."

"Me too. Listen Doctor, keep up the good work."

David knew his embarrassment would end as he took care of his next patient. He looked at the list. Oh, no. It was someone he'd secretly given the nickname, "Mr. Whiner." After checking the radiologist's report, David anticipated disclosing the results would be difficult.

Floyd Panogakos was a frail man with papery skin and a wet, sulky lower lip that shone in the overhead lights. David figured his psychosocial development was about that of a seven-year-old. More correctly, a spoiled seven-year-old.

"Mr. Panogakos, your X-rays explain why you need to use three pillows to sleep at night. And why you're so tired. It's because your heart is enlarged. But we can—"

"My heart? Now my heart is going bad, also?"

"Yes. Probably a side effect from the radiation treatment you received years ago. But—"

"Those damn treatments also made my teeth fall out. What the hell is next? My nuts?"

David's jaw tightened, but he reminded himself that Floyd was a sick, scared, and immature man. "I know side effects are bothersome, but medications can reduce them. You were first diagnosed with Hodgkin's Disease, when? Twenty-three years ago, right?"

Panogakos nodded, with a smirk.

"You're fortunate, though. Without that treatment, you'd—"

"I'd probably be better off. Your damn cure is worse than my disease."

David took a step back. "Absolutely not. Hodgkin's is a very serious disease. Don't you realize you're—"

"What? Lucky? Lucky I'm alive? All you doctors say that. But I'm falling apart. One part of my body after another!"

"I said I can prescribe medications to help strengthen your heart and—"

"How about prescribing enough sleeping pills so I can end it all, Doctor? Do you know—"

But instead of listening, David was recalling a scene from his second year at medical school. In bed, as he studied *Robbins Pathologic Basis of Disease*, he learned how recent advances in the chemotherapy of Hodgkin's Disease was permitting patients to live for twenty-five years or more. That's when David flung the book across the room, as if it were a Frisbee. The five-pound textbook shattered an old floor lamp that was his father's favorite. As his anger subsided, he felt sad. He missed his father and felt guilty about his own selfish behavior...

Panogakos' reed-thin voice jolted David's consciousness back to the alcove. "... And you're no better than the other doctors. None of you give a shit. Every new med gives me more side effects. There's only one way to end it."

"I'm sorry, Mr. Panogakos—"

"I'm sorry too. How about finding me a doctor who does care—if one exists?"

"I guess I could try, but please understand, side effects are just part—"

"Jesus, you're such a broken record. You try living with this. Do you know—"

David slammed his stethoscope down on the exam table. "You get a little tired, Floyd? Need to sleep on an extra pillow? Need false teeth? How sad. How terribly sad." David heard his voice rise, but was powerless to stop it. "You're so lucky to be alive, so fortunate that you didn't die twenty years ago, so blessed that you didn't have to leave your wife and son forever."

David stopped shouting but his heart was beating hard.

Panogakos stared at him, slack-jawed.

The alcove curtains swished aside. Tom stuck his head in. "Excuse me, Doctor, would you help me with something—out here?"

David took a breath. "Get dressed, Mr. Panogakos. I'll see you in a few minutes."

"Like hell you will," Panogakos growled.

David followed Tom down the hall to a quiet corner. "What was that all about?"

"Nothing." Sweat stung the corner of David's eye.

"Nothing?" Mendendorf frowned. "You were really spouting off."

"Panogakos was ungrateful, that's all."

"Hell, if you're going to yell at ungrateful patients, you'd better invest in a truckload of throat lozenges. Are you still upset about Becker?"

"No, that's not it. Well, maybe. I guess I just blew it, that's all."

"There's got to be more. What is Panogakos' history?"

"He's a twenty-three-year survivor of Hodgkin's Disease."

"And?"

"Well, back then, Hodgkin's patients rarely lived for more than three years."

"And you wanted him to appreciate his long-term survival?"

"Right."

"Anything else, David?"

"This whole day sucks. First rounds with Franklin. Then in the cafeteria, I blew it with the Beckers. But I was wrong to take out my frustrations on another patient."

Tom sighed. "Yes, it has been a rough day. And now, I have to tell you something that will make it rougher. Donald Becker died while you were in the library. At least he went peacefully, with his parents by his side. They, they actually seemed relieved—"

"I'm glad it went smoothly." David tried to sound like he meant it.

"David, why don't you talk to Michelle? Or maybe you'd prefer to hang out, jus the two of us, over a couple of beers?"

"No thanks, Tom. I'm glad you asked. It's not easy to lose a patient, but I'll be fine."

David waited a while for Tom to say something, but the resident just looked at his watch. Seemed like David had said enough to get him off his back. Between Tom Mendendorf, M.D., and Michelle Wintress, L.C.S.W., his life could easily become a goddamn psychotherapy marathon.

Chapter 7

Ryan Leary saw Jonathan glance at his watch for the third time. "Where the hell is Pratt?" his son said. "He promised to give me ample time to get to the airport."

"You can go now. I'll live without a nurse for a few minutes." He motioned to the phone. "There's always 9-1-1."

From his adjustable-railed hospital bed, Ryan swallowed his desire to say more. His chest gnawed as he watched his son pace. Not since he'd rocked Jonathan as a baby in this very room had the old hardwood floors of the Georgetown brownstone creaked so rhythmically.

"I'll stay just a few more minutes. Where the hell is Bruce?"

"Pratt called when you were downstairs, loading your bags. He just had a flat tire." Ryan wondered if his words sounded convincing. To him, they buzzed like a loose fan blade—Thanks to the damn feeding tube running through his nose.

"That could take a long time."

"Not him. He's a mechanical whiz. He'll probably pull in as you're leaving."

Ryan hated lying to his son. It was the first time. Ten days ago, Ryan returned exhausted from Memorial. After a dismal meeting with Dr. Cameron, he made a decision that had to be kept secret. "Go now," he said to his son. "Traffic to Dulles might be terrible. With an absolute zero level of testosterone, how could I get into trouble?" Ryan managed a wink despite deep bone pain.

"You can joke now? After being so angry at your doctors?"

"I've finally learned that anger is its own punishment."

"So you feel better now?" Jon's voice sounded desperate for hope.

"We junkies feel great all the time." Ryan forced a smile with his mouth closed, to hide his bleeding gums—a side effect of chemotherapy. The truth was, being undertreated for pain still enraged him. How ironic to discuss this on the very morning he had to fake taking meds so he could think more clearly and maximize his strength.

Jonathan's face brightened. He leaned over the bed, kissed his father's brow, and turned to pull a chair towards the bed.

"You put that chair right back. I said, 'Go!' Good luck in Boston."

Jonathan put his hand on his father's cheek.

Such a good boy, Ryan thought. The best. "Have a safe trip."

As Ryan heard Jon running down the stairs, he knew his last chance to say a real good-bye was drifting away, forever. The ache in his stomach spread upward as the garage door opened and the Volvo started....

Now he could let the tears stream down his cheeks and drop the façade of well-being. He so much wished he could have told his son how proud he was of him, how solid he thought his life-values were, how many ways he was like his mother.—His beloved Audrey. Ryan was certain she'd be waiting for him on the other side.

To shake off his sadness, Ryan congratulated himself on creating a successful ruse. When he heard the news of a multi-car accident on the traffic report, he phoned Pratt and advised him to take Route 267 between Fairfax and Georgetown. His nurse was late precisely because Ryan directed him right into that pile-up.

Ryan pressed a button to raise his bed into a sitting position and let the guardrail drop. With care, he tried to swing his legs out and down—

His spine exploded. Pain burst in every direction, flashed into every limb, crashed against the back of his skull. The room darkened and he screamed.

Two months ago, he had pleaded with Dr. Moskowitz for a higher dose of pain meds. But the doctor gave the nurses strict instructions to dole out exactly what he prescribed and no more. Later, when Ryan confronted the doctor, he learned the doctor's strong religious belief prevented him from prescribing a dose of pain killers that risked shortening a patient's life. Upon hearing his admission, the former President of Leary Industries fired Moskowitz on the spot. He would have sued, but a more urgent agenda item demanded his attention.

Ryan had to search for a replacement doctor. Patients in his prostate cancer support group whispered that a doctor named Kenard might help. But after leaving two messages on his answering machine and receiving no call back, Ryan figured he was just another worthless doctor. Then he read the headline: "MERCY KILLER TRIAL BEGINS." Evidently, the Catholic Church had found exactly what it wanted: a right-to-die M.D., ready to crucify.

Ryan felt he had zero options until two weeks ago. That's when he received an unexpected call from the Head of Memorial's new Palliative Care Center. Dr. Norman Cameron introduced himself as the PCC's specialist in *Comfort Care*. Ryan hoped this self-proclaimed leader in pain control would offer him the ultimate, permanent release. So he endured being tied into a wheelchair and shoved into a special van, to let Jonathan drive him to Memorial.

Extraordinary effort. Absolutely draining.—A total waste of time.

After a quick review of his chart and a superficial physical examination, Cameron sat down to talk. "You're welcome to come to our Palliative Care Center. But I never give patients false hopes. I'm sorry, but there is a limit to how much even we can do for you." Concern etched in the creases across the doctor's face. "It won't be easy, from here on out."

Not knowing Cameron, Ryan feared being locked up on a psych ward if he directly asked for enough morphine to end his life. So he only hinted. And Cameron acted like he didn't understand. When Ryan thought about it later, he figured the bastard knew all right. He just wouldn't admit it.

Today, he made one last-ditch call to that nice intern who referred him to group therapy. When getting another month's supply of medication did not work, he had to implement "Plan B." He'd feign willingness to check into the PCC after his son returned from Boston. But by then... no more pleading with doctors, no more humiliation from a middle-aged male nurse changing his diapers, no more feeding tube, no more Foley catheter in his penis, and no more pain.

—No more Ryan Leary.

It was a tough choice. But a rational choice.

Ryan left Jonathan a note. It asked him to forgive his subterfuge and tried to convince him not to blame himself for going to Boston. Hopefully his son would see the wisdom of sparing them both weeks of misery. For what? Christ, he had zero quality of life.

Ryan focused on the wall above the shelves that displayed his college tennis trophies. There, a crucifix of Jesus' arms extended, his fingers curled in agony. Ryan could relate to the figure now, as never before. In his mind he heard his own voice say, *This is my blood that is given for you. Drink, that ye may have everlasting life.*

Ryan clutched the sheets, and worked his legs—stalks of desiccated driftwood, every bone and tendon throbbing—inch-by-inch, over the side of the bed. He bent his knees, touched his feet to the floor, and let them support his weight. Weeping in pain, he prayed for his suffering to end.

"Father, take this cup. Oh, God, my God! Take it, take it, take it!"

As the wave of pain subsided, he realized his diaper had fallen to his ankles. He stepped over it, letting the Foley catheter drag along the floor.

On the street, he heard a car decelerate. His heart thumped as he visualized Pratt rushing in, seeing him in pain, insisting he swallow all his missed pills. Ryan would welcome the relief–though partial and temporary.

The car moved on. He sighed. His resolve returned.

In his youth, he could have crossed the room in two long strides. His youth? Three years ago. Now his tiny sliding steps sounded like hissing. He concentrated to maintain his balance.

He made his way to the foyer. Pale May sunshine fell through the beveled-glass window. It reminded him that he'd miss tonight's sunset. So what? He'd seen enough.

He stepped to the staircase and raised his right foot, intending to place it on the first step. But his left leg shrieked, forcing him to put his right foot down. Sweat poured down his back and chest. His head throbbed like a bass drum. He closed his eyes, inhaled, and raised his right foot again. This time, he used his arms to grab the banister and pulled. A thin squeal escaped his compressed lips. But when the thundering blackness faded, he was standing on the first step.

How many times would he have to repeat this, to get to the attic?

One step at a time, moving in and out of consciousness, he trudged on. Could he make it? He wasn't sure until he finally reached the top floor hallway. Surprisingly, he felt buoyant, floating above the cloud of pain. If only it would last—

It didn't.

He shuffled across the half-lit hallway to his wife's old sewing room. He grasped the doorknob, but it was instantly coated with sweat and slipped when he tried to turn it. He put his hand under his loose gown, grabbed the knob with it, tightened his grip, and twisted.

The door opened.

Inside, an intricate array of ceiling beams formed triangles that pointed to his window of opportunity. He shuffled toward it and looked out. Straight ahead, branches of a maple tree spread beyond the small extension of eaves. Below, patches of bright-green spring grass interspersed with blocks of cement.

A car stopped in his driveway. Pratt exited. Ryan stepped back from the window and held his breath. When he looked again, the driveway was empty. Pratt would be coming. And soon. He must hurry.

Ryan twisted the window latch. It creaked but turned. He grabbed both brass tabs at the bottom of the window frame and pulled. The window didn't budge.

He rested briefly, took a deep breath, then hauled up with all his strength. His entire body convulsed, jolted as though electrically charged. He had to lean against the window to keep from falling. When the spasm passed, he slumped over and sobbed. His last obstacle—

Tears filled his eyes. He shivered. The pain was too intense to try again.

The front door slammed. "Hello?" He heard Pratt's puzzled shout. "Mr. Leary? Ryan? Where are you?"

Ryan looked around the room. In the corner was an old desk chair on casters. Exactly what he needed. He rolled the chair in front of the window and turned it sideways so the backrest would be out of his way. He took one enormous lunge to stand on the chair seat, then clutched the window frame as the chair wobbled underneath him.

His teeth clenched as he tasted blood.

"Ryan? Ryan?" Footsteps, rapid thuds, racing up stairs. Louder, closer—

With his arms by his side, Ryan twisted his back to a tennis serving position, paused a second, closed his eyes, and hurled himself head first through the glass window.

A burst of glass. The whole world stopped.

His senses returned. Underneath his stomach, something hard. His eyes focused. Damn, he was barely three feet from the window. He had landed on the damn eaves. He tried to roll away from the window to drop off the eaves. But he couldn't move. He looked back. His nightgown had snagged on a stalagmite of broken window glass. He was completely exposed around the Foley.

Pratt's voice, loud and clear. "What the hell are you doing out there, Leary?"

He saw the nurse staring at him through the broken window.

Ryan opened his mouth. Blood gurgled onto his lips and chin.

Pratt's voice softened. "You poor sick jerk." The nurse put his hands between the fragments of glass and bent toward him.

Ryan strained away, but the nightgown held taut. "Let me go."

"I can reach you. Don't worry."

Ryan wondered if he'd only imagined speaking. Again he said, "Let me go!"

Pratt took a step back, then stared at him in silence. "Look at you! Leary, what a God-awful mess! Those bloody lines across your face will take months to heal. And the scars will make you a photogenic zero. You're useless." He shook his head. "You blew your chance to become our movie star."

Pratt pulled out a pocketknife and slit the nightgown off the broken glass.

Ryan slid down a few inches. Was he finally free? He took a breath, preparing to summon his last bit of energy to roll toward the drop-off.

Then he saw Pratt pull back his fist. A sledgehammer crushed into his left side and propelled him over the edge. Instantly, everything changed.

Gushes of air swirled around him, but he couldn't breathe any in.

⁂

Gazing through the window, Bruce Pratt pondered why he had paused so long. Okay, the poor old bastard looked pathetic, lying there, with his Foley hanging out. But what the hell difference did that make? He had no pity for him.

He turned from the window, walked downstairs, and entered Leary's sickroom.

He had three calls to make. But he could make only one of them from Leary's phone.

He picked up the handset and hit the numbers 9-1-1.

Chapter 8

The ER was a tsunami of activity. Patients rolled in moaning and wailing. Gurneys rattled over linoleum. "I bet it's the overflow from the pileup on Route 267," Tom shouted to David over the noise. They hurried past victims sprawled over plastic chairs, lying on the floor, on gurneys. Bruised and bloody. Some moaning, others sobbing, a few in stunned silence.

The ER supervisor shoved a tattered two-inch thick chart into David's hands. "The trauma team called the resident who had almost finished working up this patient. Send her home fast, okay? We need the cubicle."

David nodded, turned and entered the alcove.

"Olive Faulkner?"

A heavyset African-American woman pointed to the wizened lady in a wheelchair. "Yes, my mother. Where's the other doctor?"

"I'm Dr. Grainger, Mrs. Faulkner." David nodded to the daughter as he took Olive's fingers gently in his. "I'll be discharging you."

David placed the chart on the end of the bed and looked at her, before putting the stethoscope in his ear. The old lady wheezed a shrill whine every time she struggled to pull up her tiny chest. With the scope on her chest, her lungs sounded like band-saw rasps. When David stepped back again, her eyes had bulged and her mouth gaped, thrusting her dentures forward. Her face was turning blue! Her hands flew in the air, clawing wildly. In her eyes, David saw the greatest fear any human being can experience—the fear of not being able to breathe.

"Hey! Help her. She can't breathe," the daughter yelled.

David threw back the alcove curtain, ran to the medication counter, grabbed an aerosol inhaler, hurried back, and pressed the spout to Olive's purple lips. She clamped her hands over his, strained to suck in air, heaving again and again. Gradually the blue tide in her face receded. Her breathing eased. She closed her eyes as David removed the inhaler.

She moved her lips without vocalizing. "Bless you. God bless you."

"Is she all right?" the daughter shrilled. "Is she all right?"

"I'm fine now, Sweetie," Olive whispered. "I feel much, muh—" She stiffened. Again her hands rose in marionette jerks.

David replaced the inhaler and waited for Olive's breathing to stabilize. The floating nurse peeped in. David gestured for her to stay. "Don't worry, Mrs. Faulkner, I'll be right back."

He hustled out to the central desk and handed the chart to the charge nurse. "I can't discharge this lady. She needs a thorough pulmonary work-up."

The nurse nodded, opened the chart, and then shook her head. She pointed to a handwritten note on top of the chart. It said, "Call Director of Patient Services."

To David, "Patient Services" was a euphemism for the hospital's collection agency. Its Director lectured to the interns about eight months ago and should have used the title, "Maximizing insurance returns by making the most financially rewarding diagnoses." That was only one way to improve the hospital's economic bottom line. The other method sifted down to interns without a lecture: Deny admission to uninsured, indigent patients. Like Olive Faulkner.

David's call to Patient Services confirmed his suspicion. Memorial had not been paid for Mrs. Faulkner's previous ER visit so she would not be admitted unless her crisis was life-threatening. But they also warned David not to discharge her unless she was medically stable. Otherwise, the hospital could be accused of abandonment, which carries a fine of $25,000 and would open them to a potential lawsuit.

David was more worried about Olive than Memorial's legal liability. If the cause of her respiratory failure was not treated, next time she might expire on her way to the hospital.

David rarely called his mentor for clinical advice, but right now, he'd welcome Dr. Solomon's wisdom. He dialed the number, but when he heard the answering machine's message, he hung up. Olive Faulkner needed his immediate action.

He thought for a moment, picked up the phone, and knew exactly what to do.

A few minutes later, he opened the curtain of the alcove, thanked the nurse in such a way that she'd leave. He gave Olive's daughter a hard look. "I'd like your mother to get the best care. But I have to ask you if I can count on you. Can you be discreet in handling your part?"

She nodded, tentatively. "What do you mean?"

"University Hospital is way across town, but that's where your mother needs to go. The problem is, when the discharge nurse checks you out... it would be better... you know what I mean, if you didn't mention that you're taking her there."

The daughter nodded more definitely. "Oh, I see. Politics? It's everywhere."

The tight knot of pain above David's right eye eased. Todd Silver, his medical school buddy at University Hospital, had agreed to admit Olive as a teaching case so she'd get a pulmonary work-up.

David bent down to make eye contact. "Mrs. Faulkner, the doctors at University will take care of you. Okay?"

"Whatever you say, Doctor," She touched his arm. "You're very kind and—"

The squeal of ambulance tires drowned out her next words. David threw back the alcove curtain as the ER doors flew open. Two Emergency Medical Technicians rushed in, steering a rattling gurney on which arms and legs stuck out at odd angles. David looked up at the supervisor's work board. He was up for this next admission.

"Jumper," one EMT told him. "Took a header through an attic window. Really mean glass cuts. Broke almost every bone in his stupid body."

"Care to put that in more professional terms?" David trotted alongside the gurney, dodging traffic in the jammed corridor.

"Sorry," the first EMT responded. He looked at his partner to answer.

"Multiple compound fractures, probable skull fracture. Rule out subdural hematoma. Multiple thoracic lacerations. Internal bleeding. This guy actually jumped *through* a glass window. Deep facial cuts. Two units of plasma, so far."

"Lucky though," the first EMT said. "We found him lying on a small patch of grass between slabs of concrete. Had he landed on the hard stuff, we would be rolling him into the morgue, right now."

David glanced at the chrysalis of bandages and tape surrounding a motionless head above a cervical collar. Blood welled up through the cloth in long, thin lines in a way that was characteristic of sharp cuts from razors or glass. One eye peered up with a glazed expression. David took out his flashlight. The pupil reacted to light.

"He'll need thoracic surgery first, then orthopedic surgery. I'll call the plastic surgeons, also." He took the clipboard from the EMT and scanned the papers. When he saw the name, he gasped. *"Ryan Leary! Leary? My God! What happened?"*

The pain behind David's right eye exploded like a bomb had gone off. He yearned for a little time to think about the phone conversation he had with Leary a few hours ago. But there was too much to do. He stammered, "You'll make it, Ryan. I'll help you get through this."

David's reflexes kicked into automatic. He dialed the surgery secretary and gave her his long list. Then he guided Leary's gurney to X-ray. He sat down and waited. Normally, this would be the time in his routine when he'd read the patient's old hospital chart, call his other doctors to alert them that their patient had been admitted, and write the initial treatment plan. But David was too shaken to do anything but sit there, as his mind flooded with questions.

Why did Leary call? Had he really run out of pain meds? Did he request more so he could overdose? Was jumping his second choice for suicide? Did David miss a cry for help by not suspecting suicide? Was there any way David could have prevented this tragedy?

Right now, David had no information to answer any of these nagging questions. Most likely, he never would know. The dictations of other physicians would not address them. Although new to the practice of clinical medicine, David understood this reality about a patient's medical history. Although important, it is prudent to leave some facts out—to avoid lawsuits.

Chapter 9

Cameron was so focused on Barretino and Wintress as he entered the elevator that he jumped when his cell phone started to vibrate. He looked at the strange ID number. He didn't recognize the area code, so most likely, the caller was Bruce Pratt. To avoid anyone tracing their calls, the Good Life Committee gave Pratt several pre-paid cell phones. Registered around the county in a variety of fictitious names, Pratt just threw the phones away after making a few calls.

Cameron couldn't talk in public. "Is that you?" ... "Call me back in two minutes, okay?"

He had barely sat down at his desk when his phone vibrated again.

"Bad news, Doc. Leary took a high dive right through his attic window. I'm sorry that I got here too late to stop him."

Cameron said, "Oh, no," but felt himself smiling. Good thing Pratt couldn't see his face.

Privately, he congratulated himself for handling Leary's interview in such an artful way. Now, he'd win his conflict with the Good Life Committee by default. With Leary eliminated, they'd be forced to give him the extra time he needed to search for a more suitable patient to star in their ***Finale*** video. Cameron was so excited that he almost missed Pratt's next words.

". . . and the SOB's still alive."

The heavy pressing in Cameron's stomach felt like the time he was knocked flat in a college boxing match. "Alive? Where is he now?"

"Getting closer every minute, Doc. I sent him to the ER at Memorial."

Stunned, Cameron hung up. His initial remorse for Leary's botched suicide attempt turned into a feeling of validation. —Another of life's natural experiments. Leary had inadvertently become "living" proof that terminal patients need doctors to help them commit Physician-Assisted Suicide. Without such aid, they can increase their suffering instead of ending it.

The crucial question for Cameron was, how long would he live? His next move depended on whether or not Leary survived. If Leary ever told the committee how discouraging Cameron had been with him—

A noise from his front office made Cameron jerk straight up in his chair. His secretary had already left for the day. "Who's there?"

The office door swung open. Howard Hayneswurth, the silver-haired chairman of the Good Life Committee, bounded in. "Why the hell did Leary jump?"

"I don't know." Cameron caught his breath. How did Hayneswurth find out so quickly? "I just spoke to Pratt. He was also surprised."

"You have no idea?" Hayneswurth sat in the leather chair in front of Cameron's desk.

"Patients get suicidal when they're hopeless," Cameron's superior tone was designed to level Hayneswurth's power. The economist had represented the Good Life Committee when offering Cameron his job. But he knew little about clinical medicine so Cameron would rub that in. "The most frequent underlying factors that cause hopelessness are unrelenting pain, fear of losing control, a sense of increased dependency, and a belief they have become a great burden to others."

"For God's sake, Norman, just answer this: Could you predict Leary would try to take his own life, or not? Yes or No?"

"Remember Howard, I only saw Leary once. Two weeks ago he seemed impressed with my reputation in pain management. He said he was eager to enter our PCC. I even sent Pratt to make home visits. I was anticipating his admission any day now—"

"Are you saying 'No' then? You had no idea he would do this?"

"Suicide is often an impulsive act."

Hayneswurth shook his head. "Will he live?"

"Let me try to find out." Cameron tried to hide his own urgency. He keyed Leary's patient code into his computer. "He's in thoracic surgery now and is also scheduled for orthopedic surgery, They won't send him to ortho unless he does well. So we'll know in a couple of hours." Cameron stared hard. "Does that answer all your questions?"

The corners of Hayneswurth's mouth twitched. "I bet you're pleased, Doctor."

"I beg your—"

"Even if Leary survives, he'll never star in our video. So, you win. You always advised the committee against choosing a terminal patient with pain."

"Not exactly. I only encouraged us to choose the most convincing person for our ***Finale***."

Hayneswurth huffed. "You must also realize that timing is critical. End-of-life medicine is wasting hundreds of billions of dollars a year. State legislatures don't seem ready to legalize Physician-Assisted Suicide. So we must sway public opinion by producing our video now!"

"But we also must create the most dramatic appeal—"

"Cameron, if we wait too long, Medicare will crumble as fewer available young workers become strapped with paying for more old sick patients." Cameron wondered if Hayneswurth was trying to get back at him by delivering a lecture on economics. "Other health insurance companies will go bankrupt and our major financial institutions will collapse," he continued. "Clinton was right. Ignoring health-care reform will result in the end of our present way of life. But George W. was only partially right—to focus on Social Security, when Medicare is in far more trouble."

"The economic domino effect?" Cameron said, to make it appear that he was interested.

"Yes." Hayneswurth's eyes narrowed and his voice grew icy. "Our sponsors don't have the luxury of waiting any longer. Either they cut costs to increase the profits of their health and long-term care insurance companies now—or they'll lose their jobs. If that happens, we'll lose our bonuses. Got that?"

Cameron took a deep breath. Interesting how the pressure had made Hayneswurth finally admit his greed. "Okay, I understand the great pressure our sponsors are under. But Leary's disaster exemplifies exactly why terminal patients with pain are not suitable for the ***Finale***."

To stop Hayneswurth from interrupting him, Cameron raised his hand. "Using a patient with pain for our ***Finale*** video is a grave mistake. It would portray Physician-Assisted Suicide as the last desperate resort for pain relief. In turn, that would invite criticism from pain specialists, Hospice and other caregiving organizations." Cameron pointed at Hayneswurth. "To be convincing, our documentary must portray Physician-Assisted Suicide as a prudent, rational choice for *any* patient who has experienced a profound loss in quality of life. Patients who suffer from painless dementia, and unconscious patients, including those in comas or in the permanent vegetative state, as well as their family members, will all be better able to identify with a ***Finale*** star who has no pain. "

"You're right, but first, you must find such a patient, Doctor."

"Howard, I insist, the patient we select to star in our ***Finale*** must still have all his wits, so he cannot be taking narcotics to relieve severe pain. Is that clear?"

"Yes, in theory. I agree. But the type of patient you prefer seems scarce. You've kept us waiting five months so far." Hayneswurth stood up, looking impatient. "Look, I am calling a meeting of the Good Life Committee for Saturday, at 1:00 p.m. The Embassy Suites in Tyson Corners. Leary's out. And I'm done waiting, Doctor. Two days from now, Doctor, our committee will select a star for our ***Finale*** from one of your potential candidates. Got that?"

"But that's outrageous. I need more time to—."

"Yes, it's time. Be prepared to stay all afternoon, into the evening if necessary."

Cameron stared at Hayneswurth without saying a word.

As he watched Hayneswurth leave, Cameron muttered, "Shortsighted idiot." Yet his whining about how their sponsors might lose their jobs was probably accurate. The healthcare industry had been up and down for quite a while. Cameron could still remember when Oxford Health stock lost 90 percent of its value. Its shareholders were so angry, they ousted its CEO in 1998. Hayneswurth was right. Reducing end-of-life expenses was urgent. And not just for companies that sold health insurance. With the expected three-fold increase in the number of patients suffering from dementia and the relative three-fold decrease in family members available to take care of them at home for free, there will also be a crisis for companies that sell long-term care insurance.

The ***Finale*** had to be successful for Cameron to receive a full bonus. His remuneration, like that of the other members of the Good Life Committee, was based on performance. The greater the savings in insurance claims, the greater their bonuses. So Cameron's insistence on the qualities of the ***Finale's*** star was not just for pride or scientific recognition, although they too were important. Success could make the difference between two and five million. And he deserved the higher figures since he was taking the greatest professional risk. After all, he would be the ***Finale*** patient's attending physician, he'd write the documentary's script, he'd direct the action, and he'd be the co-star in the final drama. This project could not proceed without him. But he needed them, too. In addition to his monetary bonus, the committee would provide Wendy and him with new identities so they could enjoy the trip of their lifetimes. For Wendy, the last trip of her life.

Cameron unlocked the bottom drawer of his desk and took out a folder. He perused his list of potential terminal patients who were in no pain. Advanced Multiple Sclerosis, widespread paralysis from strokes, end-stage emphysema, congestive heart failure....

Any of these diseases could evoke great sympathy. But just as important as medical diagnosis was the ***Finale*** patient's ability to command respect from his social stature and personal history. Furthermore, he must possess excellent communication skills; he must arouse deep emotions in his viewers.

Cameron's handpicked list of eligible patients had originally numbered seventeen. Three had died before the PCC opened. So far, none of the others had progressed to the point where they needed hospitalization. But several were close. He scanned the list of remaining names.

One of them could be his star. The question was, *who?*

Chapter 10

Four miles from the Capital, in Arlington, Virginia, a board game was in progress.

"Check." Ben Brewster said, after his daughter snatched his Queen. "Trying to destroy your poor old pop?"

"Just once." Her eyes sparkled. "Just this once."

Ben peered at the board. "Please have my King's Bishop capture your Pawn." He allowed himself a narrow smile. "Oh, by the way, Sammie, that's check, again."

"No problem, Imperialist Swine." She immediately moved her King. "Saw it coming. You're dead meat this time."

After a moment Ben said, "You know, beating your butt at chess is not quite as exciting since I have to ask you to move my pieces. My Knight to Queen-5, please."

Sammie grabbed the black Knight, hesitated, and then looked at the board. "Damn."

He grinned. "Checkmate!"

"Not again."

"You wouldn't want me to let you win, would you?"

"Of course not, but—"

"Honey, I've played chess for forty-five years. Even with only my 'power finger,' I beat every internet opponent. Only Captain Travis can consistently beat me."

Sammie took her father's power finger, the index finger of his right hand, in hers. "It figures. Another soldier. Chess is such a man's game."

Ben laughed. A wheezing sound—nothing like the old roar that used to embarrass his wife when he let it loose in public. "But you also said that about Scrabble."

"I still say 'debriefing' is slang. Women use it as they remove their panties."

Ben laughed again. He loved his daughter's sense of humor. He twitched his finger into her palm, realizing what a poor substitute it was for those big bear hugs they used to enjoy. "Your thinking is intuitive, like your mother's. When I tried to teach her chess, she waxed artistic by moving the pieces around so they'd look best."

Sammie's laugh was a feminine version of Ben's full-throated explosion. It saddened Ben to note how rarely he heard it these days. That had to be his fault.

—His and Lou Gehrig's.

Of course, he shouldn't blame a great baseball player for having this terrible disease named after him. And Ben tried not to blame the ignorant physicians who did research on Amyotrophic Lateral Sclerosis, for whom ALS remained a baffling mystery. After decades of flawlessly sending electrical impulses to instruct muscles to contract—suddenly, the nerves stopped communicating. Why? In some cases, medical scientists could point to a gene or implicate an enzyme, but no one really knew why the nerves just stopped—unpredictably but relentlessly—one muscle group after another.

It was more than two years since Ben last carted around a golf course, almost a year since he gave his resignation speech to the Virginia State Senate. Waking up had become a daily nightmare. Each morning, he'd become aware of his disease all over again as he checked how much muscular control he had lost since the day before. Once a function was lost, it never returned. And the endpoint was clear: total paralysis.

At this point, Ben still had his voice, his facial muscles, and his power finger. With the help of some ingenious contraptions, he could still command a laptop computer fastened to the bed, and guide the joystick on his wheelchair. He got out of bed as much as possible, even though it took his caregivers hours to bathe him, dress him, and put him into his wheelchair.

"The weatherman says tomorrow will be beautiful, Sammie. Get out for a while."

"Can't do that, Dad. I gave Christine the day off."

"But this weekend is a holiday. What did you call it? The Virtual Bobby Sox?"

Sammie rolled her eyes. "If you're referring to the Vernal Equinox, Living Planet Herbs celebrated that day at the end of March. This weekend, we celebrate May Day. In pagan times, it was a festival of rebirth and replenishment."

"—Which nowadays should be a three-day weekend for a hard-working vitamin company executive," he said, "if only she'd take advantage of it."

"I will take advantage of it. By spending it with you." Her eyes had the "don't-argue-with-me" look that she had inherited from him.

Ben was both ashamed and pleased. He didn't want Sammie cooped up with him on a beautiful day. She should be out smelling the spring flowers, not tending to the decay of her father's winter. But both knew he was glad to have her company. She remained his greatest source of pleasure.

"Alice will bring her weekly care package, soon. Please, Sammie, after she gets here, take off for awhile. See your friends. Better yet, break some guy's heart."

"I'll think about it. Are you ready for dinner yet?"

"Sure. Barbecued steak, baked potato with everything, and a big Caesar salad."

"Dad—"

The baby-food slop Ben could still eat was far from appetizing. "How about a little juice? I'm not hungry yet."

"Dad, you've got to eat."

"What, and lose my new-found waistline?"

Ben watched Sammie shake her head as she turned toward the kitchen. At twenty-eight, she was a natural beauty. She parted her chestnut hair in the middle and let it hang straight to her shoulders. Her periwinkle blue eyes, which Ben called lavender, startled him every time he saw them—as had her mother's. The high cheekbones she inherited from Gloria gave her an exotic look.

She never fussed over clothes. She wore dark business suits while working as Product Information Manager for Living Planet Herbs, Inc. Today she wore one of her long, shapeless dresses that effectively hid her lithe, well-proportioned figure. She kept fit by good nutrition, swimming, walking, and yoga. Martial arts training had been a regular part of her repertoire until she became disillusioned with the trainer.

Even as a teenager, Sammie had worn only a light dusting of powder and a touch of lipstick. Three years ago, after a business trip to India, she'd declared, "I'm not going to pollute myself with chemicals that might destroy my body's natural ways."

Ben wished it was her insistence on being natural that kept eligible bachelors away. But he knew the reason–her decision to move home. He hated seeing her interests narrow down to Lou Gehrig's disease, his damned hospital bed, and his wheelchair. How much happier would she be cultivating a relationship with a young man, instead of taking care of an old one?

Ben heard the refrigerator door open and close, then the whir of the juice machine. Typical Sammie. Never bottled juice. Since her trip to India, she insisted that everything be fresh and toxin-free.

Once, Ben had jokingly asked if people in India drank from the River Ganges, in which dead cattle and human waste floated. She'd given him "the look."

Now she returned with his juice and raised the straw to his lips.

He glanced at her. "Wait. This is just plain old OJ, right? No buffalo chips or eye of newt in it?"

"Come on, Dad."

"No, really. You shouldn't use your poor old dad as a guinea pig. Those horse pills you had me on last year were bad enough, but Chinese herbs? My God."

"Dad, the Naturopathic remedies Living Planet Herbs distributes are new formulations of compounds used for thousands of years. And they work. We got great results from some botanicals from the Amazon rain forest—"

"I knew it. What's in this juice besides juice?"

She sighed but her eyes were smiling. "Echinacea, a healing herb used in the Far East since before recorded history. Even in U.S. medical journals, there's evidence for—"

"Never mind. I'll drink it. But if it tastes bad, I warn you, I'm going to jump out of this bed and turn you over my knee."

"That's the spirit." She again lifted the straw to his mouth.

Ben sucked once, then coughed. "Holy smoke, it tastes like pig manure."

"You've eaten lots of pig manure, then, have you? Drink up."

A few sips more and he blinked. His eyes widened. "Wait, wait! Oh, my God—"

"What?"

"I just moved my toes."

She wrinkled her nose. "Very funny."

He imagined himself reaching up and putting his arm around Sammie. But no part of him even quivered. He could no more physically express his anger than demonstrate love. Sometimes Ben inventoried all the gestures, leaps, and strides trapped inside his body and imagined them building up steadily, accumulating energy like radioactive waste until one day they'd reach a critical mass—Then Ben Brewster would detonate with the impact of a tactical nuclear device.

Of course he never revealed such thoughts to his daughter. It would upset her to realize how much the paralysis frustrated him.

Sammie had transformed the family room in his honor. After removing the bar, sofa, and coffee table, she renamed it his "recovery room," arguing it had "positive energy." Indeed, the patio doors let in the sunshine. Ben could smell meals cooking and hear the newspapers land on the front porch. The family room held so many memories. At night he lay with his eyes closed and imagined he could hear laughter and the bark of pets long gone.

The inevitable course of his disease, he knew, would one day force him to move to the Palliative Care Center. Then his quality of life would decline further. Hopefully that move was many months away. Meanwhile, his life had quiet pleasures. Chess with Sammie, listening to her read the newspaper aloud, and motoring his wheelchair onto the patio to gaze at Gloria's prized roses.

All the bushes were thriving, even though Gloria had been gone eight years. The roses were so much like her. Sweet yet thorny, delicate but tenacious, some colored deeply and others patterned.

If Gloria had been a rose, what now was Benjamin Brewster? A cactus? An unmoving, uncomfortable semi-animate prick?

Look what *Lou Gehrig* had done to him.

Over the past six months, his need for home-care gradually increased to full-time. Not because he'd taken a piece of shrapnel in Da Nang; not because some drunk driver had crossed the center divide and hit him head-on; not because he'd misjudged the final turn of the triple diamond run at Sugarbush. No. At the age of fifty-eight, Ben Brewster was one finger away from being quadriplegic because his own nerve cells had waged war against him.

His sharp ears picked up the crisp ticktack of heels on the walkway outside. "Uh, oh, here comes trouble."

"Is it that time already?" Sammie hurried to open the front door.

Ben reveled in the scent of wet pavement and fresh-cut grass that rolled through the doorway. Then came the perfume his sister always wore.

"Ms. Punctuality," Ben said slowly, being careful to pronounce this word. He'd begun to slur words recently. Though he could compensate for the mild impairment, it heralded future problems. His greatest worry was drowning in his own saliva. Last week he had two terrifying battles where he struggled to breathe. Of course, he hadn't told Sammie. Why worry her more?

In his war with nerve cells, there was no fighting back, no treaty possible, and only two choices before final defeat. When the muscles he needed to breathe became paralyzed, surgeons could slice a hole in his throat into which they'd insert the hose of a mechanical ventilator. Or he could suffocate to death. Slowly. The most he could hope for was the time between now, and when he would be forced to make that decision was many months away. But how many?

Alice Phillips bounced in, puffing slightly. A plump and pretty woman, she was two years older than Ben. Her reluctant merriment brightened a very proper Chevy Chase exterior. As a devout Catholic, she was tirelessly energetic when doing well. She accepted Sammie's help and they placed three full paper bags on the table. From one, she lifted an audio book. Clancy's latest. Then she pulled out two DVDs. "Here's Mozart's *Magic Flute* and Verdi's *Othello*."

"What about *Debby Does Dallas*?"

Alice looked at Sammie and groaned. "He's in one of his moods, isn't he?" She flicked a speck of lint off her flashy yellow pantsuit, leaned over, and kissed Ben on the cheek. "Lipstick looks good on you. I think I'll just leave it there."

"Big sisters," Ben grumbled. "Is this revenge for when I used to sneak down and spy on your slumber parties?"

"Like we didn't know you were there." Alice kicked off her open-toed sandals.She dropped into the recliner. "Bring me up to date, Sammie. How's our patient?"

"I'm not your patient," Ben protested, fighting off a surge of peevish anger. Lately Alice fancied herself a doctor. So did Sammie. Funny how people suddenly became medical geniuses as they orbited the burning out sun of an ALS patient.

He held his tongue. Knowing the only part of him that could leave his bed was his voice, he exercised care when using it. Sammie's fussy devotion and Alice's weekly visits complete with gifts and gab, were their ways of expressing love. He was grateful they put up with him. His burden increased almost daily.

"God's been watching over you, Ben," Alice said. "So far, you haven't needed to go to the hospital. And when you do, Memorial has its new PCC. You know, Dr. Cameron's offered you a free initial evaluation."

Sammie frowned. "I don't like hospitals. We can afford a nurse, so why think of that? Next week, I'll learn how to use the suction machine. So why—"

"Hello?" Ben spoke up. "I'm present in this room. Is anyone interested in what I have to say?"

"Sure," Alice said, but turned to answer Sammie. "Dear, when your father's ready, it's only an evalu—"

"I don't care," Sammie snapped. "Hospitals are brimming with staph germs and all kinds of—"

"I'm serious," Ben said, as loudly as he could. "Listen to me, damnit." He took a needed breath. "Sammie, testing is okay. Dr. Reynolds said it won't hurt to find out where I stand."

"Dr. Reynolds?" She looked at the ceiling.

"I know you don't care for his methods, dear," Alice said, "but he has been our family doctor for three decades. By the way, is your little problem cleared up?"

"I treated it myself. With a douche of vinegar and purified water."

"Oh." Alice's plump cheeks flared red. "Oh, my."

Ben grinned. "Vinegar and water? Dr. Reynolds prescribed salad dressing?"

"Benjamin Brewster! You just mind your own business," Alice said.

"It was just a little yeast infection," Sammie said. "Actually, he prescribed some chemical goop, but I never filled the prescription, and I'm just fine now."

"Oh," Ben said. "Woman troubles. Sorry I asked. Alice, you were right. It wasn't my business." He looked back at Sammie. "So, what about Thousand Island?"

"Ben!" Alice cried.

Sammie chuckled.

"What?" In his mind, Ben made an expansive, innocent shrug—all shoulders and arms, with a tilt of the head. "What did I say?"

Chapter 11

David likened the ending of an ER shift to passing the baton in an Olympic relay race. The outgoing runner had to keep pace with the incoming one to complete a smooth transition. David had just presented his list of unresolved patient problems to the incoming doctors.

He glanced at the clock. 6:40 AM.

"Dr. Grainger, there's a Mr. Leary wanting to talk to you." The ER nurse pointed to a middle-aged man leaning against the corner wall of the waiting room. Disheveled, he looked like he'd slept in his rumpled red windbreaker.

Leary? David had never met Ryan's son. He wondered what the man might reveal. Could David have prevented Ryan's suicide attempt? He extended his hand but received none in return. Awkwardly, he altered his gesture by pointing to a row of plastic chairs. "I'm Dr. Grainger."

The man did not budge. "I'm Ryan Leary's son, Jonathan."

"Sorry about—"

"Can we talk? In private?" His eyeballs twitched behind designer-framed glasses.

David glanced at the wall clock. Eighteen minutes until rounds.

"I think so. I'll be right back."

David found Mendendorf in the ER alcoves. "A family member wants to talk with me in the Quiet Room. I've cleared my cases. Okay?"

"Don't be late for rounds."

As they entered the Quiet Room, David motioned Leary to an oversized stuffed chair. He searched for something encouraging to say. "Your father's surgeries went well."

"I just saw my father."

"Really? I'm impressed. Few people get past our Surgical ICU nurse." David recalled the surgeons' report. "If you're worried about his spleen, don't. He'll manage fine without one. And his ribs and limbs will heal. What's most important now, is that your father has come out of anesthesia. He's medically stable."

"Stable?" Leary spoke as if the word has a bad taste. "You're right. He's stable. So stable, he faked us all out. He even tricked Bruce Pratt, his nurse, into changing routes—to avoid a traffic jam—but directed him right into it. You know why? So he'd have enough time to kill himself."

The workings of suicidal minds bewildered David. How could they simultaneously be strategic and determined to commit the most irrational act?

"We found Dad's pain pills under his sheet. He hadn't taken any all day. Can you imagine? Climbing all the way up to the attic without any pain meds? Dad must have suffered terribly. That proves how determined he was to end his suffering."

David's stomach churned. Ryan's suffering must have been intense. "I'm sorry your father suffered so much. By 'stable,' I meant only to describe your father's *physical* condition. Did you father tell you anything more?" The headshake convinced David that Jonathan did not know that his father had telephoned him. "Perhaps I could call one of Memorial's psychiatrists?"

"Dad never was a quitter," Jonathan's voice was low but insistent. "But when his Prostate Specific Antigen rose again, Dr. Moskowitz prescribed meds to lower his testosterone. That ended his friendship with a lady friend. Wasn't that when he saw you?"

"Yes," David said.

"Dad went to a prostate cancer support group, and they turned him on to an internet site where he learned that patients can refuse to lower testosterone."

"But he would have died sooner," said David.

"Perhaps, but at least he would have felt like a man to the end. Look what happened instead." Leary took a handkerchief from his pocket and blotted his forehead. "I doubt Moskowitz told him he had a choice."

So, Moskowitz did not provide Ryan the opportunity to make an informed choice. And now, this tragedy. Four years of medical school had not prepared him for this meeting. He didn't know what to say. "Aren't doctors expected to keep their patients alive as long as possible?"

"When Dad confronted Moskowitz, he admitted that he was restricting his pain meds to avoid any risk of decreasing his respiratory drive since that might hasten his dying. So Moskowitz forced Dad to suffer more... and longer... because of his own religious beliefs." Jonathan put his head in his hands.

Guilt plagued David as he wondered, *If I had asked Tom to prescribe more pain meds... maybe Ryan would not have jumped? But then—*

"Wouldn't you be mad at Moskowitz?" asked Jonathan.

David resisted his inclination to criticize Dr. Moskowitz as he could recall the exact words of a warning in a risk management's lecture. "Interns should never comment on another physician's behavior. Offering such opinions can invite malpractice suits." So David struggled to think of something to say that might be comforting. "These are tough decisions for everyone." His inadequate sounding words echoed hollow in his stomach.

"I let Dad down, just like Moskowitz did," said Jonathan. "Dad asked me to help him out of his misery, but I said no. That was terrible of me."

"But you had to say no, Mr. Leary," David said. "What else could you do?"

"Help him the way he wanted. But I just couldn't do it. I was only thinking of myself—" His voice broke and his eyes filled with tears.

Without thinking, David said, "I know how you feel. I also only thought of myself when my father died. I was nine—" David stopped himself, embarrassed for sharing personal memories.—Unprofessional.

Jonathan shot him a doubtful, half-hostile glance.

David cleared his throat. "Mr. Leary, your father's thought processes—he would never have asked you to help him die—if his thought processes were intact."

"What? His thought—? What?"

"Processes. I mean his ability to process thoughts in a rational way. That's all. But you see, your father was not rational." Relieved by finding a professional truth, David glanced at his watch. Eight minutes until rounds.

"Look, Mr. Leary. Rational people never ask their sons to help them die. The best thing now is for a psychiatrist to see your father. It's required by law, anyway, since he attempted—"

"I'll never forgive myself," Jonathan said. "I wish I had helped him."

"You followed your conscience, Mr. Leary. And if your father had been able to think rationally, I think he would thank you for doing the right thing."

"The right thing? For God's sake, Dad jumped through an attic window. Don't you get it? *See how desperate he was.* Moskowitz and I forced him to do that." He sobbed again. "Dr. Grainger, I took the path that was easier for me, not what was best for Dad."

The words, "best for Dad," reverberated. Twenty years ago, his mother had whispered those exact words as David cried in her arms.

Jonathan Leary sat up straight, composed himself, and looked directly at David. "What about now, Doctor? Dad still wants to die, but he can't. He's immobilized by casts and pulleys. All he can do is lie there and suffer." Leary's reddened eyes pleaded, "Dr. Grainger, my father needs your help. Would you help him? Can you? Would you?"

David sat frozen in place, the time of rounds starting forgotten.

"Please help him. You're his doctor so I'm asking you. I'm pleading with you."

"What you're asking for is both unethical and against the law." David stood up.

"My father needs your help. He's trapped." Leary stood in front of David, close enough to sense heat from his red face, to smell his unwashed body. "Please, help him. Please."

"I can't." David's voice was hoarse. "It's against everything I believe in."

Jonathan stared at the floor, the fire in his voice gone. "Doesn't any doctor have the courage to help?"

David wanted to defend doctors, to point out that adherence to ethical and moral principles demanded courage—but Jonathan wouldn't understand. Not now. He glanced at his watch. Four minutes to rounds.

He looked over Jonathan Leary's bent head toward the door of the Quiet Room. He was sure that he had closed it. Now it was open. In its frame stood a tall, thin man in a long white coat... looking at them.

David had no doubt who he was. His photo had appeared in the *What's New at Memorial* newsletter. The story announced the opening of the PCC.

David's only question was, Just how long had Dr. Cameron been listening?

ᘐ

Cameron hardly stepped aside, forcing David to turn sideways to get through the door. He watched the young intern sprint down the hall. Then Cameron took a seat across from Jonathan Leary positioned to study the man's face. It seemed to have aged a decade since young Leary had brought his father to the PCC.

"I'm so sorry about what happened." Cameron said. "It's a great shock. I thought your father was eager to come to the PCC."

Leary stared at the wall, without talking or even blinking.

"Have you visited your father?" Cameron asked.

Leary nodded. "Yes, in the Surgery Intensive Care Unit. I'm waiting for them to transfer him to ortho."

"Can he speak?" Cameron knew one general fact about patients who just attempted suicide. Their defenses are lowest when they first regain consciousness so that is when they will spill their guts, if they ever will. And Ryan Leary could say specific things about his prior interview with Cameron that would destroy him.

"No," Jonathan replied. "He was still out of it."

For now, Cameron thought. —A condition he had to make permanent. Before the mandatory psychiatric consult. Protocol required that every patient who made a suicide attempt had to undergo a psychiatric evaluation. Although Cameron had no idea how Hayneswurth could tap into "confidential" hospital information, he was sure the economist would have a copy of the shrink's report seconds after the transcription department had finished typing it. If this report revealed that Cameron had discouraged Ryan Leary by telling him the PCC could not help him end his life, then Cameron would not only lose his bonus; he'd also lose his job. Hell, it wouldn't even be safe for him to start his car.

"Mr. Leary, what will you do after your father recovers from his injuries?"

"Do? What do you mean, do?"

"Your father will have more pain, so he'll be out of it for a while."

Jonathan nodded.

Cameron leaned forward. "But because of his attempt, they'll consider him a high suicide risk. His psychiatrist will most likely recommend keeping him under constant surveillance, to ensure he doesn't try to kill himself again."

"Oh, God." Jonathan clutched his thinning web of hair. "Why can't they leave him alone?"

"These days, doctors must consider every legal risk, despite what they believe is right for their patients. I'm sure you're following Kenard's trial?"

"Just the headlines."

"He's facing second-degree murder for helping a patient, directly. I sympathize with your father's plight, but there's no way I can help him, directly. Understand? Not directly."

Jonathan looked at Cameron intensely. "But could something be done, Doctor? Indirectly? Is there some indirect way I can help my father? One that would be painless?"

Cameron's tone softened. "Of course. Yes, there is a way that comes from kindness, a way that would release your father from all his pain. We would not want him to suffer any more. He's suffered far too much already."

Startled by Dr. Cameron's words, Jonathan looked up as if to plead for more information.

"There is one way you can help your father, even in this busy hospital."

"Please," he implored, "tell me what I can do."

Chapter 12

"Do you ever worry about it, honey?" Ben asked.

Sammie hit STOP on the DVD remote to silence Ingmar Bergman's classic rendition of "The Magic Flute." She turned to her father. He was propped up in a hospital bed in his "recovery room." Ribbons of early morning streaming sun illuminated the sheets.

"Worry about what?"

"Mom died of cancer. I've got ALS. Aren't you afraid of bad genes?"

"No. Worry itself is harmful, and most ovarian cancers and ALS aren't genetic. My diet protects me against toxins, and meditation and yoga strengthen my *prana*, my life force." Sammie knew she sounded New Age-y, but her conviction drove her on. "We're more than our bodies."

"Oh, is that why I can sense my arms and legs are moving, but nothing happens. It's so frustrating."

"That must seem weird," Sammie wondered if Dad noticed his difficulty pronouncing "frustrating." At least he could talk. Someday, he'd need a computer to generate his speech—that is, if he chose to go on living by using a ventilator. Every moment was so precious now. That's why she was right to give the nurse the day off. Alone, they could have an intimate talk.

"At the quantum level, Dad, matter and energy are the same. Even our thoughts are energy. Changing our thoughts can change everything."

His skeptical expression reminded her of the years he spent arguing points as a Virginia Senator. "So, you are what you think?"

"That, and more."

"Does that mean you can think yourself sick?"

"It means there's always hope for healing, even when a cure is not possible. Published research shows that people with healthy emotions not only live better. They also live longer."

"I love your optimism, Sunshine. Just like your mother."

"I remember." Sammie sensed a lump in her throat but she kept back the tears. Dad had enough to deal with without seeing her cry.

She stared at Dad. His tears tore at her heart. He almost never cried. The only time she could remember seeing his eyes tear was at Mom's funeral.

His face abruptly contorted. To avoid embarrassing him, she turned away and busied herself by picking up the scattered videos. She listened to his sharp, grating breaths—obvious attempts to restrain his emotions.

After a final gurgle, Ben became quiet. Sammie gave him one additional moment to recoup, then forced a smile and turned. "Want to watch the rest of 'The Magic'—Dad? Dad! Are you okay? DAD!"

Ben's face had turned purple-red. His eyes bulged.

"Dad!" she shrieked, leaping to the side of the bed. Her hands flew ineffectually around him. Not having a nurse was a terrible idea. God help her. Could she do the right thing? Fast enough?

Her thoughts raced. Dad couldn't even gasp, let alone breathe. She opened his mouth and could see his tongue so he hadn't swallowed it. Next, if something had caught in his throat, was she strong enough to perform the Heimlich with him lying in bed?

Sammie stood motionless—watching, as her father shook violently. He drew in a long, shrill breath. A few seconds later, he exploded, coughing up a wad of phlegm onto the sheet in front of him. His eyes half closed, breathing returned. First shallow and rapid, then slower and less labored.

After a few more breaths he returned to full color.

Sammie dashed for the kitchen, grabbed the phone, and punched 9-1-1.

As she waited for an answer, she berated herself for not learning how to use the suction machine last week. "Dad better be all right or I'll never forgive myself."

Chapter 13

Cameron sat in his office. For fifteen minutes, he'd been staring at the wall, unable to focus his thoughts. He wondered why? He could efficiently handle mounds of paperwork on four hours of sleep. He had dealt with his two most pressing problems. First, he had propelled Leary's son into action. Second, he had stymied that intrusive social worker, Ms. Wintress, with a "courtesy" call to her department head that would suffice to knock her off track. Now he could let her find out about Barretino's death through normal channels. So his mind should have been free to compose a convincing presentation for tomorrow's Good Life Committee meeting.

But it wasn't.

Perhaps his mind was restless since he still needed a pain-free patient to dangle in front of Hayneswurth and other committee members. Without one, he feared they would select another damn drug-dependent patient. He picked up the phone and dialed the number of a seventy-two year-old woman with Multiple Sclerosis. He hung up before she answered. As much as he needed an appropriate patient, he refused to tarnish his professional image. No way would he lower himself to hustle patients.

Cameron released the side level on his recliner chair, slipped back, and practiced a relaxation technique, one that had worked for years. He closed his eyes, took a deep breath, held it to the count of three, and visualized a pleasant seashore scene. Then he let his breath out slowly while letting all the muscles in his body relax. He repeated the process again, and again—

It didn't work.

He sat up straight again and rubbed his eyes. When he opened them, a blue and white icon was flashing on his computer screen. He grabbed the mouse, clicked on the icon, and was shuttled into the patient database.

The name "Benjamin A. Brewster" strobbed in neon red.

Two clicks later, his adrenaline started to surge as he learned that Brewster had been assigned to PCC Room 708.

Cameron's protocol for filling PCC beds had worked again. To avoid being bothered to approve every admission, he had created general clinical criteria to pre-qualify "test" patients like Barretino. He had also listed the names of pre-approved patients, like Brewster. He clicked on "Brewster" and the screen lit up with data.

After he read the information on the screen, Cameron said, "Perfect," in a loud whisper. He shifted his gaze to Wendy's picture, blew her image a kiss, closed his eyelids, and exhaled deeply. To his surprise, his nose was wet with tiny tears.

Name: Benjamin Artemus Brewster
Current age: 58
Current address: Alexandria, Virginia

Occupation 1: Retired Virginia State Senator
Occupation 2: Retired Major, U.S. Army, Vietnam Veteran
Education: Masters Degree, Political Science, U. Maryland

Links: Articles Authored Published Speeches Articles About
Bills authored: Voting Record
Military Awards Civilian Awards
Family: widowed, one daughter, one sister

Sammie looked around the sterile-looking room. Large enough for two beds, it had only one. She thought, *Overall, an obvious failure to combine technology and warmth*, and then said, "There's no healing energy in this room."

"Goodness, dear," said Alice. "It looks like Ben's the first person to use it."

Sammie noticed her father's eyes were closed as two men in green uniforms placed Ben on the chrome-framed hospital bed. She wondered if he was dissociating from his body while being manipulated.

Alice turned to Sammie. "Ben's lucky he was admitted so quickly. Anywhere else, he would have to wait weeks—"

"And I won't be here long," Ben said. "As soon as they finish sticking foreign objects up my ass, we head straight back home."

The nurse chuckled.

"Don't encourage him," said Alice.

"I'm here only for a few tests while you two learn how to suction me. That can't take more than a day or two, right?"

A confident voice from the door said, "That sounds about right."

Sammie and Alice turned toward the distinguished looking man in a long white coat.

"Hello, I'm Dr. Norman Cameron. Welcome to our PCC."

"Hello. I'm Alice Phillips. I've heard so much about you. My husband is on Memorial's Board of Directors."

"Of course. Delighted to meet you, Mrs. Phillips." Cameron extended his hand.

Sammie was impressed. Cameron looked every inch the competent physician. He exuded an old-fashioned energy that seemed to soften the edges of this room-without-soul. His classic-looking black bag reminded her of a kindly old country doctor who carried his remedies as he made house calls. She offered her hand, and was pleased to find his warm. "I'm Samantha Brewster." She was aware of an unusual but rather pleasant smell.

The voice from the bed made Cameron turn. "Pleased to meet you, Doctor. Sorry I can't shake your hand."

Cameron reached over and squeezed Ben's right hand. "So am I."

"We're so grateful you could admit Ben right away," Alice said.

"We always try to keep a bed available, in case a patient has a dire need."

"Dire need?" Sammie said. "Dad just had a little choking episode. It was scary, but the EMT said it's not uncommon. I saw how they suctioned him. It's not that—"

"With ALS, every episode is a warning," Cameron said. "Since your father is here, we should give him a complete evaluation."

"But he's had dozens—"

"Whoa," Ben said. "My daughter's being a little protective. Perhaps she's worried since we heard your unit specializes in terminal patients."

"We also specialize in pain management and beneficial physical therapies."

"Exactly what kind of a complete evaluation?" Sammie asked.

"I'm most concerned with his respiratory function and speech." He turned to Ben. "Communication is important for everyone, but as a military man and politician, you must place a high value on your voice."

"I do," Ben said. "Especially after living through my mother's disease."

"Your mother?" asked Cameron.

"Yes, she had Alzheimer's."

Sammie was only five when her father's mother died, but she remembered that she could barely talk. The thought of her father losing his ability to speak made her so sad she could cry.

"Very interesting," Cameron said, "I'll give you some time to settle in. Then I'll return and get your family history."

Family history? Sammie thought, *Why did that subject so pique Cameron's interest?*

"Your tests will begin this afternoon," the doctor continued.

"The sooner the better," Ben said.

"I'm glad your staff works over the weekend," Sammie said. "May I ask, what I'm smelling? Is it cologne?"

Cameron shook his head. "No, it's Lancôme mixed with essential oils. I apply it after I take off Latex gloves." He turned back to Ben. "You'll find my staff quite responsive. Use the voice-activated intercom anytime—to call the nurse or even change TV channels. Don't hesitate to ask for anything you need."

"How about a new nervous system?"

Cameron smiled. "I'll see what I can do."

Three hours later, Ben heard the door creak and opened his eyes.

"You're alone?" Cameron said.

"Yes. I pretended to fall asleep in mid-conversation to get them to leave."

"Families often hover after their loved ones are admitted." Cameron pulled a tall chair to the side of the bed. "Tell me, how are you feeling?"

"Frankly, I'm exhausted. Strange, isn't it? How do I get tired if my body can't move?"

Cameron nodded. "ALS is full of contradictions. What can we do to make you more comfortable?"

"I'd rather control the TV with my finger than bother your staff by using the voice-activated intercom." Ben didn't add that his main reason was to preserve his privacy.

"Fine." The doctor moved closer. "Let me place the remote under your hand. Feel the oversized buttons?"

Ben struggled a while before sensing the small accomplishment from getting the remote to turn on the wall-mounted television. A CNN anchorman was recapping the last series of witnesses in the Mercy Killing Trial.

"Mind if I watch this?" Ben asked.

"It's hard to avoid these days." Cameron pivoted his chair to face the screen.

"Didn't Kenard work at Memorial?"

"I'm afraid so."

"You don't approve of his tactics?"

"There are pros and cons to everything. What's your opinion, Ben?"

"It depends on what that woman really wanted. If her last talk with the priest changed her mind to not commit the 'unpardonable sin,' then Kenard committed murder. But if she later pleaded with Kenard to end her suffering, I'd consider his act one of compassion. The problem is, we'll never know what she really wanted. She's gone, and it's all too obvious what Kenard must say in his defense."

"Your logic is perfect. But may I ask you a more general question? Do you believe Physician-Assisted Suicide should be available for those who need it?"

For a moment, Ben was silent. "When I was first diagnosed with ALS, I thought of putting my old .45 in my mouth. But then I began to focus on coping one day at a time. For myself? I'm not sure. But I've never given up on anything."

"I see where your daughter gets her spirit." Cameron smiled.

"My daughter Sammie is a spitfire, isn't she?"

"And very observant."

"She's 'New Age,' skeptical of modern science, but still wants me to go on a respirator."

"Have you decided about that yet?"

"No, I—Goddamn it! Sorry, I tried to shake my head. It infuriates me when I realize I can't." Ben paused. "Sorry Doctor, there aren't many people I can complain to."

"That's probably the main function of a doctor's job."

"Thanks. But I still have a lot of time before I need to decide about respirators, don't I?"

"I hope so, Ben, but ALS is unpredictable. I advise you to consider your options early. That way, you and your family can have more time to adjust."

"Isn't there some way to estimate?" Ashamed, Ben stopped himself from further begging for reassurance. Look what ALS was doing to him.

"Ben, I wish—"

"That's okay. Just for the record, I'd like to share something that surprised me. ALS had one positive effect."

"What's that?"

"It forced me to accept more flexibility in life. I used to control everything. Now everything is planned for me: what I eat, when it's time to change my position, who will do the next procedure, and so on."

"That's quite an adjustment."

"I'd thought that much dependency would depress me. Ironically, it was liberating. Doctor, I know I must decide about life support, but not today. Is that okay with you?"

"Absolutely. What I want to do is to get to know you so we can formulate a treatment plan. Are you up to it?"

"Sure." Ben realized he had little choice.

"Let's start with your family's medical history. What about your mother?"

"She developed a problem I didn't even know doctors had a term for. They called it—" Ben swallowed to articulate clearly. "Prosopagnosia."

"She couldn't recognize faces?" Cameron's eyebrows focused on Ben. "Tell me more about her, would you?"

The dozens of questions about other members of his family, his own medical history, and the physical exam took almost two hours. Cameron had asked more questions about his mother's than about Ben's history. Later, Ben wondered why.

∾

At his desk, Cameron jotted notes about Brewster.

A knock on the door annoyed him. Why didn't his secretary buzz? That's why he installed the intercom. The door opened revealing Bruce Pratt in his hospital blues, hands in his pockets. Cameron peered past him beyond the deserted reception area.

"I gave her a coffee break." Pratt locked the door. "We need to chat, in private."

As Pratt strolled over to look out his window, the back of Cameron's head pounded in synchrony with his heart.

"Your new patient—Benjamin Brewster, right? Is that 'Buffalo' Brewster?"

"I wouldn't know," Cameron replied.

"That's what we called him in 'Nam. So now he's got ALS?"

"Yes."

"Bummer for him. Maybe great for you. He's the type you were looking for, right?"

"Could be," Cameron conceded.

"I bet you're pretty jazzed. Did you tell Hayneswurth yet?"

"Well he may not be an ideal candidate. His feisty daughter is very close."

"We can deal with her."

Cameron frowned. "We?"

Pratt turned from the window. The light behind him gave the edges of his uniform a radiant blue, angelic nimbus. "I know how to solve family interference problems."

"After almost thirty years of experience, why would I need your help?"

Pratt's black eyes glinted. "Because of my training in 'Nam. The CIA—"

"The C—What?" asked Cameron.

"In 'Nam, I was in the LRRP, Long Range Reconnaissance Patrol. We worked in enemy territory doing all kinds of shit. Recon, sabotage, assassination, interrogations —men, women, children—it didn't matter. We needed cooperation and fast. Civilian types taught us. You know, guys without ID's. Get it?"

Cameron choked in disgust. Were it not for Hayneswurth's insistence, he would have transferred this low life off his PCC, stat! But he had no choice.

"Great. So you're skilled in pulling out fingernails. But this is a different world. Pratt, my mission is to allow people free choice—only if they wish to end their suffering. I would never force anyone to do anything against their will."

"But you have qualms about Major Brewster's daughter. Feisty? Listen, Doc. Only one person is closer to a Vietnam vet than his family. That's another 'Nam vet."

Cameron thought of the hundreds of veterans he treated at Walter Reed during and after the Vietnam War. Their words rang in his ears. "You weren't there, Doc. How can you understand what we went through?"

Pratt moved closer, hands out of his pockets, displaying the deformity of his knuckles like trophies. The thickened flesh made them look like horny pads on a giant cat. Cameron wondered how his hands got that way. Had Pratt been on the receiving end of "persuasion?"

"I'll keep your offer in mind, Pratt. But right now, I'll handle this myself."

"Doc, I think you're going to need me on this one."

Cameron recoiled. "It's okay to share old war stories with this patient. But on all other matters, I'll handle Brewster myself. Keep away from his family. Understand?"

"Let me know if his daughter needs some persuasion, Doc." The nurse laughed as he started for the door.

"Wait," Cameron ordered.

Pratt turned back.

"Mr. Pratt, remember this. I will only help voluntary patients who meet strict clinical criteria. I will not tolerate any form of physical persuasion. Get that?"

For a moment, the nurse just stared back, then he smiled. "We'll see, Doc. You and me, we're both here to get a job done, right? So, like I said, we'll see."

Cameron stared at the door for a long time. When he finally turned away, he began to realize just how much Pratt's offer had shaken him.

Chapter 14

To get through his thirty-six-hour day, David decided to take a stroll outside. But when he entered the elevator, his finger automatically pushed "6," the floor of the ortho ward. With so much remorse over Ryan's phone call, he had almost called Dr. Solomon. But he decided to see Ryan first. The surgeons had given him a good prognosis. Hopefully he was doing well...

On "6," he glanced at the white board to locate Leary's room number. As he opened the door, he noted the window shades were drawn, trapping a pre-dawn darkness. Hallway light rudely spilled in behind him, hurling his shadow across the bed.

Connected to monitors and IV stands by wires and tubes, with a new helmet of fresh, white bandages covering his head, Ryan lay quietly, his single eye closed.

David released the tension in his shoulders. He wished Jonathan could see how peaceful his father looked. Proof there's always hope for some degree of recovery.

Sensing a presence, David turned. His heartbeat surged. Young Leary sat in the chair on the far side of the bed. Had his thoughts conjured Jonathan out of thin air?

No, Jonathan was just very quiet. His head hung down. He clutched a pillow in his hands.

All was too quiet. David's gaze shifted to the monitors. Pulse and respiration readouts were straight lines. Temperature 95. But no alarm. *What happened to the alarm?*

David lunged to Ryan's neck and stuffed his fingertips under the bandages. Carotid pulse, absent. He pulled a small mirror from his coat pocket and held it under Ryan's nose. No fogging. He pulled out a pen flashlight, thumbed Ryan's eyelid open. Pupil fixed and nonreactive.

David backed away and noticed the glistening stains on the bandages around the nose and mouth. A closer look revealed mucous and blood.

"Your diagnosis, Doctor?"

David turned, knocking the nurse's call button off the bed. It clattered on the floor.

Jonathan slowly raised his head. "Is he dead?" Silence. "Well, is he?"

"Yes, I'm afraid so, Mr. Leary."

Jonathan rocked forward and back, shaking his head in counterpoint.

"He had quite a fall," David said. "It's amazing he survived at all."

Jonathan cried, although it sounded compressed and locked inside. "Why did it have to be so hard?"

For one selfish moment, David wished he could disappear, to avoid seeing the next inevitable scenes: Jonathan would cry, he'd sign the death certificate, and then he'd try to comfort a son who was struggling with the initial waves of grief from losing his father—

Jonathan's sobs sounded like moans from a man who felt he didn't deserve to cry.

David had to say, "Mr. Leary, don't blame yourself—" His voice trailed off as he noticed that the pillow in Jonathan's lap also had a ring of glistening mucous with a tinge of red staining the center. Oh no, David thought. His pulse raced with fear. He leaned over and twisted the volume knob on the cardiac monitor. It began to howl. Then he turned it back down.

Jonathan stared at him through foggy lenses, his eyes red and damp. "Dad is finally resting in peace." At last, the flow of tears broke through.

David swallowed hard. Both Leary and his son said they wanted this. David wondered what to do. He glanced back and forth, between Jonathan's eyes, the stained pillow, the silent cardiac monitor, and the matching stains on the bandaged face. As if from a distance, David watched himself take a step forward, lean over Jonathan, and reach toward the pillow. "Let me have that, okay?"

Jonathan looked up and automatically handed it to him.

David folded it, stained side in, walked to the door, stopped, and looked back.

Jonathan was studying his father. Both faces looked serene.

David opened the door and looked down the hall. At the far end, a petite Asian nurse nodded at him, then disappeared behind the counter of the nurses' station, leaving the corridor empty. Balling the pillow against his chest, he approached the "Bio-Waste" bin situated between Ryan's room and the nurses' station.

The bin's hinged lid popped open.

A moment later, David's hands were empty. The lid was swinging back and forth.

David walked toward the stairs to avoid passing the nurses' station, imagining his progress notes finished on the internal medicine ward, riding the bus home, dropping in bed, falling asleep. Why not? Other doctors had left a corpse for the next guy to discover. Not up to David's usual code of behavior, but these were exceptional circumstances...

A high-pitched voice reverberated through the hall. "Doctor, do you need something?"

David turned. The Asian nurse stood there, looking at him.

"Uh, yes. I need... A death certificate. Please get me one. It's for Leary. I just came from his room. Thank you."

Chapter 15

The Saturday morning traffic was predictably light. But as Michelle Wintress realized she was making every green light, she took it as a sign that confirmed it was right to visit Vivian.

She would have gone Friday night, but she stayed too long with Tom. He never said it, but his face had the *I-told-you-so* look after she revealed what her Department Head said. "It could be disruptive if you follow patients after they are transferred to the PCC. So you'll need written referrals from Dr. Cameron from now on." She was amazed how fast the head of the PCC got to talk to the head of her department. "I feel blacklisted from the PCC," she told Tom.

Michelle started to scream when Tom suggested that Cameron might suspect Michelle wanted the bounty for discovering Medicare fraud. "How in the world could anyone imagine I'm interested in money? I only care about my patients' well-being." Then she cried for almost an hour. He held her without saying another word, which is why she couldn't resist his passion.

Obviously, she was too upset to visit Vivian last night. But now, as she climbed the six flights to the PCC to avoid walking past the nurses' station, she felt ready to show compassion for Vivian. In a way, Michelle had to agree with Cameron. You must relieve your patient's pain before you can work with her on emotional and spiritual growth.

Michelle exited the stairwell, peeked down the corridor to make sure it was empty, and then headed directly for Vivian's room. Inside, the shades were drawn and the lights were off. But, inside, something seemed wrong. It was too quiet. And Vivian wasn't twisting and groaning in her futile attempts to escape the prison of her own skin. "Vivian?"

The room had an unfamiliar odor. And where were her flowers and cards?

In the unnerving stillness, Michelle crept closer. "Vivian, it's Michelle." She leaned over to touch Vivian's arm. Suddenly, the lights blazed on.

"Who the hell are you?" said a male voice.

She gasped and spun around.

The PCC nurse stood in the doorway, eyebrows knotted together, his hands floating a few inches from his sides, as if he were about to fast-draw a pair of six-shooters.

Michelle gasped in fear.

"Oh, it's you! Weren't you told to check in before seeing our patients?"

She heard her rehearsed line. “No one was at the desk.” Her heart pounded harder.

“Yeah. Of course you’d say that. Well, you’re out of here, now!”

She would have run had she not cared so much for Vivian. “Okay, but first I want to say hello to—” Michelle turned toward the bed. She halted. An emaciated black man was staring at her, eyes bulging from sharp-boned sockets, tongue working nonstop in a toothless mouth.

“Where’s Vivian?”

“Step outside. Now!” His glare moved her through the door. “You can’t barge in on a patient who is none of your business—” He opened the door for her to exit the room.

“What happened to Vivian Barretino?”

“She died.”

“But that’s impossible. When did she die?”

“Night before last. Real late.”

“But she was fine.”

Pratt smirked. “You wouldn’t say that if you had end-stage Scleroderma.”

“But she didn’t seem terminal. What happened?”

“You’ll have to ask Dr. Cameron.”

“This is terrible. Only three weeks ago she was fine.”

“She suffered from a terrible debilitating chronic disease. You call that fine?”

“But she wasn’t ready. It wasn’t her time.”

“Look, it’s time for you to leave our PCC.” The nurse clasped her forearm.

She looked down and saw his enormous knotted knuckles. She jerked away so hard she almost fell over. “Get your hands off me!”

“Get your ass off my floor. I’m not going to tell you again, Ms. Wintress.”

She tried to call upon her reservoir of professionalism, but his eyes were ruthless. She rushed to the elevators, sensing that his glare was following her. She pushed the button, wishing the elevator would come before she burst into tears.

As the doors closed behind her, she still hadn’t turned around.

Chapter 16

Cameron self-parked his car in the dingy garage. He hated the awful hotels Hayneswurth chose for Good Life Committee meetings. The elevator's brass plate had chocolate fingerprints. —Zero class. Hayneswurth's recipe for secrecy led to windowless conference rooms in middle-class hotels. Everyone had to dress like traveling salespeople—cheap ties, off-the-rack suits, and scuffed shoes. Hopefully, today's meeting would be the last before he and his wife began their own "good life."

Cameron nodded at Hayneswurth as he entered the Napa Conference Room. He suspected that, in addition to economics, Hayneswurth had a background in intelligence. His silver hair made his air imperious. His gold-rimmed glasses cut a ridge in his nose. Leaning back from the head of the boardroom table, his crossed leg revealed a pale ankle. Yet he seemed quite comfortable in his wrinkled plaid sports jacket and a tie with a lopsided knot... Was that why Hayneswurth mandated this ridiculous dress code?

Cameron looked around. The Committee's two oncologists were not present. He smiled at Margaret Chin, the Committee's PR specialist, who was employed by a Massachusetts think tank. He waved at Dr. Wesley Borysewicz, a well-known political analyst. Due to the conversation in process both returned silent welcoming gestures. Hayneswurth was saying, "I see no hope for him."

"Yes. Kenard's defense is far too weak," Chin said.

Borysewicz shook his head. "How could an ordinary doctor expect to win against both the American Medical Association and the Catholic Church?"

Resisting the urge to interrupt so he could announce his great news, Cameron feigned an interest in their discussion. "In the past, jurors have shown sympathy for doctors who reduced suffering. Remember the early trials of Dr. Kevorkian?" *

"That's true, Norman," Hayneswurth said, to stop the conversation. "Can we start with *your* recap of recent events?"

"Fine. Yesterday—"

"And if you don't mind," Hayneswurth added, "I'm making a digital recording of our meeting since the oncologists called to say they'd be late. Any objections?"

"None at all." Cameron responded in a casual tone even though he didn't believe Hayneswurth. He figured the CEOs would be listening to this recording before the sun set. Fine! Since his words would be immortalized, he decided to elaborate. "Last week, I completed my research on the psychological differences between patients who

*Jack Kevorkian, M.D., retired pathologist, did not initially break the law in Michigan because there was no law against Physician-Assisted Suicide in 1990. As of 2006, he was still in prison for committing euthanasia in 1999. That act was broadcast on CBS TV.

merely state that they desire Physician-Assisted Suicide, and patients who actually go through with the act. My clinical series ended with a woman who suffered from the pain of Scleroderma. She further increased my knowledge about what influences—"

"—Influences, you say? Really, Doctor," interrupted Hayneswurth. "Tell us, then, exactly what you learned to understand what *influenced* Leary to attempt suicide."

"Suicide?" asked Chin and Borysewicz, almost simultaneously.

Hayneswurth answered. "Yes. Our ***Finale*** candidate tried to kill himself the day before yesterday. He jumped *through* a window from his attic. It caused so much damage to his face that he'll never—"

Cameron cleared his throat to interrupt.

"Doctor?"

"Mr. Leary died yesterday afternoon, at 4:15. Here's a copy of his death certificate." He slid the paper across the table to Hayneswurth.

Hayneswurth studied the document without changing his expression, then looked up. "I don't get it. Why the hell would Leary commit suicide in such a violent way if the man knew that you would end his suffering peacefully, on your PCC?"

Cameron had anticipated this moment, planned it in fact. But he pretended to think about the question as he turned the pages on the large note pad that had been placed in front of his designated seat. Each Committee member had his own pad to share notes with the others. Cameron found the page on which he had previously created a Table. As he turned the pad toward the rest of the group, he thought how incredible it was that these otherwise bright professionals had trouble appreciating the significance of such simple concepts. He hoped using consistent fonts for categories and examples would make his points more clear.

"May I ask you all to please consider this Table again. It will help me explain what happened with Leary and also serve as a basis for deciding on our future direction. As you can see, there are four different kinds of patients, based on whether or not they are terminal, and whether or not they are in pain. There are no patient names in the Table, of course, but you know some already: The late Mr. Leary was a ***Type I***; the late Ms. Barretino was a ***Type II***; my preference has always been for a ***Type III***; and ultimately, we hope to make inroads on the millions of ***Type IVs***."

Patient Types & Diagnostic Examples		
	TERMINAL? **YES ↓**	**TERMINAL?** **NO ↓**
PHYSICAL PAIN? **YES →**	***Type I*** Cancer	***Type II*** Scleroderma
PHYSICAL PAIN? **NO →**	***Type III*** Lou Gehrig's	***Type IV*** Alzheimer's

Hayneswurth could not hide his impatience. "Doctor. What about Leary?"

"I was just about to discuss him in detail, but it just occurred to me: the oncologists will not be able to see this Table as they listen to your recording. Would you give me a few seconds so I can describe it? It's a simple 'two-by-two' grid. The 'two' on the top are 'IS terminally ill' versus 'NOT terminally ill.' The two on the side are 'physical pain IS present' versus 'NO physical pain present.' That makes four possibilities, since two times two equals four." Cameron wondered if his intent to make Hayneswurth impatient was becoming obvious so he decided to move on now rather than to belabor the obvious.

"Okay, now on to Leary. Like so many ***Type I*** patients who are terminal and in pain, when treated with narcotic painkillers, Leary's mental status was unstable. It's depressing enough to have a terminal illness. Pain itself is depressing. The disability from decreased functioning from pain is depressing. And the medications that treat pain are depressing. These medications, as everyone knows, also cloud judgment. So... if a patient is undertreated for pain, perhaps by missing a dose or two, the lapse in effective reduction in pain can lead to transient despair. Combined with depression and poor judgment, the result can lead to an impulsive act—an attempt to commit suicide." He paused. "That, gentlemen, is what happened to Ryan Leary."

"Cameron, you're amazing. But also obsessed. You never stop arguing for your ***Type III*** preference—even when you're asked directly to explain why your patient died." Hayneswurth pointed his finger at the doctor. "Must I tell you again? Our sponsors cannot... and will not wait any longer for you to find your damn elusive rare ***Type III***!"

"On that very point, Howard, I have good news." Cameron bit his cheek to prevent the smile. "But first, for the benefit of our *listening* audience—***Type III***s are patients who are 'terminal but not in pain.'" He took a moment to stare silently at Hayneswurth. "Yesterday, a fifty-eight-year-old man with ALS entered the PCC. His name has long been on my ***Type III*** list, but I did not expect his disease to progress so quickly. He is a widow, a decorated war hero, and had a distinguished career in Virginia politics. An episode of choking precipitated his admission, but his voice is still strong."

Hayneswurth's eyebrows rose. "He sounds familiar. Have we discussed him before?"

"Briefly, yes. His name is Benjamin Brewster."

"Oh yes, I remember now," said Hayneswurth. "He has one daughter. His sister is quite Catholic and her husband is on the hospital's board. Although Brewster is not religious, there could be a problem here—"

"No problem. The brother-in-law is not involved, and I've assessed his daughter and sister. I can handle them."

Borysewicz leaned forward. "I have something I must add. My staff analyzed Brewster's politics. He frequently voted against the party line, was outspoken about ethics violations, and snubbed his team if he thought they went against his personal code of ethics. Doctor, how sure are you that Brewster will cooperate?"

"Absolutely. We've talked extensively," Cameron said.

Hayneswurth leaned forward. "Are you saying he's at the point where he's ready for Physician-Assisted Suicide?"

"Yes. He has thought deeply and clearly about it. Please appreciate the difference between ***Type Is*** and ***Type IIIs***. While ALS has ravaged Brewster's body, his mind is totally intact. He is one finger away from being a complete quadriplegic, yet he *can*, and I promise you that he *will*, be exceptionally convincing when he articulates his reasons for choosing **PAS**, I mean, Physician-Assisted Suicide."

Hayneswurth merely gave him a hard stare.

Cameron stared back while running through his mind the words, *I respect you, I respect you, I respect you*—to prevent his facial expression from revealing his disgust. "In representing the sponsors, Howard, you asked me to join your Committee because of my medical expertise. Now I'm asking you to honor my clinical opinion. I recommend that we select Brewster as our ***Finale***."

Hayneswurth stared at Cameron. "Doctor, I've always been impressed with your clinical research. And I have confidence that, eventually, you could overcome any resistance from Brewster's family. If it became necessary, you could sway his opinions. But all that takes time. More time than—"

"Excuse me, but one additional factor makes Brewster an exceptional candidate." Cameron raised his voice slightly. "He was the primary caregiver for his mother. She had Alzheimer's for eight or nine years."

Hayneswurth dropped his pencil.

Margaret Chin let out a "Wow!"

"...which means we can proceed simultaneously with our ***Type IV*** project. Talk about 'time.' Do you realize how much time it will save us to use Brewster for both projects? Furthermore, by having one patient promote both, it makes the whole case for hastening dying more compelling. Could I have a moment more, to explain?" Cameron knew Hayneswurth would acquiesce.

"As a committee, we've developed a fine plan to popularize Physician-Assisted Suicide, despite all its problems—which I'll review in a few moments. We have always agreed that merely increasing awareness about **PAS** will make it more likely that other life-sustaining medical technologies will either be withdrawn, or not initiated in the first place. So the effect of our project has been, to a great extent, indirect. It's like depending on the ripple effect.

"I've always felt that the most important way to further the goals of our CEOs is to focus on ***Type IVs***. Their numbers are astounding. They include the fifty to one hundred thousand Americans in the Permanent Vegetative State and Minimally Conscious State, but that's just the beginning. Almost one-half of people 85 and older have Alzheimer's-like dementias. And once their behavior becomes unmanageable, they need skilled nursing care as family members stop caregiving without financial compensation. We're talking close to 2 million patients now, and three times that figure by mid-century, right Mr. Hayneswurth?" After the expected nod Cameron continued, "Thus, the total cost of skilled nursing care for demented patients will bankrupt not only the insurance industry, but the entire country."

"Right," said Hayneswurth, finally showing some enthusiasm.

"But they can't qualify for **PAS**," Cameron said, "since they're not even mentally competent enough to feed themselves. Yet they can be kept alive indefinitely—first by spoon-feeding and then by feeding tubes, like the one that kept Terri Schiavo alive for 15 years and might have kept her alive another 15 years, or more.

"The 'economic problem' caused by demented patients derives from their reaching a 'ripe old age.' That, in turn, is because they are medically healthy. Few are dependent on life-sustaining technology that can be withdrawn. So family members, caregivers, institutions, and health insurance companies must all passively wait for these patients—whose quality of life can be nil for several worthless years—to contract an infection. And then, these concerned people must hope that the current doctors will refuse to treat these infections aggressively. If by chance, the doctor who happens to be asked to evaluate the infection decides to start antibiotics and hydration, then the patient can often live several more months or more. Sometimes, even a couple of years or more.

"So how can our Committee make the necessary impact? Since ***Type IVs*** obviously can't speak for themselves, the best way is to seek testimonials from their close relatives. That's why finding Brewster is such a gift."

Borysewicz nodded. "I agree, but what's the plan?"

Cameron gestured so Margaret Chin would answer. "We're developing a PR plan to educate patients and their proxies—the individuals they designate to make their medical decisions—on how they can legally hasten dying by refusing all food and fluid."

"Wait a second, did you say, *refuse all food and fluid*?" asked Borysewicz. He wrote in his note pad and asked, "Do you really expect patients' *proxies*, or *caregivers*, to withhold food and fluid from their loved ones to hasten their dying?" Borysewicz asked.

"Yes, we do," said Chin, "but not necessarily directly. One of our most interesting findings points out the discrepancy between what people would decide for themselves, and what they would decide for their loved ones. We have a solution to that problem, but first, let Dr. Cameron describe how we run our focus groups. Doctor?"

"First we show videos of the enormous frustration of patients in the Minimally Conscious State as they try to, but can't, perform simple behaviors that any normal three-year-old could do in one-tenth the time. Every one can imagine a person in a coma, but this video will blow them away. They will get the point: patients in the Minimally Conscious State are just conscious enough to experience horrendous suffering. Then, we show videos of the forced spoon-feeding of a demented patient, which requires two people: one to squeeze the patient's cheeks and hold her head still; the other to spoon in the puree... Finally, we show an end-stage demented patient contracted into a fetal position with absolutely no ability to respond. Every person in our focus groups, except for those rare ultra-religious ones—and even they often waiver—will opt for refusing food and water in the future for themselves, if they ever reached a similar state."

"Defined as...?" asked Borysewicz.

"*That*, I always emphasize, is for the patient to decide. —While she or he still can. But I also provide this example from my own Advance Directive." Cameron made a fist and then released one finger at a time. (Finger 1) "If I am not able to recognize family members... (Finger 2) If I cannot respond verbally to simple questions, like the names of my family members or if it is day or night... (Finger 3) If I am incontinent of urine and feces... (Finger 4) If I am non-responsive or respond only with severe anger or depression... And (Finger 1), if I demonstrate no ability to interact in a meaningful way with my environment. Then, even if I can still take in sustenance through my mouth with another's assistance, I want my proxy to refuse all food and fluid on my behalf."

Borysewicz shook his head. "Maybe they'll stop, or won't start their own tube feeding, but loving caregivers won't starve their—"

"That's exactly where education is necessary. These patients will *not* die in discomfort from starvation; they *will* die in comfort from dehydration. Most people don't realize that the act of swallowing is really a primitive reflex. That's why nursing assistants are trained to put pureed food at the very back of the tongue. And, as we discussed many times before, there is absolutely no evidence to show that tube-feeding is of any benefit to patients who are demented.

Chin nodded in agreement. "Merging the data from all groups, only 2 out of 127 stated they would want to sustain their biological lives if their functioning were reduced to the level we described." Her face beamed with accomplishment.

"Alzheimer's is a unique disease," Cameron continued. "In the early stages of memory loss, patients retain the ability to make decisions and create their Advance Directives. In the 'Frequently Asked Questions' that Margaret and I wrote, we suggest asking a psychiatrist to consult to determine and write an opinion that the patient possesses decision-making capacity as well as to document—clearly and convincingly—precisely what patients state they do or do not want—if their dementia becomes severe. That way, there will be no challenges from 'interested' third parties, like the religious right. Also, our Frequently Asked Questions address the issue of legality by citing the case of Nancy Cruzan, the landmark decision by the Supreme Court that affirmed the right of every competent adult to refuse any medical treatment."

Borysewicz frowned. "Still, many loved ones can't even pull the plug on a patient whose life depends on a ventilator. How do you expect them to withhold the basics of food and water?"

Cameron nodded. "Good point. Very good, in fact. When you have a chance, read our Frequently Asked Questions brochure. It considers the issue of relatives who are too emotionally involved. Then it list a number of organizations whose members are willing to serve as each other's proxies. Many members have already signed up as proxies for one another. But these grassroot organizations are tiny compared to our reasonable projections of the ultimate need in this area."

Cameron's excitement rose as he realized he had established the conceptual groundwork for his dramatic ending. "Now I'd like you all to imagine Major Brewster on national TV. First, he relates the personal anguish he experienced as his mother's caregiver. Next, he expresses his deep regret for not refusing food and fluid on her behalf, so that she could have died peacefully before Alzheimer's took away all her personal dignity. Next he talks about his personal struggle with Lou Gehrig's disease and how he searched his soul regarding his own lethal choice. Finally, minutes later, he commits Physician-Assisted Suicide."

Cameron made eye contact with each person. "Can you imagine the impact? Can you? Forget the previous record audience when CBS televised Kevorkian euthanizing Tom Youk. Our ***Finale*** video will break those records in re-runs."

Borysewicz looked at Hayneswurth, but he just sat there—his silence an expression of complete agreement.

Just then, the door opened. The oncologists entered but no one turned to greet them for several long seconds. It was obvious to Cameron that the members of the committee were so stunned they needed time to fully absorb the details of his profound proposal.

Chapter 17

"Checkmate."

Sammie groaned. She covered her eyes with her hands. "Why do I even bother?"

"Because you're just as competitive as your old man."

"I am not competitive. But I will set the board up again."

Before Sammie had finished, Alice bustled in, wearing another one of what Ben labeled a church outfit. A full-skirted white dress with big black polka dots and matching black pumps.

She waved a paper bag. "Guess what I've got?"

"My rowing machine?" Ben asked.

"Very funny. No, it's a very special video."

"Not the Miracle Network Telethon, I hope."

"Ben Brewster, one of these days you will call for God, and on that day you'll get a lesson in humility. It's the old Super-8 movies transferred to DVD."

"My old home movies?" Ben was touched.

"We had them transferred to DVD. Aren't you ashamed for teasing me?" Alice stretched on her tiptoes and pushed the disk into the combo TV-DVD.

Darkness followed a burst of static, and then a bloom of warm color appeared. Deep greens, rich golds, and strangely metallic blues emerged in the distorted hues typical of old Super-8 film. A scene emerged, a small lake in the Appalachians. Massive redwood trees surrounded the water. The air seemed filled with summer sunlight and floating motes of pollen. In one corner, a dock made of planks rested on a line of empty fifty-gallon drums stretched into the lake.

"Oh, it's the cabin," Sammie said.

"And you couldn't be more than eight," said Alice.

Ben gazed fondly at the screen. Two people stood on the end of the dock. Gangly Sammie, her hair an overturned cup of gold. Young and beautiful Gloria, in a blue swimsuit and flowered swimming cap. They waved at the camera.

Ben remembered how much he enjoyed his vacations at the lake. There he stood with the firm legs of a soldier. On his left, the cabin. On his right, bright reflections from the lake. Before him, his entire life. Or so he thought.

Dubbed in was the first movement of Beethoven's Pastorale.

Cut to the view down the dock. From his bed, Ben smiled at himself in baggy swim trunks with a soldier's tan. Other than his dark face and hands, every other bit of his exposed skin was sand white. He held Sammie over his head as she thrashed and screamed silently, her face delighted, all eyes and teeth. How easily he hurled her into the green water of the lake. Spray rose like golden lace, and then fell back. Young Ben struck a He-man pose for the camera. The image quivered, probably from Gloria laughing as she held the camera.

Then Sammie's grinning face popped above the surface of the lake.

In the hospital room, Sammie giggled.

Cut to the long, dirt road leading to the lake. A tandem bicycle climbs up its slope. On the front seat of the bike is Ben, older than in the previous scene, more thickly built. A bald spot developing. He hunches over the handlebars, face intent, hips rising off the seat with each thrust of the pedals. Gloria sits behind and gives the camera a broad wink. Her hands are folded behind her head, her feet propped up off the pedals.

"I knew she was doing that," Ben said.

"Sure you did," Sammie and Alice said together.

Cut to all three Brewsters feeding apples to a quarter horse and her yearling across the wooden rails of a corral. Then, they're saddled up on their steeds. Ben's is a massive brute showing its teeth. Sammie's is a docile, long-maned palomino. Gloria's is a nimble sorrel mare.

In bed, Ben hated the lump growing in his throat. *Exercise control, no tears.*

"I remember that," Sammie said. "After that, I started riding lessons."

Ben cleared his throat. "And became a vegetarian—even though we never ate horse meat!"

They laughed as the video went on. Sammie on the lake shore, her body beginning to round out now but her movements all youthful vigor as she sprinted to scatter a family of ducks from sand to water. Gloria blowing out candles on a birthday cake, but of course they're the kind that won't go out. Gloria again, now making a sick face over the dead catfish Sammie and Ben had presented to her to clean for dinner—

So many scenes, so many moments. Snippets, really. Watching them, Ben found himself filled with regret, with erupting remorse, but didn't know why—

Yes, he knew why. There should have been many more such moments. But he'd been so busy with his career, his work. He hadn't known. How could he have known so little time was left for Gloria and him? Sadness filled from within. His ability to hold back his tears... a minor consolation.

Chapter 18

After they exchanged hellos, Hayneswurth added that he had recorded the meeting. Then Cameron said, "I am so glad you two are here now. I'd like your feedback on the next part." Cameron glanced quickly at Hayneswurth, just long enough to notice that he had *not* turned off the digital recorder. —As expected. Good.

He began slowly, to emphasize the importance of his announcement. "I am pleased to report success in solving two major obstacles to Physician-Assisted Suicide. I believe my innovations will permit us to get beyond the low utilization rate that was typical in Oregon—only about one in eight hundred people died by taking a prescribed lethal dose of pills. There are two reasons for this low rate: one applies to physicians; the other, to patients. After months of work, I've solved both. I'll start with the one for patients, since again, Brewster is so ideal. Briefly, my solution transcends the patient's lack of mechanical ability to commit **PAS**.

"As you know, the final act of committing Physician-Assisted Suicide *must* be completely voluntary; otherwise the process could be considered euthanasia. So after a family member has prepared the pudding or solution by dissolving the powder from the prescribed capsules, it is necessary for the patient to feed or to drink the lethal mixture with *no* assistance. Strictly speaking, a family member cannot place a straw in the patient's mouth. Furthermore, the patient must be able to swallow and absorb the medication without regurgitation. The sad truth is that many patients are too ill to do all this. In Oregon, some patients had the requisite mechanical ability when they made their initial request for the prescription, but then they waited and, by the time their suffering had increased to the point that they were ready to die, they no longer had the physical ability to take and ingest the prescribed drugs. Several newspaper articles described how they were then doomed to further suffering."

Cameron did what it took to make his face show compassion, made eye contact with everyone, and then went on. "My method, as will be demonstrated by Brewster, can be used even by patients who are totally paralyzed. Most importantly, the video will convince every one—doctors, family members, and law enforcement officers—that his act was totally voluntary.

"Second, the problem for physicians—"

"Wait! How is it possible... for paralyzed patients?" Borysewicz asked.

"You'll see it on the video," said Cameron, whose gaze was momentarily distracted by Hayneswurth's inadvertently pointing the digital recorder right at him.

"Physicians all over the country have reason to worry about losing their license to prescribe controlled substances, being charged with a crime, and imprisoned. The result: doctors decide to abandon their suffering patients just when they most need their help. You know my take on the real goal of federal Attorney General John Ashcroft and his successor Alberto Gonzales in bringing that case against Oregon to the U.S. Supreme Court? It was not because they really cared about the thirty or forty Oregonians who died that way each year. It was a message to doctors in every state with the threats of hefty fines and imprisonment. That's scary enough. Whether the relevant law is a newly amended federal Controlled Substances Act or new laws enacted by individual states, any time a physician writes a prescription for a medication that *could* be used to hasten dying, they are risking their profession, their life's savings, and their freedom." Cameron gestured toward the oncologists. "Don't you agree?"

"Yes I do," said one. "And this is the saddest part. After we are successful in extending the pleasurable lives of cancer victims, the way they die is often far more painful than it would be otherwise. That's the worst time to abandon them. That's why I feel your work is so important, Doctor."

"Thanks, Richard. I appreciate your vote of confidence. So now I'll explain the solution to this obstacle. Doctors need a method to hasten dying that relies on a combination of medications that do not appear on the Drug Enforcement Agency's list of Controlled Substances. Even more, doctors must feel safe that they can prescribe medications that will not raise the eyebrows of any regulator—whether federal or state."

Cameron waited for this point to sink in as he watched Richard whisper something to the other oncologist, and then direct his attention to him. "Please, Richard, don't ask what the medications are. I won't reveal this combination until I demonstrate it on the video. Suffice it to say that its acronym is '**N-A-P**' —derived from the initial letters of the three medications that, taken together, will do the job."

"I must be missing something," Borysewicz said. "Is there a difference between *prescription* drugs and *controlled* drugs?"

"Sorry, I thought you knew that. Yes there is. At the risk of over-simplifying, the Controlled Substances Act lists five categories of drugs. Schedule I includes those that are considered to be the most dangerous and that have absolutely no medical purpose. But it's not hard to argue how backwards the United States is, in this area. Heroin is used in many hospices in Europe to reduce extreme pain, and marijuana is widely recognized for its benefit in reducing nausea and vomiting in cancer patients. But you all know that.

"Skipping ahead to the least dangerous drugs... the short list on Schedule V includes medications like Lomitil, which is used to treat diarrhea.

"Schedule II includes drugs used to reduce severe pain and induce anesthesia, stimulants to treat Attention Deficit Disorder, and potent sleeping pills like Seconal—the medication that Oregon physicians most often prescribe to hasten dying. Aside from the legal threats I mentioned, doctors and patients also must worry if the dwindling number of companies who make Seconal would decide to cease manufacturing the drug. Many states require written 'triple-scripts' for Schedule II drugs, so relatively few doctors are willing to prescribe them.

"Across the county, most doctors routinely prescribe medications from Schedules III and IV—for such common indications as anxiety, insomnia, moderate pain, and to reduce appetite. Very few doctors could continue to practice medicine if they lost their licenses to prescribe medications from these two schedules. But to do that, you must have *both* a federal license and a state license. Losing either one is an insurmountable handicap.

"Now, to appreciate my innovation, consider this: While codeine in its various forms is listed more than 10 times on the schedules of controlled substances, none of the three medications in **N-A-P** that I will demonstrate are listed at all!"

Richard asked, "Must your medications be administered by IVs?"

"No, not at all. **N-A-P** can be swallowed in liquid form. Of course, patients on feeding tubes can ingest these medications administered through their tubes."

"What about your patient, Brewster?"

"Right now, he can still swallow. But only through a straw that someone must hold near his mouth. He will prove that his act is voluntary by moving his head so his lips surround the straw and then by swallowing. Yet the very reason I admitted him to this hospital is because he aspirated. Brewster is the ideal patient to demonstrate how my computer program can help a paralyzed man start the infusion of medications through tube feeding. But **N-A-P** is versatile. It can be taken by mouth, via PEG tubes, or through IVs."

Leaning far forward on his seat, Richard asked. "When can I see the video?

"By the end of next week," Cameron answered.

"And you'll name the medications right on the video?" asked Hayneswurth.

"Yes, I will. And more. I'll state the required dose of each."

"That's a real gift," said Borysewicz.

"It will make PR a cinch! We won't have to spend a penny on promotion... We'll get thousands of calls. —From all over the country."

Cameron sat down, turned toward Howard, and permitted himself a broad smile. "You can shut off your recorder, now."

Chapter 19

Ten minutes later as Cameron accelerated onto I-267, he turned on his cell phone. He wished he could have shared his triumph with his wife, but he didn't want to tempt fate. Instead, he dialed the PCC charge nurse. "How are my patients?"

"Is that you, Dr. Cameron?"

Did his voice sound different because he was happy for the first time in so long?

The charge nurse asked, "Is your phone working? Nurse Pratt was frustrated about not being able to reach you."

"Oh, I had to turn it off during the meeting."

"Here he is."

Pratt's voice was louder than usual. "Doctor, meet me in your office in fifteen."

Before Cameron could reply, the phone was dead.

Pratt let himself into Cameron's office with simple locksmith's picks. He sat on the sofa and waited in the darkness. He had lots of practice waiting. Twenty minutes later, he heard the thud of the elevator doors open, footsteps on soft carpet, the outer door of the office open, then a key rattle in the lock of the inner door. The lights snapped on.

"Jesus! Pratt! How the hell did you get in here?"

"You better sit down, Doc."

Cameron lowered himself into his desk chair.

"You know that Wintress woman? The damn social worker? I caught her sneaking into Barretino's old room early this morning. Boy was she shocked to see that old black guy in Vivian's bed."

Cameron's eyes narrowed. "What did you tell her?"

"Only that Vivian died. I referred her to you for more information. She's real suspicious."

Cameron's eyes closed briefly, then opened again. "I spoke with her Department Head yesterday. She knows the new rules."

"Yeah, well, she just broke them. She suspects something. Could be a major problem. The question is, how far will she go? Damn social workers are experts at filing reports. They started with Child Protective Services, then moved onto Adult Protective Services. She might even blow her whistle to the media—"

"But she doesn't really know anything."

"Well she might find an investigative reporter who's looking for a story—"

Pratt noticed Cameron tremble as he stared at a picture on his desk. Some old broad. Probably his wife. Finally the doctor said, "We voted to use Ben Brewster as our ***Finale***."

"Shit, what a bad time for complications," Pratt tried to sound empathic. "I know a way to *un*-complicate things." Pratt leaned back on the sofa as he watched Cameron. "What if I take Wintress' mind off her work? Give her something else to think about? —Just for a while?"

"Such as?"

"A little vacation. Nothing too fancy. How about a few days as a guest on the orthopedics ward, and several weeks in daily outpatient physical therapy?"

Cameron hesitated before he said, "Absolutely not. I could never condone that."

Pratt figured the doc had thought for a while as he vacillated. "All I'm saying, is she'll have an accident. Or get mugged."

"I wouldn't want her seriously hurt. I'd never tolerate that."

"Street crime is a reality, Doc. Happens every day in our dangerous city. By the time she's back at work, the ***Finale*** will be over. Then it won't matter what she says about Barretino."

"You're right. So much time will have passed, she'll sound hysterical."

Pratt waited. The Doc just needed a little time to convince himself. He was probably thinking he'd be out of the country by the time the social worker could talk, anyway.

"This accident?" Cameron began to ask. "Would Hayneswurth hear about it?"

"Why should he?"

"You and he have some prior connections, don't you? He brought you here—"

Pratt considered how much to say. "We've known each other, but this is the first time we've worked together. Doc, you and I are here together in the trenches, dealing with patients. Hayneswurth is just an economist. He doesn't know about clinical stuff. His job is completely separate from ours. And Wintress' vacation is part of our job." He locked his gaze on Cameron's. "Doc, I never turn on a partner. Never."

Cameron nodded.

"There is the matter of payment, though," Pratt said.

"Payment?"

"Vacations are never free. This one, I'd say, will cost two thousand dollars."

Cameron looked sour. "That's going to be hard, right now."

"That's fine. You can pay me after the ***Finale***. I have faith in our success."

Cameron looked at him in silence. "Could I ask you a question, Mr. Pratt?"

"Sure."

"What happened to your hands?"

The question caught Pratt by surprise. He raised his hands and held them out. "It's an old Japanese trick. I smashed the two main knuckles on each hand with a hammer—one at a time—then kneaded the fragments together so they'd heal like this. Nobody does it anymore, even in Japan."

"For what purpose?"

"To toughen the knuckles. And to see if I could take the punishment."

"It seems rather extreme."

"Hey, Doc, if you want a hammer, you don't make it out of rubber."

"A hammer isn't the right tool for every job, you know, Pratt."

He chuckled. "Worried about the vacation?"

"Take care not to overdo it. There's something I believe. Deeply. There should be only three kinds of deaths in this world: accidental, natural, and self-deliverance by personal choice. I will never participate in cold-blooded murder."

Pratt thought a moment. "Don't worry; you won't have to." Then he smiled. "But you know, Doc, blood is never cold."

Chapter 20

"But I have no desire to go to this party," Sammie said, as Alice zipped up the back of her dress. She had chosen a loose-fitting outfit that was comfortable, yet still elegant.

"Sweetheart, you need to get out. Tonight, I'll visit Dad for both of us." Alice went on. "He's getting a little sick of us hovering over him all the time, anyway."

"Look, Aunt Alice, I won't know anybody there."

"Goodness, you're bright, you look lovely, and this party is a wonderful opportunity to meet new people. Plus you're fulfilling your uncle's obligation as a hospital board member. Many young people will be there since the party is in honor of Dr. Solomon's son. He just returned from India."

"I still prefer to stay with Dad."

"But he wants you to go. Go. Give him the impression you still have a normal life.

Sammie sighed. "Okay, but don't be surprised if I'm back by seven-thirty."

David knew that parking would prove difficult so he took a cab to the Solomons' home. They lived in one of the venerable, red brick row houses that defined Georgetown. Every window blazed with light, people moving around inside.

The moment he rang the bell, the door was swept open by a tall, slender, bosomy woman. Her frosted hair contrasted with her rosy skin. She wore a sharply cut pantsuit of blue silk.

"David!" She drew him inside and gave him a boisterous hug. Then she held him away, looking at him. "How fabulous to see you. You look good, but tired."

David reached up to smooth his hair. "It's the 'intern' thing. Good to see you, Barbara."

"You should come around more often. Gerald misses his chats with you."

"I miss them, too."

"I hope that changes soon. David, there are several single women here. But if you want to find Gerald, look for the biggest group of devoted geeks. Of course, Ethan can't wait to talk to you." Something lurked in her eyes. A submerged laugh?

David scanned the crowd. Not many familiar faces from the hospital. He looked for his old friend, No pony tails in sight.

The doorbell rang. "I have to get this, dear. Go mingle. I'll talk to you later."

David kissed Barbara Solomon lightly on her cheek, took a deep breath and headed into the crowd.

David moved past figures wearing turbans and yarmulkes, robes and suits, gowns and Levis. He had a decision to make... to proceed toward the buffet tables, or to go to the bar...

During college, David developed a taste for Martinis but he'd pretty much sworn off alcohol because his internship showed him so many patients whose lives proved that alcohol was a velvet-lined trap with steel teeth. Still, a couple of drinks always helped his shyness. And he deserved to relax after all he'd gone through in the last couple of days. A loud snarling from his stomach made him turn toward the buffet.

Near the food table he saw an attractive young woman in a black silk cocktail dress that flowed gently around subdued curves. That image clinched his decision. As he approached, he noted the delicate way she selected portions to put on her plate. Each choice seemed to have been made after diligent consideration.

He stood behind her as he scooped up generous portions of sushi, dolmas, and blintzes. He was about to note the differences between their two plates when a familiar sounding voice distracted him. "I see your appetite hasn't changed."

David looked up. Two men stood before him, both wearing long tangerine-colored robes. Their feet were bare, their skins brown, their heads shaved. One was two inches taller than David, the other much shorter and frail-looking. His smooth head bobbed atop a wrinkled stalk of a neck.

The taller man grinned. "Hey, David."

David almost dropped his buffet plate. "Ethan?"

Chapter 21

Tonight was golden. Magic in the air.

Bruce Pratt's real skills—his true talents, natural and hard-earned in combat—had not been requested for several years. Had the world quieted down? Or did it now consider Pratt too old? Hayneswurth had thrown him a hospital drudgery job, mainly to keep an eye on Doc and the patients. Not to use his special skills. Nothing risky, Hayneswurth told him. An excuse for the meager remuneration. Only three times a regular nurse's salary. He wouldn't have taken it without the $50,000 bonus when the project was complete.

His vacation-for-the-social-worker deal with Cameron would change all that, and not just financially. This weekend, Pratt would add another invisible ribbon to his invisible uniform.

He drove from the hospital straight out to Michelle Wintress' neighborhood for a quick reconnoiter. He planned to go to sleep with the street layout in mind—ways in and ways out, possible obstacles, where witnesses might hang out, and so on—and let the plans form in his dreams. Tomorrow, he'd do the job. And feel like a man again.

He'd make Cameron his blood brother partner—forever.

Usually fate screws you in the ass, but now and then it gives you a pat on the head and says, "Do what thou wilt." Not ten minutes after Pratt turned onto Wintress' street, he saw the woman exit her apartment building. She carried a large brown bag that looked like 25 pounds of rice. She rested it on the back seat of her car and drove off.

Pratt sensed that tonight would be one of those rare occasions when all the rivers of fate run in the same direction—his direction. What were the odds for such perfect timing?

Pratt drove at a discreet distance behind Wintress. About three miles later, he watched her park, take the bag out of the backseat, and walk down the street.

As Pratt waited, he thought about the piece of crap he drove. All he could afford to drive, thanks to his greedy ex-wife and her bleeding-heart lawyer.

The worst part was how much he missed his two sons.

Never mind that now. He'd take care of Wintress, become Cameron's partner, and hire the best attorney money could buy. Then, he'd get custody of his kids again.

The way he felt tonight, no question about it. He was golden.

ᘐᘛ

Michelle felt oddly nervous since she left her place. She got out of the car and approached David's apartment using her "don't-mess-with-me walk." She'd learned that gait as a social work intern while visiting DC's dangerous areas. But David's neighborhood wasn't dangerous. She never had anxiety before, when she walked Slowpoke.

Had she not recovered from Nurse Pratt's threats? Was she still shaken by Vivian's sudden death? How she wished she could have told Vivian how much she had learned from her. Dying alone must be the worst experience in the world. No one deserves that.

She went down a few stairs and put down the bag of dog food in front of the door. She got out the key to David's apartment and heard scampering on the other side.

"Hey, girl," Michelle said as she let herself in. She put the bag in the corner, and hugged the dog. She smiled and winced at the wet slap of dog tongue.

She opened the bag and poured some into Slowpoke's bowl. Less than five minutes later, Slowpoke was sitting by the door, head tilted, round eyes staring at her.

"Okay, girl." Michelle bent to kiss her again. "Okay. Get your leash. Come on."

⁂

Pratt knew his moment had come when he saw Wintress step out of the building. She was alone, except for a skinny nervous dog on a leash. Nothing like a Rottweiler or Doberman. She was here to walk somebody's dog. A nice stroll in the dark, to let the dog take a squat. Off to the park? A perfect place to work.

Golden.

He let Wintress and the dog get quite a way down the block, the dog hauling away at the leash. Then he climbed out of his car to follow them on foot.

Chapter 22

"You look surprised," Ethan said.

"I am." David tried to compose himself. "Remember when you wore lamp shades to parties?"

Ethan threw back his head and laughed. At least that sound was familiar. His eyes were the same blue as his mother's. They flashed like sequins against the suntanned darkness of his skin. "David, meet Rinpoche Champa Daka. He's from India. Rinpoche, this is David Grainger, my old college roommate."

David had no idea what to do. Shake hands? Bow?

Rinpoche's smile showed a crooked fence of teeth. He placed his palms together in front of his chest and said, "*Namaste.*"

"That means, 'My soul recognizes your soul,'" Ethan said.

"A pleasure to meet you, sir." Rinpoche's Indian accent had a tinge of British. "Ethan has told me much about you."

"Thanks. Can I ask, what's a 'Rinpoche?'"

Ethan answered. "Precious One, or Revered Teacher."

"What do you teach, Mr. Rinpoche?"

"The Eightfold Noble Path. Buddha's path to enlightenment."

"Don't look so freaked out, David," Ethan said, eyes glinting with humor. The chandelier over the buffet table reflected a glowing ring off his scalp. "What about all the e-mails I sent, saying my interest in Buddhism was growing?"

"I thought you were just extending your comparative religion major."

Ethan laughed. Rinpoche's cheery chuckle provided counterpoint.

"Somewhere along the way I realized what I was really looking for," Ethan said. "I found it in Northern India, among the people exiled from Tibet—and the teachings of Buddha and Padmasambhava, the Tibetan Buddha."

David looked at his friend's shaved head and robe. "But your parents never told me that you went this far." He glanced at Rinpoche and back to Ethan. "Does this mean you've become a monk?"

"Only a novice. In many Buddhist cultures, men spend a limited time wearing a saffron robe and living as mendicants as they study the Dharma, which are the teachings of Buddha."

Without warning, David's memory replayed the time he'd walked into his frat room to find Ethan and a blond coed thrashing around in bed. David suppressed the image. "What do your parents think?"

Ethan's mouth formed a rueful slant. "Dad bashed me about our Jewish heritage, but I countered that we went to Temple only on High Holidays, and had more Passover Seders per year than Sabbath dinners. Buddhism is more a philosophy than a religion. So you can keep your old traditions. "

"And your mom?"

This time, Ethan didn't laugh. "She's always found multiculturalism trendy, and prefers my new haircut to that long ponytail. But to attain Nirvana, a seeker must surrender all cravings. Including cravings of the body."

"You mean—"

"Yes, celibacy. But only if I go that far. You know, Mom wants grandchildren."

"Whoa," David said. The scene with the blond flicked through his mind again.

Rinpoche waved a hand. "The decision to commit to monastic life is one that Ethan has much time to consider, Mr. Grainger."

"Ethan, can I ask, why?"

"I'd like to talk to you more about this. Just the two of us," Ethan said. Then he closed his eyes and recited, "When you know no peace, how can you know joy? When you let your mind follow the siren call of the senses, they carry away your better judgment, as a cyclone drives a boat off the charted course to its doom."

David searched for a reply. "Neat stuff, that Buddhism."

Ethan smiled. "That's actually from a Hindu scripture, the *Bhagavad Gita*."

Somewhat stunned, David's shoulder yielded as a slap brought him back.

"Listen, are you on duty tomorrow?" asked Ethan. "If you're free, we can toss a Frisbee around, like the good old days."

"Sounds great. Frisbee's okay?"

"Everything in moderation. Of course, I won't wear a robe."

"Sure. What time?"

"How about nine, in front of the Oak Creek Cemetery?"

David nodded. He watched Ethan and Rinpoche turn away in a swirl of saffron.

He couldn't believe it. Ethan Solomon the track star. Ethan Solomon the lady's man. Ethan Solomon the chug-a-lug king. And now, Ethan Solomon the stranger.

Like David Grainger, the stranger—

—Who agreed to become an accomplice to abusing the *Double Effect*...

—Who pretended to use this principle to end Donald Becker's life...

—Who failed to report Jonathan Leary to the authorities...

—Who even destroyed the evidence of smothering his own father to death.

A headache beat like a separate heart behind his right eye.

He turned and strode to the bar. "A glass of white wine, please."

Chapter 23

Once, in Vietnam, Pratt had a day like this—luminous in every detail, gilded. Every round he squeezed from his silenced .45 had gone straight home, enemy dropping like bags of rice, never seeing him, thinking a whole battalion was working them over. Later, making his silent way to the dust-off point, he came across some Marines getting chopped up in an ambush. The jarheads had driven into a minefield and now they were trying to fight back from bits of cover. One jarhead lay screaming, his legs blown to confetti, being used for target practice by invisible little men in black pajamas.

That day, Pratt didn't hesitate. He strolled straight into the minefield, lifted the Marine and strolled right on out again, slugs snarling and popping all around him. Not touching him, though. The crouching Marines stared at him in awe. Seeing a man steeped in gold, like a god.

Exactly the same feeling tonight. Nothing could go wrong. When the universe presented you with such a gift, you had to take full advantage.

He followed Wintress and the dog straining on its leash. They headed toward the darkness of Rock Creek Park. He pondered what his life had become. Working as a lowly nurse, changing bedpans and cleaning up after people who had no reason to live. Helping Hayneswurth. Demeaning grunt work. Not like Vietnam, Nicaragua, and El Salvador—where Hayneswurth sought his advice, where he was an important part of the action.

Hayneswurth was stupid to assume Pratt wouldn't find out everything. Locked doors and safes were never obstacles to Pratt. It didn't take him long to learn how much the sponsors had promised each Committee member as a bonus, including that Cameron would get the first prize of three to five million, provided the ***Finale*** was successful. That was certainly enough for the Doc to take in an equal partner.

And Pratt knew exactly how to convince him.

Up ahead, Wintress and the dog jogged across the empty street into the park.

The universe was sending him a message, right here, right now. Presenting him a gift—larger than Hayneswurth's or Cameron's. A gift from the gods, presented on a golden platter.

All he had to do was to reach out and take it.

Pratt surveyed the street. It contained a nice assortment of vehicles. Why not choose the best car available?

ℒ

Just ahead, Rock Creek Park looked dark and abandoned, not at all the joyous site it was during the day. Michelle felt another surge of nervousness. But she'd walked Slowpoke here so many times. Perhaps fewer people were here on Saturday nights.

Slowpoke's claws skidded on the pavement as she scrambled across the street to the open spaces of the park. Despite the city's leash laws, Michelle always turned her loose. Like most Greyhounds, Slowpoke was born to run. She rocketed off toward the trees. In a moment she was lost to sight.

Michelle stood at the edge of the grass, listening to the jingle of dog tags fading.

Behind her came the sound of a car cruising slowly. Very slowly. She turned her head with a snap, and then relaxed. It was an older, very large car. Very well-kept. Probably owned by somebody's grandparents. The car crept up the street before it went out of sight. She turned back toward the park.

The swift jingling grew louder. Slowpoke appeared for a moment, then hurtled past like a tiny cruise missile, just out of reach, her mouth open as if in laughter.

Michelle strolled along the sidewalk. Ahead, streetlights made a string of connected yellow pools. Nobody around. Amazing how any part of such a crowded metropolis could seem so deserted.

She glanced over at the houses across the street. Nice, well-kept houses with windows like warm yellow eyes in the night. Small front yards with concrete birdbaths and lawn ornaments. At the curb, a solid line of parked cars waiting to take their owners to church in the morning.

"Slowpoke!" Michelle shouted. "Get back here right now!"

The cheerful song of the dog tags faded, leaving silence except for the hiss of wind. Michelle scanned the gloom. Nothing. Then she glimpsed movement from the corner of her eye—distant, on the sidewalk. Not Slowpoke.

As she turned her head, a headless man stepped into view. Her heart rate quadrupled before her brain took over. The man wasn't headless. His ears were hunched down in the upturned collar of his coat. The long coat billowed around his calves.

He was walking toward her.

Michelle tried to calm down, telling herself this was just a neighbor taking his evening constitutional. But she adopted the stationary version of her "don't-mess-with-me" walk. She shouted, "Slowpoke!" knowing that *Trench Coat* had no way of knowing her dog would only play with him instead of protecting her.

He was less than a quarter block away now, walking steadily, head hunched down, hands in his coat pockets.

A person could hide almost anything under a trench coat. A penis ready to expose. A knife. A gun. A machete, for Christ's sake.

Michelle coiled Slowpoke's leash around her open hand and tried to look casual. She wished the leash were made of metal links rather than nylon. Still, it would stiffen her fist and give her more punching power.

"Slowpoke!" A shiver of adrenaline rushed clear up into the roots of her hair.

As she heard the swishing of Trench Coat's garment, she tightened her hand around the leash. Just in case.

Slowpoke materialized like a cannon shell, racing toward her. Michelle crouched and caught her, tried to hook the leash onto her collar before she could run off again. The hook slipped as Slowpoke jumped. Michelle pinned the dog under one arm. Sounds of breathing filled the air, her own, Slowpoke's, perhaps another's—harsh, thick, getting closer.

"Come on, come on," Michelle muttered, struggling with the clasp. Finally it snapped home. She shot to her feet. He was right there. Trench Coat was next to her, moving in, lifting his hand—

Michelle screamed.

Trench Coat, his hand opened toward her in casual greeting, staggered back as if her voice were a hurricane. Under thick glasses, his Asian eyes, startled. "Jesus, lady! What the hell is wrong with you?"

He turned and walked away, shaking his head and muttering.

Slowpoke lunged at the end of the leash, still wanting to play.

The adrenaline dropped out of Michelle's system, leaving her weak and shaking. "My God," she said. She bent over, hands on knees, and struggled against the urge to throw up. When the spasm passed she had to fight down laughter.

"Come on, Slowpoke," Michelle giggled, pulling on the leash. "Come on."

Dragging the dog like a kite jumping in gusty wind, she turned and stepped into the dark street. Enough adventure. It was time to get back to David's and then drive back to Tom. He'd finish moonlighting at a Redi-Care Center in a couple of hours. Although tired, he was never too tired...

She did not see the huge car until its headlights flared like exploding suns. Beyond the blazing glare she recognized its long lines and chromed angles. It was the big classic car she'd seen before. But it reappeared so abruptly...

A second later, her world filled with a deafening engine roar and headlights so close she could feel the heat. Grillwork lunged at her with shocking speed, like a lion appearing from the tall grass, jaws agape...

Chapter 24

Compared to his wife, Gerry Solomon looked like a troll, but his conversation was animated and entertaining. A small man, he had a potato of a nose, green eyes bright with intelligence, and protruding ears surrounded by unruly ringlets of black hair.

David noticed some guests centered on two hands flying in patterns like brush strokes. He decided to stay behind his mentor, to get the gist of the conversation before he greeted him.

"The outcome of Kenard's trial," Solomon said, "will have a significant influence on the willingness of doctors to offer Physician-Assisted Suicide."

"I hate that term," said an older woman. "'Suicide' is a term we psychologists reserve for medically healthy people with extreme mental problems and irrational judgment."

"Do you have another term to suggest?" asked Solomon.

"I prefer *Physician-Hastened Dying* because terminal patients are already dying. Their rational desire to hasten the process is motivated by their untreatable, intolerable suffering."

"I agree. That is a better term," Solomon said, "but Kenard's trial is about *euthanasia*."

"May I interrupt to ask a question?" It was the young woman, the one in the mauve dress whom David had noticed at the buffet table. "This is all new to me. Can someone explain the difference between Physician-Hastened Dying and euthanasia?"

David liked the direct way the woman phrased her question. She was not embarrassed to admit what she did not know, yet her dress was non-revealing.

"As we use the term, with Physician-Hastened Dying, patients must make the final decision themselves, by putting the lethal dose of medication in their mouths," said Solomon. "With euthanasia, physicians administer the lethal medications, usually into a vein. Personally, I fear giving doctors that much power."

"But you do agree—Physician-Hastened Dying can be rational?" asked the psychologist.

"Yes, it can be, provided—"

David gasped as he lost Solomon's remaining words. He couldn't believe it. His mentor was advocating Physician-Hastened Dying. He felt a tap on the shoulder. "A glass of wine?" David exchanged his empty glass for a full one. The chatter and laughter from the rest of the party were fading from his concern.

Now, a man in a suit of sumptuous fabric leaned forward. "A confidential survey of San Francisco doctors who cared for AIDS patients revealed that half had hastened patients' dying."

"They probably helped many patients," Solomon said, "but medicine should never be practiced in secret. Only open practice permits us to establish and monitor clinical guidelines, changing them as needed, for everyone's safety."

David wanted to scream. Solomon was okay with doctors killing patients, as long as they followed a monitored protocol? To control his anger, he returned to study the face of the young woman in mauve.

"But we also need safeguards for 'Dr. Heroes,'" said a lady who David recognized as an ICU nurse at Memorial. "We admitted a thirty-seven-year-old woman with terminal brain cancer. She went from lethargy to coma in two days. Her neurosurgeon boasted he could bring her out of her coma. He did. He performed a surgical shunt and gave her steroids." The nurse shook her head. "I'll never forget the horror on the woman's face as she realized she was completely paralyzed and unable to talk..." The nurse grabbed a handkerchief. "Sorry, I didn't mean to cry."

The woman in the tent dress moved toward the nurse. Empathy flowed from her as she put a gentle hand on her shoulder. To describe her, a term entered David's thoughts that had not occurred to him for years: *Flower Child.*

"I'd cry too," Solomon said. "Yes, 'Dr. Heroes' can cause additional, unnecessary suffering. But my heart also goes out to people who have no health insurance—some forty-five million Americans. Their pain and suffering are worse because they are deprived of adequate *Comfort Care.* The ideals of some politicians and religious leaders provide them no legal option to shorten their final months of suffering."

"How horrible." Flower Child's empathic voice. "Are you pessimistic about change?"

David was impressed. Flower Child could embrace both the world of feelings and the world of concepts. He looked at his glass. Time to exchange it again.

"Change is always possible," Solomon responded. "The political battle over Physician-Hastened Dying has already served as an impetus to improve end-of-life care. Oregon leads the nation in providing excellent end-of-life care, in terms of pain control, the percentage who enroll in hospice, and—"

"Gerry, you're an academic fool," said an older man. "We both know that a prescription for Seconal costs under a hundred dollars. That's not enough for even one hour's stay on an ICU! Insurance companies must answer to their shareholders' need for greater net profits. The easier way to decrease costs is '***Managed Death***.' That's the lowest cost treatment plan!"

David visualized the swinging cover of the Bio-Waste Bin with Leary's pillow inside. He downed the rest of his drink as he thought, *Probably, it cost less than fifteen dollars.*

"We must make doctors accountable for what they do," said the older man, probably one of Dr. Solomon's clinical colleagues. "Put them in jail if they break the law. And I'd start with Kenard."

"I'll drink to that," David blurted out. He bit his tongue, but it was too late.

Solomon turned. "David!" He grabbed his arm. "Step closer, son. Ladies and gentlemen, meet one of Memorial's finest interns, Dr. David Grainger. Tell us, what do *you* think?"

Now forced to say something, David's mind was flooded with images of Becker and Leary but he couldn't say anything about either. He took gulp of his drink and said, "Doctors should never write off patients, even if some of them consider their medical condition hopeless."

David noticed Flower Child cocking her head a little to the side. She seemed to agree.

A man in a maroon sweater, who had only been listening up to this point now asked, "But what if the patient concludes that she has suffered enough?"

"Doctors must never abandon their patients," said David.

"What about burnt-out doctors?" asked the older man. "Wouldn't over-tired doctors be more prone to abandon their patients? Unless times have changed, medical interns still must work thirty-six hours every other day, right?"

"Yes, but overwork and tiredness would never lead us to abandoning our patients." David recalled asking Tom a similar question.

The maroon-sweater man asked, "Want to know how I, as a lay person, define 'abandonment'? When a patient is suffering after trying everything and makes a rational request for ultimate relief, but her doctor refuses. That's abandonment!"

"No," David blurted out. "Doctors should never play God. Doctors should try to understand why their patients are so desperate. They must inquire deeply, to learn why their patients are suffering, and try to help them heal. Some are in pain. Others are depressed. But the last thing a doctor should do is kill his patient. Killing can never be healing."

"What about end-stage Alzheimer's Disease? Don't patients have the right to transcend the indignity of slowly losing all vestiges of their humanity, by avoiding years of total dependency? Doctor, perhaps you're too young to remember when we accepted paternalism from physicians as we went along with their assumption that it was their duty to deny patients their most basic civil liberty—the right to determine what happens to their bodies. Well, there has been a resurgence in that view. Have you read the 2005 report by the President's Council on Bioethics "Taking Care: Ethical Caregiving in our Aging Society"? This public document insisted that doctors, caregivers, and designated proxies ignore Living Wills since they *discriminate against a future disabled self,* if the patient was *demented.* The Council recommended *not necessarily honoring* patients' previously expressed wishes, even if they were clearly and convincingly put in writing. Instead, The President's Council stated that current decision makers should impose their own moral judgment about the patient's current condition. Only one member of the Council wrote a dissent." *Maroon* took a piece of paper out of his pocket to read, "'If you feel strongly about not living in a decerebrate state,' which means that the part of your brain responsible for memory, thinking, and reasoning no longer functions, 'you'd better kill yourself while you have control over your fate!' * How many people, with very minimal or no awareness like Terri Schiavo, would want to live 30 years instead of 15? And how many millions of patients with advanced dementia, like my mother... must be forced to live for years after they have lost their humanity?"

David didn't say anything. He just wished the man was done. He wasn't.

"Okay, I revealed that I speak from personal experience. Before my mother's Alzheimer's got too bad, she swallowed a bunch of pills in a suicide attempt. But a neighbor called 9-1-1, the paramedics coded her, the ER staff pumped her stomach, and a social worker placed her in a nursing home. A year later, her entire life was reduced to staring at a goddamn wall. Now she doesn't know the difference between food and pills. She's refusing to eat, so her doctor asked me to approve a feeding tube. My God. How long will this go on?"

"I'm sorry. Your story reminds me of the first person Dr. Kevorkian killed," said David. "Janet Adkins ** also had Alzheimer's. She played tennis the same day Kevorkian helped her die. Was it rational to commit suicide just because she couldn't keep score? Killing her was a tragedy. Experts at the trial testified that she could have *enjoyed* a few more years of life."

"Doctor, you are *not* listening. You've missed the crucial point." The man's face was turning maroon. "Sure, Adkins was still enjoying life when she chose to die, but the reason she died prematurely was because she was *afraid* to wait. She knew that eventually, she'd become unable to end her life. That is precisely what happened to my mother." He shook his head. "Society forces people like Adkins to shorten their lives because it fails to guarantee that their end-of-life decisions will be honored. I forgive your youth, Doctor. Perhaps with more experience, you'll learn to appreciate such tragedies."

David's mind wandered to his father. He rarely revealed stuff about his personal life, but heard himself say, "My father's doctors should have offered him experimental treatments instead of giving up. Hope is essential. We must never give up hope. I may be young, but I do know what leads to suicide. Loss of hope."

"No!" *Maroon*'s voice grew louder as his face got more color. "Patients suffering from end-stage Alzheimer's loose every vestige of *personhood*, not just hope."

"Then others can still hope for them. New medications are being tested as we speak. Research is our hope. Universities are conducting multi-center studies to test a Chinese herb extracted from *Huperzia serrata*, a member of the *Lycopodium species* of club moss." David hoped his memorizing the Latin words would help win his argument. "I looked this up after I learned that some patients in the early stages of Alzheimer's are not being treated because patented drugs are so expensive. Anyway, here's my point: Isn't it possible that a new combination of pharmaceuticals and herbs could stop or reverse your mother's symptoms?" David noticed Flower Girl's smile. How encouraging. "Suppose a month or two after your mother killed herself, or asked *you* to kill her, medical researchers discovered a cure for

* Janet D. Rowley, M.D., D.Sc., Blum-Riese Distinguished Service Professor of Medicine, Departments of Hematology and Oncology, University of Chicago, wrote this dissent.

** Janet Adkins was 54 years old when Kevorkian helped her die, in 1990.

Alzheimer's? What would you think then?" David noticed another full glass of wine in his hand. Two gulps, it was empty.

"I'd think that she made the best decision she could at the time." *Maroon* thrust his chin forward. "...which is better than forcing her to accept the decision of a doctor who doesn't know or care about honoring her previously expressed wishes."

David's face burned. "Do you have any children?"

"Children? Yes, three. Why?"

"Did they know their grandma? Did they have quality time with her before her Hodgkin's—I mean her Alzheimer's—got worse?" David wondered, did Flower Child notice his slip?

"Her outbursts of anger are unpredictable now. She can't recognize them, anyway."

"No I meant a year ago, when her neighbor called 9-1-1. Suppose she died then, wouldn't your children have been deprived of a few months of good memories?" David looked at *Maroon's* knuckles. They were white. Still he said, "Wouldn't your children be glad if—"

"David—" Solomon's voice.

The pressure on David's shoulder increased. People seemed to be staring at him. Was he shouting? He pulled away from Solomon as he wracked his brain for a stronger argument. "What about Stephen Hawking? The genius who wrote 'A Brief History of Time'? He has ALS. Can't even use his voice. Suppose he had asked his doctor to shoot him full of morphine when he first got ALS?"

Flower Child looked intrigued. Definitely rooting for him.

"So?" The man in maroon stepped forward. He stood a half-pace from David. "I have no problem with Hawking choosing to live as long as possible. But why should his experience prevent my mother from exercising her choice?"

"Because doctors must fight Death every way we can." He saw *Flower Child* nodding. "Doctors must never give up hope. All the rest is bull shit."

David was dimly aware of some movement behind him. Two saffron-colored shapes. "Bull shit?" *Maroon's* flushed face was directly in front of him.

"David—" Solomon's voice again.

"Doctors aren't gods," David went on. "They have no right to second-guess a patient's future. If my father had opted for an experimental protocol, he might still be alive today. Any argument that supports doctors killing patients is bull shit!"

"You're saying MY argument is bull shit?" *Maroon* turned sideways, his right shoulder lowered. Behind David, Ethan stretched out a restraining hand.

Then David saw another hand. Closed, in a fist. Becoming bigger.

A moment later, it filled his entire world.

Chapter 25

Pratt loved the way the Cadillac handled. Like a boat, gliding over streets, instead of on them. It took the impact of Wintress without swerving at all. He noticed the woman's face flared white in the beam of the headlights. Then she snapped forward in a blur. There were two soft bumps and she was gone until, in the rear-view mirror, he saw a bundle, rolling over in the street.

The dog bolted away. No screams. No barks. No nothing.

Nothing but perfection.

He took several turns over the next two miles. First fast, then slow. By now the blood should have stopped dripping. He climbed out regretfully. What great wheels.

No one would notice stains on the bumper and grille until daylight. The dent was minimal. The car's owner would be out a few hundred bucks, at most.

Pratt locked the door to prevent a scum bag from stealing the car for parts. It had to be found with blood for the police to conclude some drunken kid on a joyride did this hit-and-run.

He shoved his gloves into his pockets and strolled away, nice and casual, angling toward the block where he'd left his junker. Pretty soon he'd replace that piece of crap with something much, much better. A Cadillac. Better than what Hayneswurth would expect.

Cadillac? Screw it. He'd get a Rolls.

Chapter 26

David didn't realize he was lying down until he tried to sit up. He couldn't. His head felt enlarged three times. He opened his right eye. His mentor was hovering over him. Under him was soft leather. He was stretched out on the couch in Solomon's library. Party sounds came from the next room. The festivities were still going full-speed.

"Don't worry," Dr. Solomon said. "Your debating friend has gone."

"Who?" David sat up.

"The man in maroon. Ethan and his guru talked him into taking a cab. Pretty good jab for a computer nerd, eh? Keep this ice pack in place." David became aware of coldness pressing hard against his cheekbone.

David grunted. "Will I have to explain a black eye all week?"

"Yes." A soothing, feminine voice. "But I liked what you said about not giving up hope."

David turned to perceive the form of *Flower Child*. "You did?"

"Yes. Does your eye hurt?"

"It's not that bad." David didn't want to sound wimpy.

"Ice can be applied too long. I have something, if you're open to it. They're natural products. Let the pills dissolve under your tongue. Spread the balm over the wound. Like to try?"

Normally David would at least pose some skeptical questions if he didn't outright refuse. But the cold hurt and *Flower Child* was intriguing. He didn't want her to leave. For the small risk of accepting her style of treatment, she might continue her endearing attentiveness.

"Something new for me. Seems like a good time to try."

She opened her purse, took out a plastic bag, pinched several tiny white pellets, and placed them under David's tongue. "Let them dissolve slowly." She took the ice pack away and massaged a cream that smelled like apricots. Her touch was so gentle.

She stepped back. "Now, if you're willing. Close both your eyes and imagine you're under a waterfall. And hum like this: 'Iha.' Okay? IIIhhhaaa...."

David hummed, took a breath, hummed again. He wondered how ridiculous he looked. Did Solomon think he'd gone crazy? He opened his right eye but before he could locate his mentor, a soft gentle touch closed his eyelid.

"Continue to hum."

After three more hums, the pellets had dissolved and the balm had absorbed. "Open your eye." He saw her hand cupped near his face. On her wrist she wore a plain bronze bracelet.

"Feel any better?"

David looked up into her shining lavender eyes. His cheek pain was almost gone. His whole body relaxed. "Yes, I do. That's amazing."

"Good. If the pain returns, hum again. Now, may I ask you a question?"

"Of course."

"Do you treat pain?"

"Well I'm still an intern, but of course, I've treated a few dozen patients for pain." David glanced at Solomon. His expression: You're on your own.

"Well have you ever tried alternative modalities like chanting, creative visualization, human energy field manipulation, or magnetic therapy?"

"No, I haven't."

"But you feel better yourself now?"

David nodded. "Yes."

"Well you've just experienced them all. I thought that might interest you."

David was glad Solomon asked her, "Are you a health practitioner?"

"No, I'm in a related field. My company extracts and distributes Naturopathics."

"I see," said Solomon.

"Our compounds are accepted around the world," she continued. "But in the U.S., the medical establishment kisses the feet of the drug companies and their billions of—"

"But our FDA must establish effectiveness through controlled evaluation trials using double-blind protocols," Solomon said. "I'm sorry... double-blind pro-"

"I know what they are. Drug trials where neither patient nor doctor knows if the compound administered is active or placebo."

"Right. Unfortunately, few natural interventions have undergone such rigorous testing."

"But Dr. Solomon, you saw David improve right before your eyes. And you heard the word he used to describe his experience: amazing." She crossed her arms and glared at David, waiting for him to respond.

The last thing David wanted was another conflict. "Yes, I said that. And I do feel better."

"One patient's success doesn't eliminate the placebo effect," Solomon said.

"We also want double-blind controlled studies." Her voice changed from endearing to authoritative. "But since you can't patent Mother Nature, there's no financial incentive."

"Good point," Solomon said. "In truth, many of our tested compounds were originally isolated from Nature."

"Are you saying that just to placate me?"

David figured it was his turn. "Miss—?" His pause yielded no name. "You've made a valid point, really. Please, accept my thanks. I really do feel better. Thank you for the, the—"

She paused to let him stumble. "Yes. For what? Did you notice? You didn't even ask the name of the remedy."

"Well, no, not yet. But I was going to," said David, knowing it was too late.

"I can tell you aren't interested." She looked at her watch. "Oh, I didn't realize it was so late. I wish you complete and rapid healing. Nice meeting you both."

"Thanks for everything. I hope we'll cross paths again, soon," said David.

"Yes, I'd like that."

Blew it, David thought. No card offered, none requested. No interest. He put the ice pack over his eye and watched her leave through the front door and turned to Solomon. "I may be half-blind instead of double-blind, but my initial impression from this uncontrolled trial is that it's quite unlikely that this Naturopathic... whatever... this *Flower Child* and I will become life-long friends."

Solomon looked serious. "I must agree. I hadn't met her before although I know her aunt. Her husband is on the hospital's board. David, you haven't dated anyone for two years, have you? Is that why you were so upset?"

"No. I don't have time for a relationship right now anyway. You know what it's like to be an intern." David looked at his mentor to see if he seemed convinced. David would not admit how much he really missed female companionship.

"But tonight you were more argumentative than I've ever seen you."

David didn't want to open up. The combination of pain in his cheek and eye, shock from learning that his mentor supported Physician-Hastened Dying, and the tragic deaths of Becker and Leary made David want to escape through sleep. "I was also surprised by my strong stance."

"At one point, you mentioned Hodgkin's Disease. Your father died of that, didn't he?"

"Yes. Dad could have volunteered for a chemotherapy trial. I wonder, maybe he would have—"

"Survived longer? Possibly, but he also might have been given a placebo and put through a lot of unnecessary tests. Or even placed on a protocol that made him sicker." Solomon paused to look at David. "Have you read the book I gave you? The one by Viktor Frankl?" *

"No. I haven't had time."

"Okay. In the briefest summary, one cornerstone of his philosophy is, 'Ask not what you can get out of life, but what life is expecting of you.' You must search for meaning beyond your disappointment. Now, you're emphasizing hope. Someday, you may find meaning in your loss.

* Viktor Frankl wrote *Man's Search for Meaning* (1959)

David's head was reeling. Meaning? In losing his father? How could there be? He forced a polite reply. "I'll have to think about that for a while."

"It can take years. Want some more ice?"

"No thanks. I'll just leave it alone."

"David, we all need someone to talk to. I'm sorry our paths haven't crossed much this year. But I promise, if you make the effort, I'll be available. Tonight, you stay here, in case you start bleeding. Wake me up if your headache worsens. Understand?"

David was done arguing. "Okay. Thanks."

Once home, Sammie listened to all the messages on her answering machine, but she only responded to the one that said, "Call me, no matter how late."

"It's not even ten-thirty," Alice said.

"Dr. Solomon and his wife were wonderful. And I really liked their son, Ethan."

"Really? Any possibilities?"

"We'll get together real soon—"

"How wonderful."

"He's even handsome."

"Dear, I'm so—"

"—In his shaved head and saffron robe."

"What?"

"Ethan is studying to become a Buddhist monk."

"Oh my."

Sammie laughed. "It's okay, Aunt Alice. I really had a nice time meeting people."

"Well, then, who else did you meet?"

The woman was incorrigible. "College professors, lawyers, economists. Of course, lots of doctors."

She'd never reveal how huffy she got, walking out on that intern.

"Oh? Anyone interesting?"

"One young doctor was particularly articulate, even forceful."

"Mm-hmm."

"But not as forceful as the guy who punched him out."

"A fist fight? At the Solomon's?" A brief pause on the phone. Unusual for Alice. "I hope you're not upset with me for pushing you to go?"

"No I'm not. Most of the people were very nice."

"Well, I'm glad you got out, Sweetheart. You shouldn't lock yourself away from the outside world."

"Aunt Alice, you know what's important to me right now? To bring the outside world in, to Dad. That is my clear purpose in life right now."

Chapter 27

As Cameron walked through the reception area of the PCC, he decided to leave the lights off. A dark ambiance would permit his mind to work with greater clarity. Tonight, he would begin his plan, an important first step. He would design a strategy that would ultimately lead Brewster to believe that it was *his own* idea to volunteer for the ***Finale***.

Yesterday, instead of visiting Ben, he'd sent in the speech pathologist. This morning he'd downloaded her transcribed report. If it said what he expected, he would use it as ammunition to induce Ben to remain in the hospital. Everything was moving along nicely. He opened the door to his private office and flicked on the light—

He almost doubled over.

Pratt sat on his sofa, relaxed, unruffled, clear-eyed.

"Stop doing that! I mean it!"

"Doc, we need to talk again, in private."

Cameron sat down behind his desk. Slowly, he asked, "About what we discussed yesterday?"

"Yep. Job's done."

Something about the way Pratt said the words, "Job's done," sent a chill down Cameron's spine, like wet seaweed. "What do you mean?"

"Well, I got to thinking. I asked myself, Why send someone on a vacation when it's just as easy to get them to retire for good?"

Cameron's chair became a raft on a silky sea, rocking and twisting over the tops of large, rounded combers. "What the hell are you saying?"

Pratt opened a copy of the *Washington Post*. "Read all about it. Page 4 of the Metro Section. 'Woman killed in hit-and-run. No name, pending notification of next of kin.' Here, read it yourself." He tossed the paper at him.

"Oh my God." Cameron backed away from the paper as if it were a giant spider. He kept gazing at Pratt, but he went out of focus. He blinked and saw Pratt's mouth still moving but he couldn't hear the words. Instead the words in his head were, *What had Pratt done? What had I done?*

After a moment, Cameron asked, "What did you say, Pratt? I didn't hear you. "

"I said that she was a major hazard, Doc. That I thought real deep over it. Why take a chance? So I made a command decision in the field."

A command decision? The words reverberated in his head. What had he done? Had *he* let this crazy man loose? Then Cameron grabbed hold of an idea. Perhaps it wasn't true. Maybe Pratt was just testing him. He had searched the newspaper for a story like this only to check him out, to see if he'd be willing to go that far. Hadn't Pratt just read, "No name, pending next of kin"? Or maybe Pratt was lying about doing it himself. Wintress was dead all right, but not from any act of Pratt. It *really* had been an accident. Pratt just wanted to claim credit to get his fee. Or—

Cameron's breakfast rose into his throat. He leapt up, rushed past Pratt into his private bathroom, dropped to his knees, and spewed a sour blast of vomit into the toilet. He hung his head over it, mouth gaping, eyes closed.

Dead. A young woman. A dedicated professional. Her whole life ahead of her. And he'd set the wheels in motion.

He heaved again.

He visualized Ms. Wintress standing in front of him, outside Vivian's door, arms folded across her chest. He heaved again. Sighed. Stood up. Washed his face. Looked down into the sink, not into the mirror. He couldn't face himself. Sighed again. Sat down on the toilet seat cover, head in his hands. He felt sad, scared, and wanted to run, but Pratt was waiting. The last person he wanted to see. Or speak to. Waited. He knew the luxury of silence would not last long. As expected, words through came through the door. Distinct and impatient: "Doctor Cameron?" A first: *Doctor*, not *Doc*.

He forced himself to open the door and return to his office. Pratt sat there, looking relaxed, his gaze contemptuous.

Cameron took several deep breaths as he tried to ignore the rancid remnants of bile in his throat. He took a few large gulps of water. "Pratt, I was very clear. You were never supposed to— to, to kill her."

"It was her choice. Look at what she was doing. She kept on interfering. She just wouldn't stop. What if, after I hurt her, she still didn't shut up? What if she kept drawing attention to Barretino and the other ***Type IIs*** in your study? Think about how she acted. Be realistic Doc. Would breaking her leg really stop that bitch's motor mouth? She could have ruined everything you've worked for."

Without thinking about it, Cameron heard himself say, "That's true." His words surprised him. Pratt's reasoning sounded remarkably apt. He asked himself, how could he think so logically in the middle of a crisis? Because of his experience as a physician whose profession required him to remain calm, unflustered, and diligent. Detachment was necessary to deal with trauma patients.

Pratt was right. Wintress *was* an extreme risk. She *had* intruded despite his numerous warnings. Now, nothing could bring her back. Meanwhile, his work with Ben was so promising. His greatest dreams were about to come true. Not only for himself, but for Wendy, too.

Pratt just sat quietly. Was he waiting because he knew Cameron needed time to sort things out? He spoke only when Cameron focused on him again.

"Nobody saw what happened." Pratt's voice had a tone of reassurance. "I used a stolen car. Then ditched it. You know, it's just one more hit-and-run in our big bad city."

Cameron looked at Wendy's photo. An automatic reflex, like a plea for support. He was amazed he could still look at his wife's face without turning away in shame. Then his own logic began to creep in. Wintress' death was neither his decision nor his intent. Pratt was responsible. Only Pratt. His idea, his execution. Execution: what a word choice! Yet every major revolution requires sacrifices—

"Now," Pratt said. "About my five thousand dollars."

"*Five* thousand?" The acid from Cameron's stomach gurgled up again.

"I risked my neck last night, Doc. Above and beyond the call—."

"That's extortion."

Cameron kept himself from looking at Pratt's deformed hands, his harsh trophies of his commitment to violence. "But I specifically asked you not to. I remember my exact words—"

"Doc, don't repeat yourself. I don't need to hear anything again. What's done is done." The nurse stood up and squared off right in front of him. "Think of it this way: What I did was for *you*, for *your* project. To prevent any distractions while *you* made *your* video. It was all to benefit *you*. I took a tremendous risk, just to help you. So *you* give me a reasonable bonus. I deserve it."

Cameron stared at him, saying nothing but thinking: *A young woman. At the beginning of her life and career. With everything to live for. Dead now? Killed for what? His bonus? My video. Oh my God.*

More softly, Pratt said, "And all this... is just between... you and me..."

Cameron's gut tightened. "You'd never go to Hayneswurth?"

"Of course not, Doc. We're partners." He extended his right hand. Its knuckles bulging, ominous. "I never go back on my partner. It'd be stupid, wouldn't it?"

The word, *partner*, buzzed in his head. Cameron turned toward his wife's photo again, but this time he turned away. He couldn't keep his gaze. *Pratt's partner? What had he become? To what level had he sunk?* The shock of what happened would not wear off quickly. It would take logic and self-talk, repeatedly.

He tried to feel less guilty by reviewing how both the social worker and the nurse had acted against his specific, direct instructions. What did he tell Wintress? NOT to go Vivian's room. What did he tell Pratt? NOT to hurt her badly. Yet he still blamed himself. He could not avoid answering the "What if" question: What if he had thrown Pratt out when the nurse first suggested a "vacation"?

Pratt's mouth was still moving. "What did you say? I missed it."

"I said it's time to proceed with your work on Brewster, to convince him to volunteer for Physician-Assisted Suicide. Let's talk about your plan, okay?

"No, not right now. Later. We'll talk later."

"Are you worried about paying my fee?"

Cameron stood up. "Yes. That's it. Pratt, I cannot pay you right now."

"Doc, I understand. I know you're good for it. You see Doc, I trust you. Like no one else on earth. Hey, partner, just let me know when you're ready to work together on the Major, Doc." Pratt turned. He seemed to glide out of the office.

It was twenty minutes passed before Cameron could move from behind his desk. He looked at the phone, wanted to call Wendy, but couldn't. She'd always been his rock of reassurance, but this was one part of his life that he could never tell her about. His stomach went into spasms.

He turned on the computer and downloaded the speech pathologist's report. A quick glance indicated that it contained what he was waiting for, but he could not bring himself to read it. Instead, he went to the bathroom, washed up again, and then returned to his desk. He picked up the report and forced himself to read it, word-by-word. When he was finished, he felt partially back on track. It contained exactly what he needed. Tomorrow, at Ben's bedside, he could inform Ben of its details and then share the grim prognosis of his declining ability to speak.

He sighed and pressed his stomach. It was beginning to calm down. It was good to try to get back on track. The suffering of many people depended on his finishing his work. The social worker's death was a sad and horrible sacrifice, but it's necessity and its execution had been entirely out of his hands. It would not be easy, but he had no choice but to go forward with his plans.

Chapter 28

"Nice catch!" Ethan Called. David dropped back onto the grass, Frisbee in hand. He returned it with an underhand cast, watched it sail away, its shadow racing after it.

A perfect spring day. Pure blue sky, solid enough to support clouds like lumps of rough-hewn marble. Air laden with warm bouquets from cut grass and flowers.

It had been years since David tossed a Frisbee. His body felt creaky, as if winter lived in his muscles. He was glad to have simple fun with Ethan. Still, his enjoyment was marred by guilt. It wasn't from procrastinating on his library research or from romping in Rock Creek Park without Slowpoke, but from the tragedies of Becker and Leary.

Ten yards away, Ethan jumped up and attempted a between-the-legs catch. Wearing baggy sweat pants, a New England Patriots T-shirt, and Reeboks—his shaved head made him look more like an overzealous Marine recruit than a religious convert.

The Frisbee bounced off his hand and landed flat on the grass. Ethan thumped down beside it, sprawled on his back. David heard winded laughter rising up.

"You okay?" David asked.

"Fine." Ethan picked up the Frisbee and walked toward David, rubbing his back. "Good time for a break."

"I should head home anyway. My dog's alone, and I need to go to the library." David's left cheek still ached. "Why not walk home with me? I'll drive you back, okay?"

"Fine."

"Remember how we'd spend hours tossing a Frisbee in school?"

Ethan smiled. "Real good use of our time, huh?"

"Seemed like it at the time."

Ethan nodded. "Amazing how our priorities change, isn't it?"

"Ahh so, Honorable Kwai Chang. Like your plan to become a psychologist?"

"I still do. And eventually, I will. Want to know why I took this Buddhist diversion?"

David nodded.

"I took two seminal courses at Brown. In one, I viewed a videotape of a therapy session of a couple and their fourteen-year-old son. He had just burned down a palm tree in front of their home. During the session, the boy refused to communicate—loudly—pushing his chair right back to the wall, crossing his arms, and glaring constantly at the therapist. He hardly blinked."

"So?"

"So I learned that there is no way *not* to communicate. Then there was a course on Eastern religions. One guest lecturer was a Zen Buddhist. He sat on the desk in full lotus position, breathed slowly for an hour, then took a yardstick and slammed it on the desk and said, 'This concludes my lecture.'"

David waited for Ethan to explain. And waited. Was he pulling the same Zen trick? Finally he asked, "So these two classes convinced you to become a Buddhist?"

"No, but they forced me to examine why my mind was so flooded with chatter and negative emotions. Other students had different reactions. One coed said she floated across campus with the positive emotions of freedom and relief, unconcerned with why she experienced such joy. I realized that, before I could help anyone else, I had to search for my own personal peace."

"Is it really worth the sacrifice?" David asked.

"You bet. Haven't you had to sacrifice, to become a doctor?"

"Ethan, I've missed talking to you about real stuff. Tell me, why Buddhism?"

"To me, Judaism offers little about death. When my grandmother died, the Rabbi said, 'So long as the children remember, the parents live.' See the problem? Right now, there's no one left who can remember my great-grandparents... So in that sense, they're dead. In Buddhism, we have reincarnation, although it's not what most people think—"

David felt uncomfortable as he remembered his father so he changed the subject. "How long will you be in town, Ethan?"

"Off and on, for about a month."

They crossed the street. "David, are you ready to talk about what's bothering you?"

"Did your father tell you anything?"

"No, he'd never violate confidentiality. I can tell myself that you're upset."

After several more steps, David blurted out, "Okay. I was an accomplice to murder."

Ethan waited a moment. "Tell me the rest."

"I had an AIDS patient whose pain became unmanageable. Mentally, he wasn't competent. The faculty physician and resident gave him a lethal dose of medications after they got me to interview his parents to be sure they wouldn't file a lawsuit."

"What did the parents say?"

"His father was pissed that we had waited so long. I guess he was worn out from watching his son suffer," David sighed, "but doctors shouldn't kill their patients—"

Ethan raised the Frisbee and held it inverted in front of him, peering into it, as if it might collect something brilliant out of the air. "Is that euthanasia?"

"They'd say no because, in a few days, he would have died anyway from dehydration. He was refusing food and water and they disconnected his IVs. But he died two hours after the resident increased his meds. They'd claim they were merely treating his suffering but I think they intentionally hastened his death." He looked at his friend. "What do you think?"

"I don't know. My question is, was there anything else you could have done?"

"Maybe argued more, like I did, last night—"

"Yeah! Look where that got you."

David had to chuckle. A brief pause in the storm. "I still can't stop obsessing—"

"I think I understand." Ethan's eyebrow had that characteristic arch that often preceded his saying something profound. "Buddha's Noble Truth Number Two: You cause your own suffering... by your expectations."

"What? No way. The suffering of an AIDS patient comes from cancer, infections, wasting, dementia. His only expectation is not to have such a terrible dis—"

"I'm referring to *your* expectations... not your patient's. "

"My expectations? I only want my patients to get the best care. What's wrong with that?"

"Your expectations may be greater than that. Listen to your ego."

"My ego? Wait a—" David's shoulders tightened. He felt like another fight could begin. "Are you accusing me of being a 'Dr. Hero'?"

"No. But don't you expect your practice of medicine will meet high standards?"

"Well, of course." David's cheekbone was throbbing hard.

"Well, that's your expectation. Sometimes, you have to let go. Listen—

> *You must be smart enough to realize,*
> *That you're NOT smart enough to realize—*
> *What's always best for you."*

"What does that mean, here?"

"That when you cease being humble, and presume you know for sure what's best, then your ego is taking over, which can cause you to suffer. Big time suffering."

"I don't get it." David felt angry.

"You assumed you were smart enough to know when your patient should die, that you knew *when* was best—for him and his parents."

"That may be so. I don't know."

"Good, David. 'Don't know' means you're admitting you're not smart enough. Here's your way out: If you don't know for sure when was best, then you don't have to feel guilty."

David took a deep breath. "But also I failed miserably because the way I asked... it made the parents feel guilty that they had given permission to euthanize their son."

"Shakespeare wrote something that's consistent with Buddhist philosophy: 'There is nothing good or bad, but thinking makes it so.' Isn't it possible that his parents felt privileged by your asking them to play an important role in releasing their son from his earthly pain?"

David bit his tongue. "'Releasing from pain'? We helped him die. I thought Buddhists were against killing."

"Of course, but what's most important in Buddhism is intent."

"Intent? My intent was to talk his parents out of it."

"But you couldn't. And his father said he wished his son's suffering had ended long ago, right?"

"All right, okay, maybe you're right. I could think about this one that way and not feel so badly." David kicked a stone.

"Then why don't you sound better?" asked Ethan.

"Because I had another case that was an even greater disaster." David ran a hand through his sweaty hair. "I concealed evidence of a murder."

David stopped walking to turn and check out Ethan's look. The compassion he saw encouraged him to continue. "I admitted a man with advanced prostate cancer after he badly botched a suicide attempt. He jumped through his attic window. His son asked me to overdose him after surgery, but I refused. The next day, I found the son sitting in his father's hospital room with a pillow in his hands." He took a breath. "Ethan, he had just suffocated his own father! And I— I took the bloody pillow from him and threw it away. Then I falsified the death certificate by writing *Cardiac Arrest* instead of *Suffocation* as the cause of death."

The stroll to his apartment moved into slow motion as David waited for a response.

Ethan put his hand on David's shoulder. "So the son released his father from suffering?"

"I guess so, yes."

"If you had turned the son in, it wouldn't have brought his father back, right?"

"Of course not. But if that were a valid excuse, no accomplice would ever be found guilty."

"Wait, what I'm asking you is, what was your intention in hiding the pillow?"

"To protect the son."

"To decrease the son's suffering?"

"Yes."

"Then your act was selfless."

"Ethan, your logic makes it too easy. I still lied—"

"But his father's heart did stop, didn't it?"

"Yes, it always does." David's heart lightened. "You'll be a great psychologist."

"I will, ultimately. But I've got to do other things first—"

"Like what?"

"Like this." Ethan halted and assumed a twisted, athletic pose, cocking the Frisbee in throwing position. "Go out for a long one!"

David took off down the sidewalk, his shadow sprinting at his heels. He watched the Frisbee sail against the sky, eclipse the sun, and reappear over his head. He leaped to grab the disc and felt the soft burn of friction as it spun in his hand. He skidded for a yard on the concrete before halting. Grinning, he straightened and turned toward Ethan. Only then did he realize he was in front of his apartment. As he walked toward the entrance, he heard a voice.

"Are you David Grainger?" said a man getting out of an illegally parked car. A second man climbed out from the passenger side. Both wore white shirts, ties, and rumpled sports coats.

The first man was big and round-shouldered, dark-skinned, with almond eyes. Samoan, David thought. The other man was a thin Caucasian with small dark eyes. He looked like he just woke up from a nap.

"Yes, I'm Dr. Grainger. What is it?"

The Samoan held out a wallet that flapped open to reveal a badge and an ID card with his photo and name: Detective Geoffrey Saliamoa.

David's knees weakened. Had they found out about Leary already? And now they had come for him? His mouth wouldn't work.

Ethan came up behind him and said, "What's wrong, officers?"

Saliamoa's eyes flicked toward him. "Who are you, sir?"

"I'm Dr. Grainger's friend. What's going on?"

David held the Frisbee in front of him, like a shield.

Saliamoa took something out of his pocket and held it out to David. At first it looked like a flattened coin. On closer look, David saw it was Slowpoke's dog tag, engraved with his address. "Where did you get that?"

"Do you know a woman named Michelle Wintress?"

"She's a friend of mine. Why?"

Saliamoa glanced at his partner, then back. "Around eight last night, Ms. Wintress was killed by a hit-and-run driver."

Something fell out of David's hands. He looked down. The Frisbee lay on the ground. When he picked it up later, he realized he had folded it in half.

Chapter 29

Lunch was early. Jell-O, chicken soup, and something that resembled creamed corn. The meals at the PCC were worse than Army mess. Dr. Cameron appeared in the doorway. In the full light of day, he looked haggard. "Hi, Doc. You just missed a delicious bacon-burger with fries."

"Jell-O and soup, I see." Cameron sat on a high stool. "How are you feeling?"

"Good enough to go home, Doc."

"Did you enjoy your first battery of tests with our speech pathologist?"

"You mean Miss Repeat-after-me-repeat-after-me-now-blow-into-this-tube? Dorothy seems very sharp, but she wouldn't reveal any results."

"Ahh. That's my job."

"So how did I do?"

"How important is being able to speak for you, Ben?"

Ben looked over Cameron's head at the reflection of light and shadows cast by sunlight through the slatted blinds. No more joking. In truth, talking was all he had left.

"It's everything. I told you some about my mother's Alzheimer's. It would fluctuate so she had rare moments of lucidity when she could explain what it was like. She could see what she was going to say in her mind, but the words would just disappear and she couldn't pull them back. The words just weren't there anymore. Maybe she forgot what she wanted to say. For me, it would be the worst torture if I could not express my thoughts."

"For Alzheimer's patients, the worst time is usually when they can still appreciate how much function they've lost. But when their behavior becomes unmanageable and dangerously violent, that's when it's the worst for their families."

For a moment, Ben pondered Cameron's intense interest in Alzheimer's. Then he said, "You know what's ironic? For her last two years, my mother was all body and no mind. I'm the opposite, now—all mind and no body."

"You can be eloquent, Ben. For you, speaking is vital." Cameron's face smoothed out except for a frown. He seemed full of compassion. He took a deep breath and spoke the next words slowly: "The saddest tears are for words never said." He paused. "It's so tragic when an ALS patient loses the ability to speak before he shares his thoughts and reflections with family and close friends. I'm glad Dorothy did a thorough evaluation. Remember when she asked you to say 'Ahh' for as long as you could?"

"Two thousand years of medical progress, and that's your most definitive test?"

"Ben, I'm sorry, but the way you performed means that your breathing muscles are beginning to weaken. And when she held a mirror under your nose and asked you to repeat, 'Buy Bobbie a puppy'—"

"I so love the classics."

"It fogged up, meaning your speech is becoming hypernasal."

As his last attempt at humor failed, Ben just waited for Cameron to explain.

"I'll be honest, Ben. Right now, you still have a distinctly powerful vocal instrument. But the truth is, I'm not sure how long it will last."

Again, Ben was silent. Cameron looked as if he had more to say. What now?

"I do have one piece of good news, though. Dorothy has a protocol designed to slow down the deterioration of your voice."

"Slow down? Not stop?"

"Ben, I will never give you false hopes." Cameron's tone was sympathetic. "But if we could extend your ability to speak—for some months—wouldn't that be significant?"

Ben said the words, "It would," trying not to think what visits with Sammie would be like if he couldn't speak.

"With your approval, then, I'll ask Dorothy to start your training tomorrow. You must understand that her exercises are still considered experimental, but I believe they'll help."

"Can Dorothy make home visits?" Ben asked.

"Home? That's a problem since she's hospital-based. But we might work something out after you've completed the basic training here on the PCC."

"How long are we talking about, Doctor?"

"Just two weeks."

Ben thought about his room at home: Gloria's rose trellis outside the patio doors, his videos and CDs, the warm, familiar environment. "I'll have to think about it."

"I understand you're more comfortable at home. For an informed decision, would you like me to explain what you can expect will happen with your voice?"

Ben fantasized he withdrew his body after raising his hands to silence Cameron. "Okay."

"As your voice becomes more nasal, you'll sound effeminate. Then you'll have a soft monotone, with little dynamics. As your consonants grow indistinct, it will become more difficult for others to understand you."

Ben wished he could run. ALS was relentless. It took away his ability to enjoy life, bit by bit.

"Ben, may I discuss the respirator option now?"

Ben felt as if he had nodded. He thought he might as well hear the worst all at once. "Alright."

"For a brief time, you'll be able to speak a little by releasing the cuff in your throat, but then you'll become completely dependent on the ventilator to breathe. To communicate, you'll need a computer to synthesize speech. A program called 'Word

Plus' speeds things up a bit with a two-stage word prediction program. But with only one finger, it will still be slow."

Ben waited for him to continue.

"If—or really, when—you lose the ability to type, you'll still be able to blink your eyelids, or move your eyes left or right, to indicate 'Yes' or 'No,' and to select individual letters. However your communication will be even slower."

Ben swallowed. "How long... Can you estimate how long before—?"

"Every ALS patient is different, Ben."

"What would the speech program cost?"

"It's experimental so it's funded by research funds. If you permit us to collect data by follow-up testing, we can cover everything not paid for by your health insurance."

Ben thought for a moment. "Being a guinea pig is okay if it's free. But frankly, before I commit to spending two weeks here, I must discuss it with my daughter."

"Your—Of course, I understand." Cameron stiffened. He looked miffed. "Be sure to explain the trade-off. Leaving the hospital sooner might give you less time to speak using your own voice."

Cameron's long face turned toward the chessboard that had been set carefully aside to make room for the lunch tray. "Was your daughter here earlier?"

"Sure was. Even after a party last night. She's somewhere on the grounds."

"She's quite a girl," Cameron said. "Unmarried?"

"Yes, you wouldn't happen to have a son, would you?"

Cameron's sagging mouth tugged upward at the corners like drawn drapes. Ben had never seen so much sadness in a smile. "Unfortunately, my wife and I are childless."

"Sorry to hear that. I don't know what I would do without Sammie." Ben swallowed hard as he realizing what he just said. How true it was.

"She takes care of you at home, doesn't she?"

"Yes, but she also has her own life. She has her career." Ben's mind quickly scanned all the things Sammie did. Shopping, picking up videos, making fresh juice, playing chess, filling in for the nurses who came late or reneged. The list was endless.

"She might welcome a break. The term we use is 'respite care.' We frequently admit patients even if the only reason is to give the family a chance to catch up on their desperately needed rest, or to take care of their own lives."

"No, thanks," said a voice from the doorway. Ben turned his eyes. Sammie stood there—her arms crossed over her chest. Her face, stern and determined.

"We were just discussing if I should stay on a while," Ben said. "Dr. Cameron offered me a new program to maintain my voice."

Cameron turned toward Sammie. "Your father's voice muscles are weakening. Our speech therapist could help prolong his ability to speak."

"Not yet. Dad needs to live at home now. That's his best therapy."

"Overall, of course. But if he stayed on for only two weeks, he'd—"

"Where the mind goes, the body follows." Sammie hovered over the chessboard. "If Dad begins to think he belongs in a hospital, he may end up here."

"Of course your father doesn't *belong* in a hospital; I'm only suggesting a short stay for a specific, positive therapeutic goal."

Sammie lifted the laden chessboard, balancing it carefully. "You're talking about treating him, before he needs it? That doesn't sound like typical American medicine."

"We take pride in our PCC program being proactive." Cameron looked defensive.

"Look, don't argue," Ben said, "I'll hang in here through tomorrow night, to finish the tests I already agreed to. While I'm here, Samantha and Alice can learn how to use the suction device. When I have to return, later on, I'll consider this speech program of Dorothy's. Okay?"

Cameron's face reddened. His voice sounded strained. "Sure, you're the boss."

Chapter 30

"Slowpoke! Slowpoke!" Sunlight grew soft on his shoulders as David kept on calling out, "Slowpoke! Slowpoke!" This evening would have been David's turn to walk his dog. Instead he was patrolling the streets around his apartment toward the banks of the Potomac. No sign of Slowpoke. Earlier, he'd called Animal Rescue. No reports of greyhounds—injured or killed. David imagined Slowpoke had whimpered around the accident scene all night.

He followed the curved stone wall to the main part of Rock Creek Park. Surprised to find a gate open that was usually locked, he took that for a sign that he should search these grounds. Seeing the gently curved paths between rows of rose bushes made him think how Slowpoke would tug at her leash before he let her loose. Then she'd run in delight. "Slowpoke!"

Knowing how Slowpoke loved to explore, he traced the path's trajectories. Somehow along the way, his wandering over grassy slopes got him off the main path. The grounds were in exceptional condition, except for a large stone, which he walked around.

My God! It's a headstone marking a grave site. David was surprised. He had meandered into Oak Creek Cemetery—a place he'd never ventured into before.

Without intending, he glanced at some headstones and read several inscriptions.

Louisa Smithson, 1943-1947
Sleep Sweet Our Child
In Loving Arms.

George Detmer 1912-1967
Loving Husband and Father

His thoughts drifted to his own father. Although he missed him, David rarely visited his grave site in Connecticut. The emptiness David had for Slowpoke made him wonder how Tom was doing with the loss of Michelle. And he remembered how fond Michelle was of Slowpoke.

He had given the detectives Tom's address, phone, and pager number. Fortunately, they were either trained or sensitive enough to decide to inform him in person.

Later, Tom called David for further details. Of course, he had none to offer. No, he didn't want David's company right then. Tom had to call Michelle's parents and take care of other matters. David mused on how typical that behavior was. After a loved one dies, those close to them do the busy work, leaving the emotional work for another time. That's what David's mother did after his father died.

David was relieved when Tom did not ask him for emotional support. His training in bereavement counseling was limited to a single instruction: refer patients to hospice grief counselors and religious leaders of their choice.

In his pocket, David fingered the dog tag that had ripped free during the accident. Not "accident" but "vehicular homicide." Detective Saliamoa had sounded weary when he said, "Hopefully a witness will come forward." His message... there was very little hope.

Certainly, all hope was gone for poor Michelle. And there was little hope for Slowpoke. David recognized the old familiar feelings—of loss, of hopelessness, of sadness. But he didn't realize he was crying until he sensed his cheeks were wet. Even then, he couldn't decide whom his tears were for.

Chapter 31

Cameron couldn't call Wendy. She had a way of scanning his voice to detect even the slightest insecurity. He didn't want her to worry. So what could he do for his anxiety? He knew his relaxation technique would not work. A name kept on bombarding his mind: Pratt, Pratt, Pratt. He tried, but couldn't think of an alternative. He hated the thought of asking Pratt for anything. His sleep had been interrupted by awakening with the dread of the sight of him. He didn't expect his deep remorse about Michelle Wintress to fade soon, but why ask this low life for more help? The answer was obvious. Because he needed it. Pratt was military; he knew the military mind. Cameron sighed. His throat tightened as he looked at the phone. Despite how much he wanted to avoid all further interaction with Pratt, he picked up the handset.

Five minutes later, Pratt cruised into his office and relaxed on the couch.

"The other day you said something that intrigued me," Cameron began, "about soldiers who have a way of communicating with each other."

Pratt nodded.

"So I thought, just as an experiment, it might be interesting for the next day or so, to see how it goes, if I permitted you to work with Brewster, that is, under my supervision."

"It's the daughter, isn't it? She's wants him to go home, right?"

Cameron caught his breath. "Yes. If he leaves, he might not return for months."

"In which case, the Committee will insist on another ***Type I*** for your ***Finale***."

"Exactly."

"How soon is the Major supposed to check out of the PCC?"

"Tomorrow evening."

"A day and a half?" Pratt's left eyebrow rose. "Okay, Doc. I'll get him to stay. But I wonder, could I expect a little something extra for Christmas?"

"Naturally." Cameron tried to sound grateful.

"Perhaps something like ten percent of your bonus?"

"Ridiculous. That's—" Pratt's leer stopped Cameron from arguing.

"All right, ten percent. I'll call Nursing Scheduling so you'll be assigned to Brewster. Then I'll spend a couple of hours teaching you the basics of dealing with patients like—"

Pratt laughed, a quiet rushing sound, like wind through high grass. "Doc, I already know how to handle him."

"You don't understand. Every move is delicate. He must believe that every decision is his own. He should see us only as providers of information, explainers of the options, facilitators of his own independent thinking. He must never, never suspect that we're influencing him. That's crucial. Understand? This is very different to what you may have done before, Mr. Pratt—"

"—from what I did before in the Long Range Recon? Doc, you don't realize how similar it is. My job description was to talk people into doing things. Fast!"

"But this time, no bamboo slivers, no hot irons—"

"Don't underestimate my talent in getting cooperation," Pratt said. "Trust me, Doc. I know how to handle the Major. Trust me, like I'm trusting you."

As Cameron studied Pratt, he felt a cold fist clutch his stomach. "Bruce, if you're worried about getting your bonus, don't. I promised, and I'm a man of my word."

"That's great, Doc. It's such a pleasure to work with an honest man."

Ben opened his eyes as the front end of a cart pushed into his room. Ah, dinner time. Another Jell-O time. When was the last time he'd looked forward to eating?

The man pushing the cart said, "Evening, Major."

"What have we here? Steak? A nice New York Strip with buttered mushrooms?"

"Looks more like something from the back end of a baby to me, Sir."

Ben laughed.

"I'm Bruce Pratt."

"Greetings. What service were you in, Bruce?"

"Army, Sir. How'd you guess I was military?"

"Few civilians appreciate baby poop humor. And no offense, but you don't look young enough to have missed the Vietnam draft."

"No, Sir. But I wasn't drafted. I volunteered. Ended up in Long Range Recon."

"You're a LURP? How did a LURP end up pushing hospital carts?"

Ben saw a shadow briefly pass over Pratt's face.

"LURPS had to know how to tie off wounds and set bones. It's like nursing. Hell, everybody needs to make a living, Sir."

"You don't have to call me 'Sir,' Nurse. We're both civilians now."

Pratt took the plastic wrap off a spoon. "If you don't mind, I'd prefer to keep the 'Sir,' Sir. You were one of the few officers I respected, although I never got the opportunity to serve directly under you. Plus you're one of the rare politicians who didn't turn his back on veterans."

To his surprise, Ben's throat tightened. "Well, thank you."

The nurse sat down and began spooning yellow glop into Ben's mouth. Banana puree. Ben thought of the Gerber's puree he and Gloria spooned into Sammie's little toothless mouth so many years ago. Ben's throat constricted even more.

"You okay, Sir?"

"No, I'm not. I feel like an idiot. It's one thing to be spoon-fed information by staff sergeants and political aides. It's another to be spoon-fed baby food by a LURP."

Pratt nodded, wiped Ben's lips with a paper napkin. "Want some more, Major?"

"No, that's enough of that slop."

"Okay, Sir. You need calories, but I admire your being discriminating." He looked at Ben for a while. "Permission to speak plainly, Sir?"

"Would you stop it with the 'Sir' stuff? Of course you can speak plainly."

"Sir, if I could say... if it were me lying there, I don't know how I could stand it."

"What do you mean?"

Pratt glanced toward the open door, rose to shut it, then returned to his chair. "In 'Nam, we all thought 'Buffalo Brewster' was one of the few goddamn officers willing to get out there and bloody his hands. And in the Virginia State Senate, you were never afraid to take risks. So, may I ask, how did you end up like this?"

Ben frowned. "I got ALS. I didn't ask to retire, flat on my back."

Pratt's eyes had the ice-like coldness that Ben had seen in young men forced to survive in the jungles of Southeast Asia.

"You know what LRRPs did. Sometimes assassins; other times scouts. When necessary, we patched up bullet wounds and punji holes, snake bites and cuts from arrows. Or carried bodies out. —Unless they were too badly hurt. Then, we couldn't... because they'd risk the whole squad."

"I know," Ben said quietly.

"The thing was, we couldn't leave them either. You know what the VC did to prisoners."

"I heard stories."

"Well, I saw, Sir. I saw. So if we couldn't take the wounded out, and we couldn't leave them, that left only one choice. And we all knew it."

Ben said nothing.

"Everybody saved one .45 round for himself. One round in the old sidearm, just in case. We also carried cyanide pills. 'Being prepared,' we called it. Major, if you'd been assigned to that action, would you have come prepared?"

"Yes, I would," Ben mumbled.

"Right. So I was wondering, Sir, if I could ask... When you found out you had ALS... When you found out you'd end up crapping into a pan and being fed like a baby... Did you prepare? You're not going to let the VC capture you, are you?"

The image made Ben scowl. "Sergeant, it's not just about me. There are others I must consider."

"In the jungle we did too, Sir." Pratt remained silent as he put the eating utensils on the cart and pushed it toward the door. Then he looked back. "I didn't want to offend you, Sir. I hope what I said was alright. It's just—I'm surprised to see Buffalo Brewster like this, that's all."

"What you said was okay." Ben watched Pratt reach for the doorknob. "Bruce?"

Pratt stopped and looked back over his shoulder.

"Those men in the jungle... What happened if they were too badly hurt to use their last bullet? Or if they had run out of ammunition? What happened then?"

Pratt looked intense. "Well, Sir, we all had a certain understanding. We couldn't leave anyone for the VC. No way. So we all knew we could depend on each other to finish the job."

"Of course." Ben avoided eye contact. "But that was war."

"Yes, Sir. Yes, that was war. Different time, different place. I guess things aren't as clear here as they were back then. See you tomorrow, Sir."

Ben stared at the ceiling, concentrated on his breathing, and tried not to think. He sensed a strange taste in his mouth. Then he realized—his inner cheek was bleeding.

Chapter 32

David decided to return to his schedule at Memorial. Tending to other people's problems might distract him from his own, even though it would feel strange not working with Tom.

A four-year-old boy had gotten out of bed to go to the bathroom in his new house, and had taken a header down an unexpected flight of stairs. That was his mother's story, anyway. David had checked the boy and X-rays for past bruises from different times but there were none. He listened for a wooden recitation of the event but the mother was distraught and convincing. David had to be sure because of the legal requirement to report anything suspicious to Child Protective Services. The penalty for not doing so was stiff—loss of one's medical license, or in David's case, not getting a license. This time though, there were no tough decisions, no dire consequences. Just needle and thread.

But as he sewed, he couldn't help imagining Detective Saliamoa waiting to greet him at his apartment. "We've got a couple more questions for you. Someone found a bloody pillow in the Bio-Waste, and—"

He forced himself to concentrate on the little boy who kept rolling his eyes upward. "You'll look like Dracula for a while," David told him as he snipped the end of the thread. "Not as scary as me, though." He winked his blackened, swollen eye.

"Can I look like the Predator instead?" the boy asked.

David smiled. "Sure."

Finished, he sought out the chief resident to okay the boy's discharge.

"He'll be fine," the resident said to his mother. As they left, he looked at David and said, "You look pale. Want to take your break now?"

"Thanks, I will."

Over the weekend, Sammie had discovered that Memorial Hospital was a senseless maze. The complex had obviously evolved helter-skelter over a period of decades. Looking up, she sensed the random aesthetics of each building sitting at an odd angle to its neighbors. The result was this peculiarly shaped open space in which she now experienced a moment of serenity, of harmony and balance with the maple tree. Here she sat on a bench, transforming the hard granite into a perfect place to meditate, musing on the nearby marble birdbath.

With dismay, she wondered if someday in the future, when Dad had to return to the hospital, this pattern might become routine. But tomorrow, a transport company would take Dad home, although not as early as she wanted. The van would not be available until 8:00 PM.

She shivered and took the lid off the Styrofoam cup of boiling water—the only thing she'd consume from the hospital cafeteria. Opening her large purse, she rummaged around for a packet, opened it, and sprinkled yellow-brown powder into the cup. She inhaled the aroma and tried to relax.

"Herb tea?" a voice asked.

Sammie jumped so hard that the fluid erupted straight up out of the cup. Luckily, most settled right back. She quickly got over being surprised at the intrusion. She looked up and saw a familiar face. "Oh. Hi. How's your eye?"

"Better," David said. "I got some more Arnica cream. I've been applying it TID. I mean, three times a day."

"I know what 'TID' means. How did you find out that it was Arnica?"

"I went to a health store when my cheek started hurting again. I asked to smell a few creams that reduce pain, and bought the one that smelled the same."

Sammie tried to read the young man's name tag. "That man who hit you was such an idiot. There's never any need to resort to violence."

"I wish you'd told him that. Anyway, you found my place. I come here sometimes. I saw you sitting here and thought I'd take the opportunity to thank you for being so nurturing."

"You're welcome." She wondered what he thought of her leaving the party in such a huff, but she decided not to ask. "I liked what you said, especially about ALS."

"You mean, about Stephen Hawking?"

"Yes. Care to sit down? I hope you don't mind my saying it, but you look beat."

"It's been a tough—"

He sat on the end of the bench leaning forward. He braced his arms against his knees, letting his hands dangle. Both eyes were sunken and surrounded by dark rings that made him look sad, especially when he stopped talking.

"I am beat," he said. "You know, an intern's life."

"Sure, I understand how tired you must be. Anyway, about ALS: I saw the video of *A Brief History of Time* and was struck how—" She couldn't go on. She lowered her head, and watched the surface of her tea tremble as it embraced a tear.

The young doctor suddenly moved closer, not quite touching, but close enough for her to smell medicines and disinfectants. She looked in his face, and sensed his empathy. Was sadness drawing her to him?

"What's wrong?" he asked. Something about the way he asked sounded desperate.

For a moment, she locked on his eyes. "My father has ALS." She pointed up to the seventh story of the medical tower. "He's up there, on the PCC."

"So that's why you're here."

"Yes. He's almost completely paralyzed, although he can still breathe on his own."

"Then why is he on the PCC?"

"Trouble swallowing. Tomorrow, my aunt and I will learn how to use the suction device. Dr. Cameron wanted to do a full evaluation while he's here."

"Cameron has an extremely good reputation in palliative medicine."

"He seems quite involved in my father's case. In fact, Dad's a little concerned he's getting preferential treatment because of who he is."

"Who's that?"

"Benjamin Brewster."

The young intern just watched her expectantly. For the first time in ages, she almost smiled. "I guess he won't have to worry about your attitude, huh? Dad was a Virginia State Senator before ALS forced him to retire."

"Oh."

She put out her hand. "I'm Samantha Brewster."

He extended his hand. "David Grainger."

She took his hand, warm, almost dry. "Nice to meet you. I mean, officially meet you. But with any luck—please, don't take this personally—I doubt we'll cross paths again for a long time. My aunt and I are taking Dad home tomorrow. And I hope he won't need to return soon."

"Home is best." He looked like he might say something else, then he glanced at his watch. "Well, I guess I'd better get going." He just sat there, staring at the birdbath.

"What area of medicine do you want to specialize in?"

"I'm not sure—research, perhaps in preventative medicine."

"Have you ever considered alternative medicine?"

"Oh, yes, I remember that keen interest of yours. Herbs and natural products, right?"

"You won't get pompous like Dr. Solomon, will you? Most specialized western doctors have lost track of whole-body wellness and the mind-body connection."

"Please don't take this the wrong way, Ms. Brewster—"

"Samantha."

"—Samantha, I agree with Dr. Solomon, about the importance of controlled trials—"

"Have you checked the literature, yourself?"

He smiled. "Good point. I haven't done my own literature research."

"Glad you admitted that. But which literature? How about centuries of documentation by the Chinese and Indians? Would you consider thousands of cases just anecdotal?"

"Would I? Or most Westerners? Voluminous anecdotal evidence might not convince them—" He seemed to catch himself. "I'm sorry, there I go again."

"No, I apologize. I was also getting carried away. Tell you what. If you'll respect my opinions, I'll respect yours. How's that?"

"Fair enough."

She stared at him as he regarded her in silence. Amazing how mature he appeared in his white coat. He glanced at his watch and shot to his feet. "This time, I really have to go." Still, he hesitated. "Good luck with your father."

"Thank you."

He held out his hand. "It was a pleasure meeting you, Samantha. I mean, again."

"Same here." She rose, taking his hand. His grip was gentle but firm.

As she watched him turn toward the main building of the hospital, she wondered what she had heard him say that had made her so certain he would care about her father.

❧

"You look a hundred percent better. What did you do on your break?" the chief resident asked as he dusted some chalky plaster off his hands. Behind him in the open alcove, a drunken teenager sat on the exam table wearing a new cast on his wrist.

"Just talked to someone." David did feel much better. Then his happiness turned to shame. Donald Becker, Ryan Leary, and Michelle Wintress... All had died in the last few days. How could he feel good? Maybe it was okay. He'd helped where he could. He supported *Flower Child* by citing Hawking, a shining example of someone who chose not to give up hope. What a shame they'd never meet again. By the time her father returned to Memorial, he'd be gone on his fellowship.

David heard the chief resident say, "I'll take my break now and try to get a few hours of sleep. I want to get up early tomorrow morning. —To listen to the closing statements of Kenard's trial."

David wondered if Tom was still following the trial. For a while, it was all his resident talked about, outside of their patients and clinical medicine. The elated feeling from meeting Samantha was almost completely gone now, as David felt more empathy for Tom. Being close to a woman made David more aware of Tom's loss. He promised himself to call him this evening, on his way home.

Chapter 33

From the moment he was assigned to the Kenard case—the most publicized criminal case since O. J. Simpson—Orlando Warwick was stoked about its potential to launch his career in law. At twenty-nine, he was co-counsel to Leonard Patmore, a prestigious DC defense attorney.

—The stuff career dreams are made of.

Except for one problem. They were losing.

He glanced at Patmore as he took out his note pad. Lean, with blonde curls and a round, pensive face of a serious baby, he had the finest brain Orlando had ever encountered. And he could sit calmly without manifesting the slightest hint of worry, even though little had gone their way during the trial.

Orlando turned toward their client. Charged with Second-Degree Murder, Kenneth Kenard faced five to forty years as well as the loss of his medical license. He wore a beige suit as requested, but he refused to replace his black-rimmed glasses with contact lenses, to appear softer and more vulnerable.

Commonwealth's Attorney, Trevor Jenkins, obviously had ambitions beyond Virginia. He rose slowly. Short, with a thick midsection, he favored suspenders. As he wandered around, he took off his coat and rolled up his sleeves, which the Judge let him get away with.

Judge Barnett Williams, III—a political appointee whose electoral clout had definitely not come from the ACLU.

Jenkins ambled over to the jury box. "Ladies and gentlemen, I expect the defense to ignore every fact in this case in their final statement, including six witnesses to Juanita Mitchell's murder, the medical testimony regarding the cause of death, and the Catholic priest who counseled Mrs. Mitchell that her life—like the lives of all human beings—still had value and was worth living. I expect the defense to present instead a philosophy of twisted thinking to—"

"Objection, Your Honor." Patmore stood up. "Could the prosecutor allow me to make my own closing statement, first?"

"The court provides great leeway in closing statements, Mr. Patmore," Judge Williams said in his smoker's baritone. "Overruled."

In case a juror happened to glance over to see the defense team's response, Orlando bent over his legal pad, put a deep furrow in his brow, and made a quick notation in a shorthand he'd developed over the years. "*jg w shtd.*" It meant, "Judge Williams is a shithead."

"Thank you, Your Honor. Let's consider the famous oath of Hippocrates from 400 BC. It still sets the ethical standard for physicians' behavior." Jenkins pointed to a huge flip-chart and read,

> *"I will follow that system of regimen which,*
> *according to my ability and judgment,*
> *I consider for the benefit of my patients, and*
> *abstain from whatever is deleterious and mischievous.*
> *I will give no deadly medicine to anyone if asked,*
> *nor suggest any such counsel."*

He leaned toward the jury. "Could anything be more clear? Hundreds of generations of doctors have agreed to these ethics. But not Kenneth Kenard." He used his whole arm to point from his shoulder toward the defendant. "Dr. Kenard acted as if he were above these ethical standards, as if he were God."

Jenkins' face appeared distraught by the egregious crime. "Thank God, Father Dominguez offered Juanita Mitchell last rites before she died. But when he later returned, he didn't expect her to be dead, he could not have anticipated that Dr. Kenard would have overruled his counseling, overruled her will to live, overruled Hippocrates, overruled even God Himself!"

Jenkins made a full-circle turn, giving the jurors time to consider his words.

"Defense may argue that Dr. Kenard's action—of administering a lethal dose of medications through her feeding tube—saved Juanita from committing what Catholics consider the unpardonable sin of suicide, and therefore saved her soul—" Jenkins went back to his table and picked up a small paper bag. "But that argument has two major problems. First, it's circular. Second, there's a big hole in it." He put his hand in a brown bag, whisked out a bagel, and waved it in front of the jurors. "I call that a bagel argument!"

The jurors chuckled. Patmore shook his head. No objection. The damage was already done. Knowing that jurors remember better what they see than what they hear, Jenkins had connected an abstract argument for brighter jurors with a concrete metaphor for the others.

Jenkins continued. "Unless you find Dr. Kenard guilty, someday others will have the legal right to decide that *your* life is not worth living. Your insurance company or your grown children may save money by not providing your needed care. Your verdict in this trial will affect all of us. It's up to you to not pave the way for making it acceptable for doctors to kill their patients."

We are so lost, Orlando thought, but he turned and gave Kenard a reassuring smile.

Kenard did not smile back. His expression was deeply sad.

Now Jenkins pointed to the wall behind the Judge. "See that bronze plaque above the Judge? 'In God We Trust'? As jurors, your duty is to maintain that sacred trust.

Your duty is to find Dr. Kenard guilty as charged—of Second-Degree Murder—and leave decisions about life and death where they belong—with God."

Orlando expected the jury to applaud. Along with the audience and reporters.

Judge Williams turned toward the defense table. "Mr. Patmore, it's three-o'clock. I have another commitment tomorrow. If your closing statement is short, you can start now. Otherwise, can you wait until Wednesday?"

"Your Honor, we can wait."

"Good." The Judge smacked the gavel down.

The jury filed out and the crowd in the gallery began talking and moving around.

As Patmore gathered his papers, Kenard said, "I'm glad you have all day tomorrow to prepare an antidote to that. I guess we need a miracle."

"Honestly, it would help," Patmore said.

Chapter 34

Ben opened his eyes, pleased to see the male nurse. "Evening, Mr. Pratt. What does the hospital have for my last supper? Pork chops and corn-on-the-cob?"

"Sorry Sir. Pureed carrots, pureed apples, pureed puree."

"Ugh."

Pratt parked the cart beside the bed. "Where's your daughter?"

"She just left. She's coming back with my sister in the van."

Pratt turned toward him. "Listen, Major. I'm sorry about all that stuff I said yesterday. You've got lots of reasons to go on living. Even like this. I didn't intend any disrespect, Sir."

"That's okay, Bruce, it made me think. Do you have any children, yourself?"

"Two sons, Sir. But I'm divorced. Right now, my ex-wife has custody."

"How old are your boys?"

"Eleven and nine."

"Tell me, what's it worth to see your boys grow up?"

Pratt's face focused with intense sadness. "Everything. I'd give anything—"

"Then you can understand why I must keep on going. I hate being an invalid. And I'm not afraid of dying. But I must think of my daughter."

Pratt nodded as he spooned up the first load of slop.

"How old is she, Sir?"

"Twenty-eight. The picture of her mother."

"Ah, the mother's gone?"

"Died, almost nine years ago."

Pratt slipped the spoon into Ben's mouth. "Does your daughter live close by?"

"She moved back home after I lost my ability to walk. She helps take care of me."

"Nice to have a devoted child. So she's not married?"

"No but she's quite involved in her career." Ben felt guilty for omitting how over involved Sammie had actually become, with him and his disease.

"It's good for a woman to enjoy her job." Pratt raised a straw from the juice glass to Ben's lips. "If your daughter were married, she might not live with you."

Ben said nothing as he recalled her reluctance to go out.

"It never works anyway." Pratt looked despondent. "A whole family revolving around a sick person. When my wife's mother was dying of cancer, she insisted on providing her care. It took all her energy. At least she did what she thought was right." He shrugged. "Of course, in the end her mother died anyway. But by then, our marriage was over."

Pratt sighed as he gathered up the eating utensils. "Well, that's water under the bridge. My 'ex' would say I was the selfish one. She might be right. Sir, you're lucky your daughter's only got you to worry about." He stood up. "Want anything else to eat or drink?"

Ben realized that once he left, he wouldn't be able to talk about this with Bruce. He could be more honest with him. He wanted to ask him to stay and talk. But how could he? "Bruce, would you switch on my TV?"

"You can do that yourself, Sir."

"Pardon?"

Pratt smiled, took something out of his pocket, and gently grabbed Ben's arm. "I saw you having trouble, so I made this rig for you. I took an old wrist brace, added a metal extension, see? Anyone can strap it to your forearm with Velcro after positioning your remote control. Can you feel the buttons with your finger?"

"Yes, I can."

"Good. You're in control again. Major, take this home when you leave. It's a gift."

Ben grinned as he explored the remote with his finger. "Bruce, I owe you one."

"That's always great to hear from an officer. Is your daughter coming back soon?"

"Why do you ask? Want to ask her out on a date?"

"No, Sir." Pratt pushed the cart toward the door. "I don't think you'd want me dating your daughter. These days, I'm not having much luck with women."

Pratt took two small empty vials out of his coat pocket and held them in front of Cameron's face. He waited for the doctor to read the tiny print. One label said, "Walgreen's generic of Ipecac." The other, "$2.79."

Then Pratt said pompously, "You know the show ain't over 'till... the puking."

In his dream, Ben was scuba diving in the Azores, surrounded by silver clouds of bubbles, bright fish, and fantastic corals. Gloria's smile was visible through her mask, her eyes crinkled. She waved her hand and started rising, legs kicking easily. Ben hung back a moment, to watch her—an angel, flying toward the surface that hung above like a sheet of hammered platinum. He started moving, to follow her.

But he couldn't.

Something held him back. A twist of seaweed had twined around both his flippers. He tried to kick free, but it clung. He couldn't pull the weed loose. Then he sensed the constriction of airflow. His reserve was getting low. Drawing a breath became a struggle.

Far above, Gloria's silhouette sailed toward the sun.

His lungs convulsed, too weak to inhale against a vacuum. He kicked and thrashed, but the tenacious seaweed kept him down in the darkness.

He opened his eyes and saw a more angular, uneven darkness: ceiling tiles, light fixtures, the TV set on the far wall flickering. A dream. Thank God, just a dream. He waited for the residue of panic and strain to pass—

—waited—

The pressure on his chest increased. His head pounded intensely, a thick bubbling emerged in his throat. He was drowning *again*! Jesus! That's why he came to the hospital. And now, he was drowning on its seventh floor. Drowning in his own sour, foul vomit.

In the corner of the room, the television was changing channels fast, click-click-click. Ben realized he was pushing the TV remote with his power finger. He should have been pushing the nurse's call button. He searched for it and pushed it wildly.

In an instant, a figure appeared in the doorway, grabbed the suctioning tube. "Hang on."

He felt a tube in his throat.

Slowly, dark shapes of the kaleidoscope faded from Ben's vision.

"Hang on now." He recognized the voice. Nurse Pratt.

A few minutes later, he could whisper, "Sergeant. What happened?"

"Your airways were clogged with upchuck."

As Pratt wiped off the tube, Ben's nose curled from the vile smell.

"My God, if there was one meal I didn't want to taste twice—"

Pratt chuckled. "Don't talk. Just breathe easy. Let me change your gown."

The man worked in silence for several minutes, grabbing towels—first wet, then dry. Then he sat down.

"Major, I know you're set on going home. But you're at risk for aspiration pneumonia. Make sure your women count your number of breaths per minute, and take your temperature every four hours. And call us—or 911—if you even begin to have trouble breathing."

"Good advice. I'm sure glad you were here, Sergeant. How did you come so quickly?"

"I was next door, taking care of another patient. You all right now?"

"I'm fine now, thanks." Really, he was enraged. *Drowning in puke. It just gets worse and worse.* But he didn't want to snap at the person who just saved his life.

As Pratt continued to clean up, Ben kind of wished he had stayed down there in the seaweed in his dream. Then, his ordeal would be over. Exhausted, he almost drifted off to sleep but the harsh, burnt vomit smell kept him awake. "Sorry for my mess, Bruce." Then he blurted out, "It's amazing how little they know about this ALS. After fifty-five years of perfect functioning—all of a sudden this goddamn relentless wipe-out."

"Are you asking, 'Why did this happen to me?'" said Pratt.

"Damned straight." What a relief to talk with this man. Alice's faith made her impossibly naïve. Sammie refused to hear anything negative. But ALS *was* negative. So why shouldn't he be pissed off and complain? "Bruce, I took care of myself all my life. I exercised, ate well—"

"I know."

"Then, one day I noticed a tremor in my biceps that wouldn't go away. A few days later, another tremor in my thigh. Doctors ran every test under the sun. They can't even test for ALS, directly. Unbelievable. They can only eliminate all other possibilities. Aside from losing my wife, the most painful memory in my life was when Dr. Reynolds stared at the floor and said, "Ben, have you ever heard of Lou Gehrig's Disease?'"

Pratt said, "It's a terrible disease, but at least you don't have pain."

"But I'm like a prisoner in one of those three-by-three POW cells, except it keeps on shrinking." Ben glared at the nurse. "First I couldn't move my right leg. Then my left. Then my arms went. All I've got left is one finger, my face, my lungs. Now I can't even keep food down."

"I'm sorry, Major. I was wrong to say at least you don't have pain."

"But I can see you have something else to say. What are you thinking, damnit?"

"Permission to speak frankly, Sir?"

"Damnit. Just say what's on your mind."

"I'm wondering if you've started to surrender. Dr. Cameron told me he offered you that speech therapy program. Dorothy's training camp might be tough—"

"That's not it. I can take tough. But I must listen to my daughter, and—"

"Major, is it possible you've had too much feminine influence lately?"

Ben thought for a moment. Maybe Pratt was right. Home was like a womb—a warm, safe place—that his daughter and sister provided. He needed conversations with Pratt to sharpen his strategic plan, for whatever time he had left.

Deep inside his body, he shuddered. "Sergeant?"

"Sir?"

"Would you tell Dr. Cameron that I want to speak with him?"

Chapter 35

In the late morning light, Sammie enjoyed the little hospital garden. A couple of sparrows fluttered in the birdbath.

"You found a beautiful place." Alice looked like a pansy in her yellow skirt and blue blouse. She seemed to relish her chicken sandwich from the cafeteria.

Sammie popped open a Tupperware container of couscous. "Do you agree with Dad's decision to stay?"

"It's what he wanted."

"I'm worried. Last night he was reluctant to explain why. This morning, it took him two hours to beat me at chess. He seems miserable. So why stay here?"

"He says he likes his speech therapist."

"I can tell something's bothering him that he won't admit."

A sparrow dove out of the birdbath and landed on the walkway near the bench. Looked up, head cocked, brown eyes alert.

"Perhaps your father's finally looking inside, listening—"

"You mean God?"

"God works through everything to make His will known. Even disease."

Sammie flicked a bit of couscous onto the pavement. "I don't see Dad's disease as a sign of God's love."

"Would you see it as a sign if God took his disease away?"

"If God cured Dad, sure, I'd be thrilled. But I prayed for Mom and—"

"Oh, Sweetheart."

Sammie found herself being held by her aunt before she realized she was about to cry. She did not fight the tears. Not just because holding back would create nodes of negative energy. She just couldn't help sobbing.

Over Alice's shoulder, a white vertical blur appeared. Sammie blinked. Looking embarrassed, the young doctor started to turn away.

Sammie disengaged herself from Alice and wiped her eyes. "Hello, David."

He turned back. "Oh, hi!"

"Aunt Alice... Dr. David Grainger. The man who got punched in the eye at the Solomons' party."

David took a step back.

"I'm Alice Phillips, Samantha's aunt." She extended her plump hand.

"David's a medical intern here." Sammie said.

"How exciting to be just starting your medical career. Well, as I was just saying, I must be on my way. See you this evening, Sammie." Alice got up before Sammie could protest. "As for your father, I believe a miracle is on the horizon. The Lord can be mysterious as He performs His miracles. You'll see." She grinned at David, then scurried away.

David sat down, holding an unopened vending-machine sandwich.

"Sorry, David. I already told her about your eye. How is it now?"

"Better, especially if you like yellow tint." He opened his sandwich. "I thought your father was supposed to leave the PCC last night?"

"He changed his mind. Suddenly. And stubbornly. He's taking a two-week voice-training program. When I asked him for details, he seemed angry. I think he's holding something back."

"Is it the cost?"

"No, Cameron gave him a deal. Is that unusual?"

"Not if he's enrolled in a research program."

"I see. But I think he's depressed. Do they use St. John's Wort at Memorial?"

"Chronic patients often have mood swings as their disease waxes and wanes. It's not exactly the same as psychiatric depression. And, St. John's... I don't know for sure, but I've never seen anyone prescribe it. My guess: it's not on our formulary since the FDA hasn't approved it."

"But European studies have shown that it is effective. Compared to some other antidepressants, it has fewer side effects."

"Just be sure he's really depressed." He looked at his watch. "I'd love to discuss this more with you, but I've got to go. How about—Are you free at 5:15? We could meet in the cafeteria and talk... about helping your father?"

"David, that's so nice of you."

"In the meantime, Memorial's library has articles on depression, on ALS, and on St. John's Wort. If you like, I can go over some articles with you."

"David, you really don't have to—"

"Hey—if it hadn't been for you, I'd still be seeing the world through only one eye!"

Chapter 36

The moment Alice poked her head around the door, Ben knew something was up. Her smile was tentative, which is not typical for Alice. "Hello, Ben."

She glanced over her shoulder, then back. "I brought some visitors."

"Who?"

"Some people from Church."

Ben sighed. "Well, don't leave them standing in the hall."

Behind Alice appeared two men in black shirts and clerical collars.

"You know Father Thompson. This is Father Martin."

"Gentlemen," Ben said.

A nervous smile fluttered over her face. "I've been telling people at Church about you, Ben. They remember you—"

"—from a long time ago," Ben said deliberately.

"Well, we've been praying for you. The whole Church has. And Father Martin wanted to meet you. I knew you wouldn't mind."

Ben would have liked to say, *like hell I wouldn't.* Instead, he just grunted.

"Good to see you again, Ben." Ben last saw Father Thompson a decade ago. His hair had thinned so much it looked like strands of sticky cotton candy across a balding pate. He still had his wide build, sloping shoulders of a wrestler, and firm handshake.

The second priest, young enough to look fresh out of the seminary, had a smaller build and thick, black hair. He also pressed Ben's hand. "Father Thompson's doing a lot of teaching now, so I'm taking over many of his duties. Your sister told me much about you. May I visit, too?"

"Sure, join the party. So, what can I do for you?"

The younger priest stepped back, allowing the older Catholic priest to proceed. "The question is not what you can do for us, Ben. The question is, what can God do for you?"

"I have no idea," Ben said.

"Ben," Alice said, wringing her hands, "please don't be like that."

Father Thompson waved at her. "It's all right, Alice. Ben's in a difficult situation."

Ben swallowed hard. "Look, I stopped attending church long before I developed this 'difficult situation.' And as far as there being no atheists in foxholes, I saw too many young men lying dead in the mud to believe someone in the sky loves us. But ALS didn't help my attitude."

"God still loves you, Ben," Father Thompson said gently.

"God loves me? No offense, Father, but if a mortal man were to stand by and watch his child walk into the street and get run over by a car, they'd put him in prison for child neglect. If he used the excuse, 'I still love her,' everyone would howl for his blood. Now, if God's omniscient and omnipotent, why should he be held to a lesser standard?"

Father Thompson frowned. Alice winced. But something interesting flickered across the face of the younger priest. Was it a smile?

"Please, Ben, we're not here to argue. The Fathers want to help you."

"Help me? How?"

Father Thompson stepped forward again. "God works miracles, Ben. Always has. We want to pray with you, to ask the Lord to intercede on your behalf."

Ben raised his eyebrows. "Intercede? You mean you want to heal me?"

"No, only God can do that. But if it is His will, Father Martin and I will try to help you find your way into His healing embrace."

Ben stared at Father Martin as he recalled the much discussed Allocution of Pope John Paul II. In 2004, he stated that withdrawing food and fluid—even from patients expected to never regain consciousness—is "*euthanasia by omission.*" What nonsense. A year later, in his own final days, the Pope refused a feeding tube for himself. But the Fathers did not come to visit him to argue medical ethics. "Healing embrace you say? What's—"

"Ben, remember Mrs. Dickinson?" Alice burst in. "She's the one who brought fish and sour cream to our church potlucks? Last year she had bone cancer. The Fathers prayed for her and she was cured. Her doctors couldn't believe it, but it happened. A genuine miracle, Ben."

Ben glanced at her. "Or a spontaneous remission. It happens to atheists, too."

Father Thompson's rolling voice suddenly started reciting:

> *"Lord, look upon me with eyes of mercy,*
> *May Your healing hand rest upon me,*
> *May Your lifegiving powers flow into every cell of my body*
> *And into the depths of my soul,*
> *Cleansing, purifying, restoring me*
> *To wholeness and strength for service in Your Kingdom.*
> *Amen.*

Father Martin stepped forward waving a book. "The Bible says, 'Prayer offered in faith will make the sick person well.' We just want to offer you prayer in faith."

"Whose faith? Mine, or yours?"

"Ben!" Alice groaned. "Why not give God a chance, Ben? What can you lose?"

"My self-respect."

Father Martin smiled. "You could always claim we forced you to do it."

Ben had to smile back. —A clever way to let him save face.

"Miracles do occur," said Alice.

Father Martin said, "Aren't 'spontaneous remissions' examples of unexplained healing? Most cases of Lou Gehrig's Disease progress rapidly. But some, like Stephen Hawking's, go extremely slowly. Should we pray for something more modest?"

Ben looked past him toward Father Thompson, then at Alice. Her face was pleading, tears standing in her eyes.

Ben sighed. "Okay, what do you want me to do?"

◆

"Priests?" Cameron asked.

Pratt, at ease on the office couch, nodded. "His sister brought them in."

Cameron drummed his fingertips on the desktop. "There's no telling how they might undermine our work."

Pratt leaned forward. "I have a way to tell—in the future. I'll plant a bug in the Major's room. We can tape everything."

"Great idea," Cameron said. He wished that he had thought of it himself.

"I'll install it while Brewster is being bathed this evening. So we can begin to enjoy our entertainment tonight."

"And—?"

"What?" Asked Pratt.

"Aren't you going to ask for more money?"

"Doc, you hurt my feelings. And after all we've been through together." Pratt leaned back again, arms extended across the backrest. "I'm satisfied with our financial arrangement. But those damn priests bother me. I'd better go talk to Brewster, to check out his state of mind—"

"No, wait." Cameron had been looking for an opportunity to put limits on Pratt. "I don't want you to talk to him yet. There's something I want to do first."

Chapter 37

David rushed to the cafeteria, late for his meeting with Samantha. He raised his voice over the din. “I wish I had enough time to go to a quieter place. That’s a nice stack of articles you got.”

She nodded but gave his cup a stern look. “Coffee?”

“I plan to withdraw from caffeine, slowly, once I start my fellowship.”

“I can see that you need more sleep.”

Even when David could sleep, he’d stay awake worrying about patients. “Not till my next incarnation.”

“Do you believe in reincarnation?”

“Sorry, just an expression. I was raised Methodist, but I’m not sure what I believe.”

“Unlike your friend Ethan, huh?”

“You two have much in common. Did you talk at the party?”

“Some. I met people like him in India a few years ago. They came from all over the world, searching for hope, meaning, and understanding.”

“Is that why you went to India?”

“Personally, yes, even though I went there for Living Planet Herbs. I consulted healers from many disciplines who emphasized the mind-body connection.”

David noticed how her eyes lit up. No way did she need eye makeup. “Did they have anything for ALS?”

Her eyes narrowed.

“I’m trying to make a point,” David said softly.

Pointing, Samantha said, “What will all these photocopies say about ALS?”

“Not much, either.” He smiled. “Touché.”

“Well, most of the articles are about depression in ALS; some are about St. John’s; but none are about both. The technical ones are a bit intimidating.”

“I’m happy to read and help you—if you like.”

“What about your own research for your fellowship application?” Samantha reached out, almost touching his hand. “David, please, you’re not obligated—”

“No, really, I’d like to help. Could you tell me more about your father?”

“Until Friday, he lived at home. His symptoms began almost three years ago. Now he’s totally paralyzed except for his right index finger. I moved home five months ago. I don’t mind being his caregiver if the nurse doesn’t show up.”

As Samantha talked, David pictured his own father, lying in his sickbed, with his outstretched arms trembling. Samantha’s father couldn’t tremble anywhere. How different, the ways human bodies self-destruct—

"I've never had an ALS patient. It's rare. What do you think is bothering your dad?"

"I'm not sure. Could be fear of losing his voice. Or the decision about whether or not to go on a respirator—" She couldn't fight back her tears. David waited until she had composed herself. "Why do they even give patients that choice?" she asked. "What if he's having a bad day, just when he needs to make that life-or-death decision?"

"Maybe that's something you two could discuss over a period of time," David said.

"I know I can make Dad happier at home. This hospital is a spiritual wasteland."

David nodded. They continued to look at each other during a moment of silence.

"If I asked what you were thinking right now, would you reveal that to me?" Sammie asked.

"Sure. I was wondering, how would you define 'spiritual'?"

"Recognizing that there are forces beyond us that can influence our lives. That we are all part of a much larger plan." She leaned closer. "Now may I ask you a question? At the party, you said doctors should never give up hope. Did you really mean that?"

David liked her clarity and directness. "Yes, if you're reasonable about what to hope for."

"I agree. I'm not hoping to cure Dad's ALS. But these articles show that patients in better psychological states live up to three times longer."

"Speaking of which, has Dr. Cameron asked for a psychiatric consult?"

"Good question. I don't know. Dad's too private to tell." She focused her eyes on David. "Dad's a lot like you, David. Usually, that is."

David didn't know whether to be impressed or puzzled. "How so?"

"Both of you are skeptical and hard-headed." She laughed, tilting her head back so her hair fanned across her face. "I'm sure he'd like you. How about visiting him with me?"

"Visiting?"

"I hope it's not too much to ask."

"That's not it." He leaned toward her. "I'd like to, but Dr. Cameron might resent it."

"Not as a doctor, just as my friend."

"It's fine if you wait until he's back home. Then I could visit him without complications, as much as I want—I mean, as *you* want." He wondered if she noticed his revealing slip.

Samantha's smile didn't last long. "I'm afraid if Dad stays in this hospital too long, he may never come home. I may be overly worried, but I trust my intuition." Again, tears fell from her eyes. "Look, I need to see him now. Sorry I can't spend more time talking." She rose from the table. "David, you've been a real help."

A real help? Crying as she's leaving?

As David watched her walk between the tables, he mumbled what he had said as she left Dr. Solomon's party. "It's quite unlikely *Flower Child* and I will become life-long friends." He wondered why he felt sad. Because he saw so much in her that he liked? Because she was so spiritual? Because she could challenge his beliefs? Because she showed such devotion to her father? Or because she could be stimulating as well as nurturing?

David left without eating. The emptiness in his stomach seemed appropriate. He usually enjoyed walking Slowpoke after his shorter, ten-hour days, but she was still lost, or worse... So tonight, he'd go to the library and copy the few remaining journal articles he needed.

As he changed back to his street clothes in the Doctors' Lounge, David recalled his conversations with Tom. The resident appreciated his attempts at being empathic. Tom shared how many of their colleagues had badly bumbled their condolences. — Amazing how inarticulate the medical profession could be. Most merely apologized for not knowing what to say, instead of saying anything appropriate. Somehow, those who dealt with death every day seemed totally unprepared to talk about it.

Without intending to go there, David found himself at the little garden where he'd met Samantha. He sat under the lamppost with his articles and yellow pad. The balmy evening made this a pleasant place to work on his fellowship application paper.

He scrawled several lines on the pad, then read them, softly.

First, the title. "Who Should Make Life-and-Death Decisions?" Then, the text. "Researchers at Georgetown University School of Medicine* provided evidence showing the inaccuracy of 'Substituted Judgments.' Next of kin frequently make different decisions than the terminal patients themselves. My research will focus on the accuracy of decisions made by primary care physicians. . . ."

An important question. Samantha would be pleased. Why couldn't he stop thinking about her? An image of her face floated in front of him. Pretty. That described her, although at first, he had not been sure. But the way her eyes brightened when she expressed her opinions... He was really attracted to her mind. She was so articulate and passionate.

He heard approaching footsteps and sat up straighter. A middle-aged couple appeared and walked past. David mumbled, "Jerk," to himself. He was obviously hoping Samantha would pass by before she headed home. David regretted not being able to visit her father. He'd be a challenge for him to inspire hope. A visit could test the arguments he espoused at the party....

Damn that unwritten rule about visiting another doctor's patient. That rule did not apply to friends. And Samantha had been clear. She had not asked him to screen him for depression. He was becoming a friend of the Brewster family. After all, he had also met Samantha's aunt. So now, he'd meet her father. So what?

He glanced at his watch. Official visiting hours ended a half-hour ago. Wearing jeans, sweatshirt, and a pair of dirty Reeboks, he looked more like a college student than a doctor.

He gathered his notes, stuffed them into his briefcase, and headed off.

* D.P. Sulmasy and others

Chapter 38

Defeat settled on Orlando Warwick's shoulders like a giant carrion bird as he approached the entrance of the Patmore & Associates Building. He'd spent the last day and a half searching for new recent legal precedents. He re-read the prosecutor's closing statement too many times to count. Now, he was on his way to tell Patmore what he had found: Nothing. No new precedents. No gaps in logic. Nothing to help Patmore with the closing statement he would present in twelve hours.

As he pushed the enormous glass doors leading into the lobby, he noticed a man's reflection behind him, then a voice. "Excuse me?"

Orlando tried to slip inside quickly without an acknowledgment. He assumed the man was homeless.

But a hand clutched his sleeve. "You're one of Kenard's attorneys, right?"

Orlando glanced toward the security desk in the lobby, trying to catch the guard's eye, but his face was buried in a magazine.

"I saw you on TV. I must tell you and Mr. Patmore my story."

Hearing the names made Orlando take a closer look. Despite black stubble peppering his face and red skin around his eyes, he doubted the man was homeless. Although sweat-stained, his casual shirt and pants seemed to be high quality and his shoes were probably Enrico Bruno.

Orlando eased his sleeve from the man's quivering grasp. "I appreciate your wanting to help, but—"

"I killed my father."

"I—beg your pardon?"

"My father had prostate cancer. He suffered, terribly. No doctor would help him. So he tried to kill himself. He failed." He wiped away oily tears dribbling down his nose. "Finally, it was up to me. I had to help him. I had to. No one else would. I had to kill my own father."

"I'm sorry," Orlando glanced into the lobby again. The guard finally looked up. Orlando made a desperate "come hither" face. "Well, don't confess to any crime without adequate legal representation. Here's my card. Call for an appointment—"

"No. You don't understand. I committed no crime. And neither did Dr. Kenard. Your client is morally innocent. I just want to help."

Later, Orlando would wonder why he raised his right palm toward the onrushing guard. It wasn't merely hearing someone proclaim Kenard's innocence. After all, Orlando had been saying those words for months. It was probably the intensity of this man's unshakable moral belief. "Why are you so sure?" Orlando asked.

"People who kill intentionally have one of three reasons. They're crazy. Or they have something to gain. Or they agree to the person's request to decrease their suffering. No one should be punished for the third reason."

Orlando stood there for several seconds. "What's your name?"

"Jonathan Leary. I'm Ryan Leary's son. My father's obituary... it was in Sunday's newspaper."

Chapter 39

David yawned as he walked into the hospital at 6:45 AM. He didn't get to sleep until 3:00 AM. After two games of chess, he should have been tired, but his time with Ben Brewster inspired him to complete the outline of his fellowship paper. Strange: he'd visited Ben with the intent to give hope to a man dying slowly of a devastating illness. Yet the visit made David feel more alive.

His successful visit with her father would please Samantha. She might even call him when Ben told her about it. Then, he'd ask for her home phone number. Soon, they could arrange to meet at a quiet place, outside the hospital.

As David walked toward the counter, a nurse waved a telephone receiver at him. "Good timing, Doctor. This is for you."

Great timing. David took the phone. Was it Samantha calling him before rounds?

"Doctor Grainger? This is Dr. Cameron in the Palliative Care Center. We need to talk. Right now. Come to Suite 800. Stat!"

Stunned, David felt his knees weaken, his elbow braced against the counter.

A few minutes later he opened the inner door to Dr. Cameron's suite. David was surprised to find Dr. Franklin standing in front of the window like a great blue heron.

Remaining in his seat behind the desk, Cameron did not offer his hand. He merely gestured at the chair across from his desk. "Dr. Grainger. Please sit."

David did as he was told. The scene reminded David of his visit to the principal's office in elementary school.

"Making unsolicited visits to another doctor's patients represents a significant breach of professional etiquette," said Franklin.

"But it was a social, not a clinical visit."

"Not ethical, nevertheless."

"But I never looked at his medical chart or made any clinical inquiries."

Neither Cameron nor Franklin said anything. They just stared. Their intensity was as palpable as the hot desert sun.

As if with deep thought, Cameron said, "You're saying Mr. Ben Brewster is a friend of yours?"

"Yes, that's right."

"Mmm. So, just how long has he been your friend?"

"Well, I'm really his daughter's friend." David squirmed in his chair, hoping they wouldn't ask how long he had known her. "And I've also met his aunt. I mean, his sister."

"So then, did his daughter ask you to look in on him?" asked Cameron.

"Look in? No. Just to meet him. As a friend. Not as a doctor. I made that very clear. We only talked and played chess, basically, just two games of—"

"I don't need any details." Cameron said. "You failed to check in with the nurses before going to his room, and to follow protocol by asking his primary physician—that is, me—to obtain my permission to visit my patient. What do you think Dr. Franklin?"

From the window came the seriously toned, "I agree. Absolutely."

"But I figured, for a purely social visit, that wouldn't be necessary—"

"Not necessary?" Dr. Franklin stepped forward. "To show minimal professional respect?"

David was angry. Maybe he'd done something marginally wrong. But this was like being grilled by homicide detectives for jaywalking. "I'm sorry. It won't happen again."

"What about my patient's daughter, Grainger?" asked Cameron. "That also concerns me. Exactly what kind of relationship do you have with her?"

"We're just friends." In his mind, David added, that's none of your damn business.

"I see. Do you consider it professional to form 'friendly' relationships with relatives of Memorial's patients?"

David struggled to push back his pulsating anger. "I met her at a party before I knew her father was a patient here."

"So your relationship is new?" From behind his desk, the bluish light of a computer screen daubed Cameron's cheeks. He made a few keyboard clicks. "You're barely two months from finishing your internship and getting your medical license. What a inopportune time to muddy your professional waters. Dual relationships have brought terrible trouble to many doctors, both young and old."

David wanted to argue how there were really two separate relationships: Cameron's professional relationship, and his social relationship. But Franklin was still staring him down. Since David hadn't had much success in arguments lately he just replied, "I can see your point."

"Very well. Doctor, I look forward to seeing you in the PCC again someday. Under more favorable circumstances." Again, he made no effort to shake hands.

Franklin turned. "Rounds start in ten minutes." Then he left the room.

David gave Cameron a quick nod, then moved toward the door. But as he was about to exit, he heard, "One more word, young man."

David turned back and stood there awkwardly.

Cameron rose to his feet. "I'd like to discuss another patient, one you admitted through the ER. He died the next day on orthopedics. You know who I mean?"

David knew if he didn't make eye contact with Cameron, it would be like admitting he'd done something wrong. But he also feared his guilt might show.

"Yes, I do."

"I'm puzzled. Why did you—an intern from the ER—sign the death certificate? Why not an ortho resident?"

"Why me? Well I just happened to be there, doing a follow-up visit—to see how he was doing after all the surgeries I scheduled for him." David tried to sound professional.

"Was your visit a follow-up to meeting his son that morning?"

Of course, David realized, Cameron had seen Jonathan with him in the Quiet Room. "Right. I promised his son I'd drop by later, to see how his father was doing. When I got there, old Leary had just died. That's how come I filled out his death certificate."

"I see. How did you determine that the cause of death was *cardiac arrest*?"

David wished he could loosen his collar as he was feeling so uncomfortable. "Actually, I wasn't sure. You see, I've only signed a few death certificates—" David tried to remember what he said to Ethan.

"But you wrote, *cardiac arrest*. Why?" Cameron's eyes piercing, relentless.

"He suffered from prostate cancer, but I thought it was his internal chest trauma that caused his death. His heart had stopped. So I felt *cardiac arrest* described his final clinical state."

"Yes, it usually does." Cameron finally broke eye contact and walked around his desk. As he came toward him, David's mind flashed on pushing the pillow into the Bio-Waste bin. He was worried. Did the nurse down the hall see him? If so, had she told Cameron? Was that why Cameron was giving him the third degree?

Cameron glared right in front of David. "Anything else?"

David figured he had to respond immediately. While he hadn't said the whole truth, he might have said enough, as long as that nurse didn't see him. "No, sir. That's all I can think of."

Cameron approached closer, intentionally invading David's space. "Listen carefully, young man. Your extra visits worry me. When I was an intern, I had more than enough work with just my own patients."

"Really, Dr. Cameron, these were actually the only two times—"

"Listen very closely, young man. You are about to hear some essential advice. The extent to which you follow it will determine your future as a doctor." He stood one foot in front of David's face. "Your current behavior could abort your embryonic medical career. Do you want to finish your internship and get your medical license?" He didn't wait for David to answer. "Then stop all extra visits to any patient who is not directly under your care. In addition, cease all visits to *every* member of the Brewster family. Got that?"

Even if he could think of something to say, David couldn't answer. His mouth was as dry and sticky as an open jar of paste. The moment Cameron gestured, he jumped toward the door.

❧

As David rode down the elevator, his mind went frantic. What if Cameron learned that Ryan Leary really died from suffocation? He'd be in deep shit. He wondered, would an autopsy establish that suffocation was the cause of death? Yes, unless the pathologists were so focused on the other known causes of death that they overlooked it. Should he call the Pathology Department secretary and ask if Leary's autopsy had been scheduled? No. She wouldn't reveal that information unless he explained who he was, and revealing his name was not worth the risk. Since Leary had a terminal diagnosis and suffered multiple injuries due to his fall, requesting an autopsy had no *rational* basis...

But was Jonathan Leary *rational*? He seemed so angry at Dr. Moskowitz, he might want to sue him for malpractice. David was taught that it is almost always the angry patient or family member who sues. So Jonathan might request an autopsy to document that his father's cancer had spread widely, if he believed that he could use this evidence against Moskowitz for undertreating his father's pain.

Hopefully, it would not be too late to talk sense into Jonathan. But this was no subject for a phone call, especially from the hospital.

The elevator doors opened. The chief resident who was covering for Tom stood there. Amazingly, he had two cups of coffee and was holding one out to him.

"David, you look terrible."

"Bob, I must admit that you're right. I'm not doing well at all. Can I have the morning off? Could you tell Franklin that I'm sick?"

"You got it. Go home. Take care of yourself."

Chapter 40

David rushed home, grabbed his phone, dialed 4-1-1, and asked for Jonathan Leary's number. His fingers were shaking so badly that, for the first time in his life, he chose the ninety-nine-cent option for the telephone company to connect the call. His plan: to arrange to meet him, even go to his home.

A woman answered, "Oh, yes, Dr. Grainger, my husband mentioned you. I'm sorry, Jon's already left for court."

"Left? For court? What court?"

"The Kenard trial."

"Why?"

"He talked to Dr. Kenard's attorneys last night and we discussed it all morning. Jon decided to sign their release so they can tell his father's story in their closing arguments."

David's mouth fell open.

"Dr. Grainger? Hello?"

Still speechless.

"Are you still there? Hello? Hello?"

David slid the receiver back on the phone. He sat motionless for a minute. He got the phone directory from the top of the refrigerator and opened it. The Arlington County Circuit Court was at 1425 North Courthouse Road.

Too nervous to drive, David called for a cab. He traded his white coat for a suit jacket and went to the street. As he waited, he began to formulate arguments to convince Jonathan to withdraw permission to tell the story.

One thing was clear. His only chance to save his ass depended on getting there before Jonathan's day-in-court began.

Normally, the reverse commute to Arlington takes twenty minutes, but something was wrong on Key Bridge. After a fifteen-minute standstill, the taxi had to take Roosevelt Bridge. By the time he got to Courthouse Road, David's bladder was about to burst. He ran to the diner across the street. After he came back to the court house, he checked its directory, and then, instead of waiting for the elevator, he ran up two flights of stairs. The door to the courtroom was closed. In the one-foot square window, a yellowed sign read, "Silence. Court in Session." The door creaked as David opened it.

At the front of the room, two attorneys were approaching the Bench. David searched the room for Jonathan. He was seated on the far right. His bench, the next to last, was full, but there was space in the last bench—but not directly behind Jonathan. David tried not to be clumsy as he climbed over five people—to position himself directly behind Jonathan. He smiled apologetically, then sighed, as all five moved over to make room for him to sit down.

David tapped Jonathan on the shoulder as Patmore approached the jurors.

As Orlando watched Patmore walk toward the juror box, sweat built up beneath his armpits. Jenkins' closing statement had evoked opinions from people on street corners to so-called experts on COURT TV. None predicted Kenard could evade doom.

Upon returning from the box, Patmore glanced again at the notes he'd scribbled down as Orlando drove him to court. The twenty-seventh revision of the thumb-tabbed laser printout—the closing statement he'd been working on since the case began—was now scattered all over Orlando's back seat. Replacing this document was a yellow legal pad, complete with arrows, asterisks, and numbers—the kind of map that only its author could decipher—hopefully.

Behind Orlando, the spectators' gallery buzzed with voices predicting guilt.

Down came the Judge's gavel. Silence.

Orlando now turned all the way around to glance at Jonathan Leary. He noticed him passing a piece of paper to a jittery person behind him. Since last night, Orlando had seen numerous emotions on Jonathan's face—urgency, guilt, remorse, fear.

Now he saw a new one. Determination.

David leaned forward and tried to whisper to Leary, but the bailiff caught him. With one hand on the gun in his fancy leather holster and the other pointing a finger at him, the bailiff unmistakably mouthed, "One more time, Mister, and you're out of here."

So, in shaky handwriting, David wrote:

Please ask Patmore NOT to tell your story.

We'll both end up in deep ~~sh~~ trouble.

David quietly passed the note to Jonathan, then fidgeted as he waited for Jonathan to write back. Meanwhile, he watched the attorneys do their ritual dance.

Finally, Jonathan passed back his reply on the back of David's note:

Sorry, Dr. Grainger—

After all the suffering my father went through—

I just can't let it go for nothing.

Doctors like Kenard are my true heroes.

I must, and I will, help them.

But I promise, I'll deny you knew

anything about how Dad died.

P.S. You better destroy this note.

David was stunned by Jonathan's naiveté. Living through even one deposition teaches you the facts of life. No matter what you've promised, when an angry lawyer stares down your face and informs you how serious a crime perjury is—you tell the whole truth.

But it was too late to convince Jonathan of that.

David turned his concentration to the unfolding scene. Although this was supposed to be Kenard's drama, he felt as if it were he sitting in the defendant's box. The outcome of the trial would also determine his fate.

What would be his future? A career in medicine? Or a prison term?

Leonard Patmore faced the jurors. "Today, I'm going to be completely honest. You see, usually defense attorneys try to create a reasonable doubt in your minds. You'd expect me to argue the facts, to show how they fail to meet Virginia's legal definition of Second-Degree Murder.

"But I will not take that approach. I made that decision after meeting Jonathan Leary. His father, Ryan, died at Memorial Hospital last week." Patmore held up a newspaper. "Ryan's obituary recounts the highlights of his life but it leaves out one essential fact about his death." Patmore took a deep breath. "Ryan Leary died by suffocation from a pillow—at the hands of his own son."

David couldn't inhale. He was suffocating.

The courtroom was in commotion. Judge Williams yelled, "Quiet in the court!"

"Does that sound horrible?" Patmore continued. "Except for murdering a child, is there anything more unforgivable?" He paused. "But in this case, it would have been worse for Jonathan *not* to kill his father.

"Months ago, Ryan Leary's pain from cancer became unbearable so he asked two doctors to help end his life. Both refused. Then he pleaded with his son, Jonathan. He refused. Desperate, Ryan climbed to his attic and threw himself through a glass window in an attempt to end his life. His failure brought him more pain—multiple bone fractures, skin lacerations, and internal injuries. Worse, he was now trapped in his agony by casts and splints.

"At the hospital, Jonathan begged two other doctors to relieve his father from his living hell. Again, both refused. So Jonathan was forced to respond to his father's plea to end his suffering, forever."

David recalled the morning he met with Jonathan in the Quiet Room. Was Cameron the other doctor whom Jonathan had asked? Could that be why Cameron was so interested in Leary's death certificate?

Another crescendo of murmurs silenced by Judge Williams' gavel.

"Jonathan Leary gave me permission to tell his story because he doesn't want anyone to go through the agony he and his father went through. Are you judging Jonathan's actions? Well, he's also judging yours. He's sitting in the back of our courtroom."

David held his breath as every juror scanned the gallery. My God, was Jonathan going to stand up and take a bow? David didn't budge. Fortunately, neither did Jonathan. Not until Patmore started again did David take another breath.

"Imagine the agony Jonathan now faces. Guilt, remorse, and doubt—as he relives horrific memories. Why? Only because all his doctors refused to help when his father requested they end his suffering.

"What would you do, if your parent pleaded for that kind of help? Would you have the courage to respond with love, to end your parent's suffering? Or would you let your parent suffer? Think about it." He paused. Not a single juror glanced away. "Which course of action would cause you less guilt? Which would be best for your parent?" Patmore made silent eye contact with each juror.

"Tough questions, aren't they? Don't you wish there was another choice? How about asking your doctor, who possesses the expert knowledge and the technical means to relieve suffering? Imagine how much better off both Ryan Leary and Jonathan Leary would have been, if one brave doctor had enough courage to say 'Yes.' The father would have endured far less pain and suffering. The son, far less life-long guilt." He paused briefly. "I know it's asking a lot of you, but for just a moment, try to imagine yourselves... if you were the patient, or the adult child." He paused again.

The jurors stirred.

Patmore rubbed his temples with both hands. "On Monday, Mr. Jenkins quoted from the famous Hippocratic oath. But only part of it. And out of context. These were the sage's very next words:

> *"Physicians must refuse to treat patients who are overwhelmed by disease."*

"Today's ethicists use the term 'futile' for such treatment. And if the patient exercises the right to refuse treatment, including food and water, doctors are not permitted to start force-feeding. But choosing this scenario means that all who are involved—patient, family, and caregivers—must witness a death from dehydration that sometimes takes as long as three weeks. No wonder the former Hemlock Society used to distribute refrigerator magnets and buttons with the slogan, 'Please let me die like a dog.'"

David's heart was pounding hard and fast. He looked at the jurors, wishing he could read their faces, wishing he could understand what was stirring inside him, wishing he was as certain about these issues as he'd always been.

Patmore leaned toward the jury box. "Juanita Mitchell died, but it wasn't murder. Murder victims don't seek out their killers. Victims don't write timely farewell letters to friends and coworkers. And murderous villains don't request that all family members be present.

"You've heard from members of Juanita's family, how her life alternated between agony and a coma, with absolutely no quality in-between. For God's sake, she couldn't even let her children hug her, for fear they'd break her ribs.

"Juanita Mitchell was not a victim of murder. She was a patient who was granted her final request for a peaceful release from her suffering. Unlike Ryan Leary, she was fortunate. She had a compassionate and caring doctor who had the courage to say, 'Yes.'"

Patmore's face glowed with appreciation as he turned and smiled at Dr. Kenard. He gestured toward him. "And there he sits. This is the courageous, empathic physician who responded humanely to Juanita's last request.

"Mr. Jenkins stated that Dr. Kenard broke the law. As I began my closing argument today, I promised to be completely honest. Well, I just said, 'My client said "Yes" to Juanita Mitchell when she requested he end her life.'"

Dr. Kenard took off his glasses and squirmed in his seat. Jenkins could not hide his smile. A rush of voices swept like wind through the courtroom. Judge Williams pounded his gavel. "I hope you know what you're doing, Counselor."

Patmore turned to the jury. "Dr. Kenard administered a lethal dose of medications to Juanita Mitchell for only one reason—to stop her suffering. He thus made it possible for her to have a painless, comfortable, dignified death. Just as Juanita's family members considered it their duty of love to stay by her side as Dr. Kenard did this, the doctor knew with certainty that it was his duty to respond to her final request."

Patmore gave Dr. Kenard a gaze full of respect and admiration, an expression he kept as he turned to the jurors. "For such a selfless act, Dr. Kenard should not be condemned, far less imprisoned. He should be both thanked and praised.

"As jurors, you must therefore find Dr. Kenneth Kenard innocent of all charges—except for relieving Juanita Mitchell of terrible suffering. Thank you."

No theatrical gesture, no dramatic posing. Patmore merely nodded at the jury, then returned to the defense table. After absently straightening the edges of his yellow pad for a moment, he sat down.

The jurors continued to stare at Patmore. David couldn't guess if Patmore's words had hit their mark. But he was sure of one thing—the jurors weren't the only ones who now had a lot to think about.

As David got up from the bench, he brushed elbows with a woman who was holding a small, green spiral notebook. He glanced at it and knew immediately it was shorthand. No surprise that her badge said "Press." His chest constricted with fear. What would Cameron do when he read the newspapers and learned how Ryan Leary died?

David stumbled out of the Court House, oblivious to the commotion around him. He called a cab and wondered where to go. With Slowpoke gone, home offered only a bed. His head was churning with so many thoughts that he could never get back to sleep. He directed the cab driver to Memorial figuring he'd welcome the distraction of finishing the remainder of his day.

As the cab sped along, David's mind flooded with "What ifs?" A guilty verdict would encourage the prosecutor to accuse Jonathan Leary of murder. Under oath, his note promising to deny David's knowledge of how his father died would be worth less than a sheet of Memorial's cheap toilet tissue.

The consequence of a verdict of "innocent" was not quite as clear.

At the hospital, throughout the afternoon, David found himself strolling by TV monitors—even though he knew it was ridiculous to expect a verdict this early. On his way to one patient's room, David passed a Bio-Waste bin, blinked and flashed on Leary's bloody pillow under the swinging lid. Ten seconds of body jitters made more impact on him than the whole six-week rotation in psychiatry in medical school. Now he personally appreciated why anti-anxiety pills sell in the billions. None for him today though, not after staying up till 3:00 a.m. writing his fellowship application paper, not when it was critical for him to stay alert, not when he had to care for patients, not when he had to do everything possible to save his own ass.

Chapter 41

"So?" Ben asked Dorothy Levinson, his speech pathologist. "How did I do this afternoon?"

"Please have patience, Patient." Ben wondered if her cheeriness was forced.

She retrieved her note pad from her attaché case. Around forty-years-old, her face was round, pink, and usually smiling. She wore a swishy blue skirt and blue blazer, and balanced her weight on a pair of impossibly tiny, spike-heeled pumps. "It's only been two days—"

"-Of ar-du-ous work." Ben took extra care to not slur that word. His skull pounded. Two hours, twice a day. Of tongue-twisters, sustained humming, glottal clicks, throat-clearings. Exhausting.

"Surely you can tell me something by now," he said

"Ben, we've just begun. I can't plot a curve yet."

"I love when you talk dirty."

Dorothy concentrated on writing in her note pad.

"Something's wrong, isn't it?"

She looked up. "What made you say that?"

"After eight years in politics, I learned to read faces the way you listen to voices."

She sighed. "Your stamina is not that great. I'd like to recommend resting your voice between sessions. But how can I? For you, conversing with visitors is—"

"All I've got?"

"Yes."

"Dorothy, if you think your exercises will help, I'll save my energy."

"Good. I warn you, though. This won't be a walk in the park."

"That's okay, I almost never walk anywhere these days."

She slapped her forehead with an open palm. "Sometimes I say the dumbest things."

Ben laughed, then stopped himself. "Is laughing okay?"

Cameron was waiting for the speech pathologist's verbal report when, unannounced, Pratt waltzed in. Something was in his eyes.

"What's wrong?" Cameron asked.

Pratt settled himself deep in the couch. "Didya' hear last night's tape?"

Cameron twisted and his spine crackled. "Not yet, no."

"The Major had a visit from his daughter's friend. He's a medical intern here."

Cameron eased. He'd enjoy being one up on Pratt, so why not let him continue? "So, what did they do?"

"Do? That's not the point. Stupid chatter. They played chess. The point is who he is, and who he knew. That's the point."

"So?"

"The intern is David Grainger."

"So? I've met him."

Pratt leaned forward on the couch. "Struck me as a little convenient, you know? The Major's daughter is so pushy, and now she's got this new 'friend' who's an M.D. here. So I did some checking around this morning. Guess what?"

"Mr. Pratt, I've no time to play Twenty Questions. I knew it was Grainger. Don't worry, he's no threat."

"Careful, Doc, that's the kind of thinking that got us whipped in Vietnam."

"I already spoke to Graing—"

"Listen, Doc." Pratt bounced up from the couch. "This particular intern had a certain social worker friend walk his dog. A certain social worker who got killed in a hit-and-run accident last week. Okay, you spoke to this intern about Brewster, but did he mention that?"

Fear overcame Cameron's mind as he thought of the murdered social worker. The next time he became aware of Pratt, the nurse was standing at the door, one hand on the knob, looking back with bright mirth in his eyes.

"We may have to arrange another vacation." Pratt grinned. "As you now know, that's my specialty. Long trips at reasonable rates!"

Cameron shook as heard himself say, "That won't be necessary. I'll handle it."

But he was talking to an empty doorway.

Cameron slouched in his chair for several minutes. Then he punched the intercom button. "Becky, get me whoever the hell directs Memorial's intern program, will you? Right away!"

⁂

After finishing his work in the Out-Patient Clinic, David was free. Free to turn his concern from generalized anxiety into utter panic. But he could do nothing but wait for the jury's verdict on Kenard. Meanwhile, two questions nagged him. First, did Cameron believe his explanation for writing "cardiac arrest" on Leary's death certificate? If Kenard were found guilty and Jonathan were accused, further interrogation of Jonathan would lead to testimony that would incriminate David. Second, did the ortho nurse see him hide the lethal, blood stained pillow? If she had told Cameron about it, that would explain why the doctor drilled him so hard. To answer that question, he'd have to visit the ortho ward. If the nurse reacted normally when he said hello, he could at least stop worrying about that.

At this point, he'd do anything to reduce even some of his anxiety.

But he became more tense in the elevator ride up as he realized he had absolutely no clinical reason to visit ortho. And if the nurse had seen him hide the pillow, his visit would make things even worse... Like criminals who return to the scene of the crime. He slammed the button for the top floor and turned his back as the doors opened on the ortho floor. As the elevator rose, he turned around. His anxiety took over again. He had to know. He watched his shaking hand push the button for the ortho floor again.

Two minutes later, David was riding back down. All for nothing. The nurse wasn't there.

In the entire world there was only one person he could trust. He'd left a phone message for Ethan at lunch time. He planned to call him again from home tonight, right after he phoned Animal Rescue to ask if they had found a greyhound. And, after calling Tom again, to listen to him vent and grieve.

After dinner, Cameron held Wendy's hand as she slept in bed. "I've questioned it at times," he said softly. "Of course I have. But widespread legalization of Physician-Assisted Suicide is inevitable. I'm just helping to speed it along before our country goes bankrupt. And the same applies for all my patients. Eventually, each would have chosen to hasten their deaths. I'm not doing anything wrong. I'm merely hastening the inevitable as I reduce suffering."

He stroked her back. "Wendy, my darling, you've been so selfless for so long. You've waited for me while I've pursued my career. You've postponed your few moments of happiness. Now it's time for the trip you've always dreamed of."

He was silent for a while, feeling Wendy's wrist against his, the bones beneath, the pulse over the bones.

"You've finished your last round of chemotherapy, darling. Now you're recovering your strength. Soon, you'll be strong enough to travel. How about finding a quiet island for a little rest before we go around the world? Remember dear, this is the hardest time, so hang in there. But our timing is perfect. We'll begin your dream trip as I complete my life's work. Both are coming true simultaneously."

He was glad to see Wendy smile so much today, in part because he shared his internet research. She said, "I've always wanted to see Angkor Wat," and when he replied, "You will," bliss transcended her face as she snuggled comfortably on his shoulder.

"But there's more," he whispered, lips brushing the silk of her head-scarf. "Sometimes, when I have a little doubt, I receive a confirmation that everything will work out. Like when Ben Brewster came along. He was more than perfect because of his mother. Or that young intern. When I first interviewed him, he was so scared he actually shook. And now he'll have even more to fear. So there's absolutely nothing to worry about."

Wendy moaned. Her respiratory rate was quickening. Looking down, he saw her eyeballs rolling beneath shadow-thin lids. She made a weak, gasping sound. Cameron sat up abruptly and looked at the clock. "Oh! My fault, Sweetheart, my fault. Hang on."

Turning to the bedside table, he grabbed a syringe and gave her a tiny subcutaneous injection of Versed. Just enough not to depress her respirations.

Cameron stroked the high whiteness of her forehead. "Try dreaming of Rangoon."

∽

David hung up, disappointed that Animal Rescue had no clues about Slowpoke.

He dialed Ethan again, but got the same phone message.

He rested his head back on the sofa...

The ringing phone woke him up.

"Ethan. . . . No, no, it's not too late. What time is it? . . . Listen, I've got to speak with you. . . . Right, but not on the phone. . . . You are? . . . First thing in the morning? . . . No, no, that's okay. . . . Really, it can wait. Have a safe trip. . . . Yes, I'm fine. . . . Sure, we'll talk when you get back."

Chapter 42

After a bad night with Wendy, Cameron was late leaving for the hospital. She fell asleep only as he read her a description of the ancient hill-top temple, Wat Phra That Phangao.

Now, he was trapped in morning traffic between an SUV and a black limo.

His cell phone rang.

"Markly here." Howard Hayneswurth was using his code name.

"What can I do for you?" Cameron refused to apologize for not already being at the office, even though Hayneswurth undoubtedly had called there first.

"Turn your radio on," Hayneswurth said. "The Kenard jury is coming out."

"It's on! It's on!" A nurse called out. She stood in front of a TV in an empty room.

David knew this message would soon reach every corner of the hospital. What happened next was up to Tom. David was glad he was back, setting the priorities for their work. His moves were predictable.

Tom gestured David to follow him as he jumped into the family waiting lounge. Two nurses and an orderly were already standing in front of the monitor. David was too nervous to sit. He stood straight with his arms folded.

On CNN, the screen displayed the familiar MERCY KILLER TRIAL graphic in the foreground. In the background, an enormous black-and-white photo of Dr. Kenard. The anchorman boomed, "As most Americans know, the jury in the murder trial of Dr. Kenneth Kenard began its deliberations two days ago. This just in. They've reached a verdict. Now let's go live, to Arlington."

The scene cut to a broad, marble staircase. Men and women in suits scurrying up and down, a young reporter holding a microphone in one hand, pressing his earpiece with the other.

David squirmed as he waited for TV technicians to restore the audio. In the meantime, David mused how Kenard's destiny would soon unfold, perhaps leaving his unknown. His jitters increased to tremors. The next rumblings on this TV could herald his personal quake.

Finally, the young reporter's voice: "Despite the expectations of most legal experts, the jury has found Dr. Kenneth Kenard *not* guilty of Second-Degree Murder."

Relief came with such a draining of nervous energy that David went totally limp. His intellect began to process the good news. Jenkins would never prosecute

Jonathan, now. Funny how he couldn't process this scenario before. Now it seemed obvious. Jonathan Leary must have been counting on this result when he signed the consent for Kenard's attorneys to tell his story.

David sighed, sat down in a chair, and closed his eyes. Oblivious to several hyped conversations around him, he repeatedly mumbled to himself, "Everything will be all right."

❧

"Well, I'll be damned," Ben said.

"I beg your pardon?" Sammie said from the doorway.

Ben moved his eyes. "Kenard's been acquitted."

"I can't believe it." Sammie made a sour face at the TV and shut it off. "What's becoming of our society? A doctor admits he killed his own patient, and our justice system sets him free?"

"That's only one way to look at it," Ben said.

"Would you have legalized Physician-Assisted Suicide while you were in the Senate?"

"Don't know, honey. It's a complex issue. I would have to study it first."

"I think it's simply giving up. It's been proven, a positive attitude increases longevity."

"Sammie?"

She brought out the chess set, and looked at him. "What, Dad?"

"I won't give up."

❧

Tom was glad David asked him to go to the Doctor's Lounge. Although he was not interested in the bets or pool money, David felt grateful to celebrate with a buoyant walk. For the first time in days he could really fill his lungs completely and relax as he breathed out.

But the din in the Doctor's Lounge was so loud, David decided to duck into the mail room to retrieve his mail, which he had ignored for almost a week.

Announcements of Grand Rounds, notices of residency openings, the call list for June, late dictation reminders from Medical Records, and a light blue letterhead envelope from Memorial's Director of Graduate Education. David opened the envelope and unfolded the letter.

Memorial Hospital

Office of the Director of Clinical Training

TIME-URGENT MEMO

Dear Dr. Grainger:

It has come to my attention that you may have conducted unauthorized visits to patients for whom you have no clinical responsibility.

Please call my office at your earliest convenience to set up an appointment. Be prepared to discuss the ramifications of such behavior.

Failure to clarify this matter with me on or before May 25 will result in your suspension from all internship duties.

Paul Rosenzweig, M.D., F.A.C.P., M.P.H.

Director of Graduate Education

Chapter 43

Looking comfortable, Pratt spread out on Cameron's couch. "Your plan's not working fast enough. The Major needs more motivation."

"He still has eleven days left in his speech therapy course," said Cameron.

"You're being way too nice, Doc. He needs a more persuasive technique. We've played it your way too long. He needs one of my—"

"Pratt, let me emphasize again, I'm not only opposed to coercion. It's absolutely antithetical to the goals of my project. Know what I call success? Not only manipulating Ben into volunteering, but making sure he's convinced he came up with the idea himself. That way, he'll give his best performance."

Pratt smirked as Cameron glared.

"What if the Major decides differently, Doc? What if he makes another choice?"

"He won't. My plan may seem too psychological compared to your jungle war tactics, but as you see it unfold, you *may* appreciate it." Cameron handed Pratt a pad of paper. "Get ready to take notes. You're about to become an instant expert on Advance Directives. Then you'll share your knowledge with Ben. I can't do it myself. It'd be too obvious."

"Doc, get real. Education? That won't persuade Buffalo Brewster."

"That's only one part, Pratt. You'll see. Now, how good a student are you? Lecture today, mid-term tomorrow. If you pass, the final exam is the next day—with Brewster."

When his door opened just before 8:00 AM, Ben hoped to see Pratt bringing his breakfast. He missed brainstorming with a fellow military man. Instead it was the black moon-face of Matt, the big nurse who had originally lifted Ben into his bed. "Bringing you a roommate, Mr. Brewster." Matt pushed a gurney on which there was so much metal, wrappings, and casts that at first Ben couldn't see the human being underneath. A second nurse rolled in a tethered cart carrying something like a portable generator. From it, a one-inch plastic hose ran to the person's throat.

"What happened to him?"

"Motorcycle accident," Matt said. "Somebody pulled out in front of him. Poor guy hit the car and flew a couple of hundred feet. You know, over forty miles per hour, helmets don't help. Motorcycles ought to be illegal. That's what I think."

"Hey, I ride a bike," said the other nurse.

"Yeah, Robbie! Talk about brain damage."

"Hey, I resent that!"

"See what I mean?" Matt winked at Ben. "Robbie's new here. Can you believe... he's working a second job to buy a new bike?"

They passed from Ben's line of sight. After some grunting and rustling, all he could hear was the rhythmic sound of the ventilator's "hiss, pause, thunk, hiss, pause, thunk..."

When Matt came around the curtain divider, Ben asked, "Will he recover?"

"No way. His brain damage is too severe. But he could survive like this for years on the ventilator and feeding tubes. Poor Guy is only nineteen."

❧

Cameron had listened to some of Dorothy's afternoon session with Ben as it was being taped. Exactly what he hoped for. She'd told him his voice would not last forever. So he decided to cross her path, to justify quoting her to manipulate Ben faster.

As Dorothy was waiting for the elevator, he asked, "How's our patient doing?"

"Good and bad. His volume is good, but certain words are becoming harder for him to pronounce."

"I see. Well, all we can do is try our—"

"Dr. Cameron, may I ask you something? I'm sorry if it's outside my area." She waited for his nod. "Seeing Ben twice a day gives me a perspective, you know, of his ups and downs... Doctor, what about a psychiatric consult to rule out depression?"

Cameron cupped his chin in his fingertips. "Sounds like a good idea."

The elevator door opened and Cameron watched her tiny shoes carry her into the elevator. She held the door open with her hand. "Senator Brewster's a fine man. It's a privilege working with him since his voice is so essential. I hope we can preserve it."

"So do I, Ms. Levinson. So do I."

Cameron now wished he had not initiated this tête-à-tête. He would never order a psych consult, of course, and someday Dorothy might ask why.

❧

Pratt came in at dinner time. He paused beside the newcomer's bed and shook his head. "Jesus, that sucks." Then he approached Ben. "Speaking of things that suck, guess what's on your menu tonight?" He raised a plastic tube. "Osmolite. Goes down real easy. After all that trouble with purees, you're less likely to choke on this stuff."

"No more baby food?"

"Try it, Major, maybe it's not that bad, although I've never tasted it."

Ben felt a wave of dark humiliation as Pratt squeezed the tube in his mouth.

"Well?" asked Pratt.

"The taste doesn't justify the means, Sergeant."

"Try to think of it this way, Major. It has more protein than applesauce."

"I shouldn't complain. Look at my roommate. What's his name?"

"Jason Schaefer. Student at Georgetown."

"His parents were here earlier," Ben said. "They looked like children themselves." Or ghosts, he thought. Faces so pale they were translucent, footsteps so silent they floated across the room. From behind the curtain, the mother came out wailing so loudly that her husband had to escort her out quickly. Then sobs and screams faded down the hallway.

All the while, the persistent "hiss, pause, thunk, hiss, pause, thunk..." of the respirator, keeping him alive.

"I heard you had some visitors from a church earlier this week."

"God, I was afraid you'd find out. My sister brought them in. They prayed for me. You know, for a miracle cure."

"So how come you're not dancing around?"

"Yeah, right. What bothers me most is that, for a while, I hoped it would work. At first I was rude, but I went along while they were praying. Now, I'm ashamed." Ben was glad he could talk so frankly with Pratt. Who else could he speak to?

"Someone should string those ass holes up, Major. Selling hope where there is none. Ever see surprise on the faces of those soldiers who got shot while believing they were bulletproof because they wore *the full armor of God*?"

Ben was surprised at Pratt's vehemence. "You don't believe in God, Bruce?"

"If I did, he'd be the old-fashioned kind of God who demanded sacrifices, so you'd know where you stood." Pratt held up the tube. "Time for more Osmo—"

"Get that shit out of my mouth. I'd rather choke." Ben couldn't even turn his face away. He hated the horrible feeling of being as helpless as a baby.

"Sooner or later, you will choke even on this crap."

"And then?"

"You get a tube through your skin, direct into your stomach. It will bypass your mouth. Then, you might remember Osmolite fondly."

"Bruce, be honest with me. What do you think about respirators?"

Pratt sat on the stool next to the bed. "I wouldn't go on one. The problem is, if you don't, you'll die slowly by suffocating to death. It's terrifying to struggle to breathe. Also, once you start on a vent, you have more to worry about. Infections, abrasions, mechanical failures, people tripping over your power cord, or causing your hose to pop off. But that's not the worst of it."

"What is?"

"You can't use your own voice."

"Yeah, I know," Ben said. "Bruce, I don't know what to do."

"I do."

"What?"

"I'd do, I mean say, everything I could... while I still had my voice."

Ben looked at him.

"Major, you're a decorated soldier, a politician, you've earned so much respect. When's the last time you gave a speech?"

"It's not that easy, Bruce. Think of the logistics—"

"Major, if the VC had blown your nuts off, would you be pushing a shopping cart down the street? Hell no! You'd be demanding something from Congress, right?"

"Bruce, I'm not a spokesman for the disabled," Ben sighed. "I voted against the last batch of EEO regulations."

Pratt grinned. "Regret it now?"

"Actually, no. And I'd be a hypocrite if I changed my political views."

"So what about using your current state to speak on *not* giving the disabled more than they deserve?"

"Maybe. Except my opponents would call me pig-headed."

"Major, you've still got the two most important things—your mind and your voice. With ALS, you'll have your mind until the second you die. But the clock is ticking on your voice. I've always had respect for your ideas, Major. Can't you think of something worth talking about?"

Ben had to smile. "Now you sound like my daughter."

"She must be very smart."

"She sure is. Takes after her mother." Ben closed his eyes so Pratt would leave.

~

An hour later, Sammie came in.

Seeing the throbbing red and yellow reflections of the sunset on the wall, Ben wished he could turn his head to look out the window. He wouldn't mention it to Sammie though. It would make her unhappy. Still, he wished he were home where he could be wheeled out to the patio to see Gloria's rose bushes...

"Are you still angry at Aunt Alice over bringing in the priests?" Sammie asked as she arranged chess pieces. "It was the only way she knew how to help."

"I know."

"I found an article in the library that shows prayer improves psychological functioning. It was published in a prestigious Western journal. Impressed?"

"Anyone help you with those articles? Perhaps a young medical intern?"

"Actually, yes."

"Curious. I also met an intern one evening. We played chess. He was around thirty. And had the last bits of an old shiner around one eye?"

Her head rose from the chessboard. "That was David, I mean, Dr. Grainger."

"Right. He said he knew you."

"We met at that party a week ago."

"Reasonably good looking." Ben watched her face. "Also unmarried."

"Dad!"

Ben expected slight exasperation. Instead he saw sadness. "What's wrong?"

"I really liked him, but he hasn't called in days."

"Interns are notoriously busy," Ben said. "If he's the one, be patient."

"What did you two talk about when he was here?"

"Actually, mostly, you."

Chapter 44

Contracting ALS had left Ben's inner clock unchanged. He awakened knowing the hour was 7:00 AM. He opened his eyes, and noted the familiar drawn shades. Was he getting used to the hospital's gloomy, sterile environment?

He decided to switch on CNN, but something was wrong with the remote. Perhaps it wasn't fastened correctly over the button. Maybe the night nurse moved the rig out of position while turning him. Only Pratt treated that rig with respect.

God damnit. He was more helpless than a newborn. He tried again. Nothing. He strained his eyes to look down, but the sheet was in the way. He couldn't even see what was wrong. He was so angry that sweat sprouted across his forehead.

He was about to shout out, to hell with Dorothy and her "rest your voice" edict, when Nurse Pratt opened the door. Ben's relief at the sight of him almost brought tears. The man was amazing—always there when Ben needed him. He deserved a medal, if he didn't already have one.

"Morning, sir." Pratt switched on the lights. "Want some orange juice?"

"Bruce, check my remote control, will you? It doesn't seem to work."

Pratt leaned over and removed the sheet. He looked at Ben's hand, paused a moment. Then he raised Ben's bed so he was sitting up at a more acute angle so he could also see his hand.

Ben scanned the Velcro straps, the remote control, the nurse call button. Resting in its usual place between the buttons was his power finger—unobstructed, just sitting there, pale and bony.

"Bruce?" Ben noticed his voice slide up, both in pitch and in volume. "*Bruce!*"

Pratt leaned toward him. "Something wrong, Sir?"

"I can't move my finger."

ର୦ର

The phone rang, emptying the floating canal markets of Bangkok, smashing the Royal Palace, dissolving all of Bangkok into the Chao Phraya River.

Cameron opened his eyes.

As always, his first action was to reach over to Wendy, to make sure she was breathing comfortably. She trembled slightly at his touch, but didn't waken.

He grabbed the phone before it rang again. "Yes?" he whispered.

"Morning, Doc. Got some news." The sound of Pratt's voice made Cameron's heart plunge—so often he was the bearer of bad news.

"Wait." Cameron glanced at Wendy. Her head swathed in a pretty silk scarf. Even sleeping, she was concerned about her looks.

He walked to the den and closed the door. "How did you get my home phone number?"

"I guess some glitch in data processing let it drop."

"I see. So, what's up?"

"You know what the Major calls his 'power finger,' the only one that worked?" He paused. "Well, it just stopped." Cameron waited for Pratt to go on. "Right now, Doc, he's your basic talking head."

Cameron sat up from his desk. "That's wonderful."

"I thought you'd say something like that," Pratt said. "But there's more. It's even better. Guess who the Major asked to see?"

"Who?"

"Dr. Kenard."

⁂

Ben stared blankly at the TV images jittering across the screen. To preserve his privacy, he'd refused the voice-activated intercom. So he could no longer call a nurse using his voice. Instead, he had a sensor taped to his chest. A simple strain gauge, it would set off an alarm in the nurses' station if he ever stopped breathing for more than thirty seconds.

Great! To ask for a sip of water, he'd have to practically die.

Ben imagined he'd been killed in Vietnam. Shot, blown up, skewered in a man-trap. Sammie would have gotten over his death long ago. She'd show her husband and children photos of him—a smiling and vital young man in Army greens—and say: "What a shame you never knew him."

The irony was, he'd had plenty of opportunities to die in Vietnam. Unlike most officers, he hadn't sat behind the lines. He'd experienced his share of mud, blood, and passing bullets. He'd seen men beside him fall, yet he had escaped uninjured. At first he'd thought God spared him for a higher purpose. But the alternative was that no God existed, just hope mingled with fear and fictitiously given shape as the Great Daddy in the Sky—

—Which explained everything

—By offering nothing

—About the current condition

—Of Benjamin A. Brewster, Maj., U.S. Army, Ret.

⁂

A few minutes later, Ben heard the patter of high heels. The door opened. For the first time since he began the program, he dreaded his session of speech therapy.

"May I come in?"

"Actually, no. I'm taking a little holiday, Dorothy. I'm sorry, but this just isn't my day."

ക

"What do you mean, you haven't seen him yet? What are you waiting for, Doc?"

Cameron viewed Pratt with curiosity as he restrained losing his cool. "Sit down."

Pratt sat down but continued to glare at him.

"Ben needs time for his loss to sink in. I don't want to appear anxious to offer myself as Kenard's alternative. Get it? I'll pay Ben a visit tomorrow morning."

Chapter 45

Ben had a terrible night—dreaming, sleeping, waking, thinking, concluding that he had only one more function to lose—breathing. The loss of his power finger signaled he soon had to decide about going on a ventilator. After several bouts of near-suffocation, more than anything he wanted to know if there was a peaceful way he could leave this world before he became more of a burden and lost all dignity.

At seven, he hoped Pratt would bring him breakfast. Instead, Cameron came through the door, looking full of empathy.

"Sorry I missed you yesterday, Ben. Pratt told me about your setback."

"'Setback' you say? You call *that* a setback? What the hell will you call it when I die? A 'significant reversal?'"

Cameron looked at Ben awhile. Then, softly, "Are you thinking about that?"

"What?"

"Dying?"

"Why not? What else can I look forward to?"

Ben knew his anger was at ALS, not Cameron, but he couldn't help expressing it. The disease process of his nerves was now entrapping his mind. What inquisitor had devised such a creative torture?

"Do you have a plan, Ben? Have you thought about how you'd do it?"

"Well if the weather's nice, I'll run down to Key Bridge and take a flying leap."

"I don't blame you for being angry. Nurse Pratt said you asked about seeing Dr. Kenard. If it's not being too presumptuous of me, may I ask, why?"

Ben studied Cameron's face. If he wore a really dark suit, he could pass as an undertaker. "I wanted some information."

"About what?"

Ben licked his dry lips. "About my options, if I decide not to go on a respirator. Frankly, dying slowly from suffocation sounds horrible."

"Ben, you could discuss your options with me."

Cameron's posture and eyes reminded Ben of the intense, single-minded determination he'd seen in military commanders. Yet his facial expression was hard to read. Ben decided to take the risk. "I asked Pratt about Kenard because he has helped patients die when their pain was extreme. My question is, Do I have the same option, even though I have no pain?"

Cameron sighed. "Ben, there are different kinds of pain," he said, with warmth.

"What exactly are my options?"

Cameron's face turned more cautious. "About life support? Or about controlling how and when you die?"

"How the hell can I bail out? Is that clear enough, Doctor? I can't exactly hang myself." Ben caught his breath, wondering why Cameron was so cautious.

"Right, you need help."

"But I don't want someone to do it for me. I want to take that final step, myself. The problem is, as of yesterday morning, I can't even push a button."

"There's a way, by combining technology and medical expertise."

Ben felt a mixture of fear and relief. Relief that he could control his dying. Fear that he'd actually do it. Finally, he summoned the courage to ask *the question*. "Doctor, when the time comes, if I decide, can I ask you to—"

"Dr. Cameron?" Dorothy piped from the doorway.

Cameron spun around with a jerky movement.

The speech pathologist waggled a finger at him in exaggerated censure. "Are you messing with my patient?"

"Wouldn't dream of it." Cameron said. "Ben and I were just discussing treatment options. Right, Ben?"

"Absolutely."

Chapter 46

Sammie waited for David in a corner of the Cosi coffee shop that was less than a mile from his apartment. She had made it clear. Her purpose was professional. Aunt Alice was waiting for God's miracle. Dr. Cameron was polite but cold, and most likely considered her too "New-Age." So David was the only professional with whom she could share her concerns.

She aimlessly twirled a wooden stirrer and took a careful sip of Hoji-Cha roasted green tea. When she looked up, David was approaching in old navy blue sweats. She extended her hand. "Good to see you. Your eye is totally better."

"Yes, it is, thanks to you. How's your Dad?"

"I'm scared to death about him. Yesterday morning, he lost his last working finger, so now he's now completely paralyzed. Last night, we both cried. Yet this afternoon, he didn't seem upset at all. I don't get it."

"Have you read Kübler-Ross? About the stages of dying? I did, before I started med school. Good thing, too. Once I started medical school, I had no time to read anything outside the core curriculum. Acceptance is the last stage. Maybe that's where—"

"David, I don't want to hear that."

"I didn't mean he's accepting dying. I meant the loss of his finger."

"Oh. But Dad's always been a fighter, right to the end."

"Perhaps he's relieved that his long series of losses is over. Now he can wake up without wondering what additional motor function he's lost."

"No. His most devastating loss is yet to come. When he can't breathe on his own, he'll lose his voice." She sniffled and turned her handkerchief to find a dry section. She wiped her eyes, and wondered which of her many questions should she ask first.

"David, have you been real busy?" she asked.

"Why do you ask?"

"I was hoping you'd have the time to visit Dad, again. You made such a great initial impression. He told me he wanted to get to know you better."

"When Cameron found out I visited your father, he put me at the top of his shit-list."

"I don't understand."

Sammie noticed David biting his lip. "Some doctors get real jealous of their patients. Cameron didn't want me to get too close to Ben. For that matter—"

He stopped himself, mid-sentence. She looked at David's mouth. If he bit his lip any harder, he'd draw blood. "What is it?" she asked.

"I'm in a difficult situation. Dr. Cameron was so uptight that I visited your father that he pounded me. He came right out and warned me not to socialize with you."

"Then meeting me here could get you in trouble?"

"Yes, unless we collaborate on an alibi. If I said I was jogging in my own neighborhood, this is where I usually cool down, and we just met here by chance—would that work for you?"

"Definitely." She smiled as David sighed. They gazed into each other's eyes, and for a moment, there seemed to be no reason to talk.

Finally, David said, "If you've wondered why I hadn't called, that's why. It's not because I haven't wanted to see you, Sammie."

"That's what Dad calls me."

"What?"

"Sammie." She looked into his weary face and wondered, was she asking too much?

"I'd love to visit your dad after he returns home. Especially after I finish my internship. From July first on, there's absolutely no problem. But now? No way. Talking about acceptance—Please, Samantha, I mean Sammie, can you accept that?"

"I can accept it. But I'm not sure Dad can. I'm afraid that for him, it could be too late." She turned her handkerchief to its last remaining dry spot. "I need some way to bolster Dad's mood, to motivate him to come home." Her words sounded desperate.

"I wish there were another way I could help."

"Could you ask Ethan if Rinpoche would visit Dad?"

"Why him?"

"Dad's depression is spiritual. He needs to feel that his life still has purpose—"

"But your father didn't listen to the priests. Why would he listen to Rinpoche?"

"Dad did listen some. At his core, Dad must open himself to spirituality, to find meaning in what's happening to him. Maybe he didn't buy into Christianity since it emphasizes looking forward to the next world. Buddhism might help him find more meaning in what still remains in this one."

"Good point. I'd be glad to ask Ethan." David drained his coffee cup. "Sammie, I feel rotten about not being able to visit your father. He's a fine man and I would like to know him better."

Sammie placed her hand gently on his upper arm—the first time she initiated any touching. His face softened and brightened as she said, "Thank you."

"Hey." He put his hand on top of hers. "That's what doctors are for."

❧

"I thought you might still be awake," Pratt said as he entered Ben's room.

"I'm thinking." Ben was glad Pratt had visited, to talk.

"I hope you didn't mind my telling Dr. Cameron that you asked for Kenard."

"I was pissed until I realized that you knew Dr. Cameron would be sympathetic."

"Cameron has seen what patients and their families go through at the end—depression, guilt, anguish, divorces, careers destroyed, financial ruin. He's not like other doctors who stay far back from the battle's front lines and still think they know what's right. Cameron's right there in the trenches with you. You're lucky he's your doctor."

As Ben thought about his next question, he heard the "hiss, pause, thunk" of the boy's respirator. "Are you saying that Dr. Cameron has helped other patients hasten—"

"Major, I really can't answer that one."

"Okay. What I really want to know is, if I decided to end my life, would Cameron help?"

"I can't answer for the doctor. But I know for sure you could ask him."

What a blessing, Ben thought, to be able to talk so straight with Pratt. "I've got a Living Will," Ben said. "I filled it out after I was diagnosed with ALS. It clearly says, 'No heroics if my situation is hopeless.'"

"Absolutely useless, Major. Do you really think, when the time comes, that everyone will agree on what the words 'heroic' and 'hopeless' mean?"

"Then I'll revise them. How about if I instruct my doctors to take me off life support when I become a vegetable?"

"Still no good." Pratt pointed to the boy on the respirator. "He's minimally conscious, but not in a coma. He's beyond the Permanent Vegetative State, since sometimes, he responds to his environment. He could survive for decades like this. My guess is, if he *can* think, he'd want out. But he has no way to express himself. Like Terri Schiavo."

"Jesus. What can I do?"

"You've got two choices. Control the whole thing yourself while you still can, or appoint a proxy and hope she or he will carry through and make the ultimate decision for you at some time in the future, when you no longer can."

"Damn, who would do that for me? My daughter loves me too much. My sister would never help me after what the Pope said. You know, the ultimate mortal sin? Not to honor God's gift of life? And I have no other family members—"

"Your proxy doesn't have to be a family member, Major."

"But I can't think of anyone. Bruce... could you?"

"Nope. The law excludes people like me. There's a possible conflict of interest."

"So what can I do?"

"Think about the other choice—take action while you still can," Pratt said. "But you'd better think of a damn good way to document your wishes clearly if you want any doctor to agree to help you. After what Kenard went through, doctors have a right to be paranoid. No physician wants to risk being accused of murder."

"Yes, I'll have to think about that." After a moment of silence Ben said, "Why the hell can't I just choose to end my suffering when I want?"

"Because the reality is we don't live in a free society. It's really paternalistic. Self-proclaimed righteous legislators, governors, and attorney generals stay up nights writing last-minute laws and briefs to accuse doctors of wrong-doing. They say they are only promoting a "culture of life," trying to protect people from making the wrong decisions. But they're really motivated by power. They won't care about prolonging suffering until they, or their close family members, are dying."

"Pratt, I'm impressed. You know so much about politics and the law. How long have you been in this field?"

"I've worked closely with Dr. Cameron for a very long time."

"He must be an excellent teacher. I'd like to speak to Dr. Cameron again. We were interrupted this morning by Ms. Levinson just as we were getting down to details."

"Details about protecting the doctor who will agree to help you?"

"No. Details about what technology I can use, to control my dying, to check out of this life."

"That's your goal, Major. And it's the most important. But you might also think about how to protect the doctor who helps you."

"You're right. I need to do that. What would you suggest?"

"The Kenard trial made me think. If the jury hadn't bought the story about the son who smothered his father... do remember that tearjerker?... I'd bet ten to one that Kenard would be in jail right now, as we speak. Yet if that woman he helped, I can recall her name—Juanita Mitchell—if she had memorialized an endearing plea for exactly this kind of help before she died, then Kenard might never have been accused in the first place."

"How would she make such a plea?" asked Ben.

"There are several possibilities. She could have put her wishes in writing and had them witnessed or notarized. Then it would be her Advance Directive."

"That wouldn't work for me. I can't write."

"You'll have to think of another way then."

"What about videotaping, Bruce? Would that be legal?"

"Might be," said Pratt. "Why don't you ask Dr. Cameron? He's the expert on such things. But my feeling is that it's not simply talking into a videotape. It's what you say that counts. Before any doctor will agree to help you, my guess is that you'd have to make a clear enough statement so that he would not fear that he'd be indicted."

Chapter 47

David was tense as he ferried Ethan and Rinpoche from the ashram in Maryland Hills to Memorial Hospital. He had mild regret about setting up this meeting since he also wanted to speak to Ethan, whose time in town was limited. But Sammie's father needed an attitude change right now, while David had two weeks before his hearing with the Director of Graduate Education. David delivered "Ben's spiritual assault team" to the side entrance. He didn't wait in the getaway car. While patients always have the right to see members of the clergy, if the Director of Graduate Education discovered that it was David who set up this meeting, this sin might be added to his others and increase the risk of having his internship terminated. Life would be so much simpler once he finished and got his medical license.

David sensed a hand on his arm. "There's no rush," Sammie said. "Visiting hours are until eight tonight." He had always been a soft touch when a woman expressed her need. It began at the age of ten when his mother made him the *man of the house.*

"I know there's no rush," David said. "I always drive aggressively at rush hour."

"The purpose of Buddhism is to eliminate suffering." Rinpoche stood on one side of Ben's bed. Ethan stood on the opposite side.

Sammie had noticed Cameron's smell when she entered Dad's room. The combination of Lancôme and essential oils confirmed his recent presence. She watched her father closely from the foot of his bed.

"Your daughter and her friend David told me much about you," Rinpoche said. "You're educated and well-read. But have you delved into the subject of reincarnation?" He continued, unperturbed by Ben's silence. "Currently, over two-thirds of the world's people believe in reincarnation. Some scholars hypothesize the early Jewish and Christian leaders changed the teachings. It seemed easier to motivate people to behave righteously if they believed they had only one life to prove themselves worthy of salvation."

Ben did not respond.

Rinpoche eased back a half step, to let Ethan forward. "Mr. Brewster, I'm as American as you, but I'm impressed with the scientific evidence for reincarnation. Near-death experiences contain amazing transcultural consistencies. Children have spontaneously spoken in languages they've never heard before. Adults have described historical details about places they have never visited. Clairvoyants have predicted what archeological digs would be later discovered. And the phenomenon of *soulmates* is quite common. Not only do two people feel strongly about having known each other for a long time, but some relate detailed stories of sharing the same past life."

"How romantic," Ben said.

Sammie knew he was just being polite. At least he was listening.

Rinpoche asked, "Mr. Brewster, have you wondered why you got ALS? Have you done anything in this lifetime to deserve such punishment? If not, the answer may lie in a previous lifetime. Karma, the fundamental, unalterable law of cause and effect, states that unpaid karmic debt from a past life can cause suffering in this lifetime."

"So my getting ALS means that, in one of my previous lives, I was as bad as Attila the Hun?"

Sammie stifled a shriek of delight at Dad's sarcasm. It meant that he was listening and processing

"True, your karmic debt seems very high. But the point is, you can eliminate your entire karmic debt in the course of a single lifetime—by what you do from now on."

In her mind, Sammie yelled 'Hurray,' happy that Rinpoche emphasized this lifetime.

"Great," Ben said. "I'll fly to India and start feeding the hungry right away."

"Karma is more than physical action. The Buddha taught, 'Our life is shaped by our mind; we become what we think.'"

Ben cleared his throat. "Are you saying my thoughts got me ALS?"

"No. But I am saying your disease provides the impetus for exactly what you must do in this lifetime, to work on your past karma. I know that's difficult to accept. In Buddhism, thinking is supreme. Though strange and cruel, ALS has given you the unique opportunity to become the ultimate Buddhist—because your mind is totally unaffected."

"All mind and no body?"

"Yes. There's a fundamental difference between pain and suffering. You can learn how to train your mind to increase your capacity for happiness, and to turn suffering into peace."

As Ben stared at the ceiling, Sammie hoped with all her heart that Dad would grasp the significance of these words.

Then he said, "Mister Rinpoche, your philosophy is quite interesting, but I'm sorry, I think that's enough for tonight. But I promise, I'll think about what you said." He took a deep breath. "Frankly, there are other ways to turn suffering into peace."

Then he closed his eyes.

My God, Sammie thought. What did Dad mean by that? Was he giving up on life?

Suddenly a hand was pushing her back. Her feet were moving automatically. Ethan was escorting her through the door and down the hall. She slumped against the wall next to the elevator and covered her face with her hands. "Did you hear what he said about 'peace'? I'm scared to death."

"It is difficult to accept the Second Noble Truth," said Rinpoche, "that we cause our own suffering. But if your father decides he'd like to understand this, I'll be most privileged to help." Rinpoche placed his hands together in front of his chest and bowed slightly. "*Shanti.*"

Sammie found little hope in these words. She'd learned many mantras, but the one now repeating in her head was the voice of her father: *There are other ways to turn suffering into peace.*

"They were what?" asked Cameron, as he entered the elevator with Pratt.

"Like Hare Krishnas at airports. Bald, with orange robes."

"Where's the tape?" Cameron asked.

"On your desk. But it's an audio CD."

They were alone as the elevator ascended. Cameron would have preferred to talk in his office but they had just come from a team meeting and the other nurses might wonder why he always talked to Pratt in private. Cameron shook his head. "First priests, now them. Whose idea was it?"

"The daughter's. She—" Pratt stopped as the elevator doors opened.

A woman and a toddler entered. Both were small, round-faced, dark-haired, and handsome. Filipino, Cameron guessed. The toddler had tear stains on his cheeks and a Band-Aid on his shoulder—festive blue with a cartoon character. His mouth was turned down hard as he rubbed his shoulder.

The mother smiled apologetically at Cameron. "Vaccine. He no like."

"No one does." Cameron tried to pat the boy's head, but the boy ducked away.

Pratt's smirk stung Cameron. When he told Pratt his marriage was childless, the nurse said, "So that's why you went into geriatrics." Now that Pratt knew Cameron's experience with children was meager, the bastard was rubbing it in.

When the Filipinos got off, Pratt resumed. "The daughter egged the Major on as the bald guys went through their spiel. Too many spoons stirring the pot, Doc. Let me move him faster."

"No, Pratt. We'll follow my plan and proceed with caution."

Cameron settled onto the stool. "Good evening, Ben."

"Doctor, how can I avoid dying slowly by suffocation?" Ben really wanted to ask, *Is there some technology to enable quadriplegics to commit suicide?*

Cameron leaned closer. "Which do you want to discuss? Going on a respirator? Or controlling when and how you end your life?"

Ben's relief was profound. Cameron was willing. "Ending my life… the technology."

"First I must ask, do you have a friend who is also a doctor?"

"Not really."

"Well, you must have a physician's help." He paused and looked at Ben.

"Dr. Cameron, could you help me?"

As the doctor paused, Ben wondered what he was thinking. "That's possible if you have no alternative. But I would need some protection from lawsuits."

"I realize that. Do you have any ideas?"

Cameron's look turned serious. "In my clinical experience, to avoid legal entanglements one must usually obtain a signed, informed consent."

Ben was about to ask if videotape was an acceptable alternative to a signature when Cameron added, "Ben, I must admit I'm surprised that you're not considering the process more broadly."

"What do you mean?"

"Remember when we first talked about our experimental voice training therapy? You asked if your participation would help future patients. How come you're not thinking about helping others, as well?"

"What do you mean?"

"Take your roommate." Cameron gestured toward the boy. "He'll never move or talk again. While he previously signed an organ donor card, we can't touch his organs until his EEG shows brain death. Until then, he could 'live'—if you'd call it that—for years and cost millions.

"Ben, you still have your voice, your political savvy, and your unique way of dealing with a significant medical challenge. I'm wondering why you haven't thought more about how you could share what you've learned, to help others?"

Ben wondered if the doctor's message was an example of what Rinpoche meant. "I'll think about it." For guidance, Ben decided to ask, "Doctor, may I ask, what's your motivation?"

Without hesitation, Cameron responded, "To help others."

"Are you willing to risk what Kenard did? Your reputation, career, and freedom?"

Now Cameron paused and Ben thought he might be at a loss for words. After a sigh, he said, "Doctors don't usually divulge personal information to patients unless it's therapeutic. I had to consider if self-disclosure would benefit you. I decided it was." He took a deep breath. "When I was twelve, my baby brother died. He was only three. His death was totally preventable. My baby brother died only because my folks didn't have enough money for routine immunizations."

Ben watched a sad looking Cameron turn away for a moment. But when the doctor turned back, his expression was flat.

"Ben, think of the waste of medical resources going into your roommate. —One hundred thousand dollars a year. Or more. Think about how that money could help thousands of sick and hungry children who can't get even the rudimentary basics of medical care. Like my baby brother—"

For a moment, Cameron looked away again. "I'm not suggesting we pull the plug on terminal patients unless they make it perfectly clear that it is what *they* want. But patients should have the right to determine their own fates. Don't you agree?"

"I do. I guess I have a lot to think about."

"Good. I'll check back with you tomor—I mean, whenever—or actually if—you'd like to talk some more about this."

Ben was disappointed that the doctor had still not disclosed any specifics on how technology could make suicide possible for a quadriplegic. The ball was in Ben's court. Ben wouldn't commit to anything without first discussing it with Sammie. As a soldier, Ben had prepared to die a thousand times so he was ready for that final mystery. But Sammie wanted him to live as long as possible, to go on a ventilator, and to search for peace in his mind, as Rinpoche suggested. The question was, what would be the best way to discuss this with Sammie?

Cameron was right. He had a lot to think about.

"He's on the verge, Bruce," Cameron concluded. Since the clerical staff had gone home, he was comfortable talking to Pratt in his office. "Let's go over some details of the next part of your script for Brewster."

Cameron decided not to tell Pratt about the little fiction he'd created about having a baby brother who died. He wouldn't want to set a precedent for ad-libbing with a guy who liked to make "command decisions in the field." Things were going too perfectly to give Pratt implicit permission to take similar liberties. He might go too far. At this point, there must be no mistakes. No accidents. Not now. Not when success was so close.

Chapter 48

"Let's make a deal." David leaned across the table, peering into Sammie's eyes. "As long as you don't talk about visiting the hospital, I won't force you to order a Double Buffalo Bacon Burger."

"Okay, but first I have to thank you for bringing Ethan and Rinpoche to Dad." Sammie picked up the menu. It was shaped like the State of Texas. "And, as long as you don't mention either your patients or your fellowship application, I won't make you order a Lone Star Salad Bowl with only Balsamic Vinegar."

"Deal." David grinned. "Now, where's our cowgirl?"

Sammie looked around. Big Bend had exposed-beam ceilings and wooden tables branded with various arcane ranch signs on a shiny layer of urethane-coated plank floors. The place rang and thumped with voices, the sizzling roar of steaks hitting an open grill, and twanging country music from the lounge next door.

Sammie's left eyebrow arched. "May I ask you something? What do you think about Dad saying there are other ways to turn suffering into peace? Should I be worried?"

"We need to discuss that further."

"David, I so appreciate you."

"I'm glad to be here." David wondered if her interest was primarily professional. His queasy stomach reminded him that this was his first date in a long time.

Sammie glanced toward the cloud of mesquite smoke rising above the grill.

"Is this grossing you out?" David asked.

"Not everybody has to eat the way I do." She grinned and raised her right hand in the Girl Scout salute. "I promise. No lectures tonight."

"Do you like to dance?"

"To that?" She cocked her head toward the lounge. "I never tried, but I'm willing."

"Great. Group lessons start in an hour."

He stared at her hand for a moment. Her slender wrist had an exquisite marbling of veins barely visible beneath the surface of the skin. He rested his free hand on top of hers. Her trembling fingers reminded him of petting Slowpoke. "Do you like dogs?" he asked, and for a moment, felt sad. He had no leads from calling Animal Rescue once or more every day.

"Oh yes, very much. Medium rare!"

He loved the way she laughed.

ൠ

Ben lay wide-awake, not watching the TV that provided light and movement. With the volume off, the only sound in the room was the steady "hiss, pause, thunk" of the respirator. Unconsciously, Ben tried to match his own breathing to its rhythm, which reminded him of the sounds of drawing air from a scuba tank.

He lay there in the flickering light, not unlike the light beneath the ocean, and wished he could see his breath in the air the way he could see it underwater. He'd watch it rising, spiraling, big bubbles exploding into smaller ones, silver air alive and dancing. If he could see his breaths, he could monitor them. Count the bubbles, observe their size and shape. Make sure all the bubbles were there—

The door bumped open. "Hi, Major," Pratt said. "Care to talk?"

⁂

She shared breaded mozzarella sticks with him. "I'm not strict, like vegans," Sammie said, dipping into the barbecue sauce. Funny, when she first met David she hadn't found him handsome. But now, his sunken, exhausted eyes contributed to a sensitive-artist effect she was finding very attractive.

"Why did you become a vegetarian?"

"When I was little, we vacationed at a cabin on a lake. After I saw them bring back their catch, when I'd hear hunters banging away at ducks, I'd cry."

"Do you have any brothers or sisters?"

Sammie shook her head.

"Well, I didn't either until I went into medicine. You want siblings, try an internship. It's the world's largest codependent family."

"No offense, but I'd prefer to spend as little time in the hospital as possible—"

"Waitress!" David waved his hand. Then he turned to Sammie. "You said the forbidden word!"

A cowgirl approached, boots clomping. She wore a short denim skirt, a checkered shirt, a red bandana around her neck, and a beige Stetson. "Well, have y'all finally decided?"

"Absolutely," David said. "The lady will have the Double Buffalo Bacon Burger; I'll have the Rio Grande Steak San—"

"Hey!" Sammie said. "Wait a minute!"

David looked at her as if he'd forgotten she knew how to speak. "We had an agreement, Sammie. Remember? Not to mention the hospital?"

⁂

"Turn the TV off, will you Bruce?"

Pratt aimed the remote over his shoulder and the room darkened.

"I was thinking about what you said earlier, about making a speech as a kind of contribution, based on my condition."

"I'm sorry. I guess I shot my mouth off again."

"Dr. Cameron also suggested I think about sharing what I've gone through. He suggested it might help others, and make my experience of dying meaningful."

"But only if you think so, Major."

"The same videotape could allow me to express my wishes so they're followed, to say good-bye to my loved ones, and to protect my doctor from being charged. Also, if Dr. Cameron wanted, I'd grant permission so he could show the tape to others. It'd be a documentary proving that a rational person can decide to hasten dying. The video might help patients whose physicians are not as brave as Cameron and Kenard. What do you think, Bruce?"

"Sounds like a great idea."

"I've learned a lot from you, and from Dr. Cameron. I thought a lot about his tragedy, you know, his little brother dying."

"His what?" Pratt's voice rose. "His little brother died? Really?"

"Sorry. Was I too philosophical? I just wanted to note my appreciation."

"It's been our—at least my pleasure, Major. Your video idea sounds great."

"The video could replace my Living Will, so I'd better do it before I lose my voice."

"Major, if I may say so, your voice sounds rather determined, already."

Ben enjoyed being in control again, knowing he could still exercise his own will. "This project excites me, Bruce. I wonder, is Dr. Cameron in the hospital?"

"He might be. He often puts in long hours. I'll check."

❧

In the end, laughing, David agreed to order the Big Bend Salad for himself—and when it came, he traded it for Sammie's burger. She laughed the whole time. David was delighted to share with someone who had intense beliefs, but could still laugh like a child.

From the bar came an amplified voice.

"Dance lessons are starting," David said. "Dessert or two-step?"

Sammie got up, took his hand, and led him to the dance floor. In the changing lights, her eyes glittered with colors like the iridescent pigments of a fire opal.

❧

Pratt hung up the phone. "Cameron is coming right down."

Ben was pleased. After this enormous decision, small talk would be a relief. "I'm impressed with how well you and Dr. Cameron work together."

"Yes, we do."

"Did Dr. Cameron hire you for the PCC, or were you here before?"

"I came on when the PCC opened."

"It's great when two people of different ranks support each other so well. I like to see systems that work without animosity."

Pratt laughed. "I like how Dr. Cameron works. Like an officer and his pet non-com."

"Guess so," Ben said. But something was bugging him. What was it? He recalled his earlier conversation with Pratt. When he said, "The tragedy of Dr. Cameron's little brother dying," Pratt said, "Really? His little brother?" He seemed surprised. Yet if that was Cameron's primary motivation, how could the doctor not have shared this story with Pratt?

Ben reflected more. Yesterday, when Pratt shared his deep knowledge about Advance Directives, he said he'd worked with Cameron "a very long time." But today, he said he'd only been here since the PCC opened. That was four months ago. – Another inconsistency.

Ben long believed there was no substitute for direct observation. Five hundred years ago, his hero, Ferdinand Magellan said, "The Church says that the earth is flat. But I have seen its shadow on the moon. I have more faith in the shadow than in the Church."

Aha! The oldest trick in the book. Ben got it: leading from behind.

"You said the doctor was on his way down?" Ben asked.

"Yep." Pratt pushed a button on his watch. It triggered a bluish glow. "Should be here any minute."

". . . step, step, sidestep, slide . . ." The dance instructor's voice was a cadenced, yodeling bark, full of good humor. The floor overflowed with clomping, laughing, stumbling people. ". . . now cross-step, step, sidestep, slide . . ."

"You're doing great!" David shouted in Sammie's ear.

She laughed. "How would you know?"

"Because you've only let me step on your feet twice!"

". . . now swing your partner under . . ."

He raised his arm and spun Sammie beneath, her hair floating up long and silky, matched, farther down, by the swirl of her long skirt. He caught a glimpse of her long slender legs.

". . . bring her back and start again . . . step, step, sidestep, slide . . ."

Chapter 49

"Before Doctor Cameron arrives, Mr. Pratt, may I ask, how much of this did you and he discuss in advance? I mean, about my asking for Physician-Assisted Suicide?"

"I just knew Dr. Cameron was generally open to the idea. He's pretty liberal."

"So he didn't ask you to mention it to me?"

"No. Why do you ask?"

"I'm merely trying to remember in detail, how I arrived at my decision. That way, I'll know how to explain it on the videotape."

"Good idea," Pratt said.

Cameron appeared in the doorway. He turned the lights up and closed the door behind him. "Hello, Ben. You wanted to discuss something?"

"Mr. Pratt and I have been discussing my options. I've decided that, when the time comes, I'll opt for Physician-Assisted Suicide. But I also want to do something to help others. I've decided to create a videotape to describe how I came to my decision. This video might help other patients who may be grappling with this option. In addition, if I am clear that I wanted you to help me this way, the tape could protect you from being accused of a crime."

Cameron glanced at Pratt, then back to Ben. "A videotape? Great idea."

"But there's one thing I must insist on," Ben said.

"What's that?"

"I want to tape it at home, where I'd be surrounded by my loved ones." Ben studied their reactions.

"That's real important to me. If I can't do it at home, I won't do it."

"You're only drinking Cokes?" Sammie said.

"I never drink alcohol unless I'm engaged in a serious argument."

She grinned. In the subdued light her face was flushed from dancing. He wondered how she'd look after making love. "Sorry they didn't have green tea. How's your Perrier?"

"Refreshing, even though it's totally lacking in antioxidants and polyphenols."

"Polyphenols. Oh yes, I remember reading an FDA report on them only last week," he said.

"You mean that double-blind, controlled trial?"

"Right, the one where the only reported side effect was an increased desire to dance."

Smiling broadly, they simultaneously rose and headed for the dance floor.

❧

Ben watched Cameron closely. "Home? With your family around? But your family brought in several religious types, didn't they? Some of them may disagree with your decision."

"Good point." Ben said.

"In my experience, as soon as your family learns about your decision, they'll start grieving."

"That may be right, too. So how would you suggest I proceed, Doctor?"

"I suggest you make the videotape here, now, while your voice is still strong, but without informing your family. It would be like an Advance Directive that you write and sign and put away until the time comes. Then you go home and see how things go. When you're ready, if you still want to, you can return. Just let us know."

"Obviously, I still need to think more about the details." Ben gazed at the ceiling, controlling the silence, letting the tension build, observing Pratt and Cameron out of the corner of his eyes. If they considered him bait, he'd reel himself in and out a while. "Your idea might be best."

"You wouldn't want your family to grieve or worry until you decide it's time."

Ben noted Cameron had played the same card twice. A good argument weakened. "So I'll go home right after I finish the videotape?" Ben asked. He kept his gaze aimed upward, but concentrated on his peripheral vision. Pratt gave Cameron a hard look. The doctor twitched.

"Right," Cameron said. "We'll use the hospital's professional video equipment, and then, you'll go home."

Ben looked at him. "And we can make the tape without my family knowing about it?" Reeling out, then in.

"We can arrange videotape at just about any time of day. Yes, I think that would be best." Cameron fidgeted. "You see, there will be two parts to the videotape. You'll shoot the first part quietly, here, without worrying your family. So it would be done outside of visiting hours. Then, whenever you decide it's time, you can tell them about your decision, return to the hospital, and then, *if* you still want to, you can video the second part... to help others, and to protect me. Does that sound reasonable?"

"Absolutely." Ben closed his eyes, opened them again, but barely halfway. "I'm really tired, gentlemen. This has been an exciting day. Would you mind?"

"Of course not," Cameron said. "We'll talk more tomorrow."

"Yes, tomorrow," Ben mumbled as his eyelids drooped.

Through slit openings in his eyes, Ben watched Cameron gesture to Pratt before he led the nurse out. Pratt paused for a moment in the doorway. "Good night, Major."

The room went dark. After the door slammed, Ben heard another click—one he hadn't heard before.

Ben's heart rate quickened as his thoughts raced. They had failed his tests. First, they insisted he tape his video at the hospital. Second, they insisted he keep it a secret from his family. And every time he suggested otherwise, they had flinched, glanced, or gestured.

Whether Pratt knew Cameron for four months or for a very long time, they more than worked together. They were co-conspirators.

Ben's pulse rate increased. If their plan required secrecy, they must be scheming now to prevent Ben from revealing it to future visitors. The extra click of the door. He might be trapped!

But if they were brainstorming together, another nurse would be monitoring his respirations, perhaps one who had no special relationship with Cameron, who wouldn't hesitate to telephone Sammie for him.

No, Sammie was out on a date with that young doctor. But Alice is home. He'd ask his sister to come get him and take him home.

Ben winced at the sticky pinch of the breathing sensor taped to his chest as he took several deep breaths to build up his oxygen reserve. Then he closed his throat tightly and pinned the breath in. To alert the nurse, he'd have to hold it for more than thirty seconds.

He closed his eyes. One-one thousand . . . two-one thousand . . .

∽

"I'm exhausted," Sammie said as David held open the door of the restaurant for her. Cool, clean night air refreshed her. "It's been years since I've danced that much."

"Me too, as you could probably tell."

She laughed, thought about taking hold of his arm, but resisted the urge. Why did she feel more comfortable with David than with any other man she had dated in the last two years? Because she could talk so easily about her father? Because he was so empathic? So willing to share how he felt losing his father as a young boy? He was so genuine—

"Coming down to the hospital tomorrow?" he asked.

"Is it okay to use that word again?"

"Yes, but I still can't be seen socializing with you at the hospital. We could meet for dinner, though. I know a vegetarian Chinese place about five blocks from Memorial."

"I'd love to," she said. And, what the hell—she took hold of his arm.

∽

". . . forty-five one thousand . . . forty-six one thousand . . . forty-seven—"

Ben gasped for air in the dark room, gulped at it, mouth gaping as if to bite air.

Had the nurses not heard the buzzer? Did the sensor not work? Were all the nurses in on Cameron and Pratt's scheme?

His eyes snapped open to blinding bright light. Two faces loomed over him.

"Having trouble breathing again, Major?" Pratt said.

"Yes," Ben coughed as he tried to speak between fast breaths. "Discussing our video was real exciting."

"Our discussion left you breathless? Is that what you're saying?"

"Yes, that's right." Ben didn't know what else he could say.

Cameron leaned forward. "Any doubts about what we discussed?"

"No. Not at all. It's just, just... I was wondering how I could keep it a secret, from, from my sister. That's who. She's quite intrusive, you know."

Pratt slid in between Cameron and the bed. So you're in full agreement? You don't even have to ask your daughter?"

Ben's rate of breathing increased again. "Yes, I should. But no, I can't, and still keep it a secret."

Pratt turned to Cameron. "Look at this." He took a paper towel, sponged Ben's forehead, and put it in Cameron's hand. It was damp from perspiration.

Ben realized he could control his breathing, but not his sweating. "I'm just excited to participate," he said, "that's all."

Cameron's long jaw twisted, his eyes glowered at him. "But you seem anxious."

Now they were reeling Ben in and out. "Well, it's true, It won't be ease to, to keep it a secret from my sister, or my daughter. I was just anxious about that."

"So you tried to reduce your anxiety by holding your breath, Major?" asked Pratt.

Ben stared at the ceiling. "What do you mean?"

"Pratt, come with me." Cameron said.

Ben heard mumbling from the direction of his roommate. He heard Pratt mumble under his breath, "I think he's lying." More mumbling, not clearly heard. Then, escalating to a yell, from Pratt. "Damn it, I told you!"

Within seconds, the nurse was in his face. "How did you figure us out? More important... How much do you know?"

Ben swallowed—like razor blades twisting in his throat. "...Water..."

"Oh, sure, Maj." Pratt brought the straw to his lips, let him take one small sip, then withdrew it. "Now, answer my questions!"

"Go to hell," Ben said.

Pratt looked back at Cameron. "Now what?"

"I'm thinking."

"Okay, you think, Doc. But you listen to me, now. We're going right on with our plan!"

"Are you insane? With an unwilling participant?"

"Stubborn shithead is more like it. But I can change that. You know I can, don't you, Major? Sure I can. I'll make the Major willing, Doc. You'll see."

Cameron looked at the nurse as if he really were crazy.

But Ben knew better. He felt his heart start to thump harder and faster.

"It's finally time for me to practice my fine art of persuasion. I'm an expert. Watch me!"

Pratt bent low over the bed, so that Ben could see the blood vessels like minute red nets pulled across the whites of his eyes. He wondered how many Vietcong prisoners had seen them in just this way, an instant before they started screaming.

"Pratt—" Cameron's voice, rising.

"Shut up, Doc. I won't hurt him." He turned back, got close to Ben. "It's a real shame, Major. I bet, if we just laid it out and asked you politely, you would have gone along with our plan and helped us out. Without all of Doc's underhanded psychological shit. I told Doc, again and again. But he had to do it his way. Anyway, it didn't work, so now you're pissed, right? So you won't volunteer to help us. Right?"

Ben said nothing as Pratt smirked.

"So what can we do now? Threaten to kill you? That's ridiculous, isn't it? Threatening to kill a patient who wants to die anyway?" He paused.

"But then, there's your daughter. Right, Major?"

"You son of a bitch," Ben said.

⁂

"I parked back there," Sammie said as David drove through Memorial's parking lot. "It's the blue Celica."

David looked around. "You shouldn't park way out there at night, Sammie. It's not safe."

"I'm not usually here this late."

He drove beside her car, set the hand brake, and looked at her. "I guess this is the awkward part, huh?"

"Ordinarily." She leaned over and kissed him on the mouth.

⁂

Cameron dragged the nurse away from Ben's bed. "Pratt, stop!" His whisper was louder than he wanted due to his outrage. "There's no way we'll harm his daughter, understand? We won't hurt anyone. We're not murderers—"

"We're not, Doc?"

Pratt paused, as if he wanted Cameron to let his question sink in.

Ben heard it all and wondered, how many patients were victims of their conspiracy?

"Doc, we've got a situation here, but I can salvage it. There's no way I'm going to let you back down. Got that?"

Cameron trembled. He looked old and tired, not distinguished and wise.

"I won't be involved," he said. "You're not going to involve me in—"

"You already are involved, ass hole." Pratt turned on his heel and vanished. Ben tried to guess where Pratt went by watching Cameron's head turn.

"Pratt? What the hell are you doing?"

"Bonding again, Doc. This time, the ritual will be more public. Bonding always strengthens teams. And you and me—we're a team. At the same time, we'll make sure the Major realizes just how serious we are. One minute from now, he'll be certain we're dead serious. Got that? Dead serious. Now, let me demonstrate that I always do what I say."

For a couple of seconds Ben couldn't figure out what Pratt had done. Or didn't want to. In the center of the silent room, Cameron's body seemed locked, in a curious position of frozen intent—as if sculpted on the verge of a leap.

Complete silence. The boy's respirator was no longer running. Ben could now see Cameron shake his head sharply. Then Ben figured Pratt must have turned off the boy's alarm.

"Now what are you going to do, Doc?" Pratt said. "Turn me in? Turn yourself in? No way, Brother. We've just bonded again. Now we share two secrets."

Pratt turned to Ben. "Major, you get this? Take it as proof. I do exactly what I say I will. Always. Get that? Don't mess with me."

First, Cameron just stood there. Then he turned back, shoulders slumping. "You fool! How can this possibly work? Brewster must produce a convincing video. That's what our project is all about. You've made him angry, uncooperative, and scared. Goddamn it, he's no actor."

"You'll be surprised, Doc. I predict he'll learn acting very fast."

"What about the risk? How are we going to prevent him from getting the message out?" Cameron paced around the room. "If this ordeal has taught me anything, it's that we can't control all the variables. My God, what am I going to do now?"

Pratt slung his arm around the doctor's shoulders. "Don't worry, Doc. I've got a great idea. You'll like it, too, because it won't hurt anyone. Not one bit."

⁂

When he thought about it later, Cameron winced with regret. He should have been the one to suggest this idea. The solution to keep Ben quiet was quite obvious. The technique was similar to what many hospices use when they can't relieve extreme suffering in terminally ill patients, even after offering them extremely high doses of pain-killers. They administer a drug more commonly used to induce anesthesia. Most, but not all, patients never wake up from physician-induced loss of consciousness, which is why many professionals used the term, "Terminal Sedation."

When Cameron offered sedation to patients on his Palliative Care Center, he never used the term "Terminal." The reason: to reduce possible criticism about his underlying motivation. Instead, he wrote orders for "Palliative Sedation Therapy," a term proposed by a Japanese physician.

Pratt had not realized it, but the method he had suggested to control Ben was actually a variation of Terminal Sedation popularized by a physician in Arizona. That empathic doctor noted how exhaustion from physical and existential suffering made some patients want to die. He offered them total, but temporary, sedation. He called the technique “Respite Sedation.” In his seminars, he related how, after they regained consciousness, some patients chose to live longer.

The key difference between Terminal Sedation and Respite Sedation was to use an anesthetic whose effect was easy to reverse. Pratt knew little about pharmacology, of course, so he had to ask Cameron what specific medication to use.

Cameron knew the perfect drug. It also had a perfect name: *Brevital*!

Chapter 50

Standing at the head of the long conference table in his porkpie hat, Hayneswurth looked every bit the tourist. Given his peeved expression, also as ignorant as one, Cameron judged. It was obvious that he had no clue why Cameron had called this meeting. So Pratt had been loyal to him instead of tipping off Hayneswurth. Good.

"This emergency meeting was requested by Dr. Cameron," Hayneswurth began the meeting. "Doctor?"

"Sorry to inconvenience you on a Sunday afternoon. Don't let Howard's word 'emergency' alarm you. I just wanted you to know my underlying strategy for our ***Finale*** patient." He paused. "Let me explain why I put him into a coma."

"You what?" Chin cried.

"Brevital." Cameron waited for Chin to look puzzled. "It's a short-acting IV barbiturate that creates a completely reversible coma. But the only people who know this fact are here, in this room. His family thinks he's had a stroke. To explain—"

"A coma?" Chin said. "That's a novel way to force a guy to make a videotape!"

"Please hear me out, okay?" Cameron stopped for a long breath in, let it out slowly, and then continued. "When I permit our patient to wake up, he'll believe a coma can recur at any time, but next time the risk is very high it will be permanent. My intervention thus provides our sponsors with another significant economic benefit."

"But I thought Brewster was willing. Why does he need more incentive?" Chin asked.

"That's not the reason for the coma, Margaret. Recall my logic in choosing a ***Type III***?" Cameron opened his large note pad to *The Table of Economic Benefits*. "With no physical pain, our ***Type III*** will demonstrate his motivation for Physician-Assisted Suicide as solely due to his diminished quality of life. The economic benefit is to heighten awareness about hastening death. It's obvious that putting the ***Finale*** in a coma is the logical clinical extension. After Brewster personally lives through the experience of a coma, he will also qualify as our spokesman on the medical futility of maintaining anyone in a persistent vegetative state."

Borysewicz shifted forward. "I can see the added potential economic benefit. But your method seems like coercion—"

"Quite to the contrary," Cameron said quickly. "Brewster is grateful for my giving him the unique opportunity to make a meaningful contribution before he dies."

Chin threw up her hands. "But how can you get away with a drug-induced coma in a major hospital? What if someone checks his blood?"

"I'm the only one ordering labs," Cameron said. "And before we transferred him to a new room for better observation, I had Pratt collect a number of blood and urine samples from the patient before we started the Brevital."

Hayneswurth cleared his throat. "Doctor, I'm upset that you made this decision without consulting us first. It's so abrupt."

"Abrupt? Not at all. My timing is absolutely perfect. As Brewster finished his course of speech therapy, we fully discussed two issues—Physician-Assisted Suicide for competent patients, and voluntary refusal of food and water by proxy for victims of Alzheimer's." Cameron paused to shake his head. "I can't believe you all aren't congratulating me for the brilliant idea to add Brewster's message about the Permanent Vegetative State. Margaret, what are the latest figures on PVS?"

Margaret glanced eagerly at her note pad. "About forty thousand people currently exist in a Permanent Vegetative State, perhaps three or four times that are in the Minimally Conscious State, and some neurologists have discussed how similar these states are, to the advanced, or end-stage of dementia."

"Before you get carried away any more in your effort to establish the basis for our increased bonuses, Doctor, let alone get a nomination for an Oscar—let's see the videotape." Hayneswurth said.

"We start taping tomorrow night," Cameron said.

"Good," Hayneswurth said. "And from now on, no surprises. I want a report on your progress every day. Understood?"

To keep the look of contempt off his face, Cameron ran the thought, *I respect you*, through his mind a couple of times. He turned to Chin. "Can Margaret finish now?"

Hayneswurth nodded.

"The cost of daily care for PVS varies depending on the part of the country of course, but can be $100,000 per year or more. So the overall savings could approach 20 billion dollars a year."

"Good." Hayneswurth said. "Any other comments?" He looked around the table.

No one, Cameron noted, returned his stare.

"Okay then. Meeting adjourned."

"What is this bull shit, Pratt?"

Pratt held the cell phone away from his ear. Startled by hearing Hayneswurth shout, he asked, "What do you mean, sir?"

"I put you on the PCC to keep me informed about everything going on. I shouldn't have to go to a damn committee meeting to learn that Cameron put Brewster into a Brevital coma. What the hell is going on?"

"It seemed like an excellent idea to me, sir."

"That's not what I asked."

By this time Pratt had figured out his response. “I wasn’t aware of Cameron’s decision until early this afternoon, when he asked me to take a whole bunch of blood samples. I asked him why, but he only told me as he left for the meeting.”

“Oh.” There was a pause. “Bottom line. Do you think Cameron’s plan will work?”

“Yes, sir. Absolutely.”

“All right. But I don’t like surprises. I expect more from you in the future. Is that clear?”

“With all due respect, Sir,” he said, “I wouldn’t worry. Our operation is close to ending.”

Hayneswurth had hung up, but Pratt continued, “...and when it does end, here’s one Sergeant who’s going to retire.”

David was delayed by a patient who needed a blood transfusion so he ran all five blocks to the Chinese Dragon. He stopped in front of the restaurant to catch his breath. There he was awestruck by the balanced figure of beauty in harmony with the world. Sammie sat at a table outside, her arms braced to either side, her head bent back, facing skyward. The practice of yoga did far more than reduce stress, David thought. It centered her.

Without making a sound, David sat in the next chair. She smiled first, then opened her eyes. “Hi.” David was getting used to her “sixth sense.” She turned toward him and gave him a sideways hug.

“Thanks for taking time off to see me. And for calling me back right away this morning. I really need—David, my worst fears are coming true.”

David knew this kind of facial expression. He’d seen it when family members were shocked that their loved one was uncontrollably slipping away. Often they forgot to take care of themselves. “I’m sorry.” He noticed her unopened menu. “Have you ordered?”

“No, I’m not hungry.”

“Please, order a Buddha’s Delight. You can always take it home.”

“Okay. What did you find out?”

“I had a ‘side-walk’ consultation with the chief neurology resident. His opinion is tentative since he hasn’t actually seen your father, or his chart. But his best guess is that your Dad had a severe stroke.”

“Just as you said this morning—”

“Right. I’m sure Dr. Cameron will ask a staff neurologist to do a formal consult.”

“And?”

“A brain scan will show if there’s been damage. If there isn’t, he’ll consider other causes. There’s a standard protocol to work-up coma patients. Try to be patient, Sammie.”

“I can’t. The only thing motivating Dad to stay alive is his consciousness. Without it, he might not last much longer. I can still hear him saying there are other ways to turn suffering into peace. I can't bear the thought of letting him go..." Her voice caught and she turned away. Then she continued, "The librarian helped do a literature search but she couldn't find a single paper that connected ALS and coma." Sammie sniffed and cleared her throat.

David sighed. "Having ALS doesn't exempt a person from having a stroke."

"What are the odds my father would be the first ALS patient to go into a coma for no apparent reason?"

"The literature doesn't cite every clinical case, Sammie. Only ones of research or clinical interest. Cameron will find out what's causing your father's coma, you'll see."

She turned toward him. Her eyes were bright with tears, but hard beneath, like stones in a clear stream. Determined, like her father's eyes. "But what if they don't? Maybe they already know what happened."

"I don't under—"

"Dad was depressed, so maybe he got someone to give him an overdose."

"Sammie. Jesus. You mean, like—"

"Like Dr. Kenard."

The TV image of Kenard floated into David's mind. He heard his voice as if speaking from a distance, "But Kenard no longer works at Memorial. He left town."

"But other doctors do it, too. Secretly. They said so at the trial."

David knew that all too well. "But your father's not dead, he's in a coma—"

"Right, but wouldn't that happen if the overdose didn't work?"

David flashed on Leary, in casts and pulleys after his bungled attempt. Then he shook his head as he tried to think more clearly. "Sammie, your father would never ask for an overdose without first leaving word for you and your aunt, would he?"

"No, Dad would never do that." She took a breath. "Then maybe Cameron or one of his staff made a mistake with one of Dad's regular medications. My intuition is that his coma is not natural. It happened so suddenly. David, I've got to find out—"

David took Sammie's hands, pulled them toward him and gave her a hug. "Yes, Sammie," he said. "You've got to find out."

Tears spilled down her cheeks. "Thanks for understanding," she sniffled, "and for caring so much."

Chapter 51

The surface of the lake was a plate of thick green glass, coated with dust and pollen. Swallows knitted the air over the water. The sky was the blue-steel color peculiar to summer evenings as they hovered on the cusp of night.

"You look glorious," Ben told his wife. An obvious bit of wordplay, but he meant it.

Gloria smiled. She was sitting beside him on the long rickety dock, her knees drawn up to her chest, arms wrapped around them. Her smile caused tiny lines to materialize at the corners of her eyes—clues that she was beginning to turn into the mature woman who would leave him much too soon. She wore one of his oversized shirts and shorts. Her toes, nails painted pink, flexed against the silvery wood like the claws of a contented cat.

He wanted to touch her but didn't dare. What if she disappeared? Or wasn't real?

"Everything's real here. Jump up and down if you want."

"I just want to hold you."

She extended her arms. "Then come here, you big galoot."

He scooted across the foot-smoothed wood of the dock, his body strong, muscular, under perfect control. He held his wife and caressed the familiar contours—the soft surrender of her breasts. "Oh, God, I miss you," he whispered into her hair.

"I miss you, too." Her breath slipped into the shell of his ear. "I'm waiting for you."

He shivered. "Is this Heaven?"

"My sweet Major, always wanting to know exactly where you stand. I bet you want a map? Sweetheart, there are no recon photos for this place. But you'll find your way here when the time is right."

"When will that be?"

"You've got work to finish first. You know that."

"Work? But Gloria, I'm paralyzed back there. What can I do? I want to be with you—"

She pulled away, even though he tried hard to hold onto her. Her face was serious now, and the fading light made her skin luminous. Behind her, among the trees surrounding the lake, lightning bugs began to scratch their silent Morse code against the gloom.

"Benjamin Brewster, you've never abandoned anyone in your life—and you're not going to start now. People back there need you. And you can help even if you're paralyzed."

The lightning bugs played out in bright dashes and whorls. Ben felt a sudden, sharp pain on his left cheek, and instinctively slapped himself there. "Oh, my," Gloria said. "The mosquitoes are up. Let's get out of here before they eat us alive."

"Gloria, please—" Ben winced and slapped at his other cheek, hard enough to snap his head around. These mosquitoes by the lake were real monsters.

He slapped again and the darkness jerked around him, swirled, swept Gloria and the lake entirely out of sight. Gradually, new configurations appeared along with another sharp smack.

"Welcome back, Major," said a voice. Not a welcome voice. Not Gloria's.

"Stop slapping him, Pratt," said another voice. "It's not necessary."

Ben tried to clutch the last shreds of his dream, but they sank away.

"You don't look happy to be back with us." Ben recognized the voice. Pratt's bright eyes were staring down at him. In the shadows, Cameron hovered, like a dark ghost.

Ben's lips felt like rubber erasers, but he recalled Dorothy's lessons. With deliberate articulation, he said, "No, I'm delighted to be with you, Pratt. After all, you and Dr. Cameron are my favorite psychopaths in the entire world." He shifted his gaze to Cameron. "Now, would you mind telling me, what the hell is going on?"

Cameron stepped forward, transforming from a dark ghost into a pale, tired looking doctor. "All we've ever wanted, Mr. Brewster, is your cooperation on a project that's of utmost importance to the entire future of the United States."

"So you messed with my head for two weeks, to convince me to kill myself?" Ben said.

"Major, you're not in much of a position to defend yourself."

"Shut up, Pratt," Ben said. "At least the doctor never claimed he was an old war buddy." Ben was pleased by the spasm of anger that crossed Pratt's face.

"We just wanted to give you time to make your own, personal decision, before we revealed our entire plan," Cameron said. "We did not want your choice to be influenced by our plans. It's similar to a family member who does not want you to think of yourself as a burden. However now, it's time to reveal our goals, which I would have done anyway.

"You see, we're producing an educational video about **PAS**—Physician-Assisted Suicide, and other methods to hasten dying. Our documentary must star a well-known, respected member of our community... someone who can argue effectively from personal experience. This person must be able to explain why these peaceful methods to hasten dying should be legal and better known. Later on, when this person felt it was time, then he could, that is, if he wished, volunteer to demonstrate just how peaceful **PAS** is." Cameron paused to let that much sink in.

After no response from Ben, he continued. "As we discussed before, Ben there would be two parts to the video, first your speech, and then—when, and especially *if* you request it—your actual **PAS**. One part of your speech would present another way to hasten dying—refusing food and fluid by proxies, which is often the only option for demented patients like your mother. After we edit the videotape into a coherent whole, we'll send it out to the media, we'll broadcast it all over the country... the world. You'd be—" Cameron stopped himself, realizing that he was getting carried away.

"...I'd be your **PAS** poster-boy?" Ben wheezed a laugh. "You stupid bastard! You're like some ass holes I knew in the Army. They'd make decisions in a nice office and then expect people in the field to implement them without asking any questions."

"See, Doc. I told you. He'll never—"

"Shut up, Pratt." He turned to Ben and softened his voice. "We just wanted you to make your own personal decisions voluntarily. That value has always been my primary moral concern. Then, if you decided that you wanted **PAS**, it would make sense for you to help us. That's when we would have presented our plans about making the documentary. We never would have forced you to—"

"Never forced me? What if I hadn't figured out your ruse? Let me think a moment." Ben reviewed the pressure they put on him: Make the video *now*; here in the hospital; and keep it a *secret* from his family. Cameron was lying, but Ben decided to play along. He softened his tone. "So, it's okay if I decide not to cooperate?"

"Of course. In that case, we will just select another patient. In your case, **PAS** is obviously the best option since your specific clinical alternatives are so limited. I admit, in our rush, our intent may have appeared—"

"Select *another* patient, you said? Have you pulled this shit on others?" Ben despised paternalism, hated doctors who presumed there was no doubt they knew what was best for their patients. But Cameron's particular brand of paternalism was lethal.

Ben noticed Cameron glance toward Pratt.

"Oh, Jesus, now I get it," said Ben. "There's more than you two, isn't there? Who else? The hospital? Some insurance company? An HMO?"

"I'd be quite glad to tell you. I am not trying to hide anything from you, Ben. The goal of our group is to legalize **PAS** and to make people more aware of the legal option to refuse food and fluid, before it's too late for America. The cost—"

"Save your sermon, Dr. Mengele. Do you think you're above the Nuremberg Code? What about the first absolutely essential principle—to obtain voluntary consent?"

"I understand why you're upset, Ben. But I beg you, listen to these facts, give them some thought. Put aside your pride, your resentment for what appears to be our subtle methods of persuasion. None of that will change the reality of your alternatives, the value of this mission to our country, or the potential of your making a most unique contribution." Cameron moved closer. "Your clinical condition presents a very clear choice, Ben. Either you will die slowly by suffocation in the privacy of your family at home or you can continue your gallant public career. Your voluntary participation could have a most profound impact on society."

Cameron removed a large note pad from the shelf behind him. He opened it to a page of numbers that he turned toward Ben. "Look at this. A study at the Rand think-tank showed that forty percent of us will die slowly from chronic illnesses, mostly dementia. That means that a couple whose four parents are now alive has a seven out of eight chance that at least one parent will be dependent on them and require long-term care for years before they die... As your *mother* was dependent on you... As *you* are now dependent on your daughter. Have you thought about what kind of a life your daughter has now? Or the total cost of your illness? Imagine your scenario, and especially your mother's, repeated millions of times as our society ages. Do you see the result? Our country is speeding toward a disaster called emotional and financial bankruptcy. As a society, we must be more proactive. That's why this documentary is so important. That's why I appeal to you: Please, Ben, decide to help." Cameron took a deep breath. His face seemed to reflect the hope that his speech had totally convinced his audience... of one.

Ben just stared at both men. He decided to wait for one to make the next move, to intentionally try their patience. Pratt paced like a tiger in a cage. A hungry one.

After a long minute, Ben said, "Did you leave anything out, Doctor? Like greed? Like increasing the profits of the organizations who are behind this? You and Pratt must be nuts. You continue messing with my mind as you still hope I'm willing to help?"

Pratt became unleashed. "Oh, he believes it all right, Maj. Doc wanted this whole project to work without anyone getting hurt." He leaned over the bed. "But you and I know that real progress in this world is always paid for in blood, right Major?"

Ben wished he could take Pratt down with his bare hands.

"The bottom line, Major, whether you volunteer or not, is that you'll be the star of our video—or something terrible will happen to your daughter. Finding and hurting people was my specialty as a LURP. Like riding a bicycle, that's something I'll never forget."

Ben imagined himself erupting off the bed like a giant krait, coils unwinding, fangs sinking deeply into Pratt's neck, injecting gallons of venom. Pratt thrashing on the floor, foaming at the mouth, dying in agony. Instead Ben said, "You dinky-dau bastard."

Cameron looked puzzled.

"Old 'Nam word, Doc. Means crazy," said Pratt.

Pratt raised a hypodermic syringe and glanced at Cameron, as if waiting for a signal. The doctor nodded. Pratt brandished the syringe near Ben's face, close enough for him to see a trembling drop of fluid gleaming at the end of its needle. "You've got our proposition, Major. Why don't you sleep on it?"

❧

The phone rang and David's eyes snapped open in the dark. He was alone and scared. He swept his hands across the bed for Slowpoke. Of course she wasn't there. He picked up the receiver. "David, I'm glad you're still home. Can we talk?"

It was Sammie. He looked at the clock. It was only 6:00 AM. "Sure."

"Last night when I visited Dad, Nurse Pratt was creepy. Every few minutes, he'd open the door to Dad's room and stare at us. Frankly, he was intimidating."

"I thought your father swore by him."

"He did. And he seemed great. But last night, he gave me the third degree as soon as I got off the elevator."

"Nurses are sometimes possessive of their patients."

"He seemed different. And when I called Dr. Cameron to discuss Dad's condition, he said his first available appointment time was next week. I can't wait that long."

"Do you think Pratt made some mistake that put your father in a coma?"

"That could explain his strange behavior. David, what do you think of transferring Dad, of getting him out of the PCC?"

"Out of the PCC?"

"I mean to another hospital. If Dad can be admitted to another hospital, we'd have a second opinion right away. What do you think?"

"I think it's a great idea."

"I'm so glad you agreed, David. You're so supportive. I'll start working on it right away. See you soon. Good-bye."

After David took a shower, he picked up the phone again, almost automatically. Then he put it down as he remembered what Earl at Animal Rescue said yesterday. David had been calling three times a day. In return for his stopping, Earl took down David's hospital pager number and swore he'd contact David if any greyhound approximating Slowpoke's description showed up. The posters David put on telephone polls and the ads he ran in the newspapers had so far yielded nothing.

David missed Slowpoke terribly and that made him feel guilty. What right did he have to feel sorry for himself when poor Michelle had lost her whole life? What was his loss, compared to Tom's?

David hated his early morning ruminations. Once he got to the hospital, he could depend on the practice of medicine to distract him. But Sammie's call had awakened him earlier than he needed, and he could not fill in his extra time by calling Earl due to his promise. Thus, he had "free" time, free to worry about all the things that bothered him. Free to think about all that was causing his stress. He made a deliberate decision not to distract himself with TV or a book. He'd even start with what scared him the most: his upcoming meeting with the Director of Graduate Education, a meeting that could determine whether or not he still had a future in medicine. There were a number of relevant factors.

Attorney Patmore's closing statement revealed that Jonathan had smothered his father. So David wondered if the Director of Graduate Education would question young Leary. Not likely. The hospital's attorneys always advised doctors not to stir up things with patients or families. Even if the Director did contact Jonathan, he'd have enough courage to not implicate David in such an informal setting. Yes, that sounded right.

One key to David's fate resided in the Asian nurse. The question was, had she seen him discard the pillow? The worst possible scenario: Yes, she *had*. If she testified to that, David would be thrown out of the internship, charged with a felony as an accomplice to murder, and never be allowed to practice medicine. The best possible scenario: No, she had *not* seen him stuff the pillow. Then, David would receive a mild warning for visiting patients without authorization. He would finish his internship, get his medical license, and start his fellowship.

David considered strategies based on these two possibilities: If the nurse testified that she saw David throw the pillow away at the hearing, David would refuse to talk until he had retained legal representation. Then he'd ask his mentor to recommend a lawyer. Solomon would refer him to an attorney skillful at using delay tactics. Innocent until proven guilty, there would enough time to allow David to finish his internship and obtain his license. Most likely, the worst that would happen after that would be a temporary suspension of his license. But if the nurse did not attend the hearing, he could assume that she had not seen him. Then, he'd stick to the exact same story that he had told Cameron. He'd further point out that he had not since visited any "extra" patients who were not assigned to him. Then, he'd hope for the best.

David wondered why Dr. Cameron seemed more interested in the Brewsters than the Learys. Why had the PCC head warned him to cease contact with *every* member of the Brewster family, while he mentioned nothing about his seeing Jonathan? In both, the parent was the patient, and the issue was David's social contact with the adult child. It was probably the sex thing. But maybe not. Since Ryan Leary was dead, had wanted to die, and his son would never sue, why worry? In contrast, Brewster was alive, Samantha was feisty and sometimes non-cooperative. Was that enough difference? Whatever Cameron's reasons were, David had decided to be cautious. He would only see Sammie outside of Memorial. He planned their meetings carefully so they would go unnoticed. And he always had an explanation that Sammy knew, if they met someone from the hospital by chance. David sighed. Once Sammie transferred her father to another hospital, all this would be a non-issue.

As he stretched, David mused on how constructive it had been for him to have the courage to face each one of his fears by engaging in logical thinking. He felt far more confident about the specific actions plan for all his problems.

Furthermore, he could conclude precisely what he must do now:

Absolutely nothing!

"Give him another minute, Pratt." Cameron's heart was pounding. Last night, he finished writing the script that fit Ben's specific personal circumstances, including a reference to his Alzheimer's mother and his temporary coma. He looked forward to Ben's reaction. With great respect for Brewster's background, moral convictions, and forthright expressions of his opinions, Cameron couldn't help fantasizing that Brewster would be excited about the script. He might even volunteer additional content. That is, if Ben could get past his damn pride. Okay, the manipulation attempt was almost successful. And yes, Pratt had betrayed him. But think of the enormous contribution he could make to the world. If Ben could not see it that way, then Cameron would have no choice: he would have to implement Pratt's plan.

Ben's eyelids flickered before opening. Cameron waited until they seemed focused. "Welcome back, Major Brewster."

Ben said nothing.

"Have you decided to cooperate?" For Cameron, the ***Finale*** was critical. Last night, Wendy had sobbed in her sleep.

Ben started to speak, then cleared his throat. "Water," he whispered.

Cameron grabbed the squeeze bottle and held the straw to Ben's lips. "We kept your mouth moistened, but it's natural that your throat is dry."

He took the straw away. Ben's mouth opened. Out came only a raspy hiss.

Cameron sighed. "Come on, Ben. Don't expect me to believe you've lost your voice."

Ben opened his mouth and lisped, "Haven't done my etherthitheth . . ."

"Your exercises? Please! Any school kid could malinger better. Come on, we have a video to film."

"Can't talk. Thorry."

Cameron's palms were sweating. He turned to the nurse. "Mr. Pratt?"

"Sir?"

"Any ideas on how to handle this?"

"What kind of ideas, Doc?"

The bastard. As if he didn't know. "The way you suggested, you know, to encourage Ben to cooperate on our project?"

"I was just tossing out ideas. Do you really want me to carry through with it, Sir?"

Bastard. "Yes, if you think it'd help."

Pratt turned back toward Ben. "Doc, let me ask the Major. What do you think? Do you want to help us, or would you prefer I go after your family?"

"Athhole, I'm doing the betht I—"

"Really?" Pratt pulled out a small metal picture frame from his pocket. He held it in front of Ben's head. The angle prevented Cameron from seeing it. "Recognize this?"

Ben's eyes fixed on the photo. After a moment, his face smoothed out and became a mask. With perfect articulation he said, "Yes, I recognize it."

Now Pratt tilted the photo toward Cameron. Three people—a young Ben Brewster, a woman, and a young girl—all standing on the end of a dock in front of a smooth lake.

"Found it in his daughter's bedroom," Pratt said. "By the way, Maj, the locks you've got on that house are a joke. And please tell your daughter to buy some different underwear—the stuff in her dresser is really friggin' boring."

Ben made a short choking sound.

Cameron's palms oozed sweat. "Pratt, you didn't—"

"She was at work, Doc. She'll never even know I was there. I'll even put her picture back while she's here visiting this evening—if the Major promises to cooperate."

"You bastard. I'll make your damned video. Just stay out of our house."

Pratt nodded and turned toward Cameron. "See, Doc? Now that's the fine art of persuasion."

Chapter 52

Although he passed it every day on his way to the hospital, Cameron hadn't toured the Lincoln Memorial in years. As he trudged up the broad, marble staircase in the early morning light, he was surprised by an overwhelming sense of awe. The building loomed white against the blue sky, silent and imposing, a vast house for a man of stone. Wind inhaled and exhaled around the columns of the deserted Mall. Earlier, when Hayneswurth called to insist on meeting there, he reacted as if it were an imposition. Now, its grandeur made him feel vulnerable.

At the top of the steps, between the next-to-last and last columns on the right, he saw a figure—tall and distinguished, in a tailored gray suit, white shirt, and navy silk tie with narrow red stripes. Hayneswurth could have passed for a TV newscaster or politician.

"Good morning, Doctor." He stepped back behind the columns into the shadows. "Let's talk here." The air temperature dropped ten degrees under the overhang of marble, which kept out the early morning sun.

"Why are we meeting here?" Cameron asked, "instead of one of your horrible motels?"

"I hope the location will inspire us. We need it." Hayneswurth gestured toward the wall. The Gettysburg Address was carved above enormous murals depicting the Angel of Truth. In front, Lincoln loomed huge above, staring down the Mall.

Cameron waited for Hayneswurth to begin. He watched him look up at Lincoln.

"You promised to keep me apprised of any changes with our ***Finale*** patient."

"And I have. I've called in a report every evening."

Hayneswurth stared at him. "You really don't know?" He paused. "Norman, Brewster's family petitioned for his discharge. They want to transfer him to another hospital. My sources at Memorial told me his daughter and sister are scheduled to discuss the matter with a Patients' Advocate at 11:00, this morning."

Cameron thought quickly. "Brewster's in a coma. I won't agree. They'd have to sign him out with the Against Medical Advice form."

"Which means a hearing before the Magistrate. They can get that within twenty-four hours."

"No Magistrate would decide in their favor."

"Doctor, at our last Committee meeting you said you planned to move Brewster to a new room. Have you?"

Cameron had to nod.

"Then he's clearly up to being moved. Hospitals are reluctant to hold patients against their families' wishes. If anything goes wrong, the cost of litigation can be staggering." He paused. "I'm disappointed, Doctor. Perhaps I gave you too much leeway with this patient."

"I can use other arguments to prevent his discharge." Cameron blurted out.

Hayneswurth crossed his arms and glared at him.

"Neither woman is competent to make rational decisions concerning Brewster's health. Both are steeped in superstitious drivel. I can prove that."

Hayneswurth cocked his silvery head. "How?"

"First, his sister brought in two priests who tried to cure his ALS by faith-healing. Then the daughter brought in a couple of Hare Krishna types. I can characterize their request to transfer Ben as another desperate attempt, but with one important difference—the risk is much higher. That argument would convince a Magistrate to deny Brewster's transfer."

Hayneswurth remained silent. His gaze was distant but so intent, Cameron followed it to these words: ". . . THESE HONORED DEAD, HAD NOT DIED IN VAIN."

Hayneswurth shook his head. "Superstitious or not, if they get a reputable physician to agree to provide Brewster with continuing care, then your arguments won't work."

"What about your contacts? Surely there must be some way you—"

"I wouldn't risk bribing a Magistrate for this. No, Doctor, if the Magistrate allows the transfer, we'll have to select another patient as our ***Finale***."

"No!" Cameron's loud shout caused pigeons to flutter overhead. "We've invested so much in Brewster. He's about to make a significant impact in three economically important areas."

Hayneswurth's eyebrows raised. Cameron looked at Lincoln, hoping Hayneswurth would think he was being inspired. Actually, he was using those moments of silence to strategize.

"Howard, listen. I can finish the video in three days. And I assure you, I know how to buy that much time. Even if the hearing is held tomorrow, I'll schedule Brewster's brain scan and request a neurology consult just before the hearing so they'll happen the day after. I'll argue it would be irresponsible to move Brewster before learning the cause of his coma. No Magistrate would risk denying one more day to analyze Brewster's tests."

"I trust your ability at clinical scheduling, Doctor. But can you finish the video that quickly?"

"We're shooting a test run tonight, the real thing tomorrow."

"And Major Brewster really wants to help?"

"Yes. And I know exactly what he'll say. That's why I'm so eager. He'll be terrific."

Hayneswurth folded his arms, turned, and gazed up at Lincoln's ponderous face.

Cameron wasn't sure whose pose was more theatrical.

"Very well, Doctor, proceed. But keep these two things in mind. See the words carved into that wall? 'WITH MALICE TOWARD NONE AND CHARITY FOR ALL.' That's what our project is all about. We shall never violate that principle. Understand?"

"Yes, of course."

"Good." The bubbling chortle of pigeons came from outside the stone womb of the Memorial.

"Second," Hayneswurth faced Lincoln, "if, for any reason, our project goes sour, my first obligation will be to protect our sponsors."

Cameron was about to say "Good-bye" when he realized the interview was already over.

Hayneswurth was already halfway down the steps.

Chapter 53

Cameron was excited. Tonight would be an historic moment, for both art and for science.

"Okay, Doc, it's slow, but he's coming around," Pratt said.

Cameron feared Brewster might remain sluggish after discontinuing the Brevital. He aimed the mini-spotlight toward Brewster from slightly off-center near the front of the bed. After zooming in and focusing on Ben's eyes, he moved away from the camcorder. "Good evening, Mr. Brewster. I realize you're angry with us. But you should understand, I appear on this video, too. My reputation, my career, even my freedom—are all at risk."

"I can't tell you how much that moves me."

Cameron was relieved to hear Ben's strong, clear voice.

Brewster's eyes moved around. "Wait a—This isn't my room. Where the hell—?"

"Welcome to your new room."

Cameron double-checked the cabling between the three professional digital tape recorders. The camcorders stood on tripods aimed at different angles and ranges. He'd leave the editing into a seamless master and the addition of music, to Hayneswurth's staff. It was enough for him to function in the roles of writer, director, and main supporting actor.

"Let me explain how this will work." Cameron pointed toward the center camcorder, directly in front of the bed. "The Teleprompter screen will scroll the entire script, including my questions and your answers. We should strive for a natural sense of back-and-forth—as if there were no script. Many of the phrases come directly from our discussions, so it should all sound natural. You can ad lib freely, to add your personal touch. Any questions?"

"No, but I have one demand. Get Pratt out of here."

"I beg your pardon?"

"The sight of him disgusts me. If you want this tape to sound remotely genuine, get that shitbird out of my sight."

Pratt stood motionless.

Cameron scowled. "Mr. Brewster, if you just concentrate on the Teleprompter, there—"

"If Pratt does not leave this room, I can't be convincing."

Cameron was not surprised that Ben was still angry at Pratt. Yet he had no problem with agreeing to his request. After all, he had planned some daylight shots while Pratt stood guard in the hall. Daylight shots... early morning shots...

For a moment, the doctor mused on his artistic plans as director. He visualized the ***Finale***, when he would pan the camcorder from a close-up of the patient's eternally-reposeful face over to a wide-angle of the inside window, and then out... zooming in on the Washington Monument as it dazzled against a blue sky. Finally the camera would pan up to floating white clouds. By association, the peaceful death by **PAS** would seem a transcendence of the physical limitations of the body that deeply embraced patriotism.

"Okay, I'll agree." He turned to Pratt. "There will be times you'll have to wait in the corridor anyway. So if it will help our star shine, why not do our practice sessions this way, also?"

Pratt leaned close over into Ben's face. He said, "You're not planning to play any games are you, Major? Because if you are—"

"I know—you'll kill everyone I love. Don't worry, Pratt. I won't give you that satisfaction. But you can always stick pins in me later if it will make you happy."

The brief flash of anger that passed over Pratt's face startled Cameron.

The nurse turned. "Well, Doc, what do you want me to do?"

"First start the camcorders; then leave the room."

Pratt nodded, turned on the third camcorder, and left.

"Happy?" Cameron said.

"Ecstatic."

"Then let's begin. Concentrate on the Teleprompter, please."

ஓ

After the rehearsal, Cameron sedated Ben with Brevital. He pulled the videotapes out of the camcorders and instructed Pratt on where to hide the gear. He hurried to his office, locked the door, and shut the drapes against the strawberry blush of dawn. He loaded the tape into his the player, switched on the television, and sat back in his chair. He took a deep breath, let it out, and then raised the remote control. He pressed PLAY.

The TV monitor flickered and dimmed, then lit up with the interior of Room 812. It looked brighter on the screen than in real life. The doors of the handsome teak cabinet were closed. The video color portrayed well the intricate cream and faded blue design of the quilt, an heirloom from three generations of Camerons. The flowers and potted plants were photographed symmetrically. Overall, the ambiance was lovely. On screen, however, Cameron looked paler than Ben. He'd apply makeup before the next shoot.

CAMERON: "Good afternoon. My name is Dr. Norman Cameron, and I'm a—"

BREWSTER: "—Afternoon?"

CAMERON: "Please follow the script, Mr. Brewster. Now, again!" He paused briefly. "Good afternoon. My name is Dr. Norman Cameron. I've specialized in palliative care for more than twenty-five years, providing *Comfort Care* for patients who would otherwise suffer intensely during their final weeks or months of life.

"Today, I wish to introduce you to a very special American, Major Benjamin Brewster. His name is familiar to many Americans. He's a highly decorated officer from the Korean and Vietnam Wars. In Vietnam he rescued hundreds of soldiers from enemy territory. More recently, he was a Virginia State Senator." Cameron paused to turn from the camcorder to look directly at Ben.

"Less well-known is that Ben has suffered from Lou Gehrig's Disease for almost four years. Good afternoon, Ben."

BREWSTER: "Good afternoon, Doctor."

The sound quality was excellent. Brewster's voice was strong and he looked well—except for a tendency to squint. Perhaps the lights hurt his eyes. Shooting in daylight would eliminate that problem.

CAMERON: "Ben, would you like to explain our purpose to our viewers?"

BREWSTER: "Yes. I've always felt the core value of our American democracy is that we enjoy the right of self-determination. Our Declaration of Independence endorsed every person's right to life, liberty, and the pursuit of happiness—as each person chooses.

"So Doctors must explain the risk of every proposed medical procedure. They cannot legally proceed without the patient's consent.

"In my case, as my ALS progresses, I must eventually decide if I will undergo an operation to make a hole in my throat so that a respirator can breathe for me. Today, I'll explain why this was the most difficult decision of my life.

"For ALS patients not on respirators, some die suddenly by drowning in their own saliva. Others expire slowly by suffocating as their muscles progressively weaken. I've had a taste of each. Both are horrible."

CAMERON: "Good! That's the kind of detail we're looking for!"

Cameron permitted himself to talk out of character during rehearsals since it would encourage Brewster to be more spontaneous during the final taping.

BREWSTER: "Recently, I've endured several attacks of respiratory failure. It's a terrifying experience, worse than any I ever faced in battle."

CAMERON: "And you're a recipient of an award that is granted by Congressional decree to only the greatest of heroes—the Medal of Honor."

BREWSTER: "Doctor, every decoration I earned in the military was for my attempts to help my men stay alive. My men were out there serving their country, acting on behalf of their loved ones. My duty was to keep them safe.

"Now I find myself faced with a very serious, similar question—should I keep on using medical technology to keep myself alive? My decision will affect not only me, but also the well-being of everyone around me."

CAMERON: "What do you mean by that, Ben—?"

ஒ

"What, basically, do you mean by that, Ben?" Compared to the previous night's rehearsal, Cameron's inflection sounded friendlier. But Ben still wished he could say, *Don't call me Ben, you damn murderer.* For the camcorders however, he kept a mild expression.

Squinting at the blue-lit words scrolling down the Teleprompter, Ben spoke clearly and slowly. "What I mean, Doctor, is that physically I'm totally incapacitated. I can't move anything except parts of my face. I can't feed myself, get a drink of water for myself, let alone perform the simplest physical acts most people take for granted. As you can imagine, this makes me a terrible burden to my family and friends."

"Yes," Cameron said, following the script, "but you can still talk and—" He gave an exasperated sigh. "Mr. Brewster, please remember to look at me from time to time when I speak? This is supposed to be a discussion between us, remember?"

Ben took a deep breath and let it out. "I just didn't want to mess up my lines."

Cameron rode his wheeled stool over to the control panel, which was parked just outside camcorder range. He rewound the Teleprompter a few lines and pushed himself back beside the bed. "All right, let's try again. Okay?"

"But you can still talk and interact with people, Mr. Brewster. Surely that's more important to your family than any inconvenience caused by your condition."

Ben forced his eyes to move toward the doctor for a moment, then returned his gaze to the Teleprompter. "My ability to talk is temporary. Someday, I won't be able to breathe without a respirator. Then, I'll have to use a gadget to help me select one letter at a time. But five words a minute is barely communicating. If I go on a respirator, the supportive care can cost four hundred thousand dollars a year. It's hard to justify staying alive when the price is so high, and the rewards are so low.

"Dollars aside, Ben, how do you feel about this?"

"How do I feel? I feel terrible for being a burden, miserable for being dependent, and selfish for maintaining a life costing many times more than others. I'd feel more foolish for extending my life beyond the point after its quality reaches zero. It's difficult to think about, but I've reached the conclusion that's what I want, when I get to the point where I believe it's pointless for me to continue to live—"

Ben stopped as he heard a voice in the hallway—muted, flattened by distance and intervening walls, but clearly angry. Ben could just make out the next few words: "What do you mean I can't see my father?"

Ben opened his mouth just as Cameron's hand clapped over it.

ஒ

Brewster's daughter stood in the middle of the hallway, arms crossed over her chest. "Why not? There's no restriction on visiting during the day."

"No, you're right." Pratt restrained his voice for calmness, his movements for smoothness. He was aware of faces staring from the nurses' station, of glaring eyes from the Brewster bitch. "Aren't you usually at work right now?"

"That's none of your business. Why are you still my father's nurse? Didn't you work on the seventh floor?"

"On the PCC, we're assigned to patients, not floors," he ground out the words as he held out one arm to block her from entering Room 812. "Your father is undergoing some very delicate tests right now. Visitors would invalidate the results. I suggest you not disturb him."

"What kinds of tests?" she demanded.

"Neurological stuff. A spinal tap and an EEG. Disturbing him might skew the results. Don't you want us to find out what's causing the coma?"

Her jaw dropped. "Want to—? Of course I want to find out. I just want to see him, that's all." She made a move for the door.

Without thinking, Pratt grabbed her forearm hard. She halted, blinking, and looked down at his hand. Studied his knuckles.

"I can't," he said in a low, controlled voice, "let you in right now. Come back in fifteen minutes when they're done. I must insist for your father's sake. Understand?"

After staring at his hand for another moment, she looked up into his eyes.

Pratt noticed her face had turned pale. Was his grip too tight? He forced his fingers to loosen.

The bitch staggered back as she rubbed her arm..

"I'm going to report you. I'm going to—"

Pratt felt air pulse around him as a door opened.

"Is something wrong?" Cameron's voice sounded so concerned.

"Yes." The witch still held her arm. "Your nurse refused to let me see my father. And he manhandled me."

Pratt turned to see Cameron's deep frown. "Nurse?"

Pratt tried to think of what he could say. "She was about to disturb your EEG test, almost barged in, even though I repeatedly asked her to wait until you finished."

"Well, yes, these tests are delicate, but still—Ms. Brewster, please, do come in. We'll get this taken care of."

Pratt made himself step aside. As Brewster's daughter passed him, he glanced at her neck. Slender and graceful, it wouldn't take that big a blow. Her neck was designed to be broken. Or just tweaked, to put her in bed as a quad for life. Wouldn't that be poetic justice?

Pratt followed her to the Major's room. She went straight to her father's bed.

Pratt looked around. The lights, the camcorders, and the quilt were all out of sight. Instead, monitoring gear was exposed. Boy, Cameron really moved fast.

"What kind of tests did you run?" she asked Cameron.

"I completed a spinal tap," Cameron said, "to check for blood, protein, and bacteria. And while you were waiting, we finished his electroencephalogram."

"Did you say, 'We?'" She looked around the room as if his words implied a crowd of doctors were standing nearby.

"This is a telemetry room," Cameron said. "The same technology that transmits data to the nurses' station, to monitor your father, also broadcasts to experts outside this hospital. Their opinions will provide valuable insight into what's causing your father's coma."

She watched Cameron raise his hand to her father's forehead and remove two electrodes, as if they were the last of a complete set.

"We're doing all we can." Cameron threw the electrodes in a small trash can and turned toward her. "I hope you can see that."

The bitch sat in the chair beside the bed. "Will you leave us alone for a while?" Cameron asked. "And nurse, would you mind taking this trash can with you?"

Pratt followed Cameron back to his office. The Doc closed the door and said, "You idiot!" His voice was low but full of heat. "Pushing our patient's daughter around."

"I never hurt her." Pratt wanted to push Cameron up and down the nearest wall, but instead, he changed the subject. "Did you get much taped before the bitch showed up?"

Cameron glanced up and down the corridor. "Quite a bit, actually. I expect to finish the first take tonight."

"Finish?"

"Only the first take—the first go-through. I'd like to tape the interview several times—so Hayneswurth can choose from several takes, for the final edit. I also have to adjust the lighting since Brewster squints and blinks too much."

Pratt stared at Cameron. "He's really cooperating? I had my doubts."

"Seems as if your threats did the trick. He's very concerned about his daughter."

"So am I, Doc," Pratt said. "So am I."

David went inside the Chinese Dragon to look for Sammie and Alice but no table had two women. He was drawn to a woman sitting alone. She wore a navy suit and a white silk blouse. David noticed her long, muscular legs beneath the table. As he glanced up to the thick bun of brown hair on top of her head, he heard a voice call, "David?" Ouch, it was Sammie. His heart flip-flopped and his stomach burned.

He walked over, forced a smile, and sat down. "Where's your aunt?" Sammie wore no makeup, but the color in her cheeks and forehead was almost scarlet.

"Uncle Sid picked her up. She's very upset."

Her eyes tightened to icy slivers. "The Magistrate won't decide until 4:00 PM tomorrow—after Cameron receives the results from Dad's battery of tests."

David licked his lips. "That sounds reasonable, Sammie."

"To me it sounded like a lie."

"But it's only one more day—"

"That might be too long. Something's definitely wrong. I'm so afraid—" She leaned toward him and her jacket swung open to reveal the silken outlines of her breasts. David flinched as his stomach stabbed upward. Man, he'd better get something to eat.

"Sammie, why are you so suspicious?"

"My intuition is screaming that Dad's in danger. Cameron was so intent on keeping Dad on the PCC. Isn't it strange, right after Dad finishes his two-week crash course in speech therapy, he falls into a coma? And his creepy nurse... He was horrible. Now I'm sure he's evil."

"What happened?"

"I took the day off to go to the library to prepare for the hearing and to visit Dad. When I walked from the elevator to Dad's new room, Pratt blocked me from entering. He grabbed my arm so hard, it hurt. And he glared like he wanted to break it. He didn't let go until Cameron came out. And his hands are gross. His knuckles are deformed. They look like thick horns. He wanted me to notice them—like he was showing them off."

"Show me where he grabbed you."

Sammie rolled up her coat jacket. David nodded although he saw no evidence of bruising.

Sammie reached across the table toward him and twined her fingers through his.

"David, what if I took some of Dad's urine for an independent lab to analyze?"

"Without Dr. Cameron knowing about it?"

"I could sneak a sample from his catheter."

"Wow. You'd do that?" David slipped one hand free to rub his left temple. "The problem is that urine tests are inconclusive. To prove there's a drug overdose you'd need a blood sample."

"Fine, show me how to get one."

"That is a skill that takes time to learn. If you broke your father's vein, he'd bleed into his skin, and Cameron or Pratt would notice. Then your appeal to transfer him would be denied."

Her face sank. "I see." She stared at him for a moment. Then sweetly, "David?"

"Oh, Sammie, oh, you have no idea what you're asking. Cameron literally threatened to abort my medical career—just for visiting your father. If he caught me taking blood—"

"I'm desperate, David. What if Cameron and Pratt are hiding something, some mistake that they could be sued for? They'd never put the evidence in Dad's chart. We have to get our own—" She leaned forward and took hold of his hands again.

"I wish I could, Sammie, but—"

"Cameron is a master at manipulating the system. Dad has no one to fight for him but you and me. We are his only hope. And we need some evidence before his hearing."

"Sammie, I didn't want to burden you with my troubles, but now I'll have to—"

"David, before it's too late, please help my father. Only you can. He's in danger—"

A chill crept down David's back. He looked into her eyes, but couldn't speak. Her hypothesis could be true. But if Cameron found out he took a blood sample from his patient, his internship and medical career would be over. That's all the Director of Graduate Education would need to end his career. He had to tell Sammie what was at stake. "Sammie, I've got to tell you something—"

"David, I know your career is very important, and I do understand." Her hands slid free of his and away, across the table, down onto her lap. "Really."

"Sammie—"

"My name—" she stood up, "is Samantha."

She pushed the table back, cocked her head to the side, and stomped off.

Chapter 54

Ben swept his tongue across his sore lips. Since Cameron controlled the timing of his consciousness, Ben had to search for clues to guess how long he had been comatose. He noticed late afternoon sunlight glowing like hammered gold on the quilt that draped his body. Slowly, a memory began to emerge. "What happened, Cameron?"

"Sorry I was a little rough. I had to put you back to sleep quickly. Your daughter paid us an unexpected visit."

"So she thinks I'm in a coma?"

"Yes, she seems to be accepting that." Cameron centered the control console. "Please focus on the Teleprompter. I'll roll back a few lines from where we left off. Want some water? Let me know when you're ready, okay?"

You have no idea, Ben thought.

Cameron pushed a button on each of the three camcorders, took a deep breath, and sat back. "Let's start with your answer to, 'How do you feel about this?'"

Ben inhaled deeply and began. "After some hard thinking, I had to conclude that the point has come where it's pointless for me to continue living. That may sound shocking. It might even smack of cowardice to some, although I've never been a quitter.

"I want to be real clear. I don't want to die. If someone found a cure for ALS tomorrow, I'd be extremely happy. Unfortunately, that doesn't seem likely." Ben blinked tears.

"In wartime, when it's inevitable that a hand grenade will blow up, it's the bravest soldier who chooses to dive onto it to save his comrades. For the last three years, ALS has waged war against my body. Ultimately, it will win. Being mortal, no one wins the war with death. But sometimes we need to admit that fighting to the bitter end to preserve a life that has no quality is not brave. Instead, it's really selfish, like running away from that hand grenade.

"Our end-of-life decisions affect others. My daughter will never be rich from her career in holistic health, yet she may have children who want to attend college and graduate school. Many family members who care for terminal patients lose their entire life's savings. To me, it makes no sense to drain the assets of my estate when the quality of my life is zero.

"While I was in a coma, I had no awareness. Now, I have zero memory about that time. It was a total waste. Living through that coma increased my resolve to take action while I still can."

"Why is that, Ben?"

"Because the next time I go into a coma, I might not ever come out of it. I'm only 58, and in some ways, rather healthy. I could last another ten years, or more."

"Ben, have you ever been challenged with an end-of-life decision before this?"

"Yes. I feel tremendous guilt over prolonging my mother's dying."

"What happened?"

"For the last four of her eleven years with Alzheimer's, her mind was completely gone. Yet I instructed her caregivers to spoon-feed her, even when she resisted and would not cooperate. When the risk of pneumonia from aspirating food was too high to continue oral feeding, I signed a consent form so surgeons could insert a feeding tube directly into her stomach. Yet she never benefited from my efforts to extend her existence. Now I wish I had helped her in a different way."

"What way?"

"When she was first diagnosed with Alzheimer's and could still make medical decisions, I should have asked her if she wanted to die in peace before she lost all human dignity. I'm sure that she would have answered, 'Yes.' A one-hour visit with a psychiatrist could have prevented others from later raising the question if she was mentally competent when she created her Advance Directive. That document could have granted her proxy the legal authority to refuse all food and water on her behalf as long, as she was given *Comfort Care* including sedation. And the proxy could have either been me, or someone who could be more objective, like an end-of-life professional.

"But like most Americans, at the time I did not know that this option was legal, let alone peaceful. It's definitely not starvation. Still, some institutions and some physicians refuse to honor these last wishes—even if all family members agree that's what the patient would have wanted. Laws in many States make it more difficult to refuse food and fluid than to refuse other types of medical treatment. That's why it's so essential for patients to put specific instructions in writing in the form of an Advance Directive, to be specific, and to strive to provide reasons and examples that will be considered clear and convincing."

"Ben, if you consider Voluntary Refusal of Food and Fluid to be such a good option, why did you choose Physician-Assisted Suicide for yourself, instead, to hasten your dying?"

"The short answer? I prefer the *quicker* method. But let me explain more fully. You see, having Lou Gehrig's disease forced me to consider these options a long time.

"Doctor, there is nothing in this world that I care about more than my daughter. In just the past few weeks, she has seen me almost choke to death, improve my voice with speech therapy, and then fall into a temporary coma... For three years, she has witnessed my slowly progressing paralysis. With the loss of my last working finger, I'm now a total quadriplegic. Our relationship is very close. For the most part that's wonderful. I could not ask for a more devoted daughter. But the problem is that *her* happiness is tethered to *my* medical ups and downs. Up to this point, there was nothing I could do about her loving me too much to ever give up hope. But now, I can. And I will.

"If my situation were like those of most people, I would opt for Voluntary Refusal of Food and Fluid since its major advantage over Physician-Assisted Suicide is the ability to change one's mind as long as one remains conscious. The initial few days are critically important for those patients who have not thought deeply enough about whether or not they want to hasten their dying. During this time, their loved ones may try to convince them to resume eating and drinking. But in my case, I've thought so long about this decision, I'm sure I would not change my mind. So those extra few days would only prolong my daughter's sadness as she lets go. Since she and I have talked extensively, there is no need to prolong her process of letting go."

"Ben, your reason is both touching and compelling. —An ultimate act of giving."

"Thank you, Doctor. I know what it's like to see a parent die slowly. During my mother's last years, her disease took a horrendous emotional toll on me. Keeping someone alive whose personality and humanness have vanished is a nightmare for everyone. More than one-third of Alzheimer's caregivers are significantly depressed. Some cannot take a day off for five or ten years. Now that my mother is gone, I'm still trying to erase the horrible memories of what she became, due to the so-called 'miracle' of modern medical technology.

"If I chose to remain alive as long as possible, Doctor, I would be forcing my daughter to prolong her agony of continuing to witness my inevitable further decline. But my reasons are also for myself, as I look forward to dying of what some would term, 'Natural causes.' I refuse to die slowly by suffocation or by drowning in my own fluids, as close calls with both have convinced me how horrific they are. I also refuse to go on a respirator since I would not be able to use my own voice. Worse, I refuse to risk the horror of eventually being caught in the 'locked-in' state—where I would have no way to communicate. That is my worst fear of all."

"I agree, Ben. With a mind as active as yours," responded Cameron, "it would be torture to be locked-in and have no way to express yourself. I firmly believe that everyone has the right to request a peaceful dying. May I ask if you have any other reasons for preferring Physician-Assisted Suicide?"

"Yes, but these reasons are not for myself. In America, there are now 45 million people who do not have health insurance. Others have inadequate insurance. When they become terminally ill, their limited access to medical care in general, and *Comfort Care* in particular, could leave them in a state of prolonged and intense suffering. They need an expedient way to hasten dying. Until everyone has adequate medical insurance, Physician-Assisted Suicide should be offered as the humane way to expedite escaping from being forced to endure unnecessary pain and suffering if there is no chance of improvement. That's one reason I wanted to make this video.

"I also wanted to demonstrate that my judgment is clear, and that I am speaking with my own free will. Anyone who views this videotape should realize by now that I am depressed only because my medical situation is realistically hopeless, and that the decision I've made is a rational one." Ben's eyes teared, causing him to blink.

"I also wanted to protect you, Dr. Cameron, from any legal consequences from helping me." Ben paused to blink away a few more tears before he could resume. "I hereby grant you, Dr. Norman Cameron, permission to show this videotape to protect yourself from criminal prosecution, and to educate others on these options. So let me now ask you, in language that is as clear and convincing as I can express it: Dr. Cameron, will you help hasten my dying by offering me Physician-Assisted Suicide, when I decide that my life has become so unbearable, so intolerable, that I no longer want to continue to exist?"

"Yes, Ben, when that time comes, I am willing to help you in that way."

"Thank you, Doctor. Your promise gives me much peace. Now I can wait until the last moment to decide that it's time for **PAS**." A few more tears and blinks. "I hope that it will be many months from now."

"I also hope it will be many months, Ben, but now you no longer need to worry about slipping into the locked-in state or being a burden to your family. You have my professional commitment to ensure that your last wishes will be honored."

Ben asked, "Thank you, Doctor. Could you wipe my eyes?" as the words on the Teleprompter scrolled out of sight. Cameron remained surprised at Ben's tears. He would not have guessed this war hero would reveal so much emotion. Yet he had really probed deeply. His mother... his daughter... his own mortality... it made sense.

"Sure." He leaned over with a tissue. "And let me thank you," Cameron said in a low voice. "What you said was very moving." After a few more seconds, Cameron walked over to each of the recorders, to shut them off.

There was an uncomfortable silence for what seemed like more than a minute.

Ben looked at him. "Now what?"

The doctor gazed back with a warm, almost paternal expression. "You were excellent," Cameron said. "Just a few rough spots to re-shoot. Overall, you were quite impressive." He looked pensive for a moment. Then, there was no stopping him. "I wonder if we would be presenting too much information if we added a section on how the world is *flat* from the standpoint of allocating financial and medical resources. Unlike Europeans, most Americans do not realize the consequences of spending enormous sums on people with a limited prognosis or who have diminished consciousness, patients who won't live long, or who can't appreciate the sacrifices being made for them... Perhaps we should try to education them by comparing cost *versus* value, the utilitarian approach. What do you think? Should you say it, or me?

"Say what? That you're forcing me to do this? That's what I'd say. Damn you."

"Listen, please. The cost of maintaining one U.S. patient who suffers from end-stage dementia for one year, in round figures is about $100,000. Yet those funds have another potential use, one that I would say is better. They could purchase 10,000 mosquito nets that could potentially save the lives of 4,000 African children under age 5. These children would otherwise die from malaria. While the money saved from skilled nursing care doesn't automatically go to Africa, let alone the poor and needy in the U.S., in closed economies, like in Europe, it does. I believe Americans must start thinking this way."

Ben wanted to gouge his eyeballs out. "Don't get carried away, Doctor. You're not in the running for winning the Nobel Peace Prize. And don't congratulate yourself for my participation, either, Mr. Hitchcock. You know the reason I'm cooperating."

"I'm truly sorry about that part, Ben. Still, it's been great working with you."

"Would you please answer my question, Doctor? Now what? What next, *for me*?"

Cameron turned toward the window. The sunlight brought out all the wrinkles on his face, the depth of the lines flanking his mouth. "As I said, we'll go back and shoot a few sequences over again, decide on adding new material, and—"

"And then?"

Cameron didn't turn. "Then?"

"Give me some credit. You had us both hoping that it would be months before I ask you for **PAS**. But you can't risk putting me in and out of a coma even for weeks."

Cameron's mouth opened, then closed as he continued to stare into the sunlight. "I wish I had a daughter. Or child. You're quite blessed that way." He shivered. "Okay, I'll answer your question. In the final sequence, you'll activate a computer-controlled machine to inject a sequence of three lethal medications into your IV. I'll be standing by you the entire time, and it will all be on tape. That's why I told you before—I'm risking a great deal here, too."

"I doubt that," Ben said. "Dr. Kenard took his chances by responding to someone who requested his help. My guess is that by the time your damn video is broadcast, you'll be watching it on CNN from Rio." Ben saw this previously unspoken truth cause the doctor's jaw muscles to harden.

Cameron remained silent for a while. "Good people do bad things for good reasons sometimes. Ben, I wish you could appreciate my professional benevolence. It's just the way we went about telling you... Also, if you knew about my personal life, I believe you'd conclude I'm not selfish."

"Make sure someone puts that on your tombstone, Doctor."

Cameron pivoted on his chair. "We have more work to do. Let's get to it."

"You're not going to get away with this, Cameron," Ben said. "There's no way."

"Strong words, Brewster. But you're not exactly in a position of power here, are you?"

Ben forced himself not to show any emotion. But he was thinking how chess emulated real life. One's greatest sacrifice, like losing your Queen, may not be a mistake at all. Instead, it could be the very strategy need to win exactly what was most important.

Chapter 55

"Hello?"

"Oh hi, Ethan. It's David. Glad you're home. I can't remember your schedule."

"Rinpoche only decided today that we'd leave Woodstock."

"Actually, I called to speak to your father—"

"He's at a fund-raiser tonight, the Opera."

"Oh, I see. Well, it can wait."

"Are you okay, man? You don't sound so hot."

David glanced around his dingy little kitchen, at Slowpoke's water and food bowls still parked, empty, in the corner. "Just tired. It's been a long day."

David knew he could never fool Ethan, but as usual, he was kind and let it pass.

"Samantha Brewster called earlier. She also wanted to speak to Dad. Sorry to hear her father is in a coma. Would you tell her so, when you see her?"

"Oh, you didn't talk to her?"

"No, I only heard her message on the answering machine. How's she doing?"

"Upset, of course. Did you mean before that? She was disappointed that her father didn't ask you and Rinpoche to return."

David wondered why Sammie had called Solomon. To ask about Ben's neurology work-up? To ask if he had authority to discharge Ben? Regardless of the specifics, she would not have called Solomon if David had not refused to help. That thought made him ache.

"Pardon?" David missed what Ethan had just said.

"I asked if you want me to page Dad. Is it an emergency?"

"No, don't ruin his evening. Just leave him a note to call me in the morning."

"Will do."

"Thanks." David almost hung up, then said, "Ethan?"

"What?" His response was quiet, but immediate.

"Any further thoughts about my hiding that pillow?"

"No."

"Or about how I handled that AIDS patient and his parents?"

A long pause. "David, you don't sound settled about these patients. Let's talk some more. Do you have time this week?"

"Let me think." David knew Sammie would need his support after the hearing tomorrow. He would be on duty through the next afternoon. He asked, "Friday evening?"

"Can do. Call me as soon as you get off work."

Great, David thought. A brainstorming session with Ethan would give him a chance to go over the specifics before he had to meet with the Director of Graduate Training. But he still felt empty and restless. He needed some direction now.

"Ethan... about this karma stuff... Do Buddhists believe you can do something to make up for your past errors?"

"Hey, you got some of Rinpoche's teachings. You're correct. 'Right action' means compassion. Buddhists consider the noun 'compassion' like an action verb. First you listen with your heart, then you respond."

David wondered why Ethan had answered his call while he let the answering machine record Sammie's? Did he somehow sense that answering his call would be an act of compassion? He looked at the clock above the sink. 11:15. "Thanks, Ethan. You always give me something to think about."

"Hey, I'm always here. We'll talk more Friday evening."

David hung up and mumbled, "Right action. Compassion. Listening. Responding." If Sammie's father *was* in danger, how could he *not* respond?

He imagined sneaking into Ben's room to obtain a blood sample. He could climb the stairs to avoid passing the nurses' station. Staffing was minimal during the graveyard shift. If someone confronted him in the hallway, he could say he wanted to see Tom's patient, Max Graveitz, who was just transferred to the PCC.

Was it stupid to risk a medical career of several decades to try to save the diminished life of a man whose life expectancy might only be several months? Did he even have a true concern for Ben or was his interest more to earn points with his daughter?

David's approach to making difficult decisions was to start by making some assumptions. Then he'd project himself into the future. Finally, he'd think backwards about his "former" options.

He assumed the reason why Cameron was blocking the request to transfer Ben was that either he or Pratt had bungled Ben's medical care. If Ben eventually died because of their error, and if David could have prevented Ben's death by obtaining a blood sample to analyze... would he ever be able to face Sammie again? Could he even live with himself?

"Right action. Compassion. Listening. Responding."

Sometimes in life, one *must* take a risk. It's the only choice.

Chapter 56

The video player tugged the tape from Cameron's fingers.

Pratt sat cool in his usual spot on the couch.

Cameron picked up the remote control. "Remember, this is all from the central camcorder. There's plenty of editing work yet to—"

"Let's just check it out, before you send it off to Hayneswurth."

Cameron pushed START and watched himself on-screen. He looked like he had just noticed a visitor enter the room. His color was better than during the rehearsal. "Good afternoon. My name is Dr. Norman Cameron. I'm a specialist in palliative care, with more than twenty-five years of experience—"

The tape rolled along. Watching it critically, Cameron visualized how striking the finished version would look, with alternating angles, additional scenes cut in, close-ups, lovely vistas of mountains and oceans, inserts of photos from Ben's vigorous life.

Not to mention the heart-rending ***Finale***.

Cameron noticed that Pratt's attention tightened each time Brewster spoke.

"Wait a minute," Pratt said. "Roll it back a few minutes."

Cameron did.

"Wait! Son of a bitch!"

Cameron looked at him, alarmed. "What?"

The TV's light flickered in Pratt's cold eyes. He bared his teeth and began to chuckle. "Oh, damn," he said. "Goddamn, I knew it." Then he laughed, fell back on the couch, and hit the backrest.

"What's the matter?"

Pratt slapped his knees. "Oh, man, I knew the Maj wouldn't make this easy."

Cameron put the video on pause. "What are you talking about?"

"It's his blinking, man." Pratt wiped tears from his cheeks. "It's not lights in his eyes, and it's not crying, either. It's goddamn Morse code."

"What?"

"During the war, the gooks were always making these films of American POWs 'confessing' to war crimes. These skeletons in rags, standing in front of a microphone would say things like, 'Yes, I napalmed helpless women and children.' But one officer blinked in Morse code. While he recited his script with words, he blinked code that said, 'I had to lie. They tortured me.' The stupid gooks sent the film out, so the whole world got the real story."

The pulse in Cameron's neck beat hard. "Oh, no."

"Rewind the tape again, Doc. Just a few seconds. And mute the sound."

In the silence, Pratt slowly wrote down some letters. Then he spoke: "Cameron and Pratt forced me by threats to my daughter."

"No," Cameron said. "No, no, no."

"Yes, yes, yes." Pratt jumped off the couch. Not laughing now. He placed himself right in front of Cameron's face. "You know what we have to do now."

Cameron swallowed hard.

"We warned him. Now we have no choice."

Cameron looked into Pratt's eyes. "If Brewster's daughter dies, he will never cooperate."

Pratt straightened, flexed his hands so his merged knuckles bulged. "Don't worry, Doc. I'll make the Major cooperate. For me, that's easy. We're in my world."

Cameron felt trapped. He slumped into his chair.

"By the way, Doc. Me and you. You know, we're real partners now. Right? Which means we'll cut our bonus down the middle. Fifty-fifty."

⁂

To David, Memorial Hospital after midnight was the ER, the clamor of sobbing, blood, frantic activity, sirens. The main lobby was disturbingly quiet. He headed straight to a pay phone, deposited coins, and dialed the PCC. A nurse answered—a woman, thank God, not Pratt—and he introduced himself as Dr. Schwarz.

"Do you know—Is Dr. Cameron still in the hospital?" he asked.

"Yes, he's in his office. Want me to connect you?" A slight Filipino accent.

Damn. "No, not yet. How about Nurse Pratt? Is he there?"

"Well, he's supposed to be off duty until 7:00 AM, but he never seems to go home."

"Thank you, Nurse." He hung up.

Decision time. Cameron definitely on the premises; Pratt possibly. Definitely too risky to get a blood sample now. David walked toward the front doors, anticipating the smell of fresh night air, but he could not stop obsessing on these thoughts: What if he didn't get the sample tonight, didn't have the lab analyze it before tomorrow's final hearing, didn't help Ben… and Sammie's assumptions were true?

He made himself turn around and walked toward the Doctors' Lounge. There, he slumped in the chair, turned on the TV. A slow-moving, black-and-white '40s flick. Yesterday's newspaper. Tried to doze a bit. Couldn't. Tired, got coffee. Considered calling the PCC again, decided not to. It would cause too much suspicion.

Waited. Looked at the clock. 12:45. Late enough for Cameron and Pratt to have gone home. Grabbed his white coat. Took the elevator to "3." Gathered the equipment he needed from his ward. Went down the hall. Climbed the stairs—a good way to release nervous energy. Reached the eighth floor. Walked softly down the hall to Room 812. Opened the door.

Inside, incandescent lights outlined the monitors. A soft glow fell through the window. The Washington Monument, brightly lit outside, as Sammie described.

David closed the door. On the bed, Ben looked smaller. His chest barely moved the sheets. Something in the room reminded David of his father's last days. He felt a pang of emotional pain so deep it almost wrung a cry from his lips. He clenched his jaws and approached the bed. The IV line was flowing. Dextrose, for calories and to keep the line open for other meds. The monitor readouts... all normal.

From his pocket he took a rubber tourniquet, a tiny needle with little blue handles that looked like a butterfly, and two red-topped test tubes. No good veins in Ben's non-IV arm. Forget using the small veins in his hand. They break too easily and are always noticed. He pulled the sheets up from the bottom of the bed, tied the tourniquet around the calf, and collected blood from the vein that ran behind the ankle. Then he transferred the liquid to the test tubes. He put everything into his coat's side pocket.

The door handle rattled.

David quickly spread the sheets across Ben's feet. He skipped to the far side of the bed frame and dropped to a squat. The bed was a tangle of slats, supports, and long threaded rods adjusted into a shallow zigzag shape. Through the high spots under the head and knee areas, David watched the door open. A shadow moved across the faint hallway light. As the bar of light widened, the light blue material of a nurse's uniform appeared, then a white bulky sneaker.

A man's sneaker.

David slid under the bed. He crammed his head and shoulders into the low peak beneath the knee area, forced his legs forward. Metal struts raked his scalp, forcing him to bend his head far to the left. His neck muscles spasmed.

The room lights flickered, then came on, bright and startling.

David's left cheek grew warm. He turned his head slightly and saw a golden glow—Ben's urine bag.

To the right, the soft squeak of rubber soles on tile came closer.

David froze and held his breath. The squeaking halted.

"Incompetent wetbacks," a voice growled. The sheets began to flutter.

David noticed his left foot protruded into the light. Grimacing, he rotated his hips to force both knees to the floor, then pushed them straight, squeezing his legs under the bed frame at its lowest spot. The stress on his joints was agonizing.

The sneakers moved to the other side of the bed with the shoe tip threatening to touch David's knee. He pulled up more but a metal bolt pierced his skin. The pain forced a small gasp.

The sneakers halted. David held his breath.

After a moment, the sneakers receded. A thumping rattle of sound, as if the locked doors were being tested. The sneakers reappeared on the other side of the bed. The IV stand wobbled a bit. David glanced again at the urine bag, fearing it might need emptying. If the nurse pulled back the sheet to check it—

The sneakers didn't move. David noticed he was sweating. Was Pratt adjusting Ben's bed? Or wondering how the sheets got so messy? David's legs buzzed with dull electric pain. How much longer could he sit like this without moving?

Finally the sneakers moved away. The lights went out. A moment later, a soft click.

David remained still. His mind created a terrible image. Pratt hadn't left the room but was standing there right inside the door, staring at the bed. Waiting.

David made himself wait. He counted silently, trying to calm his mind, to ignore the pain in his cramped legs. He held his breath to listen for sounds of Pratt breathing.

He heard nothing. A few minutes later he forced himself free, limb by limb. He peered around the bed. No Pratt. His breath blasted out in a harsh gasp. He staggered to his feet, winced, and rotated his stiff neck. His legs had become rubbery.

Ben lay immobile. His face pale as polished marble. The bed sheets were smooth. A fresh IV bag hung from the stand.

David reached into his smock. The two vials of blood were still there.

He hobbled to the door, but hesitated to turn the handle. Now he visualized Pratt just outside the hallway, arms crossed, waiting like a prison sentry at the mouth of a freshly-dug escape tunnel.

Carefully and silently, David opened the door.

The corridor was empty. He let out another long breath. He ran down the hall and entered the stairwell—one hand in his jacket pocket, holding onto the tubes.

He was so anxious to descend that he missed the last step on the floor below. Thinking fast, he turned as he fell, to not break the tubes in his pocket. He walked down the rest of the way.

Chapter 57

After she left David in the Chinese restaurant, Sammie sought the distraction of dinner and watching a video with her aunt. She fell asleep on her aunt's sofa. Alice let her nap so it was after 1:00 AM when she arrived home. Her answering machine was blinking. There were seven messages. She pushed PLAY while she kicked off her shoes.

"Sammie, it's David. I just wanted to apologize. I feel bad. Would you call me?"

She smiled, until the next message began. "Samantha, this is Gerald Barnes. Your aunt called me to check on the provisions of your father's Advance Directive now that he can't make decisions for himself. I was sorry to hear that. Can you call me tomorrow between 2:00 and 3:00?" Her lips tightened.

The next call was a hang-up. Then a surprise: "Samantha, this is Dr. Solomon. I got your message. So sorry to hear about your father. Of course I'll be available tomorrow morning. If I'm not in my office, page me through extension 578."

Sammie looked at her watch. 1:40 AM. Time for sleep.

"Sammie," the machine went on. "It's David again. Are you there?" He sounded breathless. "Sorry to call so late. It's almost two. I just left your father's room. I did it! I got the blood sample. Jesus, Nurse Pratt almost caught me. I ran down the steps so fast, I almost fell on the test tubes. Anyway, I'm calling from the lobby of University Hospital. I put my name on the lab slip and told them to rush so we'll get the results by noon. Call me, please. No matter what time you get this. I miss you."

Sammie stared at the phone in amazed joy. He'd done it. They'd have the evidence they needed in time for the hearing. So she'd get her father discharged from Memorial—

An arm snapped around her throat with crushing force.

Cameron sat alone in his office. Pratt's "fifty-fifty" deal reverberated in his mind. His body trembled as he wondered what Pratt was doing to Brewster's daughter. He checked his watch. He knew it would take Pratt an hour or two, to drive to Brewster's home, and do "what he had to do," before he'd call room 812 to motivate Ben to give his best performance. To allow the most time possible for re-recording, which might be necessary, he should prepare Ben's room for shooting the ***Finale*** prior to Pratt's call. But he wanted to avoid pacing anxiously for an hour or more in Ben's room as he waited. He had hardly slept in the last four days, so he set his cell phone's quick alarm to ring in a half-hour. But nagging thoughts of the consequences of setting Pratt loose prevented all hopes for a restful nap. Although it was still too early to set up the camcorders and solutions, he decided he'd just look in on Ben.

Sitting on the stool next to the bed in room 812, Cameron stared at Ben's placid face. Waves of anger alternated with respect. This man had attempted to destroy his project—for what? Goddamn personal pride. That's all. Yet he had also proved himself the perfect spokesman—determined, convincing, and clever.

Even though only he would hear it, he said, "I wish I'd known you under other circumstances. We might have been friends. I think you'd understand why I have to—"

His cell phone rang.

Cameron jumped. So soon? Taking a deep breath, he clicked it on. "Pratt?"

"Not quite," Hayneswurth said. "Working late, Doctor?"

Cameron stiffened and turned toward the window, as if Hayneswurth's face was plastered against the glass, staring in. "How did you know I was here?"

"At Walter Reed, you always put in long hours as your projects neared completion. How is our patient?"

Cameron swallowed. "Still unconscious. I was just about to wake him up—"

"Is the videotape done?"

"We're doing the final shoot tonight."

"But the hearing is tomorrow at four."

"You'll have the tapes first thing in the morning."

"I'd better. Especially if the Magistrate permits Brewster to leave. We can't afford—"

"Don't tell *me* what we can't afford. I know what's at stake. It's my career that ends the minute this tape goes public. I'm the one who is risking arrest and prison. I'm the only one on your Committee taking that kind of—"

"And all of us appreciate you're taking those risks. I just wanted to offer help."

Cameron's anger dropped on all sides, like ash from a volcanic eruption. "Okay, Howard."

"Another reason I called is to let you know that all the travel plans for you and your wife are set."

"Thanks. Look, I'm sorry... Everything's going fine. You'll see."

Years ago, Ben had argued with Sammie about studying martial arts. "You live in a violent city. You take vitamins for your health. Well, this is also important."

So she reluctantly trained with a group of women under Eric Johnson, an ex-Army Ranger her father knew. He taught "real self-defense, no fancy-schmantzy dancing bull shit." Wearing bulky pads and a football helmet, he attacked students ferociously, expecting them to defend themselves similarly. Gouging, screaming, foot-stomping, crotch-kneeing. "Go for eyeballs and guyballs," Eric put it, "Keep it low, keep it nasty, and never, never give up."

Repulsed by the other students' excitement about inflicting pain, after two months, Sammie enrolled in an Aikido class. Their ad said: "Fighting without fighting." Aikido consisted of holds and movements designed to harness an opponent's strength, and redirect it into a controlled throw or pin. No screaming, no gouging, no clawing, no intent to injure. Her instructor, a woman of only a hundred and fifteen pounds, tossed large men around like bags of feathers, smiling the entire time. The look of shock on the men's faces had been something to behold.

Aikido techniques must become deeply ingrained to become automatic, to flow smoothly from defense to control during violent situations. Given her limited training, Sammie doubted she had practiced enough to defend herself in an actual attack. So she was surprised by her reaction when the arm wrapped around her neck.

Instead of bracing herself and going rigid, she reached up, grasped the gloved wrist, and swept her upper body forward and down in a kind of twisting bow. Her assailant's aggressive power became the force that launched him up and over her. She heard his gasp of shock, followed by the glassy crash of his feet hitting the foyer chandelier overhead.

But when he writhed like a snake, she lost her grip on his hand. The dark shape tumbled away from her.

Eric Johnson's voice was suddenly in her head: "Here's your best technique, ladies: turn around and RUN." She bolted for the front door.

Cameron disconnected the IV bag labeled "5% dextrose" that also delivered Brevital and replaced it with another IV bag. While the label also said, "5% dextrose," the color of the label was different. This bag contained only dextrose.

He missed Pratt's help with the additional details, and his standing guard. He had instructed the night nurse not to disturb him under any circumstances. For the fourth time in the last half-hour, Cameron crossed the room, picked up the rubber stopper, jerked the door open, and peeked outside. No one there.

Movie time.

The first part of the routine had become automatic. He switched on the recorders, the Teleprompter, and checked the monitors of each of the three camcorders.

Now for the new stuff. He opened the closet, rolled out an IV stand holding three small bags he'd previously labeled with a magic marker as "**N**," "**A**," and "**P**." He removed the laptop computer from his attaché case and placed it under Ben's bed. He clipped a tiny microphone onto Ben's shirt and plugged its thin cable into the computer's sound port. He connected the thicker cable from the computer's serial port to three solenoid switches labeled "**N**," "**A**," and "**P**," in the valves below the IV bags.

He rolled the wobbly IV stand so that it stood out of Ben's view. Then he checked each camcorder to make sure it was out of their range.

He sighed and said, "Okay, we're ready."

The immobile body on the bed gave no indication that he heard his cue.

Since it would take several minutes for Ben to regain consciousness, Cameron could sit down, not to relax, but to use the time to think about what he had accomplished so far, and what challenges still remained.

His original design was to administer **N-A-P** through a feeding tube, not through an IV. But he had to change that plan when Ben's strategy exposed him. Cameron had strong feelings about Ben's behavior, but couldn't find the right words... Was it idiotic? Obstreperous? Petulant? Defiant? Arrogant?

Cameron realized he was engaging in intensely negative thinking, so he stopped himself. He routinely monitored his thoughts this way. He had learned that to deal with dying patients and not get totally drained required discipline in thinking. Usually, after he caught himself, his next step would be to ask where these thoughts came from. But this time, other thoughts intruded his mind. Was it not unkind to entertain negative thoughts about a man whose dying he was engineering? Again he caught himself: Now his negative thinking was directed at himself. His further attempts to explore his feelings would led him to realize how deep they went.

In truth, he would really miss Ben. Rarely had he met someone whose intelligence, logic, and breadth of knowledge matched his own. What a challenge it had been to try to convince Ben to participate willingly. Yes, Cameron had lost the argument, but still... the battle was so intense. At this point in his life, Cameron had few friends. Having left the other researchers behind, there was now actually, no one except Wendy. So under other circumstances... Again, stop! *Regrets are just another form of negative thinking.*

Finally, he admitted to himself what he had been doing: Emphasizing Ben's negative qualities was his subconscious attempt to decrease how important Ben was to him, so he would grieve his death less. In theory, the more he trashed Ben, the valuable he'd seem, so the less grief Cameron would have when Ben was gone. Yet Cameron knew this strategy would never work. After someone dies, selective memory sets in so that survivors recall only their positive virtues.

So Cameron would grieve Ben, his last patient, more than any other. It would be his saddest loss since Michelle Wintress, in her case the grief was based on guilt, not on his longing for a continued, rewarding companionship. That poor young woman was not terminal. Every time he thought about her, he shuddered. He also had to admit that had it not been for Pratt, she would be alive today. Her death still haunted his nights.

Cameron looked over at Ben. He began to stir, but was still not fully conscious.

Cameron realized there was yet one more component that added to his sadness. He identified it as a sense of incompleteness. Cameron found himself fantasizing about the original exquisite plan he had hoped to execute today. Had Ben gone along with the plan, then a couple of weeks ago he would have warned his patient about the dangers of aspiration pneumonia from his impaired swallowing muscles. He would have explained that food and fluid could enter his bronchial tubes, go down into his lungs, and cause a potentially lethal infection. The solution was to undergo a relatively simple operation to create a percutaneous endoscopic gastrostomy, or PEG. A tube would then deliver food and fluid directly into his stomach.

If Ben had a PEG tube now, Cameron could have easily explained on the video documentary that the medications Ben was receiving by a tube, other patients could simply drink, as long as they could move their arms and swallow safely. But now Cameron had to demonstrate his three-drug method using IVs, and it would not be obvious that the technique had wide applicability. Cameron would have to "tell," when he preferred to "show." For that he had Ben's pride that led to his refusal to cooperate. So Cameron had a mixture of negative and positive feelings toward Ben. How would they change after he was gone? Only time would tell.

Cameron looked over towards the bed. Ben was becoming alert. It was time...

Pratt was amazed. He hadn't been surprised, let alone thrown—in at least twenty-five years. How the hell did that happen? Was he stiff from crouching motionless in her closet for over an hour? Was he thinking about the last phone message, how that bastard Grainger got a blood sample from Brewster?

He hit the hardwood floor and rolled, then bounced to his feet. His old instincts quickly returned with full, exhilarating power. Getting thrown was not humiliating. It was permission. It validated everything he was about to do.

As the bitch gasped for air and bolted toward the door, he launched himself into the air and came down with a kick to her left kidney. Her scream turned into a whistling gasp as she slammed into the wall and dropped to her knees. Pratt scraped his fingers across her scalp, made a tight fist, and yanked her down to all fours. He straddled her, and reached around her throat to apply a strong sleeper-hold.

But she went insane. She thrashed, bucked, scuttled backward, and almost spilled him over her head.

Furious, he moved forward, clamped his thighs around her ears, then threw himself sideways to yank her onto her side. He almost laughed as he caught his breath. This maneuver was so sloppy it could have been performed at the World Wrestling Federation.

Now her hands pummeled his legs, clawed toward his crotch.

"Bitch!" He locked his ankles and squeezed his knees together—imagining her head was an orange he'd turn into juice. She moaned. Despite a strong vice, his rayon sweatpants slipped, permitting her head to turn. A sharp, burning pain shot up through Pratt's thigh. She was biting him and really going at it, gnawing through the loose cloth to his flesh beneath. He grimaced, trying to squeeze her head with all his strength as the burning, ripping sensation grew worse. He realized how close her chewing was getting to his femoral artery. One good bite through that and his blood would explode out by the pints.

"Goddamn it!" He could have wrenched himself erect but her teeth were so tight on his thigh, it would have ripped off too much flesh. So he formed a fist contorted to make his fused knuckles prominent, raised his elbow, and aimed the strike at her temple.

But her bloody hair and the sharp angle allowed his knuckle to graze off, and his thigh deflected some of the blow's force. After a moment, she started grinding away again. Hot, sticky wetness was pooling under his leg. He cocked his arm high over his head but she saw it, deflected his blow, and then grabbed his hand. Amazing. As he yanked his hand free, she ripped her head free from his thighs. He heard a crackling, like the shredding of hair—she tore his flesh and sweatpants. He rolled onto his hands and knees, stood up, and looked at her.

She scrambled back into a crouch. Her eyes were wide, blood smeared her teeth, lips, and chin.

In one smooth, continuous motion, from a runner's start position, he ascended from his back foot, raised his other knee. Kicking toward her nose.

Contact!

The sugary crunch of cartilage felt terrific.

Her head snapped back. Her eyes rolled up.

She hit the floor like a yard and a half of chain.

Chapter 58

"What's going on?" Ben's dream world with Gloria had faded again. "Is it night?"

"Yes, it's night. Give yourself a moment. Your disorientation will pass." Cameron leaned closer and put a straw to his lips. "Here." Ben stopped drinking and Cameron put the bottle aside. "We know what you've been doing, Ben. About your blinking Morse code."

There were times that being paralyzed helped. Ben had only to control his face.

"You were warned." Cameron's voice had the same soft, almost melancholic tone he'd used during the videotaping. "You can't say you weren't fully informed... I mean, warned."

Ben's lips were dry again. He licked them. "What the hell are you talking about?"

"Our deal. You promised you'd cooperate by making the video, and I promised Pratt would leave your daughter alone. You reneged. So you forced Pratt to take action."

"You bastard. What did you do?"

"I? I did nothing. It was you who turned Pratt loose."

"If anything happens to my daughter—"

"I didn't want things to go this way, Ben. Honestly. But you left us no choice."

Ben's tears of frustration burned down the sides of his face. "All right. What do you want?"

"What I've always wanted. My videotape. Done straight. No tricks."

"All right. You've got it. Just don't let that animal hurt my daughter."

"I wish you'd thought about that before you decided to play games with us, Ben. I never wanted anyone to get hurt. Still don't. And hopefully it won't take much for Pratt to convince you... Anyway, your daughter will come out all right. As long as you agree to shoot the video tonight, and commit **PAS** at dawn."

"Fine. I don't care. Just leave my daughter alone. Just don't hurt my daughter."

"Well," Cameron said, "right now, that's entirely up to you."

Pratt stood still for a minute, breathing heavily. His internal adrenaline added to the amphetamine he had taken; the combination amped him. He clamped his hand over his thigh to check his wound, to see if a pumping rush of blood would indicate his femoral artery had been severed. No, only ragged cloth and the hot pulp of ravaged skin. Goddamn bitch.

He drew his foot back, heel aimed at the crown of her skull, but caught himself. He couldn't kill Brewster's daughter. He needed her to get Ben to cooperate.

Okay, for one point five million, Bruce Pratt's pride could take a little hurting. He lowered his foot and crawled over to look at the bitch. Blood had pooled under her mouth but her breathing was good and her pulse steady. He grabbed her by the arms and lifted her, grunting at her surprising weight. He heaved her over his shoulders in a fireman's hold and carried her into the next room and threw her into the hospital bed. Perfect, with all the bars to tie her to. He raised the back of the bed so she wouldn't aspirate her own blood.

He went to the closet, retrieved his duffel bag, and got several pre-cut lengths of nylon rope. He tied the bitch to the bed with tight knots located far beyond her reach. He lashed a length of rope across her throat, snug enough so she couldn't struggle without strangling herself. He tied a blindfold across her eyes. Finally, he checked her respirations and pulse.

Then he limped back to his duffel bag and took out a bottle of peroxide, opened it, and poured some on his wound. Then he went around the house pouring peroxide on every drop of blood he could see—to eliminate all traces of his DNA. Finally, he poured some on the bitch's mouth, gawking at how the liquid transformed dark red to foamy pink.

He snapped open a capsule of smelling salts under the bitch's misshapen nose. She snorted, thrashed her head from side to side, and tried to sit up. Pratt watched as her face changed from disorientation to terror to shock, and finally to realization.

He leaned close to her ear. "Don't scream," he whispered. He made his voice low and hoarse. "Don't make a sound until I tell you to talk. Understand?"

She nodded, snuffled blood. Her breathing was harsh and quaking. Pratt knew few things were more frightening than being blind, helpless, and at the enemy's mercy.

He took the cordless phone, dialed, raised the receiver to his ear, and listened. "Cameron," a voice said on the other end. Without replying, Pratt brought the phone down by the bitch's mouth. She had no idea it was there. Pratt leaned very close. "All right," he whispered. "Tell me something, bitch—"

❧

"Tell me something, bitch." Pratt's voice, twisted into a harsh whisper, came out of the receiver Cameron held next to Ben's ear. "Tell me how you feel."

"What do you want?"

Ben's throat locked when he heard her high, thready voice. On impulse, Ben took a breath—as if to say something—then caught himself. No more cheating. He didn't dare. There was no point, anyway. He saw Cameron flick a switch on the phone. Most likely, the MUTE.

"I want you to say how you feel, bitch," Pratt whispered.

"I—I feel—What are you going to do to me?"

"Oh, that depends. That depends, now, doesn't it?"

Click. Dial tone.

"Satisfied?" Cameron took the receiver away from Ben's ear.

Deep inside himself, Ben was shaking. "What's that psychopath going to do?"

"He's going to wait. When I tell him the video has been completed to my satisfaction, he'll leave your house. Your daughter won't be harmed. I promise you. She'll think she was the victim of a burglar. On the other hand, if I don't call and state your performance was satisfactory, Pratt will—You know the evil that man is capable of better than I—"

"Okay. Let's just get on with it."

"Yes, let's." Cameron rose to his feet and pulled a disposable lighter out of his pocket. He flicked it on. The flame danced in his eyes, reflecting like a pair of glowing slits. "Time is growing short for everyone."

Pratt looked down at Brewster's daughter and wondered if he should keep her alive. He asked himself, if Cameron knew about the blood sample that Grainger had taken, what would he do? Panic and abandon the project? Ask Pratt to "take care of things" as usual? Who cares? Obviously, it was time to make a command decision in the field. Again.

To think logically, Pratt tried to get beyond his fury. He hated missing Grainger after noticing the Major's ruffled sheets. Nothing he could do about that now. He thought about the phone message. The blood sample was submitted under Grainger's name. So only he and the bitch could connect its results to Brewster. If Grainger disappeared before he retrieved the results, that would solve one part of the problem. The other part could disappear with the bitch, later. Pratt never saw any reason for her to live. Now, there was a compelling reason for her to die. But she needed to remain alive long enough to convince Ben to tape his final scene....

Pratt would arrange the scene to look like the bitch had been murdered after she interrupted a burglary. After he pushed the ERASE on the answering machine, he rifled the house and stuffed some jewelry into his pockets.

He glanced at his watch. The three hours Cameron would take to re-shoot the video was more than enough time to take care of Grainger. Piece of cake. Meanwhile, the bitch was securely tied to the bed. She didn't need him to baby sit.

David had just fallen asleep before the phone rang. He hoped it was Sammie as he snagged the receiver off its hook. "This is David."

An unfamiliar low and quivering voice said, "Excuse me, Doctah. Excuse me, but I think you want know. Bad thing happen to girlfriend."

David stiffened. "Who is this?"

"Please, no name. I orderly at Memorial. See you leave tonight, late. I know you close to daughter of patient in room 8-1-2. I hear bad thing tonight. You need to know."

David sat up straighter. "Bad thing? What bad thing?"

"No. Can't on phone. Must talk private. I show you. You come to hospital right away."

David threw back the sheets. "Wait, are you talking about Samantha Brewster?"

"Yes, yes, Bru-stah girl. Yes, very bad danger. You come hospital right away."

"But where in the hospital?"

"In basement, in morgue. I show you."

"In the morgue?"

"Yes, I show you. Private. Not much time. Very much danger, Doctah. Come right away."

The phone disconnected.

ᔕ❧

Terror overcame Sammie. She tried to move, but couldn't. Lashed down by her hands and neck. Gagged. Couldn't expel it with her tongue. Difficult to breathe around it.

Sammie hovered between two worlds—nothingness, and throbbing pain.

Sounds of objects being thrown around, thumps and clattering. Sounds of rifling through drawers and closets. The chaotic sounds stopped. A low muffled voice from the other room, the individual words inaudible.

Sammie knew it was Pratt from the fleeting image she caught, just before he kicked her.

Then, silence. But for how long?

She could hardly breathe. Her mouth was completely blocked. The left half of her face felt like hardening concrete and the left nostril was completely plugged. On the right, only a narrow passage. Breathing was like trying to fill her lungs through a soda straw.

Calm, she thought. Calm. Breathe slowly. Calm. Like meditation. Calm.

Still her terror grew, like a tethered crow beating its wings in her chest.

She jumped, hearing a harsh whisper. Airy, close to her ear, tickling the fine hairs. "I'm going to leave you for a while, girly-girl. Don't try to get free, you understand? You'll choke yourself. Or I'll choke you, later. Either way you'll suffer. Just take it easy now, and you'll get out of this. Understand?" The band around her throat got tighter for a moment.

She nodded as much as she could. A few seconds later she heard the front door open and close. She tried to relax, to suck in air.

She hurt from immobility. She twisted her hand restraints. The ropes were brutally tight. Her fingers couldn't find the knots. She yanked her feet against their lashings—only a slight quiver of the bed.

A roaring sound of pain filled her head. She forced herself to stop struggling, to lie back, to breathe slowly through her right nostril. To rebuild her strength. To be able to fight back, when Pratt returned.

❧

Cameron wasn't stressed from the pressure of time. Instead, he saw a creative opportunity in remaking the entire videotape in one night. The candles he'd just lit were symbolic. They'd burn down as the interview neared its conclusion. Sheer genius. Beautiful ambiance, with minimal contribution from indirect lights. The timing would permit the ***Finale*** to be shown at dawn so that as he panned out the window to the Washington Monument, the obelisk would seem ignited by the first rays of the sun, like a gigantic candle for all mankind.

Brewster was following his scripted lines, needing only an occasional glance at the Teleprompter. His voice sounded sincere. Cameron was moved. He'd taken Pratt's threat to heart. There was no blinking or grimacing.

Ben gazed steadily at Cameron and said, "I've thought about this for a long time. I asked, how can you possibly calculate what a life's worth? How can you decide when keeping someone alive is no longer a reasonable choice?"

❧

As the elevator doors opened in the hospital's basement, David's constant worry about Sammie got momentary relief from a possible hypothesis. Perhaps another intern was staging a morbid prank? If so, why play? Why not turn around, go home, and get two more hours of sleep. Then, tomorrow, when somebody slyly asks how he slept, he'd say, "Never better."

Within two seconds, he had to admit this hypothesis was ridiculous .

Worry increased as he continued marching down the floor of brown Linoleum, between walls faced with ochre-colored tiles. The long, poorly lit hall was silent, except for the throbbing of forced air through the ducts overhead.

With every step, his heartbeat pounded faster.

At the end of the hall, a pair of large, swinging doors stood under the sign MORGUE. David hesitated and looked behind him. No one. He wiped his hands on his pants, reached out, and tested one of the doors. It swung in easily.

David poked his head through. The cool air smelled strongly of formaldehyde. His eyes watered. One side of the hallway consisted of six rows of stainless-steel body lockers. Did he hear a slight scraping sound? Not sure. Perhaps he'd only imagined it.

Directly ahead, another pair of swinging doors had windows of pebbled glass. No sign, but David knew what room it was. The autopsy room.

David cleared his throat. "Is anyone here?"

Was there a flicker of movement behind the pebbled glass?

"Hello?" he cried, louder. "Who's there?"

No response.

He stiff-armed the swinging doors open.

He flicked up the light switch near the door, expecting the fixtures above the autopsy tables to respond. Instead all the ceiling lights went on, washing the room in flat white light.

Four stainless-steel tables dominated the autopsy room. Next to each table stood a small instrument tray on a swivel arm.

One table had a long paper sheet covering a body. He gulped, recalling the whispered word, "Danger," over the telephone. Was it Sammie?

The hairs on his neck seemed to fill with static electricity.

He forced himself to walk to the head of the table, to grab a corner of the paper sheet, to yank it down—

—The skin from the skull was inside out, folded over the forehead and eyes.

—David staggered back, striking the instrument tray with his hip, making it rotate in a half-circle—

"Oh, Jesus." His knees went limp.

To David, the grossest autopsy procedure was brain dissection. Before the cranium could be opened with a high-speed circular bone saw, the pathologist had to remove the skin over the skull. To expose the bone, the scalp was cut behind the head and pulled up and then down over the face. After removing the brain, the skin flap was replaced to make the cosmetics more acceptable, if the family wanted an open casket.

David sighed. The thick lips and missing teeth—Not Sammie.

The pathologist had stopped his work just before sawing the cranium. The instrument cart beside the corpse held the pathologist's tools, including the cranial saw, large and small bone shears, and various sized scalpels. A pathologist had left a chipped ceramic dinner plate, a wad of crumpled plastic wrap, and a crumpled Coke can. David thought how pathologists, often treated as second-class citizens by doctors of the living, often retaliated by adopting the same macabre habits people assumed they already had.

Without warning, the room went dark.

❧

"...It's a choice I haven't made lightly," Ben said, "and it's one that no one should be forced to make. However, I do think it's one that all competent human beings should have the right to make for themselves."

"Amen," Cameron said. The candles had burned down to a quarter of their original length. The air in the room had a slightly hazy quality, giving everything a celestial halo.

"Ben, you did very well. How are you feeling now?"

"I'm peachy," he said.

Cameron glanced at his watch. Less than two hours until dawn. “Let me explain what happens next. I never got the chance to tell you how technology can make it possible for a quadriplegic to commit suicide. The basic technology came from Australia, where the first legal **PAS** took place. Australia’s main government unfortunately changed the law after 1997, so the laptop used is now in a museum. But that’s another story.” Cameron pushed the IV stand into Ben’s view.

“These bags contain the most humane chemicals for someone to die peacefully and painlessly. The computer speech recognition program provides security because only you can turn them on. First the computer will learn to specifically recognize your voice. Then, it will not respond to the voice of anyone else.

“After you say your final words of good-bye, I’ll start the computer program and you’ll say, ‘This is Ben Brewster. Activate program.’ To prove your certainty, the computer will ask you three times: ‘Are you sure you’re ready to die now?’ Each time, you’ll answer, ‘*Yes . . . I am.*’ After the third time, the computer will trigger switches to infuse the sequence of medications from these IVs. Understand?”

“Ain’t technology wonderful.” Ben’s voice sounded papery.

“All right.” Cameron glanced at his watch again. “Are you ready?”

“I need to be sure my daughter’s all right.” Fierce, fighting eyes burned from Ben’s face. “If that goddamn Pratt hurts her, I swear I’ll come back from the dead and rip both your hearts out.”

“You have my word on that, Ben. Don’t forget, my goal is to relieve pain and suffering, not to cause it. However, I can’t let you say good-bye over the phone. Your daughter must continue to think you’re in a coma.”

“Then what will she think when she sees me alert, articulate—even eloquent—on your goddamn video?”

“Here’s what she’ll believe. You spontaneously came out of your coma tonight and we discussed your options. You decided not to take the chance of falling into a Permanent Vegetative State and requested my help to commit Physician-Assisted Suicide. I had the courage not to turn you down, but insisted you protect me from prosecution by videotaping your request. As your last hurrah, you took the opportunity to wax eloquent—”

“With three professional digital camcorders? Won’t that make Sammie suspicious?”

“No, this is a research and teaching institution. We tape many things. I’ll say we decided to edit the interview only as an afterthought because of your eloquence.”

Hope flickered on Ben’s face as Cameron wished Pratt would truly let Ben’s daughter live. Though sad about Sammie’s fate, Cameron realized it was totally Ben’s fault. Had he not pulled his stubborn Morse code trick, this would never have happened. Now, there was absolutely nothing Cameron could do about it.

Anyway, the sun was due to rise. It was almost time for the ***Finale***.

Sammie could barely flex her hands and feet, or turn her head. She thought how similar her ordeal was to her father's paralysis. Ropes restricted her activity as sure as neuro-chemical inertia bound her father.

She frantically hauled air through the burning tunnel of her right nostril. Staying calm was essential. Otherwise, it was more difficult to breathe. Another similarity to what her father had to endure—

Her mind continued to churn. Why had Pratt come here? Had he come only to attack her? Why did he hide his identity with that hoarse whisper? Why tie her up instead of killing her? Was blackmail keeping her alive? He must have heard David's message. He rummaged the place after he tied her up, but he never questioned her. What was he looking for?

Pratt knew the blood sample would incriminate him. So he'd have to eliminate David. So David was in great danger. But he had no way of knowing. Only she could help—

Her usable nostril contracted. The air passage shrank to a pinhole. The darkness in the room deepened, congealed, fluttered around the edges. Sounds receded.

Calm, she thought, *calm*. But in her head, she heard many voices of many teachers over many years—Aikido, meditation, guided imagery, yoga—

Yoga.

She always kept up with basic stretching and breathing exercises. *Mind and body are one. Together, they can grow stiff and sore—or loose and supple.* Sammie recalled the complicated postures she had mastered. Being strapped to a bed no longer seemed hopeless. *Breathe*, she told herself, *relax. Become like the blade of grass bending in the wind, like the stream flowing around the rocks, like the wind even mountains cannot stop.* She filled her lungs with air. *That's it. Free your body by freeing your mind. You're only a prisoner if you believe you are.* Her respiratory rate and pulse slowed.

She concentrated on her hands. *Think of them not as flesh and bone but as energy, as ether, as an illusion in the shape of a hand. Which they really are—quantum particles, solid and wave-like at the same time, indefinable, and ephemeral.*

She visualized her hands changing shape, elongating, the thumb bending inward onto the palm, the whole hand narrowing. Becoming a tube of light. She imagined it happening. Sensed it happening.

The ropes were getting looser.

Her ex-SEAL self-defense instructor had said, "You can make yourself real difficult to get a hold of." Her father had pointed out, "Some people, like Houdini, can make their hands physically smaller than their wrists."

The loops of rope shifted against her skin. Her heartbeat began to accelerate, but she concentrated hard on relaxing. She gradually pulled her right hand against its restraints, gently twisted it from side to side, imagined her hand growing even more tapered, more narrow—

The rope clung to her skin, held on. She thought of her skin as grease, as oil. Pulled against the ropes, waggled her wrist, twisted it—

—And felt the first loop of rope pop down over her knuckles.

⁂

For a moment David was blinded by darkness. Then, across the room, he spotted the floating rectangles of the two windows in the swinging doors. They let in a wan gleam, picked up here and there by green EXIT signs.

In this uncertain light, David saw movement. A shape slipping toward him, first as a silhouette against the windows, then a pale specter in the gloom. "Who's there?" David bellowed, his voice cracking. "Who are you?"

"Shhh! Is me. Is me." The voice, low and urgent—as it sounded over the phone. "Don't want you see face. Just want tell you about girlfriend." The ghostly figure moved sideways, circling the autopsy table farthest from David. There was a slight scraping sound, like metal on metal, and an instrument tray glinted as it shifted on its wheels.

"Wait," David said. "Don't come any closer. Someone—"

"I know, I know, bad people here," the man said. "Hear talking. Hear things very important for you." He drifted closer.

"I said stop!" David took a step back, felt the instrument cart shift against his hip again. "Stop right there. Talk to me from there."

"No, no, must show you something." The pale shape came around the foot of the autopsy table. "Must show you—this!" And it hurtled forward.

The large knife would have entered David's thorax but he was standing in front of the instrument stand and it deflected its trajectory. David jerked to one side, responding to a spine-deep reflex, grabbed some instruments off the tray and threw them at the oncoming figure. There was a crash, a furious shout. David turned and scrambled around the head of the autopsy table, and ran toward the swinging doors.

His foot caught on a dangling cord. It coiled around his leg and he toppled forward, throwing out his hands to fend off the stainless-steel corner of the next autopsy table. He landed flat on his chest. The air punched from his body, his chin cracked against the floor, and the world erupted into a ball of molten red light.

I can't pass out.

He started crawling—unable to breathe or get to his feet. His chest seemed wrapped in iron bands, his limbs trembled like an infant's. His hand struck something flat and hard lying on the floor—the ceramic plate from the instrument tray. He picked it up.

He heard a footstep behind him and flew to his feet, spinning halfway around. His lungs opened with an explosive gasp, and his vision began to return in disassembled cubes.

A figure stood not five feet away, wearing a black sweat suit, eyes glinting. He raised something metallic, like a huge scalpel, except for the cruel hook at its point. "Lots of handy tools around here, aren't there?" he asked. Now he had no accent at all.

"Pratt!"

The large hooked blade tilted, creating a small nova of light. David's eyes drew to the gleam, aware of nothing but the thundering of his heart in his ears.

He had never been so afraid.

"This might sting a little," Pratt said, and lunged forward, blade extended.

David unwound his body with a snap, his right arm flying up and out at the last instant, releasing the dinner plate like a Frisbee.

With a crack like a well-hit baseball, Pratt's upper body reversed direction—going backward while his legs continued forward. For a moment he hovered on his back in mid-air, then he dropped. Shards of broken crockery clattered to the floor around him.

David didn't wait. Turning, he headed toward the doors.

Pratt scrambled like a crazed man, so fast that he put himself between David and the doors. David turned back, sprinting to protect himself behind the autopsy table.

Chapter 59

After she freed herself from her father's hospital bed, Sammie discovered that all the phones were dead. Pratt must have cut the main line. Her cell phone was in the car. Wincing from the pain of returning circulation, she grabbed her keys. In the garage, she leaped into her car and pulled open the glove box.

She automatically punched in David's number, as she started the engine.

The car weaved down the driveway in high-speed reverse. With every heartbeat, her nose throbbed with pain. She turned down the street and looked up. The clouds in the east outlined the approaching dawn.

"Hello," a cheerful voice said in her ear, "this is Dr. Grainger. I'm only home for about six minutes a week, so if you're a burglar you've got lots of time to—"

She pushed the END button, pushed down hard on the gas, and hoped out loud. *Please, David, be sleeping peacefully in bed. Be ignoring your phone—*

What should she do? Go to David's, to see if he was all right? Head straight for the hospital and her father? Either way, twenty minutes. She clutched the steering wheel in anguish. Her father was the prime target, the nexus of all this violence. David didn't answer so he might not even be there.

Call the hospital? Demand that security send guards to her father's room? No, they'd take her for a crazy woman and connect her to the psychiatrist on call.

Call the police? They might just call the hospital and be connected Cameron.

And what if the wrong people intercepted her call? She had no idea who else at Memorial was involved in this conspiracy. Giving herself away could be disastrous.

She took a corner on two wheels. Never a fast or aggressive driver, she remained calm as the horizon tilted, then dropped back into place.

She needed help that she could trust. Someone who had clout at the hospital, who could rally the troops up to the PCC right away—

Of course!

~

Cameron asked, "Give me an idea of what you'll say in the final scene, okay?"

"Well, it will be hard to say good-bye to my daughter on videotape, but as long as I'm not looking at you, it will come from my heart." Ben wanted to transcend his anger, and his fear. He knew he would have little time so he hoped he could express his positive feelings. "Then I'll say good-bye to my sister, some friends, and the people I've worked with over the years."

"Fine. Feel free to talk as long as you wish."

"Give me a break," Ben said. "You'll just edit out most of what I say anyway."

"You're a very intelligent man. A real loss to humanity. I really mean that."

"I'm sure you do."

Cameron closed the closet doors and wheeled the cart toward the bed. He lifted its wheels over a camera cable snaking across the floor. He connected the tubing from the triple IV setup to the shunt in Ben's arm.

"All right," Cameron said. "I'll start the camcorders so you can say your good-byes. Then I'll stop the camcorders for our rehearsal, which will allow me to demonstrate the technology to you. Then, I'll restart the camcorders and explain the technology to the viewing audience. Understand?"

"Yes, I understand," Ben said. "I'm a very intelligent man, remember?"

"Intelligent enough, I hope, to understand what this production means for mankind. You're making the greatest contribution of your life, right now."

Ben quirked his upper lip. "And for all this, I have you to thank, don't I?"

⁂

Near the head of the autopsy table, David tripped on something soft but firmly attached to the floor. He toppled forward, but managed to catch himself on his hands and protect his aching chest from hitting the floor. Directly in front of him, the tile was illuminated with pre-dawn light that fell from the high, narrow autopsy room windows—a long, bright carpet reaching down from freedom.

Something hard slammed into his ribs. Pain shot through his lungs. His torso floated up, then collapsed onto the floor. He opened his eye. The toe of a nurse's white sneaker pointed right at his eye.

"I'm tired of getting hurt by you stupid-ass amateurs," Pratt said in a matter-of-fact voice. The toe flicked David's chin. He moaned, flopped onto his back, saw Pratt as enormous, almost ceiling-tall from his perspective. Blood ran down the nurse's nose.

"Usually," he said, "I like to kill using local tools. It throws the cops off. Like when I ran down that social worker with a stolen car."

David was stunned. Pratt killed Michelle. "You?"

"But sometimes, it's best to use your own tools and get the job over with. Like now." Pratt reached behind and brought his hand back again for David to see a large hunting knife.

David pawed around for something to use as a weapon. A shard of broken plate. Anything. Desperate, all he could find was the cord he'd tripped over. It dangled from the darkness, terminating at a moderately heavy, unanchored object. He couldn't see what it was, but he pulled on the cord—

Pratt bent low. "You know, this is just business, down here. Like what's going on upstairs with the Major. At least the pay for my giving vacations keeps on getting better." Pratt raised the knife toward David. "'Bye now."

David tugged the cord again. An object suddenly came to his hand—the cranial saw. He grabbed the saw and raised it.

The jagged circular saw met Pratt's forearm as he came down with the knife. For a moment, they were in a metallic arm wrestle. As Pratt leaned his whole body weight with his knife from above, David pressed the sharp blade of the cranial saw against Pratt's forearm from below. For the moment, it stopped Pratt's knife.

The harder Pratt pushed, the harder the saw gashed into his forearm. Pratt gritted his teeth, hesitated, then pressed even harder.

The knife inched closer to David's throat.

❧

"...And finally let me say good-bye to all those people who, like me, are suffering, or will suffer, from incurable, chronic diseases. May you all have the opportunity to make your own decisions about when and how you will die."

Out of sight, from behind, Cameron said, "Your words were heartfelt. Perhaps I should have kept out of other portions of this video." But as he said these words, Cameron was taking the opportunity to remove one tie and put on another that had a different color.

Cameron leaned over to come back into the view of the close-up camcorder. He smiled and nodded to Ben, and said, "Your life included a richness of many warm relationships, Ben. I am sorry to have met you only recently."

Cameron glanced toward the window. Only minutes until dawn. His spirits felt ready to take flight with the first light of the sun.

As Cameron walked toward the camcorders, he looked back at Ben and said, "Okay, I'm shutting off the camcorders." But he was merely pretending for Ben's benefit. Standing between Ben and each camcorder, he covered the red lights with small pieces of black electrical tape.

"Are you ready now, Ben?" he asked.

"Yes. I'm ready."

"Good. First, we'll set the computer security so that only you can activate it. Then, we'll have a brief rehearsal to make sure the final part goes smoothly."

❧

Pratt forced down the knife so it was only three inches from David's carotid artery. David's knew his upward pressure with the cranial saw blade could not stop Pratt for long. Pratt had both positional advantage and high tolerance for pain. David tried to equalize their positions. He braced his leg to the side and strained to push the saw against Pratt's forearm. He used all his strength to roll Pratt over. Pratt's body went through a peak of resistance and then rolled more easily.

As they rolled, David's shoulder squeezed against a round, soft object attached to the floor.

A startling whine. Shrill. A smell like burnt plaster filled the air. Warm mist spattered David's face. What happened? The cranial saw blade had abruptly started. David's shoulder had rolled over and activated its foot switch.

Pratt's severed hand—still holding the knife—fell onto David's chest.

Pratt shrieked with disbelief. He reared back, looking at his detached hand. The sleeve of Pratt's sweatshirt was torn, red and black, glistening. Blood poured from the middle of his forearm. Pratt screamed again and collapsed on his back, his left hand jerking wildly...

David pulled himself up to his knees, panting, the saw motor singing and trembling in his blood-gloved hand, the whirling blade a pink disk of light. After a moment, he used his hand to push down on the foot switch and the shrill whining stopped. Now, only Pratt's grunting could be heard.

"Happy?" Pratt tried to sit up. "Think you're hot shit?" He got half-way up to sitting, but then fell straight down with startling totality, a marionette released, the back of his head thumping against the floor next to the autopsy table. He crumpled into a disjointed heap.

David stood up over Pratt, reached into his side pocket, found the tourniquet, tied it as tightly as possible just under Pratt's elbow. He began to examine the wound itself more closely, until he realized what he was doing. Tending his wounds? Jesus!

Then David recalled Pratt saying something about the business of what's happening up there. Ben was in danger.

David kicked the cranial saw out of his way, turned and stumbled toward the swinging doors, which he hit at a shambling run. He ran through the morgue into the hallway beyond. He grabbed the wall phone. "Operator, no time to connect me. Listen. A man down in the Morgue just lost his hand. Severed by a saw. Call the ER staff to send someone down to help him. Also alert the hand surgeon team. Got that?"

As he heard the PBX operator respond, David wondered if she'd believe him if he told her what was going on in Ben's room so all he said was, "Send security to room 812. This is Dr. Grainger. I'm on my way there to explain why."

His arms and legs felt cold. The cuffs of his jacket were dripping with blood. He jolted over to the hallway doors and crashed through them.

He ran to the elevator, stopped, and caught his breath.

A few seconds later, he exited the main floor.

Chapter 60

After the "practice session," Cameron approached each camcorder and pretended to turn it back on, but all he really did was remove three pieces of electrical tape. He aimed one camcorder at the laptop and zoomed in to capture its screen.

He removed the lapel microphone from Ben's shirt, looked directly into the middle camcorder and said, "Before we proceed, I want to demonstrate our *speech-recognition program*. Its purpose is to make sure that only Mr. Brewster has control over what will happen next, not I. If any final decision about life and death is made here, it will be made by Mr. Brewster, no by me. Let me demonstrate how technology can prevent euthanasia and allow only Physician-Assisted Suicide. This same technology makes Physician-Assisted Suicide possible for patients with severe physical disabilities. Ben, as you know, is a total quadriplegic.

"First note how the computer does not respond to my words. Note the laptop." Cameron paused briefly and then said, "This is Ben Brewster. Activate program."

The laptop screen did not change.

He replaced the microphone to Ben's shirt. "Now, Mr. Brewster, if you want to, if you are sure, you must say those words."

Ben took a deep breath. "This is Ben Brewster. Activate program."

Almost immediately, the computer screen changed to show the words, "PROGRAM SUCCESSFULLY ACTIVATED." A robotic-sounding monotone pronounced the same words.

Then the computer voice asked, "Has your life reached the point where you no longer want to live? Are you ready for self-deliverance now?"

Ben closed his eyes. "*Yes . . . I am.*"

After a pause, "Are you really sure?" the computer asked.

"*Yes . . . I am.*"

Cameron leaned over Ben.

The computer said, "Listen carefully as this next message is extremely important. If you answer '*Yes . . . I am*' one more time, the computer will activate the switches to send lethal doses of medications into your bloodstream. This is your final warning. Do not answer '*Yes . . . I am*' again—unless you are absolutely certain that you are ready for peaceful death. Do you want to die, now?"

A second later, Ben said, "This is Ben Brewster. Activate program."

Cameron's energy slumped. Damn it, Brewster had not said, "*Yes . . . I am.*"

The computer repeated its final routine. "Remember, if you answer '*Yes . . . I am*' one more time, the computer will activate the switches—"

"Doctor, I must ask you one question," Ben interrupted.

Cameron uncapped a syringe he held hidden in one hand. "Yes?"

"I must have proof that my daughter is alright. Let me hear her talk on the phone one last time, to assure me that she's all right. Then I promise, I'll go through with it."

Cameron smirked. Now he could not give the tapes to Hayneswurth. There was no problem giving Howard tapes with good-byes that were too long, or side comments about standing out of the way. But threatening Ben's daughter could never be revealed. Cameron would have to edit all three tapes. That would take at least an hour. He sighed. —Just one minor, but annoying detail. Ben would be dead, the video would be complete, and he and Wendy would be embarking to the other side of the world.

"Sorry, Ben, you have no choice but to trust me. See this syringe? It contains five times the amount of Brevital I've given you to induce your temporary comas. This high a dose won't just put you to sleep. It will kill you instantly. Like vets use for dogs. I'm ready to use it, if I need to. And it won't be hard to edit in one of your practice '*Yes . . . I am*' statements for the benefit of our viewing audiences. You see, Ben, I never turned off the videos during our *rehearsals*."

"You bastard!"

"Major Brewster, please, now. If you want your daughter to stay safe—Once more, with feeling!"

Pratt didn't want to open his eyes, to see his severed hand. He had to focus, to think through how to salvage his situation. He didn't have to see how screwed up he was.

He thought about the time in 'Nam when he'd taken a punji stake through the heel. Hell, the goddamned thing had burrowed straight up through his ankle and calf muscle before popping out through the skin behind his knee. Nasty, nasty, wound—especially because the stake had been smeared in human excrement. Pratt had feared the smell of gangrene would give him away before he got out of Indian Country.

But he got out. And despite what the medics told him, he even kept his leg.

But this time he wouldn't be so successful. The amputation was squeaky clean, of course. But it was so high up that no surgeon could reattach his arm so that it'd work. Forget his right forearm. It was gone. Perhaps he could count all his money with his left hand—

If he survived.

How could he get out of here? He was too dizzy to stand up, let alone run. It wasn't the pain. He always could handle pain. It was the dizziness from losing so much blood. Goddamn, he was still oozing where the bitch first bit him. Then, that enormous gush from his forearm—

Pratt heard Grainger call the ER. Too bad he admitted so much... The social worker, the Major, the bitch, and Grainger himself. Too many completed or attempted murders. Not good. Life without parole would be the best to hope for.

Maximum security, federal style, with only one hand? No picnic. Not being able to defend himself, he'd be at the mercy of every hard-up homo in the whole prison. That image disgusted Pratt. Even though most are amateurs, some are hardened criminals. Even amateurs... Look what the last two had done to him.

The men who returned from torture by the Cong motivated the others to carry cyanide pills to avoid fates worse than death. Now, Pratt faced one.

Pratt never thought he'd see the day when he'd give up. Figured he'd offer his cyanide to some other sad bastard. But the thought of spending the rest of his life trying to fight off being used like a male whore...

Pratt's capsule was deep in his right pant pocket. His right arm just hung there, throbbing with pain, still trickling blood. He rolled onto his left hip and strained to reach his right pocket with his left hand. He twisted his back and leaned his shoulder over toward his right knee. Not even close. He still couldn't reach into that pocket. Damn!

Frustrated, exhausted, leaning back to rest a moment, he heard sounds from down the hall: Elevator doors opening, two men talking. "Watch the stretcher on that door. There he is, down there."

Time was running out. He had a choice to make. Suffer a life of indignity, or opt out as an honorable soldier. Pratt unbuckled his belt with his left hand, pulled down his pants, and reached into the pocket. Removed the capsule, put it between his front teeth.

Honorable? Tried to pull his pants up before the final bite into the capsule. Sat up, to pull up on the waistband. Became dizzy, let go of his pants, fell over. His head hit the cold floor. The impact through his chin crushed the capsule. Some of the powder spilled onto his lips and the floor.

He swallowed the rest, even though he knew the lower dose would make his death slower, more conscious, and far more painful.

Pratt heard someone approach. He could no longer suck in air, like a vise had closed in on his chest. The cyanide hit his stomach. His gut spasmed with the greatest pain he'd ever experienced. He convulsed, then gagged on vomited blood. He squirmed across the floor—as if it would help him escape his misery. He snarled, clawed upward with his bloody fingers, then just lay there, motionless.

He was dimly aware of two men standing over him. "Lenny, you jerk. You left the Ambu bag upstairs." The other, "Hey, nobody told us he couldn't breathe." The first bent down, looked at Pratt's mouth. The other yelled, "Wait, don't give mouth-to-mouth. Smell bitter almond? And there's powder on his lips? Could be cyanide."

A minute later, Pratt felt himself being rolled onto the gurney. His darkness had turned utterly white.

David ran toward the PCC wing. A few strolling people seemed unalarmed as they stepped out of his way.

Waiting, waiting ... in front of the PCC elevator, David's previous experience seemed surreal. Cutting off a murderer's arm with a cranial saw... David's aching chest and side, his throbbing, bruised chin, the congealed blood made it seem more real. Still, a severed hand ... holding a knife ... about to cut David's jugular—

Pratt's words replayed in his mind about the Major's business, up there...

A minute later he was riding the elevator up to the PCC.

David paused to ask the Filipino nurse on the eighth floor, "Is security here yet?" She looked bewildered and shook her head. "Call them," he yelled. "Tell them, go to Room 812. Right away." He dashed down the hall.

❧

As Sammie sprinted into the lobby, she saw a gnomish figure running down the hall in an overcoat. Were those pajamas under his coat? Running beside him were two security guards and an orderly. —All toward the elevators.

"Dr. Solomon!" she yelled.

❧

Relief washed over Cameron when Ben finally said, "Yes . . . I am." Now he breathed deeply as the word "INFUSE" flashed on the computer screen. He heard a soft click as the first solenoid relay opened. The bag with the letter "N" started to tremble slightly, as it began delivering the first of the three medications. It emptied in a minute. Then, the bag with the letter "A" began to infuse. When it finished, the final bag with the letter "P" would infuse.

As Cameron watched the automatic process, he thought how, within less than five minutes, Ben would slip into a very deep sleep. Within a half-hour, his heart and lungs would stop, peacefully, and forever.

Cameron watched Ben close his eyes and mused how no one had yet invented an instrument that could measure a person's serenity as they were finally freed of their suffering.

It was now time to reveal to his viewing audience, the names and the dosages of **N-A-P**, the three medications he had just used, how none of them were particularly lethal when taken alone, but how in combination, they could hasten dying—as they would now witness—

And then—

A rattling sound. Something crashed into the door so hard the upper corner bent in sharply, then sprang back. The shock wave shook the rubber wedge loose.

The door burst wide open, whacking it into the wall.

Cameron stared at the young man barging in.

"Stop!" he said, "Stop!" The doctor's whites were bloodstained, his hair unkempt, his eyes wild. What was familiar about his face? Fear. As if threatened. Cameron knew him.

"Grainger!" Cameron yelled. "Get the hell out of here. You have no right—"

"Help me!" Ben croaked. "Get this thing out of my arm! He's trying to kill me!"

Grainger glanced at the three-bag infusion set-up, hit Cameron in the side of his chest to move him away, and leaped toward Ben's IV.

"No!" Cameron made a fist with the emergency syringe, raised it and walloped Grainger in the abdomen. He pushed the plunger in, to empty its contents.

With a stunned look, the young doctor's eyes closed as he slumped to the floor.

For a moment, everything was quiet.

Then the door banged against the wall again. Solomon rushed in, followed by the Brewster girl who yelled, "What's going on?" Solomon went to Grainger. Two security guards entered the room and moved steadfast toward Cameron who stood there, behind the bed—

Then, a loud voice at the door. One of the newer orderlies. "Can I help?"

"Get the crash cart," Solomon yelled, "He's not breathing. I need the Ambu bag." Solomon picked up the syringe lying near David and turned to Cameron. "What was in this?"

The question hung in the air as Cameron ducked between the two security guards. He tried to bolt for the door, but one guard caught his arm from behind. Cameron went wild, kicking their shins, flinging his arms at everything within reach.

The guards were twisting Cameron's arms as Solomon shouted, "Call the psych ward. Tell them to send some of their big guys. With major tranquilizers. Stat."

"I've already got some Versed in the crash cart, if you want," said the orderly.

"I have to continue squeezing David's bag. Take my order to inject an ampule IM, into Dr. Cameron, okay?"

"Yes, Sir," said the orderly.

Cameron tried to squirm away from the security guard's hold as someone cut through his coat and shirt sleeves.

As he heard the words, "Don't move," Cameron felt a stick in his left shoulder muscle. He was aware of taking his first deep breath since the door burst open. He thought, maybe it's time to give up. He struggled less, expecting to soon experience that sweet loss of consciousness he'd so often observed in his patients.

But a moment later, his heart was pounding, strong and fast. "I've got terrible chest pain. And it's traveling down my left arm." He was overcome with fear. "I'm—I'm—"

"Hey look, he's short of breath and sweating," said the orderly.

"My God!" Cameron clutched at his chest. "I'm having a heart attack. Help me."

"I could put him on a gurney," the orderly said, "and have him down at ICU in less time than a code blue team would take to get here."

"Let him," Cameron said. "We've never done CPR on the PCC."

Solomon looked up. "Okay. Guards, you go along."

As Cameron was being helped on the gurney, he grabbed his chest and closed his eyes. To him, the chest pain represented the loss of all his dreams. He thought of Wendy. She needed him. He couldn't die. Not yet.

The next time Cameron opened his eyes, he was looking at an elevator ceiling. "Please. Go fast."

❧

A warm hand caressed David's forehead, gently closed his eyes, and smoothed out his eyelids. They infused love. A strange repeating hissing and thunking were the only sounds.

He opened his eyes.

"Thank God." A woman's voice, interspersed with crying.

Another voice, "He'll be able to breathe on his own soon. He'll be fine."

David tried to talk, but couldn't. Something was blocking his throat.

"David?" The woman's voice again, now joyous.

Again he tried to talk but he couldn't even smile. He closed his eyes as something slid up his throat and out of his mouth. Then he opened them again.

"Come on, David," the woman said. "Keep coming back. Keep coming back."

He tried to answer, but his breaths seemed too short. He needed more air—

Gradually he became aware of a reddish glow in front of him. Darker areas moving across it. He opened his eyes.

The room was full of light and people. Everyone was surrounded by a corona. Bandages on the woman's face and nose. Staring at him, her mouth trembling between a smile and a sob. Sammie! But her face... Something terrible had changed one side of it. What happened? Why couldn't he remember?

He struggled to take in air. "Hello."

The uninjured half of Sammie's face broke into a radiant grin. "You'll be okay."

Dr. Solomon's face appeared. "That was a close call. It's been years since I used an Ambu bag."

"Thanks," David croaked, as his memory returned. "How's Ben?"

"He's fine. He's upstairs. Before you fell from the Brevital that Cameron pumped into you, you grabbed Ben's IV and ripped it out of his arm. You saved his life."

"What happened to Dr. Cameron?"

"He had a heart attack and was on his way to the ICU and..."

David waited for Solomon to continue, wondered why he paused. "And?"

"Somehow he never got there. The police are looking for him now. He couldn't have gone too far. Given what Ben said, he'll face charges of at least attempted murder."

"Right. What? Ben can talk again? I don't understand?"

"His coma was induced by Brevital, part of Cameron's plan."

"Oh my God. Sammie, you were right. What about Pratt?"

"They couldn't save him despite infusions of nitrite and thiosulfate."

"Infusions? For what? I asked for hand—or arm surgery."

"He took a cyanide pill. The emergency department tried the usual antidotes but they didn't help. His blood pressure was too low and he had lost too much blood. He died about an hour after he arrived in the ER."

He heard Sammie say, "He didn't deserve to live."

David nodded. He was exhausted. It would take him a while to put all this together. He took a big breath and let his eyelids close. He felt lips pressing softly to his and he smelled Sammie's sweetness. In his ear, a soft whisper. "You'll feel better soon, and then, we'll go dancing."

He wasn't sure whether he really said, "Yes," before he fell back to sleep, but when he woke up later, he remembered his dream. Sammie and he were dancing.

⁂

Robbie had a part-time job in addition to working as an orderly at Memorial, so he never had time to visit the Lincoln Memorial. Tonight's meeting could have been an awesome treat, with the floodlights creating harsh shadows between its columns. Yet he paced with anxiety as he wondered if he'd gotten himself into deep shit. There were two possibilities—

A figure emerged between the next-to-last and last columns on the right. It extended a piece of paper. "Here's the title to your brand new Harley. Thanks. Good job."

"A favor for a favor, eh boss? Seems like old times, doesn't it?"

"In a way. Have a nice ride—"

"Wait a sec. I've got to know—What happened to Dr. Cameron?"

"Robbie, trust me. The less you know, the better. But don't worry, you have my word. Your injection just raised his blood pressure to *simulate* a heart attack. You did not kill him. And that's all you need to know."

"I'd feel better if I knew he was alive. He looked awful when you took him from the elevator. After all those articles in the newspapers... Is he missing or dead?"

"That's not for you to know. Just forget it. Enjoy your bike. Have a nice, long ride."

"Can I explain why it makes a difference to me? It's because—"

Robbie stopped talking when he realized that the figure was already halfway down the steps.

Chapter 61

Sammie lingered outside after saying good-bye to their last guest. She smelled her mother's roses through the muggy August air. This afternoon's engagement party was a success. Most important, she was happy that she'd finally found the right man to share her life with. But that was tempered with sorrow for her father as his power faded. She glanced at the photos on display, as she walked down the hallway. Pictures of Dad crouched before hulking choppers full of bullet holes, surrounded by grinning soldiers, decorated in dress uniform with medals, shaking hands with politicos and celebrities. And now—

She opened the bedroom door and watched Dad turn from David to her. "What a wonderful party./ You are so beautiful. / I wish you both / so much / happiness."

Over the past two months, Ben's ability to breathe had declined dramatically. Reduced lung capacity limited him to a few words between short gasps for air. He tried to compensate by more judicious choices of words, but Sammie still missed his convoluted rhetoric couched in complex sentences.

"Did Solomon / say anything / about the search / for that bastard Cameron?"

"Now the FBI is assisting the DC police," said David. "They say they have some leads."

"What leads?"

"Cameron's wife has advanced breast cancer, so the FBI notified all the major medical centers. Admitting departments are now on alert for new patients with her specific diagnosis, especially if they show up without previous medical records. And the FBI is on the alert for overseas shipments of her anti-cancer drugs. Of course, there are always reported sightings of Cameron, but so far—"

"Nothing solid," Ben grunted.

"It's so amazing. By the time they identified the new orderly as the one who wheeled Cameron away on that gurney," said David, "the guy had died in a freak motorcycle accident. With Pratt dead, there's no one left to sue, except the hospital. Human Resources should have done a better job on background checks."

"No suing. / Anger is its / own punishment. / It would only / make it worse. / Pick up that little book / from my night table. / Read page one / out loud."

Seeing David behave like an obedient son warmed Sammie's heart. It had been so long since David had enjoyed a father-son experience. Her intended took a deep breath and read from a small book,

"For hatred can never put an end to hatred.
Love alone can.
This is an unalterable law.
People forget that their lives will end soon.
For those who remember, quarrels come to an end."

David looked up and turned to Sammie. She saw the love in his eyes. Now her father spoke.

"That's from Buddha's / *Dhammapada.* / Now, there's something I want / to talk to you both about. / It's important."

Something important? Sammie nodded, but her stomach was a churning mess. Was this the conversation she'd been dreading? Would Dad announce he'd decided to refuse a ventilator? She looked at him. Probably not. His expression did not seem that foreboding.

"What is it, Dad?" she forced herself to ask.

"Dr. Kenard / called me / earlier today."

"Oh no!" Sammie said. "You're not considering—" Her concentration was so intense, she hardly noticed his pausing for breaths. David said he felt the same way, after a while.

"**PAS**? / No honey, / I'm not. / It's Kenard. / He's in trouble. / He's facing another / hearing for **PAS**."

"Dad, can't you talk about anything else? Talk about living, not dying!" Sammie found David's arms around her. Crying embarrassed her. "I'm sorry Dad. It's just hard for me." She sat down as David let her go. "You can go on. I'll listen."

"Thanks Sammie. / I thought the prosecution / would leave Kenard alone / after losing their last case, / but now they've got a group / with great potential / to arouse a jury's sympathy. / *Still Alive* claims / to represent disabled people / even though many disabled are / actually in favor of **PAS**. / Kenard hopes what I say / on *Nightline* will help / his attorney convince the judge / to approve a / summary dismissal. / Honey, all I want is / your opinion on / what I plan to say."

Sammie was worried. If Dad really needed feedback in this area, others were more knowledgeable than she. Her habit was to always consider his strategy. Was he laying the groundwork for his own ultimate decision? She was afraid to ask. She fidgeted to snuggle down into her favorite stuffed chair, a place she'd listened to hundreds of her father's ideas.

"First, I believe / the decision / to hasten dying / can be rational," Ben said. "Certainly it would have been, / for your grandmother.

"Second, the truth / is that **PAS** is practiced / in secret every day. / Without monitoring / there's no way / to be sure / there's no abuse. / Many patients are vulnerable." He looked at Sammie. "And now for my / personal touch. / Not long ago, / I almost died / because of / such abuse. / It may sound ironic, / but legalizing **PAS** / is necessary / to protect the disabled.

"Third, if **PAS** were legalized, / the reporting rate / must be 100%. / An anonymous survey / in The Netherlands / showed only 60% / of the doctors / reported the events." Ben stopped to smile at David. "I owe this idea, / which is brilliant, / to David / who suggested a way / to assure compliance."

Sammie looked at her fiancé. He beamed with Ben's approval. Still, she worried that her Dad's interest was more than what to say on a TV show. Would he decide on **PAS** someday?

David took Ben's cue. "It seemed obvious," he said. "Legislators can make the penalty for not reporting **PAS** the same as the penalty for not reporting suspected child abuse to Child Protective Services: professionals would lose their licenses."

"What do you think?" Ben asked.

"Oh, Dad. Don't ask me. I don't know." She left the room so they wouldn't see her cry. She remembered the words of her best friend from high school: "It isn't easy, being intuitive."

⁂

"Rinpoche says / two things are / most important / at the moment of death." Ben loved sharing what he learned about Eastern philosophy as much as David loved benefiting from his new learning. Ben had asked Rinpoche to visit right after he appeared on *Nightline.*

"The first is / what we've done / in our lives. The second is / our state of mind / during our final moment," said Ben. "The more peaceful / we are when we die, / the more success we will have / in our afterlife. / So I'm studying meditation." Ben's mouth quirked. "I'm the perfect student. / I can stay still / a very long time." Ben gave a feeble laugh. "Seriously, / I feel at peace / with what I've / accomplished in my life." Ben's stare was penetrating. "David, I'm ready..."

David shuddered as he realized why Ben wanted to speak to him alone.

"Once my voice goes, / I won't be able / to enjoy life. / And that could happen any time."

David didn't want to hear this, but forced himself to stay. "But you know that I believe a doctor's role is to preserve life. How could you ask me?"

"Remember our talk / about Catholic organizations / who take over / community hospitals? / After they forbade / staff doctors / to educate patients / on how to prevent / sexually transmitted diseases, / the incidence / of AIDS increased / in their community. / That made you indignant. / You said no religious group / should impose its / beliefs on others. Right?"

David shook his head. "Yes, but what does that have to do with—"

"Apply the same principle to us. / You're entitled to believe / doctors should never / give up hope. But you're not entitled / to impose that / belief on others, / including me."

"Okay, but then you shouldn't force me to act contrary to my beliefs."

"No, I would / never force you, David. / I'd only ask. / Even plead. / Who else can I turn to? / Who else can I trust?"

"But why now? We're still having fantastic conversations."

"Yes, but if I wait too long, / I'll no longer be able to ask."

❧

"I lunched with Jonathan Leary yesterday." David sat beside Sammie on the porch swing. He put his arm around her shoulders. Her skin was softer than her silk sundress.

"Really? Why?"

"I asked how he felt about helping his father make his final transition."

"That's a rather generous way to put it." She looked straight into his eyes. "And?"

"His only guilt was for not responding earlier, so his father would not have had to jump from the attic."

Sammie's shoulder stiffened. "Have you talked to Dad about this?"

"Yes. And he asked me to help him—with **PAS**."

"Oh my God! No! What did you say?"

"That I'd think about it."

"Think about it? I can't believe that. Why didn't you flat out just say, 'No'?" Her face tightened as she stood up. The swing rocked drunkenly, like an oarless boat. "How could you? You're a doctor. And we—David, how could you?" She clapped a hand to her mouth. Tears spilled down her face. She started to walk away, but David grabbed her hand.

David waited for her to calm down, then said, "Remember Dad's paraphrase of Descartes? 'I talk, therefore I am'? If he goes on a respirator, he'll lose his voice. But if he refuses, the fear of suffocation will terrify him. Plus, he's committed to dying peacefully."

She lowered her hands. Glossed with tears, mottled red and white, her face was so beautiful, so natural. David's heart ached.

"I know Dad's great at debates, but I never thought he'd change your mind on **PAS**."

"He hasn't." David reached for her hand and pulled her so she would sit next to him. "Not yet."

❧

Sammie entered her father's room. She felt like a little girl again. "Daddy, you can't do it." She choked up with tears.

"Sammie, / I knew you'd / be upset. / Let's talk. / I want you / to understand."

"David told me your reasons. I won't argue against your wish to control the way you choose to die, Dad. But I will argue about the timing. Why now? You have so much life left."

"But if I wait, / I may lose / the ability to—" Ben looked at her a long time. "Honey, / if I were on a ventilator, / could you imagine / yourself someday / pulling the plug?"

Sammie shook her head. "To be honest, I don't know."

"What if I / completely lost my ability / to communicate?"

"Dad, I don't want to talk about it right now. You're not there yet. And—" She couldn't hold back the tears. The thought of her father not being able to talk to her, of losing him completely, of pulling the plug—it was too much for her to deal with.

"Sammie, / there's one more / reason to do it now. / To help Kenard. / If I videotaped / my PAS, / and showed / how peaceful / it can be, / it could help."

Sammie's profound sadness turned into rage. "I don't believe it! You're planning to do exactly the same thing that Pratt and Cameron wanted you to."

"I disagree. / But I do want to make / my death meaningful. / This is my last chance / to do something / of real value. / It's not just / for Kenard. It's for / everyone. / There's got to be a reason why I, / a politician, / was stricken with ALS. / Do you remember / the Sufi master Rumi?"

"Please Dad, tell me what you feel. Don't quote another so-called sage."

"It's short. / Please listen:

"'So man has come into the world
For a particular task.
And that is his purpose.
If he doesn't perform it,
He will have done nothing.'"

"Dad, that *sounds* so noble. But you've missed one essential point. One of your major purposes is to be my father." She leaned forward and nuzzled her face into the curve of his neck. "I've already lost Mom. I don't want you to go." She shook as she sobbed. She wished he could put his hand on her head like he did when she was a little girl. Just one more time. To be held by her father, just once more. Was that too much to ask? She listened to him breathe, waited for him to say something.

"Sammie, / I think I know where / I'm going. / I have dreams / of what's on the other side. / There, I'm with your mother, / on that old dock / near our vacation lake. / I can throw her / into the water again. / I can swim after her. / I can give her a great big hug. / I believe that's / what it will be like. / I'm not sure. / But I am sure / I don't want the alternative—"

"Which is—?" she mumbled.

"The 'locked-in' state, / where I'm totally paralyzed / and have no way to communicate. / That horror / would be worse / than anything. / Understand?"

"Yes, I think so."

"So, let me ask, / if I ever got to that state, / could you / pull the plug? / Sammie, / only answer if / you're absolutely sure."

Sammie tried to say the assuring words Dad wanted to hear, but only these would come out: "I think so."

Ben responded promptly. “That doesn’t sound / like an / ironclad promise.”

“It’s the best I can say right now. Sorry Dad. I have to be honest.”

“We’ve always / been honest / with each other. / I love you.”

“I love you too.”

“Sammie, / there’s something / I want you to know.” His voice took on a deep intensity. “And I don’t want you / to ever forget it. / Wherever I go / after I leave / this useless body, / remember this: / Love never dies. / I really believe that. / Love never dies. / Now, please, / I want / to hear you say it.”

Through tears, her voice soft, but deep, she said, “Love never dies.”

Chapter 62

Holding a tissue to her eyes, Sammie came out of the bathroom in David's small apartment.

"Is something wrong?" David asked.

Alice had asked for some private time with Ben after lunch. She claimed she wanted to talk about his estate but Sammie guessed Alice wanted to create an opportunity for Sammie to have some alone time with David.

Now, Sammie stood there, asking, "Would you hold me?"

David got up from his laptop at the dinette table and put his arms around her. "Wow. You smell wonderful. You've never worn perfume before. How come?"

"It's the anniversary of Mom's passing. I'm wearing her Chanel № 5."

"Oh, I'm sorry."

"No, it's good to remember her. When I smell like her, I feel close to her." She took his hand and led him to the couch. "David, this may sound weird, but sometimes I wonder how, or if, I'll be able to continue living after Dad is gone."

"Well, he's been the major focus of your life for a long time."

"I'm not suicidal." Sammie took off her shoes and moved closer. "But our relationship is so precious—I'm scared about what it will be like after—Do you understand?"

"I think so. You're talking about feelings, not anything you'd do."

Sammie nodded. "Precisely." She closed her eyes.

As David watched her meditate, he reflected on how wonderful it was to be so open with her, to have the type of relationship he'd always wanted with a woman. In the past, he pushed women away, often with regretting it later. Like the regrets for how he behaved toward his dad—

Sammie opened her eyes. "David, what was it like when you lost your father?"

David wondered if, years from now, he might get used to Sammie's ability to read his mind. "That was over twenty years ago," he said.

Sammie brought her knees up to her chin and gazed at him, relaxed and patient. "Please share, David—If you want to, I mean. I sense I need to hear it as much as you need to tell me. But it's up to you."

Calm was unusual for David when someone asked him to reveal feelings. He wondered why. Because her love would be there, even if he decided not to share? Because he believed she needed to hear his story for herself? Never before had he shared what made him feel most guilty. With trust, he closed his eyes and went back in time.

"I came home from my fourth grade school and went directly into my father's bedroom. As always, I asked him if he felt better. He never did. I was always disappointed that he broke his promise to take me to the zoo. He said he would take me when he felt better, but he never did, so I continued to bug him about it. Do you see how selfish I was? —I've felt guilty ever since. Instead of showing him how much I cared about him, I only cared about him taking me to the zoo.

"But that day was different. I had barely entered the room when Dad motioned for me to come close. Usually, he ended our visits with a hug. But that day, he started off with one. He always felt warm. But then, he was cold and wet. Usually his hugs were limp, but this hug was shaky. He hugged me for a very, very long time. Then he did something he'd never done before. He held both of my shoulders in his hands and he placed me straight, right in front of him, and looked at me very hard. It seemed like his gaze was trapping me. I was scared and wanted to look away, but I couldn't. Finally, he nodded towards Mom and let me go. When I turned to her, she was crying. She told me to come with her. Strange... even though I had wanted to get away a few moments before, now I felt an even stronger pull to stay with Dad. I really wanted to stay. But I didn't say that. I couldn't say anything. I just let Mom take me to the foyer, where Aunt Sylvia grabbed my hand and took me for a walk. I can't even remember where—" David took a tissue out of the box.

"When we returned, everyone was crying. And Dad was—He was—gone."

David put his head in his hands and sobbed. Sammie has put her hands over his. After a moment, he looked up. "A little later, Mom sat down with me in the kitchen. She told me that Dad had gone to a better place. I wasn't convinced, especially seeing how she acted. How could it be better? She trembled so badly that Uncle Sid had to take her to another room.

"That's when Aunt Sylvia took me back to my bedroom. We sat on my bed and she told me this would be the last time I could ever see Dad—if I wanted to. She said she could take me to his room, and that it was okay to see him because he was at peace. I asked her to decide for me. She took my hand and walked me to his bed. He didn't really look different except that his face was pale and he didn't move. His ankles stuck out from below the sheets. They were so swollen—

"Aunt Sylvia had taken a bottle of Royal Blue from my paint set. She spread some of it on Dad's hand, and some on mine. Then she pressed both our hands on a sheet from my sketch pad. I'd forgotten about that until I was in high school, when my aunt got sick. That's when she gave me the handprints. I thanked her, but I just put the paper away. I didn't even look at it. Sammie, I still feel guilty about the way I treated my father. I only cared about what I wanted." He sniffled and wiped his nose. In Sammie's eyes, he saw tenderness and acceptance. He waited for her to say what she thought.

"I see what made your dad's death so hard. For God's sake, you never had a chance to say good-bye."

"No, Sammie, I was a spoiled child. I harassed Dad while he was fighting for his life."

"But you were only a child. David, could you get those handprints?"

A few minutes later, David unfolded the sketch pad sheet on the table.

"Give me your hand, David." Sammie put his hand next to the smaller print on the sheet of paper. "See how small your hand was, when your dad died? You were just a kid then. You did the best a nine-year-old could. Don't judge yourself by adult standards. You didn't know your dad was dying. You couldn't have understood what it was all about."

As David gazed at his hand next to the painted print, he found himself turning slowly, folding into the soft embrace of Sammie's arms. Her gentle squeeze felt warm, tight, steady, and dry—the opposite of his father's last hug. He cried under her hair, nestled in the valley between her neck and shoulder. The aroma of her mother's perfume filled his heart. "I'm sorry, Sammie, I thought I was supposed to be helping you."

"Actually you did. Far more than you realize."

⁂

Although deep in his inner world, Ben opened his eyes as he sensed someone in his room.

Sammie took the seat next to the bed. "Were you sleeping, Dad?"

"No, meditating. / Preparing for tomorrow." He saw her glance across the room, where the digital camcorder was set up. "Sammie, sweetheart. / You're not going / to try to talk me / out of it again, / are you? / That look in your eye—"

"No, that's not why I'm here. It's just—Daddy, I have a confession."

"Don't tell me / you're—"

"Daddy!" Color climbed high in her cheeks. "It's about the way I've been. Fighting you so hard about what you want to do."

"What else would / I expect / from you? / That's the way you are."

"Don't make excuses for me." She shook her head. "You know, my dreams about Pratt, about being tied up in this bed? Sometimes I wake up and fear I can't move. It scares me to hell.

"Pratt taught me what it's like to be paralyzed. I couldn't bear it, even though it only lasted an hour. But you've been paralyzed for many months. Daddy, I feel so guilty. Now I realize: when I argued with you to stay alive, I was thinking only of myself. I wanted to enjoy your company for *myself* when I should have considered how much *you* were suffering. And I hoped that you would decide to go on living for another reason. It would mean that your suffering wasn't that bad, so I wouldn't need to feel guilty. See how totally selfish I was?" She covered her face with her hands. "I'm sorry, Daddy. I'm so sorry."

Ben fantasized he and Sammie were in a movie, for this would be the moment. His hand would quiver, rise, float over, and caress her cheek. His love, her love, their love together—would overcome disease. A miracle.

But his arm lay still, beside him. His fingers didn't even twitch. "Sammie," he said. "We're all selfish, / that's just / part of love."

Her sobbing continued, hidden by the shimmering cascade of her hair.

"Sammie, listen to me."

She turned and Ben saw her reddened eyes, her glistening cheeks.

"When I ran parajumper / missions in Vietnam, / to avoid guilt / from leaving a soldier in the jungle, / I did some stupid things. / I risked not / ever coming back, / making your mother a widow, / not bringing you into this world. / You know those / medals I received? / They were for avoiding guilt, / not for being brave."

Sammie seemed unaware that she was wiping her eyes with a handful of her hair. Ben smiled. It had been years since he'd seen that childhood habit.

"A little guilt is okay, / Sammie. / But you must get on / with your life. / I can't tell you how much / I want that for you. / More than anything / I don't want you / plagued by guilt."

"I know, Dad. I won't let it get to me." She bent over to kiss his cheek and whispered, "I love you, Daddy."

"I love you too, Sammie. / And don't forget / what I told you."

"I won't forget." She gazed at him tenderly, and said the words he wanted to hear. "Love never dies."

❧

David's mind was churning as he gazed at the ceiling. What was keeping him from sleeping? An hour passed before an answer emerged. His heart ached for stimulating discussions with Ben in the future. In their last argument, Ben won with the premise, "Every individual has the right to say when enough is enough." So, David agreed to help Ben commit **PAS**. But he was still anxious and troubled... How could he be sure it was right?

He gave up on sleep, got up, and wrote Sammie a note that he'd gone for a walk. Oak Creek Cemetery would be a good place to talk out loud to himself and debate the issue from both sides.

After some deliberation, David concluded that he had agreed only to provide the technology so Ben could exercise *his* choice. The setup was designed so that only Ben could make the ultimate decision. The strategy of involving several others not only spread the legal liability, it also provided some degree of emotional comfort in that each person will have made some contribution to empower Ben so he could make *his* lethal choice.

The time alone had been fruitful. So now, David could go home. But he wasn't tired. He decided to take a moment to appreciate his surroundings. He took in a refreshing breath of cool night air, noticed the clear sky, saw the willow trees blowing softly in the wind, and then—he heard a rustling in the bushes. First he was scared, then surprised.

Something leaped at him. What was it?

A leaping bundle of bones and sloppy tongue jumped toward him. Slowpoke, disheveled and thin, couldn't stop giving David unbridled affection—

He couldn't wait to tell Sammie. But it was after 3:00 AM by the time he returned and Sammie was fast asleep. He fed Slowpoke and looked forward to their reunion in the morning, when they both woke up.

Restless from all the excitement, he turned on his laptop to check his e-mail. There was a new message from the FBI agent, whom he hadn't heard from in over a month.

The e-mail read: "Bureau notified of an advanced breast cancer patient admitted to an unaccredited clinic in Puerto Rico. Identity initially withheld. Washington authorized appropriate paper work. Current plan: Search for Cameron in the Caribbean."

Chapter 63

"Are you okay / David? / You look so / serious," said Ben.

"Well—I—I just want so much to make this as peaceful as it can be, for you."

"I want to make sure / that none of you / will be named as accomplices. / Someday, I hope / all this legal worry / and secret planning / won't be necessary."

"I know. But our plan will work, for now. It's almost time for us to leave. We'll return right after the two volunteers from *Compassionate Friends* leave, after then hook up your IVs."

"Right. Can you / absolutely prove that this / was my decision?"

"That's why we're using old video tape on only one camcorder, which will never be turned off. So a forensic expert can prove we did no editing."

"No shenanigans / like Cameron?"

"Exactly." David held up something that looked like a big wad of bubble gum. "Second, inside this piece of plastic is a 'momentary switch.' If you choose to activate the pumps for the IVs, you must bite down on it continuously, for five seconds."

"So simple. / No way to fake."

"Precisely. Third, another person will place the switch in your mouth after I leave the room. When I return—if you still want to—" David looked hard into Ben's eyes. "Do you, Ben?"

"I appreciate / your asking again. / Yes, David. / I do. / Enough now. / I'm sure."

"I had to ask."

"I know," Ben said.

"So when I return, this plastic will be in your mouth. I'll focus the camcorder down on the switch in your mouth as you bite down—to photograph your voluntary choice."

David turned to glance toward the patio. The group he now called "The Crew" was waiting. It included Ethan, Rinpoche, Father Martin, Alice, and Sammie.

"Ben, if you're ready, I'll talk to the others."

"Fine. Tell them what I said."

David's gaze lingered on Ben. He understood his feelings without any words.

David walked out to the patio. The Crew turned toward him.

"We'll leave now so the volunteers can do their part," he said. "When we return, we'll all talk to Ben as a group. Then, we can each say good-bye individually. After that, Ben wants to be alone with me. And... and then, you may wish to see how peaceful he is."

Sammie's grip tightened on his fingers. He turned. Her eyes were floating in tears. "Ben considers us as his mid-wifes. He wants us to celebrate his transition."

"His rebirth," added Rinpoche.

"Thank you. Now, does anyone want to add anything?"

Nods. Uh uhs. No smiles. No words.

"Okay. I guess we can leave now." David began to turn.

"What about—after?" Alice asked.

Rinpoche answered. "In Buddhist tradition we don't move the body right away."

"I want to stay with him for as long as I can," Sammie said.

"You'll have some time," said David. His mind switched to the details he did not need to share with the Crew—hiding video equipment, disassembling IV switches, disposing empty bottles in separate dumpsters around town....

"Ethan will call the hospice nurse. She will call the coroner to certify the death. Then she'll call the mortuary to come. No one should call 9-1-1." David took a breath. "It should take about three hours."

"What if someone asks what happened?" asked Sammie.

"Just say that Ben stopped breathing. That's all anyone needs to know. After the morticians and nurse leave, call me on my cell phone to let me know it's safe to return. Since no one will have seen me here, it's unlikely anyone would suspect that I was involved. We won't contact anyone from the media until after he's cremated and we've spoken to our attorneys."

"Come back with food," Alice said.

"Taking nourishment together is a statement that life goes on," said Ethan.

"Ben would want that." David looked at each person in turn. "Anything else?"

The Crew was silent. David looked at Father Martin who stepped forward and said, "Let's recite together—

"'The Lord is my shepherd,'"

Rinpoche was the first to join in.

"I shall not want."

And then the others:

"He maketh me to lie down in green pastures,
He leadeth me beside the still waters. . . ."

The open windows in Ben's bedroom let a whisper of breeze flutter the curtains and carried the scent of Gloria's roses into the room.

"Are you ready now, Ben?" David asked.

"Yes."

David checked that the camcorder's power light was on, and that the volunteers from *Compassionate Friends* had connected the cables to the IV bags.

He took a deep breath, and heard his voice ask the question he most dreaded asking, "Ben, are you sure you want to die now?"

"Yes, I am."

"Okay, I'll leave the room now."

The three-inch screen on the camcorder showed Ben's face—waiting, resolved, and calm. Then a smile of sadness mixed with joy. On the screen, a thin hand appeared. Its distinct delicate soft marbling trembled as it placed a piece of pink plastic into Ben's mouth. Gently, it stroked Ben's cheek. And then, it disappeared from view.

A moment later, David returned. He zoomed the camcorder on Ben's mouth. Then he turned on the text-to-speech program on his laptop. It would sound the words that David had previously written. He had shown the script to an attorney, but was advised to use the computer to avoid revealing his identity.

"Ben, are you still sure?" asked the laptop computer.

Ben hummed, "Uh huh."

"In that case, Benjamin Brewster," the computer continued, "if you are certain you want to exercise your lethal choice, bite down on that switch for more than five seconds. You can stop anytime, but if you continue to bite down, you'll activate a pump that will send a lethal dose of medications into your bloodstream. The medications will put you to sleep, then paralyze your breathing, and finally stop your heart. The result is certain: you will die. Do you understand that completely?"

Ben hummed again.

On the screen, David saw Ben bite down.

Then he couldn't look any more. He just held his breath... and tried not to count to five.

Chapter 64

"Do you, David, take this woman, Samantha, to be your wife? Do you promise to love her through good times and bad, in sickness and in health, and forsaking all others, as long as you both shall live?"

"I do," David said.

"And do you, Samantha, take this man, David, to be your husband? Do you promise to love him through good times and bad, in sickness and in health, and forsaking all others, as long as you both shall live?"

"I do." Sammie wore a simple white dress with several of her mother's red roses woven into the long tumble of her hair. David couldn't stop staring at her beauty.

Father Martin turned toward the audience in St. Mary's Church. "My hope for you two, who've shared that you've *fallen in love*, is that you'll now learn to *rise in love*. Before I pronounce you 'man and wife,' there's something special planned for you to begin learning."

Father Martin's face lit brightly as he turned to the side and nodded.

With an electronic whir, a wheelchair trundled away from the wedding party and into the central aisle. Alice stood behind it.

A strangely flat, stilted monotonic voice said, "GOOD AFTERNOON. I'M BENJAMIN BREWSTER, FATHER OF THE BRIDE. WONDERING HOW I CAN SPEAK WITHOUT MOVING MY LIPS? BY USING A COMPUTER-GENERATED VOICE. DO I SOUND LIKE DARTH VADER?"

A chuckle ran through the congregation. A lump was burning in David's throat. He swallowed hard and clutched Sammie's hand.

"THIS MESSAGE WAS PREVIOUSLY RECORDED SO THERE WILL BE NO Q's-AND-A's."

More chuckles.

"THESE TWO YOUNGSTERS MEAN MORE TO ME THAN LIFE ITSELF. WITHOUT THE POWER OF THEIR LOVE FOR EACH OTHER AND THEIR LOVE FOR ME, I WOULD NOT BE HERE NOW. THEIR LOVE FOR ONE ANOTHER IS THEIR ULTIMATE EXPRESSION OF GOODNESS AND STRENGTH."

Ben blinked twice—causing the computer voice to pause. His eyes sparkled as he made eye contact with the people around him.

David recalled that hot day three months ago, when Ben had planned to commit **PAS**, but stopped biting down on the switch....

That evening, everyone recovered from the ordeal in his or her own way. Alice served more tea and sandwiches. Ethan and Rinpoche meditated. Father Martin prayed. David took Sammie and Slowpoke for a walk.

Later, David held Sammie as they talked about Ben's "spiritual epiphany."

Ben had explained, "I tried to follow Rinpoche's suggestions by doing a life analysis and making peace with my unresolved issues. I thought I had settled everything, but I was wrong. As I was biting down on that switch and reflecting on my thoughts, I realized that instead of imagining my consciousness was merging with a deity, I visualized how this very scene would not only save Kenard's ass, but be aired as the sequel to my appearance on *Nightline*—to break all previous audience viewing records. I even visualized wheelbarrows of mail pouring in!

"I had to admit that spiritually, I was not ready to die. I was filled with too much pride, too attached to my own self-importance, too invested in proving I was a hero."

Then Ben opened a great smile as he said, "Finally, I wondered, if I did follow my doctor's orders, might I survive long enough to attend a very special wedding?"

David's memories were interrupted by the sound of Ben's computer voice. He looked at his new father-in-law and saw bliss shining in his eyes. David hung on his next words.

"I WISH SAMMIE AND DAVID AS MUCH JOY AS THEY'VE GIVEN ME, AND AS MUCH HAPPINESS AS I EXPERIENCED WITH SAMMIE'S MOTHER. AND NO MATTER WHAT, IT'S MOST IMPORTANT THAT THEY, AND ALL OF YOU, ALWAYS REMEMBER THIS: LOVE NEVER DIES."

David glanced at Sammie, biting her lower lip, tears wetting her cheeks. Oh, boy, David thought, blinking fast. He looked back at Ben. He was crying, too. He never thought I'd see that. And then he couldn't hold his own tears back anymore.

Chapter 65

Ben held Gloria's hand as they stood at the end of the dock. Autumn had progressed into winter and the twilight air off the still water had grown colder. "It's almost time to start using our fireplace. I'm looking forward to it."

Gloria slipped her hand into his. "So am I."

"I mean all the time. I want to stay here with you."

She looked straight into his eyes. Behind her, a crescent orange moon hung over the silhouette of the pines against the sky.

"When I'm here with you, Gloria, it seems real. But when I'm on the other side, it seems like a dream. I don't know which to believe."

"You'll see how real it is, when you get here."

"How will I get here? I waited too long. I no longer can bite down, let alone for five seconds."

"If you're ready, spiritually, you'll find a way. How's your anger with Dr. Cameron?"

Ben Brewster let forth his full body laugh. "You never cut a guy any slack. I'm still meditating on Buddha's *Dhammapada*:

> *"'He was angry with me, he attacked me, he defeated me, he robbed me.*
> *Those who do not dwell on such thoughts will surely become free of hatred.*
> *For hatred can never put an end to hatred.*
> *Love alone can.*
> *This is an unalterable law.'"*

Ben took in a deep breath. "It helps." God, it felt so good to breathe on his own. Gloria stroked his cheek. "Remember the ending of the prayer of St. Francis?"

She nodded, and together, they recited,

> *"For it is in giving that we receive;*
> *It is in pardoning that we are pardoned;*
> *It is in dying to self that we are born to eternal life."*

Ben squeezed her hand. "All my life, I've heard these words, but only now do I really appreciate what they mean." He turned to her. "Gloria, it's time. Sammie and David haven't taken a proper honeymoon. It's been two months."

"Major Brewster, are you certain you're not planning your last heroic gesture?"

He just gazed at her.

She pulled his right arm forward as if ballroom dancing, and turned her back toward his chest. She brought his arm in front and snuggled close to him with her head back on his shoulder.

He put his other arm around her waist, and squeezed. "To be honest, in a way, yes, I am. But there's one important difference. This time, only you and I know what I've planned."

As they looked up at the same part of the sky, her arms suddenly tightened over his. "Look, look," she said. "A shooting star."

Chapter 66

While taking his shower, David wanted to rehearse the critical parts of the speech that he would give at lunch today. His anxiety came not from the place he would lecture—the Medical Society of Virginia. Nor was his anxiety due to feeling obliged to excel since the fellowship committee had waived the requirement of the application paper. Given all that had happened, they decided to accept his oral presentation in place of that paper. What was making David nervous was the content of his message. Although supported by the facts, his theory would definitely not make his medical colleagues happy. David never wanted to become a renegade, but he could not deny where his observations had led him.

He planned to start his lecture with its conclusion. In his mind, he went over the exact words that he planned to use:

The ironic truth is, when patients or families inquire about ***PAS*** *or other interventions to hasten dying, the* ***last*** *professional they should ask to carry out this act might very well be their own primary physician.*

Anxiety over the lecture added to David's ongoing deep concern about Ben and Sammie. Over the past few months, his mind was plagued by intrusive thoughts about his father-in-law's condition as Ben sadly continued to deteriorate. Meanwhile, his wife's way of coping was to increase her denial.

Intrusive thoughts about Ben and Sammie did not keep David off track for long, however.

Like all people, physicians have biases. But when people turn to them for professional advice and the stakes are as high as life and death, doctors have a fiduciary obligation to be aware of their biases. Ideally, when patients consult them, physicians should respond to the patient's values, not to their own beliefs.

Until nine days ago, Ben's ability to blink permitted him to select letters one at a time for the computer to generate speech. The last sentence he blinked had brought tears to Sammie's and his eyes. It was the now familiar refrain, "Love Never Dies."

One type of bias is relational. The closer and longer a physician knows the patient, the more likely the doctor will predict a high likelihood for survival and quality of life. To refer to this kind of bias, I suggest using the term, "Dr. Friend."

David had always been Ben's friend. Now they were family. First there was admiration, now love. After Ben's last loving message, his eyelid muscles stopped working so the only way he could communicate was by using a clear board on which letters were written. Sammie would hold the board up and stare at him through each letter. If Ben moved his eyes to the left, it meant "No," and she'd go on to the next letter. If Ben moved his eyes to the right, she'd write down that letter. Communicating was exceedingly slow and tedious.

Whether conscious or not, many doctors embrace the fallacy of the "self-fulfilling prophecy." They behave as if by merely telling patients that they will do well, the prediction itself will make this come true. For this type of bias, the appropriate term is "Dr. Optimistic."

Other doctors avoid telling their patients bad news. Some may be motivated by saving face if treatment attempts fail. Others want to encourage the rest of the healthcare team to work harder. Since these doctors give patients a poorer prognosis than is warranted, so we'll call them, "Dr. Pessimistic."

Throughout Ben's decline, Sammie's devotion had been touching, but sad. Prior to his using the letter board, Ben's thinking was clearly intact. Now, it was hard to tell.

Another bias is monetary. The infamous Dr. Norman Cameron, wherever he is hiding now, was over the top in this area. But many doctor-owned HMOs have an economic structure where the less money spent on treating patients, the larger their bonuses. —"Dr. Wallet."

David subsequently learned that Dr. Cameron would qualify for an additional kind of bias—"Dr. Ego"—since he desperately wanted to be recognized as *the* physician who discovered how to permit a totally paralyzed man to commit suicide voluntarily, and who devised a combination of medications that would individually pass under the radar of the drug enforcement agencies but in combination, would be lethal. After deliberating for a while, David wondered if the "Ego" bias reflected the unique frustration of a deranged researcher, so he could omit it from his lecture. Since he wasn't sure, he asked Ben. When his brilliant father-in-law agreed to leave it out, David felt validated.

David's mind moved onto Tom Mendendorf. Now a nephrology fellow, his old colleague had called to say he was too busy that day to attend David's lecture. David was disappointed. But at least Tom promised to read and critique the written version of David's lecture, before he sent the article to the journals.

One insidious form of bias is that tired and overworked doctors might be more likely to agree with **PAS** *and other ways to hasten dying, given the lure of getting fewer middle-of-the-night calls and of having to endure less frustration from performing unsuccessful procedures. —"Dr. Burn-out."*

David wondered if Dr. Moskowitz, Ryan Leary's urologist, would be in the audience. If so, would he be open to consider the lecture's next message?

Some physicians believe that suffering is necessary for salvation, and that only God can decide when a life is over. Their bias can result in the prolongation of dying and more suffering by undertreating pain. —"Dr. Religious."

In preparing earlier versions of this lecture, David and Ben had developed a daily routine. David would give his father-in-law notes each morning; Ben would spend all day recording his well-considered responses. That evening, the two would discuss them. To speed up their interchange, Ben would prepare a series of responses that anticipated several different tracks that David might follow. Once David replied, Ben would save time by selecting the response that applied. For Ben, it was like playing chess several moves ahead. The process permitted Ben to fire one question after another as David stumbled in his search for answers.

One night, Ben confronted David by asking if he had left out any types of bias. David then remembered the story that the ICU nurse told at Solomon's party...

Some doctors never give up on their patients, even if their attempts to save patients only causes more suffering. When other physicians consider such treatment would be futile, this term may be too kind, if the additional treatment causes more suffering. In any event, the term is "Dr. Hero."

David worried if Ben would pin this type on David. Perhaps a well-tempered "Dr. Hero" would not be that bad. But no, Ben had something else in mind. He stimulated David to consider another area of bias, one that is often overlooked.

Many physicians are afraid of being sued for not following the direct treatment requests of family members who will survive their patients. Other doctors are afraid they will be charged that they overdosed their patients with drugs or made them into addicts, even when they just wanted to adequately treat their pain. Scared of malpractice suits... scared of criminal charges... scared of losing their license... scared of being imprisoned... —"Dr. Scared."

Still, Ben was not satisfied. He would only give David a hint, that this type of bias was a subcategory of "Dr. Scared." Instead of revealing it that evening, however, Ben encouraged David to spend the next day pondering this question: Why was he seriously considering withdrawing from clinical medicine, thinking of this fellowship as the beginning of his career in research?

In what turned out to be their most challenging discussion since their argument about whether David would help Ben with Physician-Assisted Suicide, David learned about another type of bias... and about himself.

In dealing with dying patients and their families, some doctors are so scared of making a mistake... of saying the wrong words... and by the emotional toll... that they decide to withdraw from clinical medicine... —"Dr. Too Sensitive."

David initially felt insulted when he saw the words, "too sensitive," on Ben's computer. But as he mulled over Ben's logic, he gradually accepted his insight, even though the label still nagged him.

David felt relieved when Ben agreed with his reasons to omit "Dr. Too Sensitive" from his lecture. In one of the few arguments he ever won with Ben, David pointed out that the term applied only to doctors who were no longer in clinical practice. Yet David still felt some anxiety. Might he reveal his "too sensitive" trait during his lecture? He wondered if Ben had intentionally allowed him to win this argument. Why? —Perhaps to give him more confidence. David often reminded himself that Ben's strategy skill could not be overestimated.

David so wished he could discuss his personal biases further with Ben. There was so much Ben could have taught him. What a loss, to realize he would never have challenging conversations with him again. How awful, to see this once brilliant man sinking down a narrow well. With each passing day, Ben was becoming darker, more distant, and more depressed.

Then he heard something...

Sammie's voice from the other end of the house. Through the hiss of water, her words sounded sharp and tense. Was she scared? He couldn't make out her words. He shut off the water and listened.

"Dad?" she shouted. "Are you awake? Dad? Can you hear me?"

In a flash, David was out of the shower, grabbed a towel and ran wet.

Sammie was leaning over her father's hospital bed, staring into his face. "Dad, look to the right. Look to the right, will you?"

As David approached, he saw Ben's open eyes. They were fixed.

Sammie patted Ben's cheeks. "Dad! Wake up! Wake up! David, his eyes won't move. What can we do?"

David positioned himself in front of Ben. "Good morning, Dad. Can you move your eyes to the right?"

No response.

"Ben? Hello, Ben?" David called more loudly. He took Ben's bony wrist, palpated the pulse. Light, but regular. "Ben, move your eyes to the right, okay? Please? To the right?"

Nothing.

David looked at Sammie. Her lips were trembling, steel-blue in color. "He put his hand on her shoulder and led her to the chair. "Breathe deeply, Sammie. I'll find out what's wrong." David hurried into their bedroom, yanked on a robe, and grabbed a pocket flashlight from his doctor's bag.

When he returned, he shined the flashlight directly into Ben's left eye. Then he shifted the beam to the right eye. "Pupils constrict equally. That's good. He's still there."

"Thank God," Sammie whispered through a sigh.

David held the flashlight about twelve inches in front of Ben's nose and moved it slowly from side to side. Ben's gaze remained fixed. "Follow this, will you?" Gaze still fixed. David shook his head, and walked around the bed. He heard Sammie gasp and looked back. Ben's eyes had followed his move. David then moved his whole head slowly, back and forth. This time, Ben's gaze did not follow him. He moved to Sammie, looked back, and again, Ben's eyes had moved toward him.

"He moved," Sammie said, "he moved his eyes."

David straightened up. He knew exactly what she was thinking, and why. Being able to move was the critical trigger in Ben's Advance Directive.

"Sammie, we need to talk. Let's go have some juice."

In the kitchen, Sammie remained silent as she poured two glasses of fresh-squeezed juice. Then she looked up. "So he's okay. For a minute, I was really scared. But he's okay. He can still move his eyes."

David kept himself from shaking his head as he put his glass back on the counter. "Sammie, listen. I wish I didn't have to say this sweetheart, but Dad's gone."

Her hand whitened around her glass. "That's ridiculous. You said, 'He's still there,' when you shined the flashlight in his eyes. And he moved his eyes to follow you around the room. We both saw that. So he's not gone!"

David kept his voice low and even. For months he knew that someday he'd have to say these words. So why couldn't he find the right ones, now?

"Pupil contraction proves only that he's not totally brain dead. And Ben's eye movements don't mean anything. They're pure reflex. Like when your leg jerks after the doctor taps your knee with a mallet. It doesn't mean you can walk."

"But didn't you see—He looked right at you."

"Dad's eye reflexes have nothing to do with his ability to communicate."

"You don't know that for sure. How can you be so sure?"

"Sammie—"

"Movement is movement. Who are you, to pass judgment on what it means?"

David felt helpless. God! Talk about denial. Hers was unshakable. He looked out at the bare rose vines through the kitchen window. "Want a second medical opinion? Shall I call Dr. Solomon?"

"No, he agrees with you on everything."

"Honey, how can we resolve this?"

"I don't know."

"What about calling the Crew?"

She nodded.

"I'll be done with my speech by 1:30, after that I'll help you make the calls."

"I'll be finished calling them all by the time you arrive at the Medical Society. Just come home as soon as you can."

Alice served hot tea and apple pie. David figured it made her feel better to do so. She didn't seem to notice that no one was eating.

David handed out the photocopies. "This is Ben's Advance Directive. Only Sammie and I have seen it before. Alice, would you read it?"

"No, I couldn't. I'd be too emotional. How about Ethan?"

"Yes," said Sammie. "But first give him time to say hello to Dad. Otherwise, it just doesn't seem right to me."

"Sorry I was late. Terrible traffic," Ethan said. "After David called this morning and explained Ben's situation, I did a meditation for him."

"But I'd still appreciate it if you paid Dad your respects in person," said Sammie.

Alice bounced up. "I'll boil more water in the meantime."

By the time Ethan returned from saying good-bye to Ben, everyone had a full cup of tea. He took so long that David wondered if he had done another meditation. But before he could ask, Ethan cleared his throat and started to read:

To my dearest Sammie and David

Please accept this expression of my last wishes as **durable**:

Unless I die from another cause, my ALS will progress to the point where I can no longer move. With no means to communicate, I will then enter the "Locked-In" state. I'm horrified by the thought of existing in this state indefinitely. That is why I wrote this Advance Directive.

I believe the exact time of my natural death has already been set. However if I am on life-support apparatus, you will not know when that moment has arrived.

When I can no longer move, assume my consciousness has entered the worlds between lives that Buddhists call the *Bardos*, or that my soul has left my physical body. I frankly admit that my choice of words is neither traditional Buddhist nor strictly Catholic, but what is important, and what I humbly ask you to respect, is my belief that the moment of my death has arrived, even though this will be hard for you.

Please honor my final wishes when I can no longer move. I do not want to chance feeling extreme fright from air hunger as my last sensation. I want to experience only positive emotions as my spirit leaves my body. So I ask you David to please administer a sufficient dose of sedatives to keep me asleep and then turn off my respirator. Sammie, please graciously permit David to do these two things. This is how I want both of you to demonstrate your love. I know it will be difficult for you. But rest assured, it is what I really want. If I had the physical ability to do so, I would take the sedatives and turn the respirator off myself.

I love you both and thank you for letting me trust you to carry out my last wishes. Knowing that you will respond as I have asked is precisely how you can provide me with my last moments of peace.

Love, Ben

"And then, on the next page, there's the signature of a notary—" Ethan blotted his eyes with his handkerchief.

Tears streamed down Alice's face. David looked at Sammie, curled up beside him on the sofa, with her thumbnail between her teeth, sobbing softly.

David tried to remain calm. "This is why we are here. As you know, Ben has been communicating recently by moving his eyes. Today, although his eyes sometimes followed me as I moved around the room, after many repeated attempts, Ben did not move his eyes in response to our requests. I believe Ben's residual eye movements were merely reflexes, not the deliberate movements Ben mentioned in his Advance Directive, which had been allowing him to communicate. In many discussions with Ben, he emphasized his belief that the ability to communicate with loved ones was the essential component of *personhood.*" David looked with sorrow at his wife. "Sammie disagrees with me, so, here is our question: Do you believe Ben has reached the point mentioned in his Advance Directive, that he's in the *Locked-In* state?"

"David, first let me ask... How do you feel about this?" Father Martin asked.

"I *feel* very sad, but I *think* the time has come to carry out Ben's final request. Ben is counting on me, now. He put his trust in me for exactly this kind of situation. He's relying on me to make sure that his last wishes will be honored." He sighed. "The last thing in the world I'd want to do is to hurt Sammie. Yet it seems clear to me, absolutely clear now, what Ben wants me to do."

Beside him, Sammie remained absolutely still.

Father Martin nodded. "Sammie?"

"Not now. Maybe later."

"Rinpoche?" Father Martin said.

"*Namaste.* As long as Ben is alive, he is evolving spiritually. We are only outside observers. Hence we must accept our limitations in observing this mysterious process. None of us can judge whether Ben has finished his karmic work."

David frowned. "Rinpoche, are you saying that you want us to leave him on that respirator indefinitely?"

"No, I am saying this: Do not judge Ben's condition too quickly. You've concluded his life has ceased to have value because he cannot communicate. But I—"

"Wait!" David gulped down his anger. "I didn't conclude that. That was Ben—"

"David," Father Martin waved his hand. "Please let him finish."

Rinpoche gave a tiny bow. "David, listen carefully to what I must say. There is *no* way not to communicate. Even now, Ben is communicating with us. How? By *not* moving his eyes. Understand? Ben is asking all of us to do more spiritual and karmic work here together. He communicated this so well that we are all having this intense discussion. Can you see that?"

David knew there was no possible rebuttal to Rinpoche's words, so he continued to listen.

"See how much power Ben has over all of us?" Rinpoche continued. "Certainly, his style of communicating is unusual. But 'unusual' does not justify ending his life."

Sweat popped out on David's forehead. "I haven't decided to end Ben's life. Ben put his trust in me—He wrote his Advance Directive precisely to—" David stopped himself. He realized that he'd only be repeating himself.

"I'll go next." As she talked, Alice twisted her copy of Ben's Advance Directive. "To me, it's very simple. To communicate with God, Ben need not speak, need not blink, need not move his eyes. God is all. God knows all. When God is ready, he'll call Ben Home. No machine can stop that. It is not for humans to make this decision. So, as long as Ben is alive, he deserves to live. Our role is to allow him to live, and leave the ultimate decision where it clearly lies... in the providence of God." She stared at Father Martin.

"Yes, you're right, Alice," Father Martin said. "Ben did not discuss the specifics of his Advance Directive with me. But for most of his life, he did share these same beliefs about God."

David's back was cold with sweat. He was losing. Ben was losing. He couldn't think of another argument if *his* life depended on it.

The room became uncomfortably quiet.

Ethan's staccato voice broke the silence. "We must not overlook one important point," he said. "Ben has known for a long time that he'd lose his ability to communicate. That's precisely why he composed his Advance Directive."

David said, "Right," and watched the others nod.

"So let me ask," Ethan continued, looking alternately at David and Sammie, "in all the months since he dictated his Advance Directive, did Ben ever indicate he had second thoughts? Did he ever say for example, 'Hey I'd like to reconsider the supreme importance I've placed on being able to communicate?'" He paused for a moment of silence. "Or did he ever express any doubt along this line? For example, did he ever say something like, 'I may have been a bit hasty in what I wrote about this suicide where I ask David to sedate me and turn of the ventilator, so I'd like to revise my Advance Directive?'"

"Ethan, you've used the wrong term. What Ben asked for is not suicide," David said. "Through his Advance Directive, Ben has asked me to withdraw life-prolonging treatment. If Ben could speak for himself right now, he could exercise his legal and moral right to refuse medical treatment and demand that we pull the plug."

David waited for Ethan to nod before he continued. "But you're right. Ben has never wavered about these wishes. His Advance Directive described the precise situation where he'd consider further treatment to prolong his life as futile. And I'm sad to say, very sad, that's where he is now."

David stared at Sammie for a response. A slight nod. Did she agree?

"Okay, then," Ethan continued. "If Ben could speak for himself right now he might possibly say, 'Hey, I've changed my mind.' And that would be that. But he can't. Since he can't communicate now, we must accept his last clear statement—the one he wrote in his Advance Directive. He designated David as his agent, and gave him specific, *durable* powers."

Ethan gave a soft look to Alice, to Father Martin, and Rinpoche. "All your arguments are sound, and if you could discuss them with Ben, he might change his mind. But it's too late for that. Since Ben gave David sole authority to make this medical judgment, the rest of us must accept David's definition of 'movement.' Now we must support David, and Sammie, as they honor Ben's final request."

Ethan slumped in his chair, looking completely drained.

David stared at him for a moment, "Your logic was impressive, Ethan." Then he turned to Sammie. "Sweetheart?"

She turned to him with glistened eyes. "It's so hard. I don't know."

"Look, maybe none of us really knows what's best for Ben," David said. "Ben himself just made his best guess. But his Advance Directive clearly put all his trust in Sammie and me. So we must—we're obligated—it's our duty to carry out his last wishes."

Father Martin got to his feet. "David, can I—?"

"Thank you, Father. Thank you all, but it would be best if everyone left. Sammie and I need to talk. We'll call you if we need you."

He buried his face in the honey of Sammie's hair, and listened to the shuffle of passing feet. A hand squeezed his right shoulder. He guessed it was Ethan's.

David held Sammie until she stopped crying and trembling. Then she sighed, a sound as long and quiet as the rush of wind through grass. "Tonight, I want to sit with Dad," she said. "It will take me some time to get used to the idea. Maybe by tomorrow morning, I'll be strong enough to do what Dad requested."

❧

She sat beside her father's bed all night long. She held his hand. She talked to him in a low voice. She watched the shape of his eyes beneath his closed lids. She told him how terrific her childhood had been, what a great father he'd been—especially after Mom's death. She told him how much she always loved him.

She meditated, sent him good energy, and prayed every prayer she could think of, including her mother's favorite, the prayer of St. Francis.

She wept. She giggled. In one moment of bare honesty, she confessed that she'd lost her virginity in this very room at the age of sixteen, to a long-haired teenager Ben never liked.

There was no response to any of it.

She apologized for arguments that occurred long ago, particularly the vehement ones over Vietnam. She expressed again her intense guilt for being so selfish for wanting him to stay alive, despite all of his suffering.

Still no response.

She sobbed bitterly, clutched her father's hand, and told him how much she'd miss him.

No response.

Chapter 67

At dawn, David dressed before he entered Ben's room. He felt disjointed from his surroundings, not sure if he'd slept. He'd spent most of the night wondering if he should join Sammie, but deciding over and over again not to. This morning, he found her asleep with her head on the mattress beside her father's arm, her hair spilling down her back.

Gently, he touched her shoulder. She shivered, then snapped erect. One side of her face was mottled red and creased from the folds of Ben's sheets. Her eyes were instantly alert. "Is it time?"

David nodded. "Want me to call Father Martin and Rinpoche?" He touched her cheek.

"Just Father Martin. Rinpoche already taught me the 'Position of the Lion.'"

David sat on the stool she'd vacated. Her warmth was still there. He looked at Ben's face. "Well, my friend," he said softly. "Are you ready for your final transition?"

Of course, there was no response.

Sammie washed her face, brushed her teeth, combed her hair, and changed into the belted blue dress that was Dad's favorite. She put on some of her mother's perfume and jewelry. She took her time. Finally, she could think of nothing else to do.

She returned to Ben's bed. She waited. She heard David open the front door, then the low tones of Father Martin. She stood aside and witnessed the anointing ceremony. She heard the prayers and joined in the responsive reading from the Book of Common Prayer.

"We sinners beseech you to hear us, Lord Christ." Father Martin's voice had the deep resonance of a tolling bell. "That it may please you to deliver the soul of your servant from the power of evil, and from eternal death.

"We beseech you to hear us, good Lord.

"That it may please you to grant him a place of refreshment and everlasting blessedness."

Oh, yes, please God, thought Sammie.

At the conclusion, she let Father Martin squeeze her hand.

A moment later she heard the front door close.

David now stood on the other side of the bed with a sealed plastic bag in his hand, looking down at Ben. She looked into David's glistening eyes, and bit her lip. Her own eyes felt wet, but not yet teary. She extended her hands toward David.

David took her hands in his. Without a word, they nodded to each other in synchrony.

David emptied the contents of the plastic bag onto the tray attached to Ben's bed.

"Sammie, your father loves you. And I love you. You don't have to watch this."

She stood in silence for a while. Then her knees weakened so she sat down on the stool. "I have to be with Dad now."

David raised the syringe and pulled the shield off the needle. He looked into Sammie's eyes. "Are you ready?"

"How long will it take?" she whispered.

"If Ben were awake, we could see him fall asleep in a minute or two. I'll wait three minutes to be sure. Ready?"

"As soon as I give Dad my last positive affirmations."

"Not your last. Rinpoche said you can still help him as he travels through the *Bardos*."

"I remember. Every week for the next seven weeks, at the same time of day—"

She knew her talk was a stall—buying time against her father's wishes. She motioned to David to help her roll Ben onto his right side, placed Ben's left hand on his right thigh, his right hand under his chin. That way, he would have the same posture as The Buddha did as he died.

She leaned close and said, "Dad, it's time. Time to say good-bye. You need to go to another place. And, not that you need my permission, but I want you to know that I am— Yes, I really am—Finally willing to let you go. You know how much I love you."

She glanced up. David, standing still, syringe in his hand, tears in his eyes.

"One more thing, Dad. You're not the only one with poignant quotations. I've saved William Blake's poem for this time.

> *"'He who binds to himself a Joy,*
> *Does the winged life destroy;*
> *He who kisses the Joy as it flies,*
> *Lives in Eternity's sunrise.'"*

She looked back at her father's face. "Okay," she whispered to David. She bent down, put her face next to her father's, and closed her eyes.

She heard David moving about. As she meditated, a part of her mind couldn't help picture a needle entering her father's IV line, seeing its fluid being dispensed, imagining David checking his watch—

Still, she jumped when she heard, "All right. He's asleep now, for sure."

There was a soft click, and then something profound. Silence. The "hiss, pause, thunk" had stopped. Finally. David had shut the respirator off.

She heard birds singing outside, greeting the new day.

She watched her father's chest slowly empty with a long, gentle sigh.

It did not rise again.

Sammie pulled away from her father's face. She looked at his peaceful face. Nothing about him had changed, really, other than the stillness of his chest. He looked exactly the same as he had five minutes ago.

And yet... something was different.

It was.

It had to be—

Weeping now, she leaned forward to give her father a last kiss.

At first, she assumed they were *her* tears that had dampened his cheeks. Then she reared back. "David! Look! He's crying. Look, he's crying! He doesn't want to go! My God, my God! Turn on the respirator! Turn it back on! Turn it back on!"

David didn't move. "No, Sammie. I couldn't, even if I wanted to. He's been without oxygen for too long. He'd be severely brain damaged. It's too late."

She stared at David, shocked, disbelieving. How could he just stand there? Couldn't he see what was happening? Was he blind?

She lunged around the bed, reaching for the switch on the respirator.

David stepped in front of her.

"Don't do this, Sammie. Please, let him go. It's like you said, 'It's time...'"

"But he's crying! He's communicating with us! You said communication was the key. Well? Didn't you?"

As David reached out to her, she felt a wild impulse to shove him out of the way, to get to the ventilator before it was too late. Really too late.

But David's hands were on her shoulders, gentle but strong, holding her back. "Sammie, listen. Let go. Let your father go. Please. That's what you need to do, now."

She kept her eyes on the bed, on her father's damp cheeks, but she permitted David to guide her to the couch. She let him ease her down and sat close to her.

Now her voice was loud. "We let Dad down. His consciousness had not left. His soul had not left. He could still communicate. Damn it! He was crying. David, what did we do? We killed him! Dad was still there, crying. Crying, because he didn't want to die."

She turned away and buried her head in her arms.

"Sammie, it's hard to be sure, now. Remember what Rinpoche taught? 'Learning to live is learning to let go'? We only did what Dad wanted. —Exactly what he wrote in his Advance Directive. Now, we have to learn to let go." He brushed a damp strand of hair from her cheek.

"But he was crying—Dad must have changed his mind. Like he did last time. Maybe, as he saw the end coming, he regretted leaving those instructions in his Advance Directive. Maybe he wasn't ready to leave, but he had no way of telling us—"

She paused to reflect, to give David a moment to say something, words that might help. She held her breath, hoping.

"We only did what Dad wanted, Sammie. Think of it that way and you'll feel better."

"No, David. We did exactly what Dad wrote four months ago. But we don't really know what he wanted today. You want me to feel better?" She took a deep breath.

"There's only one way I could possibly feel better. That's to be assured that Dad really wanted to die."

She shook her head, and looked at David.

"And that—Until my dying day—Is the one thing that I will never, ever know."——

Chapter 68

All the orchids from the U.S. Botanical Garden couldn't make this a pleasant place for me," Sammie said. "And those morticians—I know they're trying to be nice, but—"

Her only comfort was David's hand on her waist as they walked into the coolness of the funeral parlor.

Ethan waved at her from across the room. He stopped talking to his parents and began moving toward her. As he approached, she saw empathy in his face. Was there also urgency? But a hand took her arm—Aunt Alice had decided to escort her to the ladies' room.

When she returned, David and Ethan seemed intense. "He's got something to tell us," David said. "Let's go to that little room behind the sanctuary, okay?"

They entered the private room. Ethan chose a Queen Anne chair and moved it so he was sitting directly in front of Sammie. She sat next to David on a small sofa. Sammie noticed how soft and caring Ethan's eyes were. She wanted to cry.

"David told me about your father's tears. I think you need to understand something—"

"I already understand," Sammie said. "I've thought about it deeply. Dad's tears prove two things. First, that he was still conscious.

"Second, that he didn't want to die. It's terrible to admit, but that means that David and I— We— I can't even say the word— What we did to him." She trembled and teared as David held her.

Ethan waited until she nodded that she was ready to listen.

"Sammie, in part, you are right. What I must say may shock you. Remember when you asked me to pay my respects to your dad in person?"

"Of course."

"Did you wonder what took me so long?"

"Yes, I did," said David. "I figured you did another meditation."

"That wasn't it." Ethan sighed. "Here's what happened. As soon as I entered your father's room, he moved his eyes to the right. I moved real close—to be sure. I asked him if he could move his eyes. He moved his eyes to the right, again. And again. That surprised me, so I asked him, 'Do you want Sammie and David to know you can still move?' Then, he moved to the left." Ethan looked at her. "For greater certainty, I asked if he wanted to keep it a secret from you two, that he could still move and communicate. Guess what? His eyes went to the right. You see, even with only 'Yes' and 'No' answers, if you ask enough questions, you can trust the answers.

"So I thought a while, and got the courage to ask your father the ultimate question, 'Do you want to die, now?' He moved his eyes to the right—not once, not twice, but three times! For him, that was like shouting."

Sammie let out a deep sigh. The tension in her body was draining away.

"But why?" David asked. "If Dad wanted to die, why would he keep his ability to move a secret? Why didn't he simply communicate his wish to us?"

"Initially, I had no idea," said Ethan. "But then I read his Advance Directive and as everyone else discussed it, I was trying to figure out the answer to that very question." He turned to Sammie. "Your father's main fear was the 'Locked-In' state, wasn't it?"

Sammie nodded.

"I figure your dad's logic went like this: If he waited too long, he wouldn't be able to communicate 'Yes' or 'No,' so he had to do it before he lost that ability. That's why he had to fool you into thinking that he was already locked in. See?"

"That's only part of the reason," David said, as he held Sammie's hand. "Honey, this may be hard for you to hear—but Dad told me he was worried that you'd never let him go as long as you thought he still had conscious thought."

"That's true. I never could promise him that I'd be able to pull the plug."

"Might I ask, how were you able to put the momentary switch in your dad's mouth—to give him the option of committing **PAS**?" said Ethan.

"Because then, the final choice would be Dad's. And look what happened. He changed his mind!" She cried. "Like he wanted to change his mind this time, but we didn't let him."

"How can you be so sure he changed his mind?" asked Ethan. "I'm just wondering."

"Because of his tears." Sammie shuddered.

David put his hand gently on her face and turned it to him. "Sammie, listen. Think of how infrequently Dad cried. Can you ever remember him crying over his own losses? Not once, as he lost battle after battle with ALS. For his whole life, Dad only cried for the losses of others."

Relief seemed to ascend Sammie's body as if she were being immersed into a hot tub. No more arguing with Ethan and David's interpretations. True, she never could promise Dad that she'd let him go. David was kind not to remind her that she almost sabotaged Dad's last wishes. She would have, had David not held her back. And Dad's tears... Could they have been for her?

"Okay Ethan," she said. "You said you thought about this? So tell me, what would have happened if you had not gone in to see Dad?"

"His plan would still have worked perfectly if he hadn't cried," Ethan said.

"Let me think a moment." She took a tissue from her purse, dried her nose and closed her eyes. "There's another, important reason why Dad set things up this way," she said. "He wanted, more than anything, to spare David and me from feeling any guilt from pulling the plug. So, if his plan had worked, he would have fooled us into believing he had no consciousness left. Remember his Advance Directive? Something like 'my soul would have already left my body?'"

"Aha!" said Ethan. "Your father's last act of compassion. Truly a remarkable man."

They all sat in silence for a moment.

Ethan cleared his throat. "There's one more thing that your dad communicated that evening. He kept staring at the letter board with eager eyes, so I picked it up. I hadn't used it before, so it took me a long time. Eventually, he selected three letters. When I got them, his eyes twinkled with delight and he looked to the right, twice. I asked him if he'd explain, but he looked away from the board, as if he did not seem interested in selecting any more letters. I asked him if he wanted me to share the letters with you. This time, he looked straight ahead, right at me, every time I asked. And I asked three times. For a while, I was confused. I thought and thought... If the answer is not 'Yes' and not 'No, then ' what was the alternative? Finally I asked your Dad if his intent was to let *me* to make that decision. He smiled with radiant eyes as he looked to the right. Until this very moment, I did not realize why. He didn't want me to share the letters with you, unless you already knew he could communicate."

"Again, that seems logical, Ethan. So what were the three letters?" asked David.

"Right. Maybe you'll know their meaning. They were, **L - N - D**."

Sammie gasped. It took several seconds for her to catch her breath. "That's Dad, all right. Always the strategic chess player. Always setting things up to win—either one way or the other."

"And always with love," said David.

"Yes, loving to the end," said Sammie.

"Even from beyond," said David.

Sammie smiled. "Want me to explain **L - N - D**? Sure. I'd love to."

Epilogue

Wendy loved the soft humid breeze caressing her sun-tanned body as it came off the long curving shoreline of Karon Beach. Slower paced than the hotel district, the north end was still used by local fishermen to cast their nets in the lagoon.

Phuket, Thailand... with its lush green hills, coconut groves, and rubber plantations... What an amazing place to heal. Especially since Norman was doing absolutely everything to assure her happiness. He arranged for four women to take care of every possible need—a nurse, a personal assistant, a maid, and a cook.

Sitting under the shade of a large umbrella, Wendy took a sip of sweet Thai iced tea. She felt blessed. Now that she could enjoy food again, she was learning how the Thais combined spicy Indian curries with Chinese rice and noodles. Her renewed energy allowed her to delight in Thai art and dance—other ways that reflected the local melding of diverse Asian cultures.

But, as she had always expected, her greatest delight was to enjoy spending time with Norman. It wasn't hard for her to pretend that she was unaware that they couldn't afford to take the promised around-the-world trip. She went along with the façade that they had to wait until she regained more strength. What was important was being away from all the pressures of Washington and getting him to laugh. It seemed like the first time in decades.

Soon after they arrived, Norman carefully explained why they had to assume new identities. He knew she would read accounts of the allegations on the internet. After several lengthy discussions, she understood how his vision for the way the world needed to change fit with what had happened back in Washington. The U.S. Supreme Court had refused to let the Attorney General punish physicians who followed Oregon's Death With Dignity Act. She never expected perfection from her husband. Norman's worst trait had always been impatience. All he wanted to do was to decrease unnecessary end-of-life suffering. His heart was well-motivated and his cause was noble. But his method was severely criticized because others misunderstood. Regardless of what newspaper reporters had said, Norman never intended to kill anyone. She believed him... it was an accident that Grainger fell on that syringe full of barbiturates. And Norman only had it ready to ensure that Brewster's dying would not be prolonged with unnecessary suffering.

How sad that now, her husband would never get the recognition he deserved. Plus, he had lost his identity and his profession. Wasn't that punishment enough? At least they were together, in this Asian paradise. —A lot better than spending years alone in jail, like Jack Kevorkian.

And he was so good to her, more patient than ever. She was content with her daily routine. She'd bring a couple of computer batteries to the beach, plug in a wireless modem on her laptop, connect to the internet, and keep up with the latest in art and world news. What a relief... it'd been five months since she read an article saying terrible things about her husband.

But as the months passed, she sensed an increase in Norman's underlying restlessness. She figured he missed discussing research with his colleagues so she continued to scan the internet for articles in his field. Early on, he'd sometimes react with envy or anger. She could empathize with how hard it was to give up his role as a leader in this field. Now, to protect him, instead of sending the articles directly to his computer as she did in Washington, she'd first summarize them verbally and watch his reaction. If he didn't seem upset, she'd e-mail him the article. Wendy was pleased at how beautifully her protocol was working, how she was able to enrich her husband's life in this special way.

She looked up as Norman picked up a towel. Wet from a vigorous swim in the Andaman Sea, he looked refreshed and young again. "You look so wonderful," she said.

"You do too, sweetheart. Find anything interesting on the Internet?"

"Your place or mine? Art or medicine?"

He chuckled. "Start with medicine."

"I could have guessed. Okay. An Australian doctor is now sending out instructions for do-it-yourself chemistry kits to terminal patients who want to kill themselves. What do you think of that?"

"Ahh, I know him. His idea is awful. I'd never promote that. If even one teenager used this method to commit suicide after a disappointing romance, I couldn't live with myself."

Good reaction, she thought. *I'll send him this article.* "I just began reading an abstract of a paper on doctors' biases. The bottom line is rather curious: 'Patients and family should consider their personal physician *last* when they face the challenge of a life-or-death decision.' What do you—?"

"Who did that study?"

"Give me a second to scroll down." She hit the PgDn key on her laptop. *Oh no, it's David Grainger. What can I say?* "Uh... Well, there are several authors. You probably don't know—"

"Let me see." He crouched behind her chair, to view the screen.

Impatient again. Oh my God, what will he think?

Suddenly Norman plopped on the blanket beside her. At first she hoped he had just lost his balance, but when she saw his face grimace with pain, his hands grab his chest, his forehead bead with sweat—she got scared.

"Norman, Norman are you okay? What's wrong?"

"Don't panic honey," he gasped, "it's probably just a Coronary Spasm. I'll be okay. They're some Nitroglycerin tablets in my attaché case. —In the zippered compartment."

Wendy jumped out of her chair, picked up the attaché, and unzipped the front compartment. *Have I been in denial? She recalled the newspaper accounts of his having a heart attack as he left Memorial.* She ran her hand around the bottom of the compartment. Instead of a bottle, she found some loose papers, which she put aside. “I can’t find them.”

A desperate voice, “Not the big zippered compartment. The small one, in the front.”

She unzipped the small compartment, found the bottle of tablets, shook a few into her palm, and offered them to Norman. He picked up two tablets and put them under his tongue.

Millions of people keep Nitro on hand for situations just like this and do fine. He’ll be all right. He better be all right...

A long minute later he said, “My pain’s almost gone. I’m fine.”

As Wendy watched him relax, something in the papers she had just retrieved from the first compartment caught her eye. *Nutrition Today?* Norman had never shown any interest in that journal. As she looked closer a familiar name popped out of a one-paragraph story. *Grainger!* The headline read, “Samantha Grainger promoted to regional sales director. Relocating to Norfolk, Virginia...”

A feeling of nausea, like the worst side effect from chemotherapy, swept over her. And a question began to nag her—one that would not go away...

Why is Norman so interested in the whereabouts of Samantha Grainger?

L-N-D

Acknowledgments

I was not born a writer. My parents encouraged me to study science so I could become a physician. My resistance to their plan succeeded only in my first becoming a research scientist. So I have many people to thank for contributing to this novel.

This story was prompted by two radio news announcements I heard in close proximity in 1996: Dr. Jack Kevorkian killed his 33rd patient, and a politician predicted Medicare would be bankrupt within three decades. From those two snippets, the idea for the plot of **Lethal Choice** emerged: An insurance company's conspiracy to save money by forcing a patient who was all brain and no body to serve as their "poster boy" to promote Physician-Assisted Suicide. It "only" took ten years and much help for many people for this basic idea to take the form of this medical thriller.

My first general writing coach was Shirl Thomas. She wrestled with my tendency to write like medical scientist. I sincerely hope she won. Then, Mark Clements worked patiently with me for almost a year. He made contributions that only a professional author could offer: convincing dialogue, fast pacing, alternating scenes, and vivid imagery—goals that I hope we achieved. The books that Mr. Clements had previously authored could not have been more different than the style of writing with which I was familiar: his several awards and nominations were in the fields of horror and the supernatural—the ultimate thrillers.

I learned that even during its creation, art reflects life. In **Lethal Choice**, the evil male nurse says to his victim with whom he shares a military background, "Doc here wanted this whole project to work without anyone getting hurt. But you and I know that real progress in this world is always paid for in blood." Similarly, seasoned author Mr. Clements had to convince me, a budding novelist, that for this story to be convincing, I would have "to commit murder." —At least in fiction.

My next collaborator was Drusilla Campbell, a writing teacher who wanted to be psychologist—a complementary match for a psychiatrist who wanted to be a novelist. She helped strengthen the characters' motivation to achieve their goals and make the action more compelling. The next edit was crafted by Michaela Hamilton, now editor-in-chief of Kensington Publishing Company. She helped me streamline, polish, and shorten the novel. In addition to these personal coaches, I attended about two dozen writing conferences. At one, Richard Walters of UCLA taught me that "story" is paramount. The author's message must emerge from the story, not the other way around.

Over the past decade, the landscape of the intense conflict between the opposing camps of the right-to-die *versus* the sanctity-of-life factions moved from the conflict over implementing Oregon's Death with Dignity Act, and the 1997 U.S. Supreme Court decision that Physician-Assisted Suicide was *not* a Constitutional right, to the saga of Terri Schiavo, and another round at the U. S. Supreme Court. Yet the plot of **Lethal Choice** remained virtually unchanged as I added new relevant facts.

Meanwhile, I became better acquainted with my characters and what was frustrating them from achieving their goals. All my writing teachers taught me that you can only write about what you know, and I needed to know more. So I did a "tour of duty" at the San Diego Hospice, where especially Dr. Charles von Gunten, a recognized leading teacher of hospice and palliative care, provided the clinical opportunity to learn about the multidisciplinary field of end-of-life care. In addition, the "ashram" came to me for a year. I was privileged to welcome in my home, a Buddhist monk and physician who trains hospice doctors and nurses in Thailand, the Venerable Mettanando Bhikkhu, M.D., Ph.D., a specialist in the fields of medical ethics and healing meditation.

I must also thank neurologist Dr. Richard Smith, not only for sharing some of his internationally recognized expertise about lower motor neuron disease (ALS), but also for referring to me, some of his clinical patients and families, from whom I learned first hand, what it is like to deal with the awesome challenge of this disease. What these physicians and patients taught me influenced not only what specific information actually made its way onto the pages of this book, but also the way I wrote it... or sometimes, as it seemed, the way the book wrote itself.

On the technical side, I wish to thank Mark Janssen for library research and copy editing, and Simon Warwick-Smith for consulting on so many aspects of the business of publishing. Thanks to Amy Bartlett, who created the audio version of the book, the process of which permitted me to "hear" the drama and help mold the final product; to K. Lorraine Graham and Janelle Diters, who diligently performed the typesetting; and to Matthew Windwer, who created the web site.

Many other people helped, inspired, read, critiqued, and influenced the final product, directly or indirectly, especially Ronald Baker Miller, M.D., Michael S. Evans, J.D., M.S.W., and members of several ethics committees. Ronald Miller also commented and edited the Position Paper on Legalizing Physician-Assisted Suicide.

Finally, I thank my wife and three children for putting up with my obsession to write about what may have seemed like a morbid topic. To me, the subject of dying inspires a deep evaluation of all that is meaningful in life.

But more than anyone, it was my dear friend, Ronald Ferris, M.D., who influenced me to apply my psychiatric skills to end-of-life care. His gracious appreciation for my attentiveness during the last ten months of his life taught me, along with his family, "how to die" in the context of knowing "how to live." Without the privilege of knowing Ron Ferris, I doubt I would have discovered this new direction in my life, now represented by the non-profit organization, Caring Advocates.

I hope my writing will help readers find more meaning in their lives, as well as their own choice of peaceful paths when their lives must come to a close.

Stanley A. Terman, Ph.D., M.D.

Legalizing Physician-Assisted Suicide: a position statement

In the novel, **Lethal Choice**, the main character presents two different ways to hasten dying. One is Physician-Assisted Suicide. Over the past two decades, this option has been debated almost as heatedly as abortion. Why? Because it is almost as difficult to say when a life has ended, as when a life begins. Increased interest in legalizing Physician-Assisted Suicide was due in part to a 2006 U. S. Supreme Court ruling that affirmed that individual states have the right to decide what constitutes "legitimate medical practice." Yet at the same time, opponents of Physician-Assisted Suicide were seeking to restrict the prescription of the lethal medications at the state level, or considering amending the federal Controlled Substances Act of 1970. That would end the practice, they think. Actually, the focus on those medications listed as "dangerous," the ones monitored by the federal Drug Enforcement Agency, is misplaced. As the novel indicates—but does not name—there is a combination of drugs that are not considered lethal individually, so they are not listed as "controlled substances"—but they could still be used to hasten death instead of barbiturates. These prescription medications could slip under the radar of federal and state agencies.

The other method to hasten dying is Voluntary Refusal of Food & Fluid. This option is much less well known and discussed, yet it is already legal in every state. In my experience, few non-professionals are aware that Voluntary Refusal of Food & Fluid is not only comfortable but also peaceful. Although true, I have never heard this stated publicly: Voluntary Refusal of Food & Fluid has the potential to help hundreds of times more people than Physician-Assisted Suicide. That's because it can help patients with severe physical or mental impairments. Voluntary Refusal of Food & Fluid can be an important part of advance care planning for the future, while Physician-Assisted Suicide is only available in the present.

As the novel, **Lethal Choice**, points out, Voluntary Refusal of Food & Fluid may be the only way to prevent the long, irreversible descent into the indignity and total dependency of Alzheimer's disease and related dementias—diseases that will affect increasingly huge numbers of elderly people and their families in the future. Various aspects of Voluntary Refusal of Food & Fluid are discussed in greater depth in the companion self-help book, **The *BEST WAY* to Say Goodbye**, and the web sites, www.TheBestGoodbye.com and www.CaringAdvocates.org offer detailed information and forms to let your family and doctor know that you may someday wish to choose this method.

This position statement primarily focuses on the issue of *legalizing* Physician-Assisted Suicide. **The *BEST WAY* to Say Goodbye** compares this method to hasten dying with Voluntary Refusal of Food & Fluid in several ways, including:

- How soon one can expect to die, starting from the first request?
- What is the relative effectiveness and safety of each method?
- What types of patients most need each method?
- What types of patients should avoid each method?
- How reversible is each method, for patients who change their minds?
- How aesthetic are the two methods?
- What is the potential for guilt and for healing among survivors?
- What is the potential of each method to change the nature of the healing relationship of physicians? and,
- What is the relative moral toll of the two methods?

Opponents of legalizing Physician-Assisted Suicide often cite these two issues: It will begin a "slippery slope" that will lead to a "culture of death"; and the old, needy, and vulnerable will be forced to hasten their dying. Basically their warning comes down to one fear with two consequences. They say that giving people the choice to hasten dying will neither respect the patient's voluntary wishes nor the sanctity of life. I agree; both are possible. We do need "guardrails" to prevent the slippery slope, and the "ultimate decision" must be voluntary. However I do not agree that the best course of action is to make the practice of Physician-Assisted Suicide punishable as beyond professional ethical practice or even criminal. Instead, to prevent potential abuse, I offer two specific recommendations in the form of professional practice guidelines. Although untested, I believe they could solve many objections to Physician-Assisted Suicide. Yet even if both strategies were successfully implemented, I would still consider Voluntary Refusal of Food & Fluid as having significant advantages over Physician-Assisted Suicide in most but not all situations. I therefore describe those advantages. My final comments relate to the intensity of effort to legalize Physician-Assisted Suicide. Specifically I ask, how much time, money, and energy should be devoted to changing the present laws, when it would be more prudent instead to educate both professionals and the public on an alternative peaceful way to reduce end-of-life pain and suffering that is already legal?

Preface

Our democracy is based on protecting individual liberty. Each person has the right to freely choose what seems best, which defines autonomy; that is, as long as that decision does not hurt or endanger others. Our society also places the highest value on the "sanctity" of life, which may conflict, although there is more than one way to define this term. Over two-thirds of us will endure a slow dying process. Many will suffer from a chronic terminal illness that causes unbearable suffering, either from physical pain or from total dependency and indignity. It is therefore not surprising that about 70% of those surveyed indicate they would want some means to hasten their dying.

Clinical experience for over 8 years with Oregon's *Death With Dignity Act* that legalized Physician-Assisted Suicide is consistent with a psychological theory that is widely underappreciated and misunderstood. Worse, those who oppose offering patients any means to hasten dying often mischaracterize such options with fear-tinged slogans that allude to paying homage to the "culture of death."

Here is the **ironic truth**: When terminally ill patients who are competent are given the compassionate choice to decide WHEN and HOW to die... when they possess the knowledge that they *can exert control over the dying process...* many will choose to live longer. Yes, **longer**! Why? Because every day that they wake up and choose ***not*** to exercise their choice to hasten dying is a day that they instead consciously make the choice to continue living as **voluntary survivors**... a day that they need not worry about being forced to exist as **involuntary sufferers**... a day they need not feel anxiety about devastating loss of functioning to the point where the future holds only prolonged indignity and dependency. Relief from worry and anxiety permits more enjoyment of whatever precious time remains. It allows people to use this time to seek deeper meaning in their lives. Some will create or expand the legacy of values by which they want others to remember them. Yet the most important consequence is also the most ironic:

Offering people the **compassionate choice** to hasten dying can—and often does, lead to the choice to **live longer**. When people know that others will honor their Last Wishes, they can live with less anxiety. Most importantly this knowledge will prevent the great tragedies of violent, of illegal, and especially, of premature deaths.

Here are more details:

1. The position paper focuses on the word "legalizing" because confidential surveys have documented that some doctors facilitate Physician-Assisted Suicide even when, or where, the act was not legal.

2. In terms of terminology, I prefer the term **Physician-Hastened Dying,** or even better, **Physician-Facilitated, Patient-Hastened Dying** to the usual term, Physician-Assisted Suicide. (I elaborate further on terminology in **The *BEST WAY* to Say Goodbye.**) Both alternate terms reflect the truth that we all must die someday and that we can only hasten the process. The second term is clearer about the roles: the physician only facilitates; the patient is responsible for the hastening. It is up to the patient to decide if and when to ingest the lethal dose of medication the physician prescribed. The longer term importantly distinguishes this act from euthanasia, however for brevity I will use the shorter term.

Although assisting suicide is a crime in many states, the act of suicide is not. Patient-Hastened Dying can be accomplished without a physician's *intentional* facilitation. One physician told me this story: Almost three years before her death from an overdose, a woman was diagnosed with terminal cancer. Every month, she asked her doctor for a prescription of a small dose of medications. But instead of taking them as prescribed, she stored them and took them all one evening in the presence of her family, after she had come to the conclusion that her pain and suffering were unbearable. The physician who told me this story did not assist her in any way, but he did agree with her final decision. He also felt that she had made this decision diligently.

3. Opponents of Physician-Hastened Dying worry about the "**slippery slope**," defined as "once any law permits people to control dying, its use will expand." Let us consider the next "stop" along this slope:

Active Voluntary Euthanasia by a physician is when a patient requests his or her doctor to administer a lethal dose of medication that causes a rapid "good death," which is the classic definition of euthanasia. Although this practice is legal in a few countries, I believe it should not be legalized. Euthanasia opens a potential door that is antithetical to individual autonomy. While physicians may provide important advice to patients, doctors should not have the power to effect the final act. Why? Because the minds of some physicians might be biased, and some bias is unconscious. Any bias can lead to misuse. The novel, **Lethal Choice**, illustrates several examples of *physician bias*, although not all lead to hastening death. The novel "names" these biases as: Dr. Friend, Dr. Optimistic, Dr. Pessimistic, Dr. Wallet, Dr. Ego, Dr. Burn-out, Dr. Religious, Dr. Hero, and Dr. Too Sensitive. One type of bias even has subcategories: Dr. Scared includes physicians who fear sanctions from their professional societies, lawsuits from surviving family members, and criminal charges from regulatory bodies.

4. A major protective virtue of Physician-Hastened Dying is that right up to very last moment before they ingest the medication, patients can voluntarily change their minds and continue to live. The fictional action in **Lethal Choice** shows that patients can do this even under extreme duress. In this story, a deranged physician has a back-up plan: **to force involuntary euthanasia**, an illegal act that is better known as "murder." In Oregon, under the *Death With Dignity Act*, only 246 out of 390 patients ingested the prescribed pills. The other 144 waited so long that they died from natural causes, without ever taking the pills. Yet they still benefit greatly because they lived with less anxiety and worry during their final weeks or months. One point cannot be emphasized strongly enough: **The ultimate decision to ingest the pills is ultimately, and always, the patient's.**

5. Some people question how certain physicians can be when they state the patient's prognosis is terminal, They ask, how accurate is the prediction that the patient will for live six months or less? This time frame is the typical criterion to qualify for Physician-Hastened Dying. Even if physicians' estimates were wrong, the relevant safeguard here is that patients have the final say over when and if they take the medication. They will NOT do so until and unless they decide their *quality of life is nil*. Here is another essential safeguard: Before patients hasten dying, they should be encouraged to enroll in **hospice** where they can be given every opportunity to reduce their physical suffering. In Oregon, 90% of patients who took advantage of the

Death With Dignity Act had enrolled in hospice. That figure compares to the national average of less than 25%—a difference that is truly astounding.

6. Opponents of legalizing Physician-Hastened Dying raise another relevant point; that all we know about such acts is derived from data provided by those physicians who *voluntarily chose to report the acts*. Opponents point out that the only consequence to physicians who fail to report, under *Oregon's Death With Dignity Act*, is loss of immunity from prosecution, and if acts were "successfully" performed in secret, physicians would not need immunity. While there is no hint of any under-reporting in Oregon, this criticism should still be taken seriously.

I believe that currently, there is adequate oversight since the medications prescribed for Physician-Hastened Dying are barbiturates, and they are listed on Schedule II of the Federal **Drug Enforcement Agency's** list of Controlled Substances. The acts of writing and filling prescriptions for barbiturates by physicians and pharmacists, respectively—especially in the large quantities necessary for lethality—serve as red flags to the Drug Enforcement Agency. These days, physicians rarely prescribe *barbiturates* for sleep or anxiety anyway, because of the danger of unintentional overdoses, and of emotionally-based suicides. While the U.S. Supreme Court ruled that the States, not the Federal government, have jurisdiction over determining what constitutes "legitimate medical use" of medication, its January 2006 ruling left open the possibility for Congress to amend the Controlled Substances Act of 1970. If Congress did amend that act, it would effectively overturn this 2006 decision. Also, individual states could pass restrictive laws about the use of barbiturates. If they did, doctors could then re-act:

Physicians could use a combination of medications that are NOT listed on the Drug Enforcement Agency's Schedules. As mentioned previously, the novel **Lethal Choice** indicates that such a combination exists, but it does not name the specific medications. In theory, doctors could participate in Physician-Hastened Dying in secret without waving a red flag, and not report. What is the problem with this? Most professionals agree that medicine should be practiced openly. That way, the actions of physicians can be reviewed and improved... to maximize life (safety), liberty (freedom), and the pursuit of happiness (minimize suffering).

Proposal 1: To solve the problem of possible under-reporting

The requirement for mandatory reporting is not a *new* concept. Some States have laws that invoke severe penalties for failure to report *suspected* child abuse. New laws could similarly require "mandatory reporting" of Physician-Hastened Dying. The penalty for failing to report could be the same: the loss of their license to practice their profession. If applied to Physician-Hastened Dying, those required to report could include all health professionals including physicians, psychologists, nurses, pharmacists, social workers, physical and respiratory therapists, dialysis technicians, physician assistants, and pastoral counselors.

Morally, this plan makes sense since facilitating a patient's desire to hasten death is as important as preventing *suspected* acts of child abuse. *Legally*, it is sound to endorse this fiduciary responsibility of professionals to their patients and clients. And *pragmatically*, it would be effective. Since professionals from several fields typically contribute to end-of-life care, if the law applied to all professionals who had been involved in the patient's previous assessment and treatment, then each professional would be aware that the other professionals would report, and that in turn, would effectively encourage all to comply with the reporting requirement. The requirement to report would help provide an "effective guardrail" to prevent further descent down the slippery slope to Voluntary Active Euthanasia. However, it would not, by itself, prevent another type of possible abuse, which is discussed next.

7. Another relevant criticism about Physician-Hastened Dying is the potential for *implicit* and *explicit pressure*. This criticism rarely acknowledges that similar pressure may be exerted on patients to refuse any life-sustaining treatment. Such refusal is already legal for any competent adult. Here is the problem. Some patients may incorrectly come to believe that their lives are worthless. Others may feel they have become too burdensome for their caregivers. The worst scenario is when unfortunate patients are subjected to a type of *elder abuse* called *undue influence*. Typically, heirs to the patient's estate wish to preserve whatever financial assets remain instead of continuing their care. Yet there are patients who voice their preference to use the funds in their estate for their grandchildren's college education, for example, rather than to prolong their diminished, anguished existence in an Intensive Care Unit. We must be sure that a patient's judgment is sound and that his or her decision to hasten dying is voluntary?

To prevent potential abuse, laws that legalize Physician-Hastened Dying must require that all patients be assessed to assure that A) they possess the capacity to make medical decisions; and that B) their decisions to hasten dying are voluntary, in their intricate web of personal goals and relationships.

Proposal 2: To make sure the patient's choice is sound and voluntary

I will be specific in terms of the way some proposed laws have been written:

The decision to refer to a psychiatrist or to a psychologist should not be left to the discretion of two physicians who have practiced *any* specialty of medicine, whose primary function is to certify medically that the patient has six or fewer months to live, or to the unknown expertise of whatever hospice staff specialty happens to perform the initial evaluation when a patient is admitted. Routine psychiatric or psychological examinations and assessment of family dynamics can prevent premature deaths, which would justify their reasonable cost. They should be performed along with a thorough assessment of the adequacy of *Comfort Care* to reduce physical suffering. I therefore propose:

A) Any one who wishes to hasten his or her dying should have a mandatory psychiatric or psychological examination. Legislators must appreciate that non-psychiatrists are not expert at making the diagnosis of depression. Even psychiatrists find it challenging to assess terminally ill patients when it is realistic not to have hope in certain areas. One of the worst reasons to attempt suicide is to use the act to express anger toward a specific family member or loved one.

Note: A less stringent, but possibly adequate requirement would be to require each of the two certifying physicians to sign a statement such as this: "In my clinical opinion, it is NOT necessary for a psychiatrist or a psychologist to rule out such mental problems as depression, anorexia nervosa, disturbed judgment, or impaired capacity to make sound medical decisions. With respect to these areas, I feel confident about certifying this patient to exercise the option of Physician-Hastened Dying."

B) The evaluation of decision-making capacity, the clinical term for competence, can be so obvious that most physicians will make the correct call. At one extreme is perfect lucidity; at the other, inability to express a consistent choice. But there are clinical cases or circumstances where a psychiatrist or psychologist who specializes in such determinations would be needed. Experts realize that having a psychiatric diagnosis and lacking the capacity to make medical decisions are distinctly different impairments that require separate assessments; and that one type of impairment does not necessarily imply the other. For example, a patient in the early stage of the mental disorder of Alzheimer's disease may still be able to make medical decisions; while a patient who has a medical disorder that creates a fever of 104 degrees may temporarily not be able to make a sound medical decision.

C) A valid argument can be made for the rights of loved ones to know that the patient intends to hasten dying. Survivors may experience increased guilt if they are denied the opportunity to make final amends and to say their last good-byes. Unless there are compelling reasons not to inform family members, they should be informed and given the opportunity to discuss the decision to hasten dying. While it can be reasonable for a patient to decide that continued existence is too much of burden, it is also possible that one or more family sessions may result in the decision to prolong life. For example, the patient's motivation might be based on inaccurate perceptions of being too much of a burden; may be due to subtle or explicit coercion; or may be based on anger stemming from feelings of abandonment. The psychiatrist, the psychologist, or the primary care physician, or palliative care physician can recommend, or at least notify all concerned, that family sessions for these purposes are available. At times, it might be appropriate for a professional to insist on family sessions. In any event, the refusal to inform the family that he or she has decided to hasten dying, that should be taken as a red flag for further inquiry.

Let me share a true story. It indicates that it is not always clear how the rights of a patient should be balanced with the potentially conflicting rights of their loved ones:

A forty-six year-old man had long-standing anger with his parents. When I first met him, he had AIDS, although he was not dying. Early on, he clearly asked me *not* to notify his parents as death approached. Yet when he was imminently dying, I *did* inform his parents.

I was there when his parents entered his room, and I noticed that he welcomed them, warmly. That was the point at which I left. Later, his parents informed me that the three of them shared for hours, exchanging healing good-byes. I saw the patient only one more time after that but he *not* did ask me how his parents happened to appear just then. Obviously, the result was definitely best for all. Still, I questioned the ethical soundness of my action.

I asked myself, did I violate this patient's rights? —Not an easy question to answer. Here is one way: I believe that I acted in the patient's "best interest." I formed the psychiatric opinion that his *mental capacity to make this specific decision* was impaired at the time he made it several months previously, or at least that at that particular point in time, it did not apply. When the issue came up again, we did not have the luxury of time to spend several sessions to reach a diligent decision that he would be comfortable with, after taking in consideration that whatever decision he made would be irreversible. Under the circumstances of his imminent dying, I formed the psychiatric opinion *to not bring up the issue that related to his past anger*. Instead, I deferred to what I did know for sure, that his parents *definitely* wanted to see him. I doubted that the patient would *not* welcome them, but he still had the capacity to do so. So I took the patient's instruction as one made in a different context; I presumed that in his current situation, of imminent dying, he might want to change his mind but probably did *not* want to discuss the issue since doing so would bring up his past anger. Although there is even a term for this type of action, "therapeutic privilege," I have to admit that if someone criticized my action as being paternalistic, I would have to agree.

What did I learn from this experience? —That delicate situations should be professionally evaluated on a case-by-case basis. (Permit me to suggest reading the story, "Whose Choice Is It, Anyhow?" in **The *BEST WAY* to Say Goodbye**.)

Although hospice programs assess the usual types of family pressures and conflicts, motivation and influence can be quite complex. Elder abuse, at its worse, may require evaluating *undue influence* by a team of professionals drawn from the disciplines of psychiatry, law, family therapy, and social work.

D) Some people champion their interpretation of "sanctity of life." They argue there is only *one way* to honor God's gift of life: to accept it is not moral for human beings to hasten dying. Others disagree. They argue that "sanctity" does not reside in biological existence but in the Creator and in human beings' relationship with their Creator. Clearly, someone who has severely diminished consciousness is no longer capable of having a relationship with the Creator. Some religious people feel it is morally wrong to use modern medical technology to prolong biological functioning when it is God's will to end a person's earthly existence. Less religiously inclined people may emphasize spiritual or philosophical aspects, or invoke utilitarian arguments. Dying can be seen as the process by which space is made available for new human beings; scarce resources must be used where they can do the most good;

and it is *noble* to consider the ethical principle of *social justice*, which should extend to the poor and needy around the world. (Professor Ronald Dworkin has much to say on a secular concept of "sanctity of life," which stimulated the Conclusion to **The *BEST WAY* to Say Goodbye**.)

Non-judgmental physicians and others should respect patients who consider evaluating "quality of life." Many people believe that the allocation of enormous resources to patients with little or no benefit, to patients who cannot even appreciate the sacrifices being made for them, should be considered in the context of the "sanctity" of depriving basic medical benefits to huge numbers of patients who would benefit enormously. In America, 46 million people have no health insurance; others have inadequate insurance. The result is that many terminally ill patients receive such inadequate *Comfort Care* that they die in extreme pain. Chapter 12 and the Conclusion in **The BEST WAY to Say Goodbye** consider the global inequality of allocating resources. For what it costs to maintain for one year, one patient in the United States who has no or virtually no consciousness, such as one in the persistent vegetative state or in end-stage dementia... about 4000 African children under the age of five might be saved from dying from malaria by purchasing mosquito nets. This is an illustration of considering the principle of medical ethics called "social justice," which could be seen as respecting the "**sanctity of *many* lives**."

Let me pause to summarize the main points. I propose two changes in professional practice guidelines for Physician-Hastened Dying:

1) Require *mandatory reporting* by laws that punish the failure to report by loss of professional license;

2) Require a psychiatric or psychological evaluation to determine that the decision to hasten dying is *sound* in terms of judgment, and is *voluntary* in terms of will.

Now for the last major point: to assure that the patient's decision for Physician-Hastened Dying is voluntary...

E) Decisions cannot be voluntary unless patients are fully informed. Patients should be informed of all alternatives to Physician-Hastened Dying as required by the clinically accepted standard of providing informed consent for any medical procedure. They should especially be informed about the option to hasten dying by the method of **Voluntary Refusal of Food & Fluid**:

Advantages of Voluntary Refusal of Food & Fluid

i) **Voluntary Refusal of Food & Fluid** is legal for all competent adults, is peaceful, and is not violent. In contrast, the stories in the Prologue and Epilogue in **The *BEST WAY* to Say Goodbye** provoke serious consideration of an alternative view; in some cases, the term "murder" might be appropriate.

ii) The first several days of the final fast are often experienced by competent patients with alertness and lucidity.

iii) To continue their fast during these days, patients must demonstrate their consistent resolve. To postpone their decision to hasten dying, they need only ask for something to eat and drink, as long as their request is made early enough. (See the story, "She changed her mind twice. She was ready only after she had created her loving legacy," in **The *BEST WAY* to Say Goodbye**.)

iv) These initial days provide an opportunity that can be precious for healing among family members as they say their last good-byes.

v) Patients who received a prescription for a lethal dose of medication, but who plan on taking it at a much later date, must worry if their physical or mental functioning will subsequently decline to the point where they can no longer voluntarily take medication on their own. In contrast, the "act" of Voluntary Refusal of Food & Fluid is passive and does not require physical capability. (See the story, "She could no longer swallow," in **The *BEST WAY* to Say Goodbye**.) While the novel, **Lethal Choice**, illustrates a method for Physician-Hastened Dying that could be used by a totally paralyzed man, this method is not generally available.

vi) Patients and families who ponder the future loss of capability to ingest the lethal medication may thus face one or more of these undesirable alternatives:

a) Patients may feel forced to decide to ingest the medication *when they can*, instead of *when they want to*. But *premature dying* is a tragic outcome that should always be avoided. (See the story, "How much longer might she have enjoyed life?" in **The *BEST WAY* to Say Goodbye**.)

b) The situation could get worse. Some of the proposed new laws for Physician-Hastened Dying require patients to self-administer the lethal dose of medication. "Assistance" would not be permitted. A disproportionately large number of patients with Lou Gehrig's disease (Amyotrophic Lateral Sclerosis) use Oregon's *Death With Dignity Act*. But many of these patients would not be permitted to do so if the law required "self-administration."

c) If loved ones or caregivers secretly administer the medication, they may experience more intense and prolonged guilt, and, depending on the law, also risk being accused of a crime.

d) In these scenarios, the alternative would be to die prematurely, to die illegally, or to die violently... or for others to risk increased guilt and being accused of a crime... or, for the patient to continue existing despite prolonged pain and suffering, which is precisely what the patient wanted to avoid.

A Perspective on the Prudence of Attempts to Legalize Physician-Hastened Dying

A) Surveys over the past two decades repeatedly have demonstrated that, under some end-of-life conditions, between 60 and 70% of people would like the option to ask their doctors for assistance in dying.

B) Yet many politicians are aligned with causes or interests that may compete with those that solely serve the people's will.

C) Campaigns, especially when directed to a popular vote, can be extremely expensive compared to passing a bill in a State Legislature). Even worse, such campaigns have, in the past, publicized much misinformation, and have thereby done the public a great disservice.

D) Both voter-passed initiatives and State Legislature-passed bills can be held up in the courts for years, at additional cost.

E) Such laws may ultimately benefit relatively few people. In Oregon, only about 1 in 900 died this way. That amounts to less than three dozen people per year. And this number would be even lower if new laws require "self-administration."

F) Putting the money and effort into educating the public (and professionals) about Voluntary Refusal of Food & Fluid may be far less costly, and at the same time, benefit many more people. Not only can people with severe physical impairments opt for Voluntary Refusal of Food & Fluid, but people can decide *now* to what extent they are willing to experience the *irreversible descent into the indignity and dependency of dementia*. They can decide at what predetermined point... they wish to have their Proxy on their behalf... **Refuse Food & Fluid**. The amount of quality life saved by *preventing premature dying* in cases where the patient feared increasing dementia can be *years*, rather than months. (Read the story about Judge Robert Hammerman, "Many Care *about* Me—But None Will Take Care *of* Me," in **The *BEST WAY* to Say Goodbye.**) In the few states and other countries where Proxy Directives (Durable Powers of Attorney for Healthcare) are *not* recognized, a Living Will, with a well-documented treatment directive to the future physician, can be used instead, and may specify the reasons for asking the doctor to **Withhold Food & Fluid** under specific circumstances.

G) While the **Refusal of Food & Fluid by Proxy** is fraught with greater challenges than a competent person's **Voluntary Refusal of Food & Fluid**, those who are motivated can learn how to diligently create the appropriate documents. They are: a **Proxy Directive** supplemented with **Empowering Statements for My Proxy** designed to meet the high legal standard of ***clear and convincing*** evidence.

In states and countries where Proxy Directives are not authorized, a **Living Will** (Directive to Physician) can provide instructions that describe the diminished level of functioning where the patient would want his or her future doctor to **Withhold Food & Fluid.**

The clinical and legal backgrounds, as well as strategies and guidelines on how to accomplish the goal of having others honor one's Last Wishes, are included in the book, **The *BEST WAY* to Say Goodbye: a Legal Peaceful Choice at the End of Life.**

People and affiliated groups can also consult with professionals in the field for specific, individualized advice. One such organization is **Caring Advocates**, a non-profit corporation whose staff provides clinical and legal advice on the creation and implementation of end-of-life decisions and whose goals also include doing research on the extent of the public's knowledge about Advance Directives. Caring Advocates develops programs to educate lay people and professionals to fill in these gaps of awareness. These include offering lectures, seminars, and workshops; and distributing relevant material via the mail and Internet.

Disclaimers:

Dr. Terman is the principal author of **The *BEST WAY* to Say Goodbye: a Legal Peaceful Choice at the End of Life**.

Dr. Terman is the Executive Director of **Caring Advocates**, a 501(c)3 non-profit organization whose educational mission is to conduct research on gaps in knowledge about end-of-life options and to fill in those gaps. Dr. Terman may derive income from some of the activities of Caring Advocates.

Why also a self-help book with memoirs on the same topic?

The answer is far beyond the traditional reason, that some readers prefer to be entertained (hence, the medical thriller), while others prefer to be taught (hence, the self-help book with memoirs, advice, and guidelines). I hope, if my writing goals succeed, that both books will educate and entertain. The more substantive reason is that each book attempts to solve two very different end-of-life challenges:

Lethal Choice shows how an adult who is mentally competent but extremely impaired physically can determine if and when he will decide to ingest a lethal dose of medication to hasten his dying. One reason why so few people use Oregon's *Death With Dignity Act* (approximately three dozen a year), is that many patients are too ill to put the pills (or even the powder from the pills) in their mouths, and swallow. The medical thriller also asserts that a combination of prescription medications that are *not* listed on the Schedules of the Drug Enforcement Act, which are individually *not* even thought of as having lethal potential, can when combined, effectively and peacefully hasten dying. This could be important if individual States impose restrictions given their right to determine what is "legitimate medical use" now that the U.S. Supreme Court has affirmed that State right. The U.S. Congress may also pass new laws to amend the Controlled Substances Act of 1970. (Note: The novel does not reveal the names of these medications, nor will its author publish them to prevent their misuse by patients who are physically well but suffer from psychiatric illnesses.)

In contrast, **The *BEST WAY* to Say Goodbye: A Legal Peaceful Choice at the End of Life**, does more than serve as a general guide to creating effective Advance Directives (where success is defined as setting the stage so that others will honor your Last Wishes). It details all aspects of **Voluntary Refusal of Food and Fluid**—the peaceful alternative to Physician-Hastened Dying that is legal everywhere for competent adults. The book also describes specific strategies so that adults who currently possess the mental capacity to make medical decisions, including some in the early stages of Alzheimer's disease, can trust that at a specific end-point of their own choosing (for example, loss of the ability to recognize or to communicate with loved ones, or indignity from loss of bodily control)—their designated Proxy can overcome potential challenges from others to honoring their end-of-life decision to **Refuse Food and Fluid by Proxy**. A diligently prepared set of documents should permit patients not only to refuse tube feeding, but also (if that is their choice) to refuse forced feeding at the hands of nursing assistants via the mouth, when the process has become an unpleasant and unrewarding ordeal; for example, when restraints must be used.

How to Hasten Dying by Voluntarily Refusing Food & Fluid, the Legal Peaceful Alternative to Physician-Assisted Suicide, an introduction for competent, terminally ill patients

(See Disclaimers, below.)

Often, people can just stop eating and drinking without encountering any conflict, to experience a legal peaceful transition. Others, such as the anonymous person who wrote the story, "But They Just Want To Save Me," in **The *BEST WAY* to Say Goodbye: A Legal Peaceful Choice at the End of Life** [in Chapter 9] feel the need to write a strongly worded document similar to the one below. This author wrote that his brother, a priest, "alleges that my suffering benefits other souls in Purgatory, and that makes him feel morally obligated to fight my expressed wishes." He is not alone. The position of the current administration is reflected in the report of The President's Council on Bioethics, "Taking Care: Ethical Caregiving In Our Aging Society" [2005]. This report fully supports the intrusions of others that disrespect the previously expressed Last Wishes of vulnerable dying patients, even if these wishes were written clearly and convincingly. As I write this, at least twenty-three States are considering adopting the "model law" proposed by the National Right Committee. These laws would make it illegal for physicians to withdraw *artificially administrated* Food & Fluid from incompetent patients for whom such treatment is far more a burden than a benefit. Thus, many people will feel less anxiety if they know they have diligently taken the necessary steps to prevent future challenges, even if those challenges are not currently anticipated.

The document below summarizes some of the major strategic points in **The *BEST WAY* To Say Goodbye**. Implicit are the reasons why I strongly prefer **Voluntary Refusal of Food & Fluid** as the legal peaceful alternative to the hotly debated method of Physician-Assisted Suicide. This short document does not consider how to create a set of strategic documents to accomplish the far more complex task of **Refusal of Food & Fluid by Proxy** in the future, as would be needed by patients suffering from severe dementia. The legal, clinical, political, religious, and relational aspects of this method are considered in detail in **The *BEST WAY* to Say Goodbye**. Suffice it to say here, if terminally ill but mentally competent patients may find great challenges to currently exercise their Constitutional right, how much additional effort will it require for all of us, as we worry about a prolonged existence with dementia that may begin five to fifty years from now, or worry about brain damage from a sudden car accident, to feel sure that our Last Wishes will be honored after we can no longer speak for ourselves?

This document expresses my **Constitutional right to decide what happens to my body**. In the area of end-of-life decision-making, the practical application of this right leads to a well-known standard of practice in both medicine and the law:

> **Any adult whose judgment is not impaired by mental illness may refuse any medical treatment, even if such refusal hastens dying.**

I am aware of this ethical position stated by the American Medical Association: "The social commitment of the physician is to sustain life and relieve suffering. Where the performance of one duty conflicts with the other, **the preferences of the patient should prevail**." In that spirit, I request my physicians to provide me with the best available *Comfort Care* regardless of any other decision I make about what happens to my body (even if they personally disagree with my decisions), and even if they hold the opinion that because of those decisions, I need additional *Comfort Care*.

I am aware of the important research of Dr. Linda Ganzini and her co-workers that was published in 2003. They asked experienced hospice nurses to rate the quality of dying for their last competent patient who was capable of drinking fluids but chose **Voluntary Refusal of Food & Fluid** at the end of their lives. On average, these patients experienced a **good death**, with a score of **8**, where "**9**" was the highest score for "a very good death," and "**0**" was a very bad death. They rated their **peace** higher, and their **suffering** lower than for patients who opted for physician-assisted suicide (which was legal in Oregon). Moreover, 70% of surveyed nurses stated they would choose **Voluntary Refusal of Food & Fluid** for themselves if they were terminally ill.

Based on what I consider a realistic view of my current and future medical and mental conditions, I have therefore made the decision detailed below. The first part my decision is indicated by my writing my initials in one of the boxes below (or by directing someone to do so for me, with witnesses, if I am physically unable to initial):

|_________| (*Your initials*) I have decided **NOT to enroll in hospice** but I am willing to discuss both my decision not to enroll in hospice and my decision to **Voluntarily Refuse Food & Fluid** with a psychiatrist. I will also permit this psychiatrist to evaluate my capacity to make these medical decisions and to rule out the possibility that a mental illness is affecting my judgment.

OR

|_________| (*Your initials*) **I have enrolled in hospice** hoping that their team of

palliative care doctors and nurses, who are expert at delivering *Comfort Care*, can reduce my pain and suffering to the point where I will want to continue living. After I have given the hospice staff what I consider is a reasonable amount of time for this last treatment effort however, if I still feel my condition is unbearable and intolerable, I may then want to **Voluntarily Refuse Food & Fluid**.

Regardless of whether or not I have chosen to enroll in hospice (as indicated above), I am willing to cooperate with a psychiatrist to evaluate these beliefs: My decision to **Voluntarily Refuse Food & Fluid** does not arise out of my being depressed, anorexic, angry, or suicidal in the usual sense. To explain: I would love to go on living if I felt better, but in my present condition, I find my continued existence intolerable. I also believe that I possess the mental capacity to make sound medical decisions. **If any person, agency, or facility doubts the validity of these beliefs, I am willing to have a psychiatrist verify them, as long as the process of evaluation is completed within seven days of my signing below**. (If I disagree with the first psychiatric evaluation, I can request a second evaluation. If these two opinions disagree, then I can request a consultation from a third psychiatrist, or ask for a consultation from an ethics committee.)

I have had the opportunity to discuss the options of further aggressive palliative care with my physicians, to make final arrangements with my legal and financial advisors, to make my peace with my spiritual and pastoral counselors, and to resolve emotional issues from my past regrets and disappointments with my psychological counselors. I also have had an opportunity to make amends and say good-byes to as many friends and relatives as is reasonably possible. For them, as well as for those whom I have not had a chance to talk to directly, I have had an opportunity to consider creating an *ethical will* that can serve as my *loving legacy* as it contains my personal expression of values; that is, what I have learned in life. The statements in my *ethical will* are the essence of what I want people to remember about me.

As I begin my **Voluntary Refusal of Food & Fluid**, I hope that those who care about me may find comfort in the knowledge that I can change my mind and postpone the process to hasten my dying as long as I remain conscious (typically, a few days). I realize that I must not wait too long to change my mind; otherwise, I may experience irreversible organ damage. Otherwise, I can reverse the process to hasten my dying merely by asking for something to eat and to drink. I realize that I may need extra care from my physician. The potential for reversibility is one reason why I have chosen **Voluntary Refusal of Food & Fluid** to hasten my dying over physician-assisted suicide (even where it is legal), and why I have notified the people who care about me about these Last Wishes.

Important: I wish to be clear about one point: **I do not authorize anyone to reverse my decision to alter the course of my decision after I can no longer speak for myself**; for example, after I slip into a coma. To those lay or professional people, or institutions and agencies who would try to reverse my decision, please read and respect this: I emphatically state that my wish to Refuse Food & Fluid is **DURABLE**, by which I mean I want this decision to remain as the final statement of my end-of-life wishes that transcends my mental competence. After I lapse into unconsciousness, I forbid anyone from attempting to reverse MY decision by going to a court of law or to an ethics committee to argue that placing a feeding tube or an intravenous line in me would be in my "best interest." I want to avoid such attempts since I consider such attempts "to delay" as tantamount "to deny" my Last Wish.

I now list those people I wish to be present at my bedside if they are available and able. They can remain at my bedside for as long as *they wish* |__| or as long as *I remain conscious* |__|. I look forward to our final opportunity to dialogue in general. I understand that some of them may feel a moral obligation to try to talk me out of continuing my resolve to **Voluntarily Refuse Food & Fluid**. While I will permit them to do so, I ask them to balance their attempts with **respect** for my wishes so that these discussions do not turn into arguments that cause me further anguish. If that situation arises, I reserve the right to ask others to honor my request to ask them to leave my bedside.

______________________________, ______________________________,
______________________________, ______________________________,
______________________________, ______________________________.

I now provide a partial list of individuals whom I wish to explicitly exclude from having any power to reverse my **durable** decision to **Voluntarily Refuse Food & Fluid**. (I may make additions to this list orally at any time.) They are entitled to follow their own beliefs for themselves, but I insist that they respect mine.

______________________________, ______________________________.

I have attached three statements to this document:

The first contains some suggestions for *Comfort Care* that specifically may reduce any additional suffering as I **Voluntarily Refuse Food & Fluid**.

The second illustrates the kinds of experiences that others or I have had, that provide the basis for why I have made this decision. (These can be personal experiences or selected from the stories and movie summaries in the book, **The *BEST WAY* to Say Goodbye: A Peaceful Legal Choice at the End of Life**.)

The third is a form called **Physicians' Order for Life-Sustaining Treatments (POLST)** that my doctor has signed. This form communicates my wish to refuse emergency life-sustaining treatments; for example, Cardio-Pulmonary Resuscitation and admission to an acute care hospital.

(This form would be signed, notarized, and placed with the three attachments.)

Note: The experience of author, Stan Terman, during his four-day total fast of Food & Fluid, and ways to decrease discomfort, by both over-the-counter remedies and by prescription medications that are not only effective but also require a minimal amount of liquid to administer, plus memoirs attesting to the peaceful experience of the transition by Refusing Food & Fluid are included in the book, **The *BEST WAY* To Say Goodbye**. This book also presents strategies to plan for this option to be exercised by Proxy in the future. It also deals with the legal, political, and religious aspects of Refusing Food & Fluid. Importantly, it explains why a physician must oversee the process, and how to reverse the process if you change your mind and decide to postpone your dying.

General Disclaimers

This publication is designed to provide information with the understanding that the author and the publisher are not engaged in rendering medical, legal, or other professional services by the sale of this book. If professional advice or assistance is required, readers should consult local experts in their respective fields. This product is not a substitute for medical or legal advice.

It is the responsibility of each reader to consult with qualified professionals for medical advice that meets the standard of care in his or her community, and for legal advice that complies with the laws of his or her state of residence, and which takes into account, his or her specific situations and goals. Such action is necessary before reader make medical or legal decisions, or sign documents.

None of the information in this book is designed for minors, or for people with serious emotional disorders, or for use for illegal purposes.

Certain suggestions in this book are designed for consideration by people who wish to avoid prolonging their dying process, but these suggestions are only directed to patients who are terminally ill or who suffer from an incurable progressive condition that will eventually lead to death, and none of these suggestions should be followed without first discussing them with the reader's personal physician, and psychological, spiritual, religious, and legal counselors.

The mission: To promote a culture of extended quality of life

Life's greatest irony is that the freedom to control ***when*** we die, can—and often does—lead to choosing to ***live longer***. In contrast, the greatest end-of-life tragedy is to believe that our only choices are to die illegally, violently, or prematurely—lest those in power force us to endure months or years of unbearable pain and suffering, or to merely exist as our indignity and dependency increase.

The mission: to continue to enjoy whatever remains in our lives by promoting *a culture of extended quality of life*. Given our great end-of-life fears, we must be assured that others will honor our Last Wishes when we cannot speak for ourselves. The challenges are daunting and increasing: We might suffer more pain if new laws criminalize doctors for prescribing medications at doses that non-medical regulators "judge" as intentional overdoses to hasten dying. Recalling private conversations around our kitchen tables will no longer be considered evidence of our enduring wishes, if 23 (or more) States pass laws to restrict family members from making the end-of-life decisions that they know we, their loved ones, would want..

What can we do? Compose strategically effective Living Wills and Proxy Directives. **The *BEST WAY* to Say Goodbye** can be your guide. Start by modifying your State's form, a popular form like "Five Wishes," or use a form in the book. Add new approaches for future success: attachment "Empowering Statements for My Proxy," designate a "Living Will Advocate," and have your Proxy sign an "Acceptance Agreement." Such refinements, while based mostly on legal cases from United States' courts, can also apply globally.

Beyond pragmatism, **The *BEST WAY* to Say Goodbye** considers all aspects of a subject that will affect us all—first, with our loved ones, and then, for ourselves. The book covers the psychological, practical, clinical, religious, ethical, moral, legal, and political aspects of dying. Its clear, step-by-step guides and poignant personal memoirs are spiced with humor and wit, to make the provocative subject matter also enjoyable to read.

Embracing and then transcending the personal-centered, high-profile political controversy of *autonomy* (freedom to choose **not** to prolong your suffering or indignity) versus *faith-based discipline* (freedom to follow the teachings of your religious leader), the book views Advance Directives as *moral documents* and introduces this noble goal,

To honor the sanctity of ***many*** *lives.*

About the author

Stanley A. Terman received his B.A. from Brown University, his Ph.D. from M.I.T., and his M.D. from U. Iowa. A board-certified psychiatrist, he was on the faculty of the University of California, Irvine. before he moved to San Diego. Now he heads Peaceful Transitions® and Caring Advocates™, whose staffs of clinical, legal, and spiritual professionals assist patients and families facing end-of-life challenges.

Dr. Terman has participated actively in three bioethics committees in San Diego, and is on the consulting staff of the San Diego Hospice. He has appeared before California's Law Revision Commission and has served as chief of staff at a local psychiatric hospital. He sometimes testifies in civil cases as an expert. In his clinical practice, he assesses patients' judgment when they wish to create Advance Directives, appoint a power of attorney for medical or financial decisions, or Refuse Food & Fluid.

In these days of political polarities, Dr. Terman tries to maintain a balanced approach. He provides advice to those who wish to avoid prolonged, unnecessary end-of-life suffering or the progressive indignity and dependency of Alzheimer's disease and other dementias by exercising the legal peaceful choice of Voluntary Refusal of Food & Fluid (sometimes, by Proxy). Yet he has also criticized the actions of Dr. Kevorkian and declined to join the former Hemlock Society.

If asked what beliefs he holds most dear, his answers are, "We are morally obligated to honor a patient's previously expressed wishes," and "Do everything possible to learn directly from the patient, what she or he wants." In the latter context, Dr. Terman's declaration was submitted to Florida Judge Greer in the fiercely litigated case of Terri Schiavo.

In addition to the medical thriller, **Lethal Choice,** he is the primary author of **The *BEST WAY* to Say Goodbye: A Legal Peaceful Choice at the End of Life**. This "book-within-a-book" strives to meet the needs of both general and professional readers with memoirs, humorous tales, cartoons, practical guidelines, and over 250 medical references and legal citations. Dr. Terman is also the contributing editor to ***Last Wishes*: Memoirs and Professional Advice on Peaceful Transitions**, a forthcoming anthology.

Dr. Terman's interests in part are reflected by the titles of his lecture offerings: "Do We Need to Legalize Physician-Assisted Suicide"; "Why Refusing Food and Fluid may be the *BEST WAY* to say goodbye"; "How to plan ahead for a dignified death if the diagnosis is Alzheimer's"; "A Critique of The President's Council on Bioethics report, *Taking Care*"; "The Sanctity of *MANY* Lives"; and "Does art accurately reflect the last chapter of life?" (how Hollywood portrays end-of-life decisions).

Dr. Terman's family includes Elias and Alex (his sons); Sharon (his daughter); Alex's wife, Nadine; their son, Leo; and Emily and Lauren (Beth's daughters). He lives in Carlsbad-by-the-Sea with his wife, Beth Gardner, and two Pomeranian dogs.